ROBERT LOUIS STEVENSON, novelist, poet and essayist, was born in Edinburgh on November 13, 1859, and died December 3, 1894, in Samoa. His parents were upper-middle-class Scots and, like his devoted nurse Alison Cummingham, were of dour Calvinist stock. At birth Stevenson showed signs of pulmonary trouble, and ill health interrupted his formal education at Edinburgh University and plagued him throughout his life. Leading a bohemian existence during his twenties and thirties, his travels throughout Europe formed the basis of his first two books, *An Inland Voyage* (1879) and *Travels With a Donkey* (1879). In 1875 he settled into the artists' colony at Barbizon and began writing for English magazines. There he met Fanny Van de Grift Osbourne, a married woman ten years his senior, with whom he fell in love. In 1879 he followed her to San Francisco (which gave rise to *An Amateur Emigrant*)—a trip which proved disastrous to his health. After Mrs. Osbourne obtained a divorce, they married and for the next eight years traveled a great deal in Europe and America in search of good health. Stevenson remained industrious and during this period wrote *Treasure Island* (1883), his first successful and popular book, which established him as a prominent writer. *Dr. Jekyll and Mr. Hyde*, which sold 40,000 copies in six months, and *Kidnapped* soon followed in 1886. The Stevensons finally settled in Samoa, where he became involved in politics and was known as Tusitala, the Teller of Tales. He was dictating *Weir of Hermiston* on the day he died of a cerebral hemorrhage.

The Body Snatcher and Other Stories

Robert Louis Stevenson

EDITED AND WITH AN
INTRODUCTION BY
Jeffrey Meyers

A SIGNET CLASSIC
NEW AMERICAN LIBRARY
NEW YORK AND SCARBOROUGH, ONTARIO

NAL BOOKS ARE AVAILABLE AT QUANTITY DISCOUNTS
WHEN USED TO PROMOTE PRODUCTS OR SERVICES.
FOR INFORMATION PLEASE WRITE TO PREMIUM MARKETING DIVISION,
NEW AMERICAN LIBRARY, 1633 BROADWAY,
NEW YORK, NEW YORK 10019.

Cover painting, "Portrait of Robert Louis Stevenson" (detail)
by John Singer Sargent, 1887. Bequest of the Mr. and Mrs.
Charles Phelps Taft; The Taft Museum, Cincinnati, Ohio.

SIGNET CLASSIC TRADEMARK REG. U.S. PAT. OFF. AND FOREIGN COUNTRIES
REGISTERED TRADEMARK—MARCA REGISTRADA
HECHO EN CHICAGO, U.S.A.

SIGNET, SIGNET CLASSIC, MENTOR, ONYX, PLUME, MERIDIAN
and NAL BOOKS are published *in the United States* by NAL PENGUIN INC.,
1633 Broadway, New York, New York 10019,
in Canada by The New American Library of Canada Limited,
81 Mack Avenue, Scarborough, Ontario M1L 1M8

Library of Congress Catalog Card Number: 87–61822

First Signet Classic Printing, February, 1988

1 2 3 4 5 6 7 8 9

PRINTED IN THE UNITED STATES OF AMERICA

CONTENTS

INTRODUCTION

Robert Louis Stevenson, who came from a repressive Calvinistic background and spent his adult life as a restless invalid in search of health, was born in Edinburgh in 1850 and died in Samoa in 1894. His great themes are romantic love, rivalry and vengeance, passion and renunciation, the supernatural and the macabre, the temptation of the forbidden, the torments of conscience, the strain of savagery beneath the veneer of civilization, the influence of ancestry, the conflict between fathers and sons, the double or alter ego and the dual nature of man.

He is excellent at evoking the setting—in a few vivid paragraphs—of London and Edinburgh, the Scottish moorlands and highlands, France and Spain, Hawaii and Samoa. He writes in many genres: black comedies, historical fables, moral allegories and folk tales. His stories, an odd mixture of the adolescent and the sophisticated, combine atmosphere and action, adventure and morality. Many of them take place in nocturnal darkness or crepuscular light. He employs an archaic style to evoke the past, and is stronger at inventing than concluding his ingenious plots.

His dashing and decent heroes fall instantly in love, usually in lonely landscapes. Most of his women, compromised in some strange fashion, are noble, beautiful and boring. In "The Sire de Malétroit's Door" the protagonist chooses marriage over death; in "The Pavilion on the Links" he defeats a vicious rival in love; in "Olalla" he renounces his love for an attractive lady in a bestial family; in "The Bottle Imp" he overcomes adversity and is reunited with his devoted wife; in "The Beach at Falesá" he accepts domesticity with a native woman; in the unfinished "Weir of Hermiston" he is destined to be rescued from prison and escape to America with his beloved after killing a friend who had seduced her.

The subtly controlled tone, perfect diction and grim ironic humor make "The Body-Snatcher" a minor masterpiece. A frame story (or story within a story)—in which Fettes confronts and accuses Macfarlane, his old confederate in an unnatural occupation that runs counter to funerary convention—leads into the fictional equivalent of Rembrandt's *Anatomy Lesson.* Fettes' pathological duty in the Edinburgh school of medicine had been "to supply, receive, and divide the various subjects" who "supplied the table" in the anatomy class. He frequently noticed "the singular freshness of the bodies" and, when a personal acquaintance is delivered in a sack, is forced to admit that almost all his corpses had been murdered.

Macfarlane encourages his progressive immersion in evil by urging Fettes to suppress and ignore the truth. When Macfarlane produces a corpse he himself has murdered, forces Fettes to conceal the crime ("The more things are wrong the more we must act as if all were right") and briskly announces: "Richardson may have the head," Fettes realizes the thin partition between life and death, the gruesome contrast between the physical and spiritual aspects of man: "To bodies that had been laid in earth, in joyful expectation of a far different awakening, there came that hasty, lamp-lit, terror-haunted resurrection of the spade and mattock," which exposed the body "to uttermost indignities before a class of gaping boys." Fettes' exclamation at the beginning of the story, "I wished to know if, after all, there were a God; I know now that there is none," illuminates the meaning of the supernatural transformation at the end. If there is no God, then the devil is free to do evil.

A historical romance set in France in 1429 during the Hundred Years' War, "The Sire de Malétroit's Door" opens as Denis de Beaulieu, feeling his way through the darkness ("the touch of cold window-bars . . . startles the man like the touch of a toad"), is pursued by hostile men-at-arms and finds refuge through a door that suddenly opens behind him. Malétroit's character is revealed in his countenance: "equivocal and wheedling . . . greedy, brutal, and dangerous." Their dialogue begins with a misconception ("I have been expecting you all the evening") and ends with Beaulieu's realization that he has been mistakenly snared for an impromptu marriage.

Malétroit's niece Blanche, whose name, "white," suggests her innocence, explains that her recent flirtation with a young captain, which Malétroit feels has dishonored their ancient family, has led Beaulieu into the trap set for her lover. Forced to choose between hanging and nuptials, Beaulieu at first feels honor-bound to refuse matrimonial coercion. They debate the niceties of the situation during the two hours allowed by her wicked uncle and, as dawn breaks, Beaulieu does the decent thing and opts for life rather than for "a dark and dusty corner, where a man gets into his tomb and has the door shut after him till the Judgment Day." "Though I will die for you blithely," he confides to Blanche, "it would be like all the joys of Paradise to live on and spend my life in your service." The wildly improbable plot can be read as Stevenson's ironic commentary on the chivalric ideal.

"The Pavilion on the Links" is as thrilling and intriguing as "The Sire de Malétroit's Door" is pleasantly absurd. For the former contains all the romantic elements: a remote setting, keen suspense, mysterious strangers, hidden crimes, fatal quicksands, dangerous attacks, a passionate love triangle, a destructive conflagration and a rescue ship that arrives too late to help.

Cassilis, after nine years of wandering, returns to the links ("a Scottish name for sand which has ceased drifting and become more or less solidly covered with turf") where he had once spent a lonely winter and then quarreled with his friend, Northmour. A puzzling misogynist and lover, Northmour is both handsome and repulsive, brave and cowardly, and "combined the vivacity of the south with the sustained and deadly hatreds of the north." On the links, Cassilis witnesses a number of enigmatic events and asks: "Why was the pavilion secretly prepared? Why had Northmour landed with his guests at dead of night? . . . Why had he sought to kill me? . . . How had he come to have a dagger ready in his hand?"

Cassilis saves the beautiful Clara from the quicksands and falls in love with her. As their courtship develops, she elucidates the baffling incidents. Her father, Bernard Huddlestone, a dishonest and ruined banker, is fleeing from his enemies. In return for marrying his daughter to his savior, he is about to escape to the South Seas in Northmour's yacht. In a neighboring village, Cassilis discovers three Italians in pursuit of Huddlestone. Ominous seagulls—who "wheeled over his sepulchre with their usual melancholy piping" and continue to hover and circulate throughout the story—indicate that one of the Italians has fallen into the deadly sands. Northmour is enraged when he discovers Cassilis embracing Clara. He reveals that Huddlestone had gambled away a huge sum of money deposited in his bank by a group of Italian revolutionaries who have now come to Scotland to murder him. For Clara's sake, the two suitors agree to suspend hostilities and to risk their lives in defense of the thieving banker. The Italians move in to attack the fortified pavilion, call for the blood of the traitor Huddlestone and promise to spare the others if they will hand him over.

There are some surprising and perverse sexual moments, swirling beneath the conventional romance of the novel, which excite the men and reinforce their bond at the expense of the passive girl. Northmour, realizing that he has lost Clara to Cassilis and will probably be killed, declares: "By God, I'll have a kiss!" He rudely and repeatedly embraces the woman as Cassilis looks on impotently, and then urges his rival to take a kiss himself to square accounts. When Cassilis contemptuously refuses, Northmour justly exclaims: "You've been a prig in life; a prig you'll die." After they have been driven out of the house by the fire and Huddlestone rushes into the avengers' bullets to save the others, Clara faints. The next moment, as Cassilis cries "Shame!" Northmour, still eager for sexual compensation, "was straining Clara to his heart and covering her unconscious hands and face with his caresses." Not to be outdone by his passionate rival, and also taking advantage of his beloved's unconsciousness (though under the guise of assisting her), Cassilis, in a wonderful phrase, "loosened, as well as I was able, her dress and corset." Though Northmour warns him to keep his hands off the girl, he again falls to his knees and plants a chaste kiss on her brow. Cassilis' comparative restraint takes the wind out of Northmour's sails. Defeated in love, he atones for gross lechery by sacrificing himself for the cause of Italian freedom. Years later, he is killed in the Austrian Tyrol, fighting under the patriotic colors of Giuseppe Garibaldi.

"Markheim," influenced by Poe's theme of the double self and by the murder of the old pawnbroker in Dostoyevsky's *Crime and Punishment*, is Stevenson's macabre contribution to the genre of the Christmas story. Markheim (whose German name makes him seem more sinister) enters a London curio shop and rejects a mirror, or hand-conscience, as a Christmas gift. He then anticipates the "double" theme by observing his reflection in a series of mirrors and in several large pier glasses. He muses that life is short and insecure and, in an unmotivated and gratuitous act, kills the dealer with a dagger. Staring at the body of his victim, "where it lay both humped and sprawling," he notices that it looks "incredibly small and strangely meaner than in life."

After the murder the story moves inside the tortured mind of Markheim with considerable psychological penetration. The sense that he was not alone "grew upon him to the verge of madness." He is confronted by his alter ego or evil conscience in the form of a commonplace yet odd devil-figure, who says he lives for evil and debates the meaning of the murder. He urges Markheim to steal the dealer's money and to stab his maid, and offers to help him escape. Yet Markheim, with a resurgence of moral awareness in his corroded heart, rejects this advice. He moves from justifying his evil deed—"about God Himself he was at ease; his act was doubtless exceptional, but so were his excuses, which God knew; it was there, and not among men, that he felt sure of justice"—to an acceptance of his guilt. Though he does not admit responsibility and repent at the end of the story, he struggles with his conscience and decides to resist evil: "If I be condemned to evil acts . . . there is still one door of freedom open—I can cease from action." Knowing the consequences of his crime—the dock, the prison, the gallows and the black coffin—he has the moral courage to spare the maid and tell her: "You had better go for the police. . . . I have killed your master."

The opening of the vastly underrated "Olalla" anticipates the beginning of D. H. Lawrence's story, "Sun," and has srikingly Lawrencean themes: sun worship, primitivism, "blood-consciousness" and the ghastliness of Catholic iconography (as in Lawrence's essay, "Christs in Tirol"). Stevenson's "Lawrencean" belief, expressed in a letter to his cousin Bob, suggests the theme of the story, for he wrote that man should "honour sex more religiously. THE DAMNED THING of our [puritanical] education is that Christianity does not recognize and hallow sex."

The English hero of the story is sent to recover from a war wound in the salubrious mountain residence of an ancient but decayed Spanish family. Stevenson recreates the Spanish landscape (perhaps the Sierra de Guadarrama north of Madrid), which he had never seen, with consummate skill. Before leaving for the mountains, the hero learns that the wild mother of the family broke with all tradition and married (or perhaps never bothered to marry) a muleteer or smuggler. Her half-witted son Felipe—still a common type, whom Spanish villagers today call *mental* and treat with unusual sympathy—conveys the hero to the decayed mansion and is chastised by him for torturing a squirrel.

The mother's nearly mute and exceptionally hedonistic behavior is subtly portrayed. She spends her days brushing her hair and lolling in the sun with "an expression of almost imbecile good-humor and contentment," her vacuous face "a moral blank expressing literally naught." Her beauty and stupidity soothe and amuse the hero, though she is bored by him, yawns in his face and falls asleep while he is conversing with her: "She lived in her body; and her consciousness was all sunk into and disseminated through her members." When the scirocco blows in from Africa, everyone in the house becomes tense and depressed. Late at night, the hero is shocked to hear an outbreak of atavistic cries of pain and rage, but he is unable to discover where they came from or what caused them.

The hero is introduced to the elusive and mysterious daughter, Olalla (whose name echoes the disturbing ululations), through her books and poetry that present a complete contrast to the rest of the feral family. The first words she speaks to him are an order to go away, and the rest of the story explains why he must unwillingly obey her command. The good soldier immediately responds that he "would gladly forswear my country, my language, and my friends, to live forever by her side." The deeper vision of Tolstoy's realistic *Anna Karenina* shows how the romantic love of Anna and Vronksy is destroyed by precisely these sacrifices.

In an extraordinary brutal scene, the hero (perhaps punishing himself, seeking a nurse or searching for a reason to remain) slashes his wrist on a casement window. (Both Stevenson and Lawrence were obsessed by blood, which recalled their nearly fatal tubercular hemorrhages.) When he shows his bloody wound to the bestial mother, she thrusts his hand in her mouth, bites it to the bone, utters the monstrous cries that had awakened him on the night of the hot wind and is pinned to the floor by Felipe. Her screams, the hero realizes, "were the death-cry of my love. . . . This savage and bestial strain ran not only through the whole behaviour of her family, but found a place in the very foundations and story of our love."

Olalla believes that she can end her cursed inheritance ("the hands of the dead . . . guide me") only by refusing to propagate her race. Though she is the great exception in the degenerate family, she persuades the hero to accept her Christ-like renunciation: "We must all bear and expiate a past which was not ours." Unlike the muleteer who damned himself with her mother, the hero—guided by the Christian precept that pleasure is "not an end, but an accident"—abandons love, marriage, sex, procreation and the concept of earthly happiness.

A fable and folk tale, written with engaging simplicity for a Polynesian audience in Hawaii, "The Bottle Imp" is fired by Stevenson's Calvinistic sense of damnation and incites the fears instilled in the islanders by hellfire missionaries. The gentle hero Keawe—who wanders between San Francisco, Honolulu and Tahiti—buys the "round-bellied bottle with a long neck; the glass of it was white like milk, with changing rainbow colours in the grain. Within-sides something obscurely moved, like a shadow and a fire." Though the bottle imp grants every wish at once, there are two conditions: The bottle must always be sold at a loss, and if a man dies before he sells it, he must burn in hell forever.

The bottle is sold five times in the story. Keawe, having fulfilled his desire for a magnificent house, sells it to a friend who wants to own a schooner. After falling in love with a beautiful maiden, Kokua, Keawe discovers he has leprosy and buys back the bottle to rid himself of the disease. But he fears he will not be able to sell it for less than one cent and imagines the fire burning him in the bottomless pit. He marries Kokua, tells her that he dared hell in order to possess her and is overjoyed by her suggestion that he sell it for French centimes. But he does not want to save himself by the eternal ruin of another man. Kokua repeats Keawe's sacrificial act by buying the bottle back from an old man who has bought it from her. Stevenson invites the reader to anticipate, rather than merely read about, a satisfactory solution that would enable Keawe to achieve a happy ending. The story suggests not only that a man's character is revealed by his material desires and that human greed finds it impossible to resist the temptation of unlimited and immediately gratified desires, but also that crass materialism can be transcended by noble altruism.

The two longer and more substantial stories, "The Beach at Falesá" and "Weir of Hermiston," show a considerable advance in realism, depth of characterization and narrative skill, and show Stevenson working at the height of his powers at the end of his tragically curtailed career. "The Beach at Falesá," a South Seas *Heart of Darkness*, helped to create the image of the innocent and degenerate tropical islands that is also found in the work of Melville, Gauguin and Maugham. (The story was transformed into a film script by Dylan Thomas.) The opening paragraph of the salty first-person narrative instantly evokes the fresh and exotic setting and brings the hero, John Wiltshire, to an atmosphere heavy with menace and to a place where white men die suddenly. Like Conrad, Stevenson exposes the corruption of the white man's colonialism—Wiltshire exclaims: "It would be a strange thing if we came all this way and couldn't do what we pleased"—and his crude exploitation of the gentle island people.

Though he learns about the disastrous fate of his predecessor and sees in the drunken Captain Randall (who has "gone native") a warning of his future fate, Wiltshire clings to his optimistic expectations. He naively accepts the lies of Case, a rival trader, who provides a wife, Uma, a bogus marriage contract and false reassurance that everyone is honest in Falesá. In the course of the story, Wiltshire moves from passive persecution by Case to a decision to retaliate, from exploitation of the native woman to a recognition of her generosity and appreciation of her love.

Though Wiltshire pours his case of gin over the edge of the verandah in order to make himself worthy of his new wife, things immediately begin to go wrong. Valuable stock is stolen; the natives gather in a circle to stare at him; they refuse to buy anything in his store; he learns that Case has poisoned a previous trader, Johnny Adams; the native pastor is terrified of Wiltshire's appearance; and he is taboo for mysterious reasons. Case, who can speak the local language, offers to help; but Wiltshire finally realizes that Case has turned the people against him. Uma then reveals that she has been jilted by her suitor and rejected by the village, and that she too is responsible for the taboo. Nevertheless, Wiltshire's love for Uma grows, and he is properly remarried by a missionary. The missionary tells Wiltshire that Case has also corrupted the native pastor, driven one trader off the island and buried a second one alive.

In order to defend himself against Case's evil, Wiltshire seeks Case's devilish shrine—the source of his power over the natives, who are caught in the uneasy transition between paganism and Christianity. In the bush, Wiltshire finds eerie noises made by Aeolian (he calls them "Tyrolean") wind-harps that Case placed in the trees and demonic idols burnished with luminous paint. When Wiltshire exposes Case's fraud to the young chief Maea, Case's rival in love, Maea lifts the taboo and buys from Wiltshire's shop.

To complete the destruction of his enemy, Wiltshire returns to the bush to blow up the shrine with dynamite. As he passes through the jungle, "the light of the lantern, striking among all these trunks and forked branches and twisted rope-ends of lianas, made the whole place, or all that you could see of it, a kind of puzzle of turning shadows." Uma follows him to warn him of danger, they are both wounded by Case and Wiltshire stabs him to death—taking considerable sadistic pleasure from the extinction of evil: "His body kicked under me like a spring sofa; he gave a dreadful kind of a long moan, and lay still. . . . The blood came over my hands, I remember, hot as tea."

At the end of the story, Captain Randall dies after his hand is accidentally blown off and Black Jack (who had performed the bogus wedding ceremony) is eaten by cannibals. Wiltshire finally restores to the island the simplicity and innocence he had originally hoped to find there. He abandons his plan to return to England and open a pub, and remains loyal to his wife and children: "There's nobody thinks less of half-castes than I do; but they're mine, and about all I've got."

Stevenson was dictating "Weir of Hermiston" on the day he died of a cerebral hemorrhage. But his notes and conversation anticipate the conclusion of the novel (see Appendix). Adam Weir, the father of the hero, is based on a notorious eighteenth-century hanging judge, though the bitter quarrels with his son Archie reflect the young Stevenson's arguments with his father. There are four Elliott brothers in the story, three Weirs, two Kirsties (aunt and niece) and one rival for young Kirstie's love, Frank Innes.

The marriage of Archie's parents is an unnatural union of opposites: the father coarse and cruel, the mother refined and religious. The father is hostile to the son, the mother adores him. In a finely wrought, almost Shakesperean scene, the older Kirstie is forced to announce the wife's death to the husband:

> "The Lord peety ye, Hermiston! the Lord prepare ye!," she keened out. "Weary upon me, that I should have to tell it." . . .
>
> "Has the French landit?" cried he. . . .
>
> "Is onybody deid?" says his lordship. "It's no Erchie?" . . .
>
> "It's the mistress, my lord; she just fair flittit before my e'en." . . .
>
> "Weel, it's something of the suddenest," said he. "But she was a dwaibly [infirm] body from the first."

Adam begins to decline after his wife's death—"he became less formidable and infinitely more disgusting"—and, as the animosity between father and son increases, Archie seeks out the wise and sympathetic Lord Glenalmond as a substitute parent.

Archie attends a trial at which his father pronounces the death sentence—"the loathsomeness of Duncan Jopp enveloped and infected the image of his judge," publicly denounces "this God-defying murder" and also condemns capital punishment at a university debating society. (It is a great pity that Stevenson, unlike Orwell, did not give a detailed description of the hanging.) Archie's subsequent interview with his father, which parallels the talk with Lord Glenalmond and shows Adam in a more favorable light, is the high point of the fragment. Instead of defending his principles, Archie, overawed by his father's personality, admits he has made a fool of himself and promises filial obedience. Outraged by his son's disloyalty, Adam disqualifies him from the bar and sends him to manage their country estate at Hermiston. This concludes the first part of the story.

Archie's ephemeral opposition to his father leads to independence as laird of Hermiston, a complete contrast to Adam's house in Edinburgh, and allows him to fulfill his emotional destiny. His wooing of the young Kirstie is strikingly different from his parents' courtship. He finds in her the qualities of his dead mother; she discovers in him the gentleness so notably absent in her four brothers. Though they come from different social classes, Kirstie's father, like Archie's, "had never been loved, but he had been feared in honour." The brothers' honorable vengeance of their father's murder—one "rode his horse to and fro upon the human remnant" of the attacker—foreshadows Archie's projected vengeance on Kirstie's seducer, Frank Innes.

Archie and Kirstie first see each other in church and are immediately attracted, though the torn page in her psalm book warns of their danger. Their fate is hastened by the arrival of the mephistophelean Frank Innes, a casual university friend who sponges off Archie when he runs out of money. He resents Archie's indifference to his visit, quarrels with his friend, slanders him and discovers his secret courtship of Kirstie. Old Kirstie, who had established a satisfying friendship with her master before he met her niece, repeats—for equally selfish motives—Frank's criticism of Archie's love for Kirstie. Both Frank and old Kirstie resent the loss of his favor and both are emotionally frustrated. In a final interview with Kirstie, before the story breaks off, Archie rejects her embraces and pedantically warns her that they must not risk scandal by their supposedly secret meetings. Archie's rather priggish lecture will provoke Kirstie's desire to punish him and lead to her tragic involvement with Frank Innes.

The bleak moorland setting of "Weir of Hermiston" is very different from the lush tropics of Samoa, where he wrote the story; yet the contrast stimulated Stevenson to recall the memories of his Scottish childhood. He lies buried under a simple but solid tombstone on a mountaintop above his grand house Vailima and the town of Apia, on the island of Samoa. Ten years ago I climbed for several hours through the creeping lianas of the jungle, up the steep slippery paths and past the freshening spray of cascading waterfalls till I left the dense foliage, reached the clearing at the peak and saw the magnificent view of the landscape, sea and sky over which the brilliant, gentle spirit that suffused the stories still seemed to preside.

—JEFFREY MEYERS
University of Colorado

The text of these stories is from the Swanston Edition of Stevenson's *Works* (London: Chatto & Windus, 1911–12).

The Body-Snatcher

EVERY NIGHT in the year, four of us sat in the small parlour of the George at Debenham—the undertaker, and the landlord, and Fettes, and myself. Sometimes there would be more; but blow high, blow low, come rain or snow or frost, we four would be each planted in his own particular armchair. Fettes was an old drunken Scotchman, a man of education obviously, and a man of some property, since he lived in idleness. He had come to Debenham years ago, while still young, and by a mere continuance of living had grown to be an adopted townsman. His blue camlet cloak was a local antiquity, like the church-spire. His place in the parlour at the George, his absence from church, his old, crapulous, disreputable vices, were all things of course in Debenham. He had some vague Radical opinions and some fleeting infidelities, which he would now and again set forth and emphasise with tottering slaps upon the table. He drank rum—five glasses regularly every evening; and for the greater portion of his nightly visit to the George sat, with his glass in his right hand, in a state of melancholy alcoholic saturation. We called him the Doctor, for he was supposed to have some special knowledge of medicine, and had been known, upon a pinch, to set a fracture or reduce a dislocation; but beyond these slight particulars, we had no knowledge of his character and antecedents.

One dark winter night—it had struck nine some time before the landlord joined us—there was a sick man in the George, a great neighbouring proprietor suddenly struck down with apoplexy on his way to Parliament; and the great man's still greater London doctor had been telegraphed to his bedside. It was the first time that such a thing had happened in Debenham, for the railway was but newly open, and we were all proportionately moved by the occurrence.

"He's come," said the landlord, after he had filled and lighted his pipe.

"He?" said I. "Who?—not the doctor?"

"Himself," replied our host.

"What is his name?"

"Doctor Macfarlane," said the landlord.

Fettes was far through his third tumbler, stupidly fuddled, now nodding over, now staring mazily around him; but at the last word he seemed to awaken, and repeated the name "Macfarlane" twice, quietly enough the first time, but with sudden emotion at the second.

"Yes," said the landlord, "that's his name, Doctor Wolfe Macfarlane."

Fettes became instantly sober; his eyes awoke, his voice became clear, loud, and steady, his language forcible and earnest. We were all startled by the transformation, as if a man had risen from the dead.

"I beg your pardon," he said, "I am afraid I have not been paying much attention to your talk. Who is this Wolfe Macfarlane?" And then, when he had heard the landlord out, "It cannot be, it cannot be," he added; "and yet I would like well to see him face to face."

"Do you know him, Doctor?" asked the undertaker, with a gasp.

"God forbid!" was the reply. "And yet the name is a strange one; it were too much to fancy two. Tell me, landlord, is he old?"

"Well," said the host, " he's not a young man, to be sure, and his hair is white; but he looks younger than you."

"He is older, though; years older. But," with a slap upon the table, "it's the rum you see in my face—rum and sin. This man, perhaps, may have an easy conscience and a good digestion. Conscience! Hear me speak. You would think I was some good, old, decent Christian, would you not? But no, not I; I never canted. Voltaire might have canted if he'd stood in my shoes; but the brains"—with a rattling fillip on his bald head—"the brains were clear and active, and I saw and made no deductions."

"If you know this doctor," I ventured to remark, after a somewhat awful pause, "I should gather that you do not share the landlord's good opinion."

Fettes paid no regard to me.

"Yes," he said, with sudden decision, "I must see him face to face."

There was another pause, and then a door was closed rather sharply on the first floor, and a step was heard upon the stair.

"That's the doctor," cried the landlord. "Look sharp, and you can catch him."

It was but two steps from the small parlour to the door of the old George Inn; the wide oak staircase landed almost in the street; there was room for a Turkey rug and nothing more between the threshold and the last round of the descent; but this little space was every evening brilliantly lit up, not only by the light upon the stair and the great signal lamp below the sign, but by the warm radiance of the bar-room window. The George thus brightly advertised itself to passers-by in the cold street. Fettes walked steadily to the spot, and we, who were hanging behind, beheld the two men meet, as one of them had phrased it, face to face. Dr. Macfarlane was alert and vigorous. His white hair set off his pale and placid, although energetic, countenance. He was richly dressed in the finest of broadcloth and the whitest of linen, with a great gold watch-chain, and studs and spectacles of the same precious material. He wore a broad-folded tie, white and speckled with lilac, and he carried on his arm a comfortable driving-coat of fur. There was no doubt but he became his years, breathing, as he did, of wealth and consideration; and it was a surprising contrast to see our parlour sot—bald, dirty, pimpled, and robed in his old camlet cloak—confront him at the bottom of the stairs.

"Macfarlane!" he said somewhat loudly, more like a herald than a friend.

The great doctor pulled up short on the fourth step, as though the familiarity of the address surprised and somewhat shocked his dignity.

"Toddy Macfarlane!" repeated Fettes.

The London man almost staggered. He stared for the swiftest of seconds at the man before him, glanced behind him with a sort of scare, and then in a startled whisper, "Fettes!" he said, "you!"

"Ay," said the other, "me! Did you think I was dead too? We are not so easy shut of our acquaintance."

"Hush, hush!" exclaimed the doctor. "Hush, hush! this meeting is so unexpected—I can see you are unmanned. I hardly knew you, I confess, at first; but I am overjoyed—overjoyed to have this opportunity. For the present it must be how-d'ye-do and good-bye in one, for my fly is waiting, and I must not fail the train; but you shall—let me see—yes—you shall give me your address, and you can count on early news of me. We must do something for you, Fettes. I fear you are out at elbows; but we must see to that for auld lang syne, as once we sang at suppers."

"Money!" cried Fettes; "money from you! The money that I had from you is lying where I cast it in the rain."

Dr. Macfarlane had talked himself into some measure of superiority and confidence, but the uncommon energy of this refusal cast him back into his first confusion.

A horrible, ugly look came and went across his almost venerable countenance. "My dear fellow," he said, "be it as you please; my last thought is to offend you. I would intrude on none. I will leave you my address, however—"

"I do not wish it—I do not wish to know the roof that shelters you," interrupted the other. "I heard your name; I feared it might be you; I wished to know if, after all, there were a God; I know now that there is none. Begone!"

He still stood in the middle of the rug, between the stair and doorway; and the great London physician, in order to escape, would be forced to step to one side. It was plain that he hesitated before the thought of this humiliation. White as he was, there was a dangerous glitter in his spectacles; but while he still paused uncertain, he became aware that the driver of his fly was peering in from the street at this unusual scene and caught a glimpse at the same time of our little body from the parlour, huddled by the corner of the bar. The presence of so many witnesses decided him at once to flee. He crouched together, brushing on the wainscot, and made a dart like a serpent, striking for the door. But his tribulation was not entirely at an end, for even as he was passing Fettes clutched him by the arm and these words came in a whisper, and yet painfully distinct, "Have you seen it again?"

The great rich London doctor cried out aloud with a sharp, throttling cry; he dashed his questioner across the open space, and, with his hands over his head, fled out of the door like a detected thief. Before it had occurred to one of us to make a movement the fly was already rattling toward the station. The scene was over like a dream, but the dream had left proofs and traces of its passage. Next day the servant found the fine gold spectacles broken on the threshold, and that very night we were all standing breathless by the bar-room window, and Fettes at our side, sober, pale, and resolute in look.

"God protect us, Mr. Fettes!" said the landlord, coming first into possession of his customary senses. "What in the universe is all this? These are strange things you have been saying."

Fettes turned toward us; he looked us each in succession in the face. "See if you can hold your tongues," said he. "That man Macfarlane is not safe to cross; those that have done so already have repented it too late."

And then, without so much as finishing his third glass, far less waiting for the other two, he bade us good-bye and went forth, under the lamp of the hotel, into the black night.

We three turned to our places in the parlour, with the big red fire and four clear candles; and as we recapitulated what had passed, the first chill of our surprise soon changed into a glow of curiosity. We sat late; it was the latest session I have known in the old George. Each man, before we parted, had his theory that he was bound to prove; and none of us had any nearer business in this world than to track out the past of our condemned companion, and surprise the secret that he shared with the great London doctor. It is no great boast, but I believe I was a better hand at worming out a story than either of my fellows at the George; and perhaps there is now no other man alive who could narrate to you the following foul and unnatural events.

In his young days Fettes studied medicine in the schools of Edinburgh. He had talent of a kind, the talent that picks up swiftly what it hears and readily retails it for its own. He worked little at home; but he was civil, attentive, and intelligent in the presence of his masters. They soon picked him out as a lad who listened closely and remembered well; nay, strange as it seemed to me when I first heard it, he was in those days well favoured, and pleased by his exterior. There was, at that period, a certain extramural teacher of anatomy, whom I shall here designate by the letter K. His name was subsequently too well known. The man who bore it skulked through the streets of Edinburgh in disguise, while the mob that applauded at the execution of Burke called loudly for the blood of his employer. But Mr. K—— was then at the top of his vogue; he enjoyed a popularity due partly to his own talent and address, partly to the incapacity of his rival, the university professor. The students, at least, swore by his name, and Fettes believed himself, and was believed by others, to have laid the foundations of success when he acquired the favour of this meteorically famous man. Mr. K—— was a *bon vivant* as well as an accomplished teacher; he liked a sly illusion no less than a careful preparation. In both capacities Fettes enjoyed and deserved his notice, and by the second year of his attendance he held the half-regular position of second demonstrator, or subassistant in his class.

In this capacity the charge of the theatre and lecture-room devolved in particular upon his shoulders. He had to answer for the cleanliness of the premises and the conduct of the other students, and it was a part of his duty to supply, receive, and divide the various subjects. It was with a view to this last—at that time very delicate—affair that he was lodged by Mr. K—— in the same wynd, and at last in the same building, with the dissecting-rooms. Here, after a night of turbulent pleasures, his hand still tottering, his sight still misty and confused, he would be called out of bed in the black hours before the winter dawn by the unclean and desperate interlopers who supplied the table. He would open the door to these men, since infamous throughout the land. He would help them with their tragic burden, pay them their sordid price, and remain alone, when they were gone, with the unfriendly relics of humanity. From such a scene he would return to snatch another hour or two of slumber, to repair the abuses of the night, and refresh himself for the labours of the day.

Few lads could have been more insensible to the impressions of a life thus passed among the ensigns of mortality. His mind was closed against all general considerations. He was incapable of interest in the fate and fortunes of another, the slave of his own desires and low ambitions. Cold, light, and selfish in the last resort, he had that modicum of prudence, miscalled morality, which keeps a man from inconvenient drunkenness or punishable theft. He coveted, besides, a measure of consideration from his masters and his fellow-pupils, and he had no desire to fail conspicuously in the external parts of life. Thus he made it his pleasure to gain some distinction in his studies, and day after day rendered unimpeachable eye-service to his employer, Mr. K——. For his day of work he indemnified himself by nights of roaring, blackguardly enjoyment; and when that balance had been struck, the organ that he called his conscience declared itself content.

The supply of subjects was a continual trouble to him as well as to his master. In that large and busy class, the raw material of the anatomist kept perpetually running out; and the business thus rendered necessary was not only unpleasant in itself, but threatened dangerous consequences to all who were concerned. It was the policy of Mr. K—— to ask no questions in his dealings with the trade. "They bring the body, and we pay the price," he used to say, dwelling on the alliteration—"*quid pro quo*." And, again, and somewhat profanely, "Ask no questions," he would tell his assistants, "for conscience' sake." There was no understanding that the subjects were provided by the crime of murder. Had that idea been broached to him in words, he would have recoiled in horror; but the lightness of his speech upon so grave a matter was, in itself, an offence against good manners, and a temptation to the men with whom he dealt. Fettes, for instance, had often remarked to himself upon the singular freshness of the bodies. He had been struck again and again by the hangdog, abominable looks of the ruffians who came to him before the dawn; and putting things together clearly in his private thoughts, he perhaps attributed a meaning too immoral and too categorical to the unguarded counsels of his master. He understood his duty, in short, to have three branches: to take what was brought, to pay the price, and to avert the eye from any evidence of crime.

One November morning this policy of silence was put sharply to the test. He had been awake all night with a racking toothache—pacing his room like a caged beast or throwing himself in fury on his bed—and had fallen at last into that profound, uneasy slumber that so often follows on a night of pain, when he was awakened by the third or fourth angry repetition of the concerted signal. There was a thin, bright moonshine; it was bitter cold, windy, and frosty; the town had not yet awakened, but an indefinable stir already preluded the noise and business of the day. The ghouls had come later than usual, and they seemed more than usually eager to be gone. Fettes, sick with sleep, lighted them upstairs. He heard their grumbling Irish voices through a dream; and as they stripped the sack from their sad merchandise he leaned dozing, with his shoulder propped against the wall; he had to shake himself to find the men their money. As he did so his eyes lighted on the dead face. He started; he took two steps nearer, with the candle raised.

"God Almighty!" he cried. "That is Jane Galbraith!"

The men answered nothing, but they shuffled nearer the door.

"I know her, I tell you," he continued. "She was alive and hearty yesterday. It's impossible she can be dead; it's impossible you should have got this body fairly."

"Sure, sir, you're mistaken entirely," said one of the men.

But the other looked Fettes darkly in the eyes, and demanded the money on the spot.

It was impossible to misconceive the threat or to exaggerate the danger. The lad's heart failed him. He stammered some excuses, counted out the sum, and saw his hateful visitors depart. No sooner were they gone than he hastened to confirm his doubts. By a dozen unquestionable marks he identified the girl he had jested with the day before. He saw, with horror, marks upon her body that might well betoken violence. A panic seized him, and he took refuge in his room. There he reflected at length over the discovery that he had made; considered soberly the bearing of Mr. K——'s instructions and the danger to himself of interference in so serious a business, and at last, in sore perplexity, determined to wait for the advice of his immediate superior, the class assistant.

This was a young doctor, Wolfe Macfarlane, a high favourite among all the reckless students, clever, dissipated, and unscrupulous to the last degree. He had travelled and studied abroad. His manners were agreeable and a little forward. He was an authority on the stage, skilful on the ice or the links with skate or golf-club; he dressed with nice audacity, and, to put the finishing touch upon his glory, he kept a gig and a strong trotting-horse. With Fettes he was on terms of intimacy; indeed, their relative positions called for some community of life;

and when subjects were scarce the pair would drive far into the country in Macfarlane's gig, visit and desecrate some lonely graveyard, and return before dawn with their booty to the door of the dissecting-room.

On that particular morning Macfarlane arrived somewhat earlier than his wont. Fettes heard him, and met him on the stairs, told him his story, and showed him the cause of his alarm. Macfarlane examined the marks on her body.

"Yes," he said, with a nod, "it looks fishy."

"Well, what should I do?" asked Fettes.

"Do?" repeated the other. "Do you want to do anything? Least said soonest mended, I should say."

"Some one else might recognise her," objected Fettes. "She was as well known as the Castle Rock."

"We'll hope not," said Macfarlane, "and if anybody does—well, you didn't, don't you see, and there's an end. The fact is, this has been going on too long. Stir up the mud, and you'll get K—— into the most unholy trouble; you'll be in a shocking box yourself. So will I, if you come to that. I should like to know how any one of us would look, or what the devil we should have to say for ourselves, in any Christian witness-box. For me, you know there's one thing certain—that, practically speaking, all our subjects have been murdered."

"Macfarlane!" cried Fettes.

"Come now!" sneered the other. "As if you hadn't suspected it yourself!"

"Suspecting is one thing—"

"And proof another. Yes, I know; and I'm as sorry as you are this should have come here," tapping the body with his cane. "The next best thing for me is not to recognise it; and," he added coolly, "I don't. You may, if you please. I don't dictate, but I think a man of the world would do as I do; and I may add, I fancy that is what K—— would look for at our hands. The question is, Why did he choose us two for his assistants? And I answer, Because he didn't want old wives."

This was the tone of all others to affect the mind of a lad like Fettes. He agreed to imitate Macfarlane. The body of the unfortunate girl was duly dissected, and no one remarked or appeared to recognise her.

One afternoon, when his day's work was over, Fettes dropped into a popular tavern and found Macfarlane sitting with a stranger. This was a small man, very pale and dark, with coal-black eyes. The cut of his features gave a promise of intellect and refinement which was but feebly realised in his manners, for he proved, upon a nearer acquaintance, coarse, vulgar, and stupid. He exercised, however, a very remarkable control over Macfarlane; issued orders like the Great Bashaw; became inflamed at the least discussion or delay, and commented rudely on the servility with which he was obeyed. This most offensive person took a fancy to Fettes on the spot, plied him with drinks, and honoured him with unusual confidences on his past career. If a tenth part of what he confessed were true, he was a very loathsome rogue; and the lad's vanity was tickled by the attention of so experienced a man.

"I'm a pretty bad fellow myself," the stranger remarked, "but Macfarlane is the boy—Toddy Macfarlane I call him. Toddy, order your friend another glass." Or it might be, "Toddy, you jump up and shut the door." "Toddy hates me," he said again. "Oh, yes, Toddy, you do!"

"Don't you call me that confounded name," growled Macfarlane.

"Hear him! Did you ever see the lads play knife? He would like to do that all over my body," remarked the stranger.

"We medicals have a better way than that," said Fettes. "When we dislike a dead friend of ours, we dissect him."

Macfarlane looked up sharply, as though this jest were scarcely to his mind.

The afternoon passed. Gray, for that was the stranger's name, invited Fettes to join them at dinner, ordered a feast so sumptuous that the tavern was thrown into commotion, and when all was done commanded Macfarlane to settle the bill. It was late before they separated; the man Gray was incapably drunk. Macfarlane, sobered by his fury, chewed the cud of the money he had been forced to squander and the slights he had been obliged to swallow. Fettes, with various liquors singing in his head, returned home with devious footsteps and a mind entirely in abeyance. Next day Macfarlane was absent from the class, and Fettes smiled to himself as he imagined him still squiring the intolerable Gray from tavern to tavern. As soon as the hour of liberty had struck he posted from place to place in quest of his last night's companions. He could find them, however, nowhere; so returned early to his rooms, went early to bed, and slept the sleep of the just.

At four in the morning he was awakened by the well-known signal. Descending to the door, he was filled with astonishment to find Macfarlane with his gig, and in the gig one of those long and ghastly packages with which he was so well acquainted.

"What?" he cried. "Have you been out alone? How did you manage?"

But Macfarlane silenced him roughly, bidding him turn to business. When they had got the body upstairs and laid it on the table, Macfarlane made at first as if he were going away. Then he paused and seemed to hesitate; and then, "You had better look at the face," said he, in tones of some constraint. "You had better," he repeated, as Fettes only stared at him in wonder.

"But where, and how, and when did you come by it?" cried the other.

"Look at the face," was the only answer.

Fettes was staggered; strange doubts assailed him. He looked from the young doctor to the body, and then back again. At last, with a start, he did as he was bidden. He had almost expected the sight that met his eyes, and yet the shock was cruel. To see, fixed in the rigidity of death and naked on that coarse layer of sackcloth, the man whom he had left well clad and full of meat and sin upon the threshold of a tavern, awoke, even in the thoughtless Fettes, some of the terrors of the conscience. It was a *cras tibi* which re-echoed in his soul, that two whom he had known should have come to lie upon these icy tables. Yet these were only secondary thoughts. His first concern regarded Wolfe. Unprepared for a challenge so momentous, he knew not how to look his comrade in the face. He durst not meet his eye, and he had neither words nor voice at his command.

It was Macfarlane himself who made the first advance. He came up quietly behind and laid his hand gently but firmly on the other's shoulder.

"Richardson," said he, "may have the head."

Now Richardson was a student who had long been anxious for that portion of the human subject to dissect. There was no answer, and the murderer resumed: "Talking of business, you must pay me; your accounts, you see, must tally."

Fettes found a voice, the ghost of his own: "Pay you!" he cried. "Pay you for that?"

"Why, yes, of course you must. By all means and on every possible account, you must," returned the other. "I dare not give it for nothing, you dare not take it for nothing; it would compromise us both. This is another case like Jane Galbraith's. The more things are wrong the more we must act as if all were right. Where does old K—— keep his money?"

"There," answered Fettes hoarsely, pointing to a cupboard in the corner.

"Give me the key, then," said the other calmly, holding out his hand.

There was an instant's hesitation, and the die was cast. Macfarlane could not suppress a nervous twitch, the infinitesimal mark of an immense relief, as he felt the key between his fingers. He opened the cupboard, brought out pen and ink and a paper-book that stood in one compartment, and separated from the funds in a drawer a sum suitable to the occasion.

"Now, look here," he said, "there is the payment made—first proof of your good faith: first step to your security. You have now to clinch it by a second. Enter the payment in your book, and then you for your part may defy the devil."

The next few seconds were for Fettes an agony of thought; but in balancing his terrors it was the most immediate that triumphed. Any future difficulty seemed almost welcome if he could avoid a present quarrel with Macfarlane. He set down the candle which he had been carrying all this time, and with a steady hand entered the date, the nature, and the amount of the transaction.

"And now," said Macfarlane, "it's only fair that you should pocket the lucre. I've had my share already. By-the-bye, when a man of the world falls into a bit of luck, has a few shillings extra in his pocket—I'm ashamed to speak of it, but there's a rule of conduct in the case. No treating, no purchase of expensive class-books, no squaring of old debts; borrow, don't lend."

"Macfarlane," began Fettes, still somewhat hoarsely, "I have put my neck in a halter to oblige you."

"To oblige me?" cried Wolfe. "Oh, come! You did, as

near as I can see the matter, what you downright had to do in self-defence. Suppose I got into trouble, where would you be? This second little matter flows clearly from the first. Mr. Gray is the continuation of Miss Galbraith. You can't begin and then stop. If you begin, you must keep on beginning; that's the truth. No rest for the wicked."

A horrible sense of blackness and the treachery of fate seized hold upon the soul of the unhappy student.

"My God!" he cried, "but what have I done? and when did I begin? To be made a class assistant—in the name of reason, where's the harm in that? Service wanted the position; Service might have got it. Would *he* have been where *I* am now!"

"My dear fellow," said Macfarlane, "what a boy you are! What harm *has* come to you? What harm *can* come to you if you hold your tongue? Why, man, do you know what this life is? There are two squads of us—the lions and the lambs. If you're a lamb, you'll come to lie upon these tables like Gray or Jane Galbraith; if you're a lion, you'll live and drive a horse like me, like K——, like all the world with any wit or courage. You're staggered at the first. But look at K——! My dear fellow, you're clever, you have pluck. I like you, and K—— likes you. You were born to lead the hunt; and I tell you, on my honour and my experience of life, three days from now you'll laugh at all these scarecrows like a High School boy at a farce."

And with that Macfarlane took his departure and drove off up the wynd in his gig to get under cover before daylight. Fettes was thus left alone with his regrets. He saw the miserable peril in which he stood involved. He saw, with inexpressible dismay, that there was no limit to his weakness, and that, from concession to concession, he had fallen from the arbiter of Macfarlane's destiny to his paid and helpless accomplice. He would have given the world to have been a little braver at the time, but it did not occur to him that he might still be brave. The secret of Jane Galbraith and the cursed entry in the daybook closed his mouth.

Hours passed; the class began to arrive; the members of the unhappy Gray were dealt out to one and to another, and received without remark. Richardson was made happy with the head; and before the hour of freedom rang Fettes trembled with exultation to perceive how far they had already gone toward safety.

For two days he continued to watch, with increasing joy, the dreadful process of disguise.

On the third day Macfarlane made his appearance. He had been ill, he said; but he made up for lost time by the energy with which he directed the students. To Richardson in particular he extended the most valuable assistance and advice, and that student, encouraged by the praise of the demonstrator, burned high with ambitious hopes, and saw the medal already in his grasp.

Before the week was out Macfarlane's prophecy had been fulfilled. Fettes had outlived his terrors and had forgotten his baseness. He began to plume himself upon his courage, and had so arranged the story in his mind that he could look back on these events with an unhealthy pride. Of his accomplice he saw but little. They met, of course, in the business of the class; they received their orders together from Mr. K——. At times they had a word or two in private, and Macfarlane was from first to last particularly kind and jovial. But it was plain that he avoided any reference to their common secret; and even when Fettes whispered to him that he had cast in his lot with the lions and forsworn the lambs, he only signed to him smilingly to hold his peace.

At length an occasion arose which threw the pair once more into a closer union. Mr. K—— was again short of subjects; pupils were eager, and it was part of this teacher's pretensions to be always well supplied. At the same time there came the news of a burial in the rustic graveyard of Glencorse. Time has little changed the place in question. It stood then, as now, upon a cross road, out of call of human habitations, and buried fathom deep in the foliage of six cedar trees. The cries of the sheep upon the neighbouring hills, the streamlets upon either hand, one loudly singing among pebbles, the other dripping furtively from pond to pond, the stir of the wind in mountainous old flowering chestnuts, and once in seven days the voice of the bell and the old tunes of the precentor, were the only sounds that disturbed the silence around the rural church. The Resurrection Man—to use a byname of the period—was not to be deterred by any of the sanctities of customary piety. It was part of his trade to despise and desecrate the scrolls and trumpets of old tombs, the paths worn by the feet of worshippers and mourners, and the offerings and the inscriptions of bereaved affection. To rustic neighbourhoods, where love is more than commonly tenacious, and where some bonds of blood or fellowship unite the entire society of a parish, the body-snatcher, far from being repelled by natural respect, was attracted by the ease and safety of the task. To bodies that had been laid in earth, in joyful expectation of a far different awakening, there came that hasty, lamplit, terror-haunted resurrection of the spade and mattock. The coffin was forced, the cerements torn, and the melancholy relics, clad in sackcloth, after being rattled for hours on moonless byways, were at length exposed to uttermost indignities before a class of gaping boys.

Somewhat as two vultures may swoop upon a dying lamb, Fettes and Macfarlane were to be let loose upon a grave in that green and quiet resting-place. The wife of a farmer, a woman who had lived for sixty years, and been known for nothing but good butter and a godly conversation, was to be rooted from her grave at midnight and carried, dead and naked, to that far-away city that she had always honoured with her Sunday's best; the place beside her family was to be empty till the crack of doom; her innocent and almost venerable members to be exposed to that last curiosity of the anatomist.

Late one afternoon the pair set forth, well wrapped in cloaks and furnished with a formidable bottle. It rained without remission—a cold, dense, lashing rain. Now and again there blew a puff of wind, but these sheets of falling water kept it down. Bottle and all, it was a sad and silent drive as far as Penicuik, where they were to spend the evening. They stopped once, to hide their implements in a thick bush not far from the churchyard, and once again at the Fisher's Tryst, to have a toast before the kitchen fire and vary their nips of whisky with a glass of ale. When they reached their journey's end the gig was housed, the horse was fed and comforted, and the two young doctors in a private room sat down to the best dinner and the best wine the house afforded. The lights, the fire, the beating rain upon the window, the cold. incongruous work that lay before them, added zest to their enjoyment of the meal. With every glass their cordiality increased. Soon Macfarlane handed a little pile of gold to his companion.

"A compliment," he said. "Between friends these little d——d accommodations ought to fly like pipelights."

Fettes pocketed the money, and applauded the sentiment to the echo. "You are a philosopher," he cried. "I was an ass till I knew you. You and K—— between you, by the Lord Harry! but you'll make a man of me."

"Of course we shall," applauded Macfarlane. "A man? I tell you, it required a man to back me up the other morning. There are some big, brawling, forty-year-old cowards who would have turned sick at the look of the d——d thing; but not you—you kept your head. I watched you."

"Well, and why not?" Fettes thus vaunted himself. "It was no affair of mine. There was nothing to gain on the one side but disturbance, and on the other I could count on your gratitude, don't you see?" And he slapped his pocket till the gold pieces rang.

Macfarlane somehow felt a certain touch of alarm at these unpleasant words. He may have regretted that he had taught his young companion so successfully, but he had no time to interfere, for the other noisily continued in this boastful strain:—

"The great thing is not to be afraid. Now, between you and me, I don't want to hang—that's practical; but for all cant, Macfarlane, I was born with a contempt. Hell, God, Devil, right, wrong, sin, crime, and all the old gallery of curiosities—they may frighten boys, but men of the world, like you and me, despise them. Here's to the memory of Gray!"

It was by this time growing somewhat late. The gig, according to order, was brought round to the door with both lamps brightly shining, and the young men had to pay their bill and take the road. They announced that they were bound for Peebles and drove in that direction till they were clear of the last houses of the town; then, extinguishing the lamps, returned upon their course, and followed a by-road toward Glencorse. There was no sound but that of their own passage, and the incessant, strident pouring of the rain. It was pitch dark; here and there a white gate or a white stone in the wall guided them for a short space across the night; but for the most part it was at a foot pace, and almost groping, that they picked their way through that resonant blackness to their solemn and isolated destination. In the sunken woods that traverse the neighbourhood of the burying-ground the last glimmer failed them, and it became necessary to kindle a match and re-illumine one of the lanterns of the gig. Thus, under the dripping trees, and environed by huge and moving shadows, they reached the scene of their unhallowed labours.

They were both experienced in such affairs, and powerful with the spade; and they had scarce been twenty minutes at their task before they were rewarded by a dull rattle on the coffin lid. At the same moment, Macfarlane, having hurt his hand upon a stone, flung it carelessly above his head. The grave, in which they now stood almost to the shoulders, was close to the edge of the plateau of the graveyard; and the gig lamp had been propped, the better to illuminate their labours, against a tree, and on the immediate verge of the steep bank descending to the stream. Chance had taken a sure aim with the stone. Then came a clang of broken glass; night fell upon them; sounds alternately dull and ringing announced the bounding of the lantern down the bank, and its occasional collision with the trees. A stone or two, which it had dislodged in its descent, rattled behind it into the profundities of the glen; and then silence, like night, resumed its sway; and they might bend their hearing to its utmost pitch, but naught was to be heard except the rain, now marching to the wind, now steadily falling over miles of open country.

They were so nearly at an end of their abhorred task that they judged it wisest to complete it in the dark. The coffin was exhumed and broken open; the body inserted in the dripping sack and carried between them to the gig; one mounted to keep it in its place, and the other, taking the horse by the mouth, groped along by wall and bush until they reached the wider road by the Fisher's Tryst. Here was a faint, diffused radiancy, which they hailed like daylight; by that they pushed the horse to a good pace and began to rattle along merrily in the direction of the town.

They had both been wetted to the skin during their operations, and now, as the gig jumped among the deep ruts, the thing that stood propped between them fell now upon one and now upon the other. At every repetition of the horrid contact each instinctively repelled it with the greater haste; and the process, natural although it was, began to tell upon the nerves of the companions. Macfarlane made some ill-favoured jest about the farmer's wife, but it came hollowly from his lips, and was allowed to drop in silence. Still their unnatural burden bumped from side to side; and now the head would be laid, as if in confidence, upon their shoulders, and now the drenching sackcloth would flap icily about their faces. A creeping chill began to possess the soul of Fettes. He peered at the bundle, and it seemed somehow larger than at first. All over the country-side, and from every degree of distance, the farm dogs accompanied their passage with tragic ululations; and it grew and grew upon his mind that some unnatural miracle had been accomplished, that some nameless change had befallen the dead body, and that it was in fear of their unholy burden that the dogs were howling.

"For God's sake," said he, making a great effort to arrive at speech, "for God's sake, let's have a light!"

Seemingly Macfarlane was affected in the same direction; for, though he made no reply, he stopped the horse, passed the reins to his companion, got down and proceeded to kindle the remaining lamp. They had by that time got no farther than the cross-road down to Auchenclinny. The rain still poured as though the deluge were returning, and it was no easy matter to make a light in such a world of wet and darkness. When at last the flickering blue flame had been transferred to the wick and began to expand and clarify, and shed a wide circle of misty brightness round the gig, it became possible for the two young men to see each other and the thing they had along with them. The rain had moulded the rough sacking to the outlines of the body underneath; the head was distinct from the trunk, the shoulders plainly modelled; something at once spectral and human riveted their eyes upon the ghastly comrade of their drive.

For some time Macfarlane stood motionless, holding up the lamp. A nameless dread was swathed, like a wet sheet, about the body, and tightened the white skin upon the face of Fettes; a fear that was meaningless, a horror of what could not be, kept mounting to his brain. Another beat of the watch, and he had spoken. But his comrade forestalled him.

"That is not a woman," said Macfarlane, in a hushed voice.

"It was a woman when we put her in," whispered Fettes.

"Hold that lamp," said the other. "I must see her face."

And as Fettes took the lamp his companion untied the fastenings of the sack and drew down the cover from the head. The light fell very clear upon the dark, well-moulded features and smooth-shaven cheeks of a too familiar countenance, often beheld in dreams of both of these young men. A wild yell rang up into the night; each leaped from his own side into the roadway: the lamp fell, broke, and was extinguished; and the horse, terrified by this unusual commotion, bounded and went off toward Edinburgh at a gallop, bearing along with it, solo occupant of the gig, the body of the dead and long-dissected Gray.

The Sire De Malétroit's Door

DENIS DE BEAULIEU was not yet two-and-twenty, but he counted himself a grown man, and a very accomplished cavalier into the bargain. Lads were early formed in that rough, war-faring epoch; and when one has been in a pitched battle and a dozen raids, has killed one's man in an honourable fashion, and knows a thing or two of strategy and mankind, a certain swagger in the gait is surely to be pardoned. He had put up his horse with due care, and supped with due deliberation; and then, in a very agreeable frame of mind, went out to pay a visit in the grey of the evening. It was not a very wise proceeding on the young man's part. He would have done better to remain beside the fire or go decently to bed. For the town was full of the troops of Burgundy and England under a mixed command; and though Denis was there on safe-conduct, his safe-conduct was like to serve him little on a chance encounter.

It was September 1429; the weather had fallen sharp; a flighty piping wind, laden with showers, beat about the township; and the dead leaves ran riot along the streets. Here and there a window was already lighted up; and the noise of men-at-arms making merry over supper within came forth in fits and was swallowed up and carried away by the wind. The night fell swiftly; the flag of England, fluttering on the spire-top, grew ever fainter and fainter against the flying clouds—a black speck like a swallow in the tumultuous, leaden chaos of the sky. As the night fell the wind rose, and began to hoot under archways and roar amid the tree-tops in the valley below the town.

Denis de Beaulieu walked fast, and was soon knocking at his friend's door; but though he promised himself to stay only a little while and make an early return, his welcome was so pleasant, and he found so much to delay him, that it was already long past midnight before he said good-bye upon the threshold. The wind had fallen again in the meanwhile; the night was as black as the grave; not a star, nor a glimmer of moonshine, slipped through the canopy of cloud. Denis was ill-acquainted with the intricate lanes of Château Landon; even by daylight he had found some trouble in picking his way; and in this absolute darkness he soon lost it altogether. He was certain of one thing only—to keep mounting the hill; for his friend's house lay at the lower end, or tail, of Château Landon, while the inn was up at the head, under the great church spire. With this clue to go upon he stumbled and groped forward, now breathing more freely in open places where there was a good slice of sky overhead, now feeling along the wall in stifling closes. It is an eerie and mysterious position to be thus submerged in opaque blackness in an almost unknown town. The silence is terrifying in its possibilities. The touch of cold window-bars to the exploring hand startles the man like the touch of a toad; the inequalities of the pavement shake his heart into his mouth; a piece of denser darkness threatens an ambuscade or a chasm in the pathway; and where the air is brighter, the houses put on strange and bewildering appearances, as if to lead him farther from his way. For Denis, who had to regain his inn without attracting notice, there was real danger as well as mere discomfort in the walk; and he went warily and boldly at once, and at every corner paused to make an observation.

He had been for some time threading a lane so narrow that he could touch a wall with either hand, when it began to open out and go sharply downward. Plainly this lay no longer in the direction of his inn; but the hope of a little more light tempted him forward to reconnoitre. The lane ended in a terrace with a bartizan wall, which gave an outlook between high houses, as out of an embrasure, into the valley lying dark and formless several hundred feet below. Denis looked down, and could discern a few tree-tops waving and a single speck of brightness where the river ran across a weir. The weather was clearing up, and the sky had lightened, so as to show the outline of the heavier clouds and the dark margin of the hills. By the uncertain glimmer, the house on his left hand should be a place of some pretensions; it was surmounted by several pinnacles and turret-tops; the round stern of a chapel, with a fringe of flying buttresses, projected boldly from the main block; and the door was sheltered under a deep porch carved with figures and overhung by two long gargoyles. The windows of the chapel gleamed through their intricate tracery with a light as of many tapers, and threw out the buttresses and the peaked roof in a more intense blackness against the sky. It was plainly the hotel of some great family of the neighbourhood; and as it reminded Denis of a town-house of his own at Bourges, he stood for some time gazing up at it and mentally gauging the skill of the architects and the consideration of the two families.

There seemed to be no issue to the terrace but the lane by which he had reached it; he could only retrace his steps, but he had gained some notion of his whereabouts, and hoped by this means to hit the main thoroughfare and speedily regain the inn. He was reckoning without that chapter of accidents which was to make this night memorable above all others in his career; for he had not gone back above a hundred yards before he saw a light coming to meet him, and heard loud voices speaking together in the echoing narrows of the lane. It was a party of men-at-arms going the night-round with torches. Denis assured himself that they had all been making free with the wine-bowl, and were in no mood to be particular about safe-conducts or the niceties of chivalrous war. It was as like as not that they would kill him like a dog and leave him where he fell. The situation was inspiriting, but nervous. Their own torches would conceal him from sight, he reflected; and he hoped that they would drown the noise of his footsteps with their own empty voices. If he were but fleet and silent, he might evade their notice altogether.

Unfortunately, as he turned to beat a retreat, his foot rolled upon a pebble; he fell against the wall with an ejaculation, and his sword rang loudly on the stones. Two or three voices demanded who went there—some in French, some in English; but Denis made no reply, and ran the faster down the lane. Once upon the terrace, he paused to look back. They still kept calling after him, and just then began to double the pace in pursuit, with a considerable clank of armour, and great tossing of the torchlight to and fro in the narrow jaws of the passage.

Denis cast a look around and darted into the porch. There he might escape observation, or—if that were too much to expect—was in a capital posture whether for parley or defence. So thinking, he drew his sword and tried to set his back against the door. To his surprise, it yielded behind his weight; and though he turned in a moment, continued to swing back on oiled and noiseless hinges, until it stood wide open on a black interior. When things fall out opportunely for the person concerned, he is not apt to be critical about the how or why, his own immediate personal convenience seeming a sufficient reason for the strangest oddities and revolutions in our sublunary things; and so Denis, without a moment's hesitation, stepped within and partly closed the door behind him to conceal his place of refuge. Nothing was further from his thoughts than to close it altogether; but for some inexplicable reason—perhaps by a spring or a weight—the ponderous mass of oak whipped itself out of his fingers and clanked to, with a formidable rumble and noise like the falling of an automatic bar.

The round, at that very moment, debouched upon the terrace, and proceeded to summon him with shouts and curses. He heard them ferreting in the dark corners; the stock of a lance even rattled along the outer surface of the door behind which he stood; but these gentlemen were in too high a humour to be long delayed, and soon made off down a corkscrew pathway which had escaped Denis's observation, and passed out of sight and hearing along the battlements of the town.

Denis breathed again. He gave them a few minutes' grace for fear of accidents, and then groped about for some means of opening the door and slipping forth again. The inner surface was quite smooth, not a handle, not a moulding, not a projection of any sort. He got his fingernails round the edges and pulled, but the mass was immovable. He shook it; it was as firm as a rock. Denis de Beaulieu frowned and gave vent to a little noiseless whistle. What ailed the door? he wondered. Why was it open? How came it to shut so easily and so effectually after him? There was something obscure and underhand about all this that was little to the young man's fancy. It looked like a snare; and yet who could suppose a snare in such a quiet by-street and in a house of so prosperous and even noble an exterior? And yet—snare or no snare, intentionally or unintentionally—here he was, prettily trapped; and for the life of him he could see no way out of it again. The darkness began to weigh upon him. He gave ear; all was silent without, but within and close by he seemed to catch a faint sighing, a faint sobbing rustle, a little stealthy creak—as though many persons were at his side, holding themselves quite still, and governing even their respiration with the extreme of slyness. The idea went to his vitals with a shock, and he faced about suddenly as if to defend his life. Then, for the first time, he became aware of a light about the level of his eyes, and at some distance in the interior of the house—a vertical thread of light, widening towards the bottom, such as might escape between two wings of arras over a doorway. To see anything was a relief to Denis; it was like a piece of solid ground to a man labouring in a morass; his mind seized upon it with avidity; and he stood staring at it and trying to piece together some logical conception of his surroundings. Plainly there was a flight of steps ascending from his own level to that of this illuminated doorway; and indeed he thought he could make out another thread of light, as fine as a needle, and as faint as phosphorescence, which might very well be reflected along the polished wood of a handrail. Since he had begun to suspect that he was not alone, his heart had continued to beat with smothering violence, and an intolerable desire for action of any sort had possessed itself of his spirit. He was in deadly peril, he believed. What could be more natural than to mount the staircase, lift the curtain, and confront his difficulty at once? At least he would be dealing with something tangible; at least he would be no longer in the dark. He stepped slowly forward with outstretched hands, until his foot struck the bottom step; then he rapidly scaled the stairs, stood for a moment to compose his expression, lifted the arras, and went in.

He found himself in a large apartment of polished stone. There were three doors; one on each of three sides; all similarly curtained with tapestry. The fourth side was occupied by two large windows and a great stone chimney-piece, carved with the arms of the Malétroits. Denis recognised the bearings, and was gratified to find himself in such good hands. The room was strongly illuminated; but it contained little furniture except a heavy table and a chair or two, the hearth was innocent of fire, and the pavement was but sparsely strewn with rushes clearly many days old.

On a high chair beside the chimney, and directly facing Denis as he entered, sat a little old gentleman in a fur tippet. He sat with his legs crossed and his hands folded, and a cup of spiced wine stood by his elbow on a bracket on the wall. His countenance had a strongly masculine cast; not properly human, but such as we see in the bull, the goat, or the domestic boar; something equivocal and wheedling, something greedy, brutal, and dangerous. The upper lip was inordinately full, as though swollen by a blow or a toothache; and the smile, the peaked eyebrows, and the small, strong eyes were quaintly and almost comically evil in expression. Beautiful white hair hung straight all round his head, like a saint's, and fell in a single curl upon the tippet. His beard and moustache were the pink of venerable sweetness. Age, probably in consequence of inordinate precautions, had left no mark upon his hands; and the Malétroit hand was famous. It would be difficult to imagine anything at once so fleshy and so delicate in design; the tapered, sensual fingers were like those of one of Leonardo's women; the fork of the thumb made a dimple protuberance when closed; the nails were perfectly shaped, and of a dead, surprising whiteness. It rendered his aspect tenfold more redoubtable, that a man with hands like these should keep them devoutly folded in his lap like a virgin martyr—that a man with so intense and startling an expression of face should sit patiently on his seat and contemplate people with an unwinking stare, like a god, or a god's statue. His quiescence seemed ironical and treacherous, it fitted so poorly with his looks.

Such was Alain, Sire de Malétroit.

Denis and he looked silently at each other for a second or two.

"Pray step in," said the Sire de Malétroit. "I have been expecting you all the evening."

He had not risen, but he accompanied his words with a smile and a slight but courteous inclination of the head. Partly from the smile, partly from the strange musical murmur with which the Sire prefaced his observation, Denis felt a strong shudder of disgust go through his marrow. And what with disgust and honest confusion of mind, he could scarcely get words together in reply.

"I fear," he said, "that this is a double accident. I am not the person you suppose me. It seems you were looking for a visit; but for my part, nothing was further from my thoughts—nothing could be more contrary to my wishes—than this intrusion."

"Well, well," replied the old gentleman indulgently, "here you are, which is the main point. Seat yourself, my friend and put yourself entirely at your ease. We shall arrange our little affairs presently."

Denis perceived that the matter was still complicated with some misconception, and he hastened to continue his explanations.

"Your door—" he began.

"About my door?" asked the other, raising his peaked eyebrows. "A little piece of ingenuity." And he shrugged his shoulders. "A hospitable fancy! By your own account, you were not desirous of making my acquaintance. We old people look for such reluctance now and then; and when it touches our honour, we cast about until we find some way of overcoming it. You arrive uninvited but believe me, very welcome."

"You persist in error, sir," said Denis. "There can be no question between you and me. I am a stranger in this countryside. My name is Denis, damoiseau de Beaulieu. If you see me in your house, it is only—"

"My young friend," interrupted the other, "you will permit me to have my own ideas on that subject. They probably differ from yours at the present moment," he added, with a leer, "but time will show which of us is in the right."

Denis was convinced he had to do with a lunatic. He seated himself with a shrug, content to wait the upshot; and a pause ensued, during which he thought he could distinguish a hurried gabbling as of prayer from behind the arras immediately opposite him. Sometimes there seemed to be but one person engaged, sometimes two; and the vehemence of the voice, low as it was, seemed to indicate either haste or an agony of spirit. It occurred to him that this piece of tapestry covered the entrance to the chapel he had noticed from without.

The old gentleman meanwhile surveyed Denis from head to foot with a smile, and from time to time emitted little noises like a bird or a mouse, which seemed to indicate a high degree of satisfaction. This state of matters became rapidly insupportable; and Denis, to put an end to it, remarked politely that the wind had gone down.

The old gentleman fell into a fit of silent laughter, so prolonged and violent that he became quite red in the face. Denis got upon his feet at once, and put on his hat with a flourish.

"Sir," he said, "if you are in your wits, you have affronted me grossly. If you are out of them, I flatter myself I can find better employment for my brains than to talk with lunatics. My conscience is clear; you have made a fool of me from the first moment; you have refused to hear my explanations; and now there is no power under God will make me stay here any longer; and if I cannot make my way out in a more decent fashion, I will hack your door in pieces with my sword."

The Sire de Malétroit raised his right hand and wagged it at Denis with the fore and little fingers extended.

"My dear nephew," he said, " sit down."

"Nephew!" retorted Denis, "you lie in your throat"; and he snapped his fingers in his face.

"Sit down, you rogue!" cried the old gentleman, in a sudden, harsh voice, like the barking of a dog. "Do you fancy," he went on, "that when I made my little contrivance for the door I had stopped short with that? If you prefer to be bound hand and foot till your bones ache, rise and try to go away. If you choose to remain a free young buck, agreeably conversing with an old gentleman—why, sit where you are in peace, and God be with you."

"Do you mean I am a prisoner?" demanded Denis.

"I state the facts," replied the other. "I would rather leave the conclusion to yourself."

Denis sat down again. Externally he managed to keep pretty calm; but within, he was now boiling with anger, now chilled with apprehension. He no longer felt convinced that he was dealing with a madman. And if the old gentleman was sane, what, in God's name, had he to look for? What absurd or tragical adventure had befallen him? What countenance was he to assume?

While he was thus unpleasantly reflecting, the arras that overhung the chapel door was raised, and a tall priest in his robes came forth, and, giving a long, keen stare at Denis, said something in an undertone to Sire de Malétroit.

"She is in a better frame of spirit?" asked the latter.

"She is more resigned, messire," replied the priest.

"Now the Lord help her, she is hard to please!" sneered the old gentleman. "A likely stripling—not ill-born—and of her own choosing too? Why, what more would the jade have?"

"The situation is not usual for a young damsel," said the other, "and somewhat trying to her blushes."

"She should have thought of that before she began the dance! It was none of my choosing, God knows that: but since she is in it, by Our Lady, she shall carry it to the end." And then addressing Denis, "Monsieur de Beaulieu," he asked, "may I present you to my niece? She has been waiting your arrival, I may say, with even greater impatience than myself."

Denis had resigned himself with a good grace—all he desired was to know the worst of it as speedily as possible; so he rose at once, and bowed in acquiescence. The Sire de Malétroit followed his example, and limped, with the assistance of the chaplain's arm, towards the chapel door. The priest pulled aside the arras, and all three entered. The building had considerable architectural pretensions. A light groining sprang from six stout columns, and hung down in two rich pendants from the centre of the vault. The place terminated behind the altar in a round end, embossed and honeycombed with a superfluity of ornament in relief, and pierced by many little windows shaped like stars, trefoils, or wheels. These windows were imperfectly glazed, so that the night-air circulated freely in the chapel. The tapers, of which there must have been half a hundred burning on the altar, were unmercifully blown about; and the light went through many different phases of brilliancy and semi-eclipse. On the steps in front of the altar knelt a young girl richly attired as a bride. A chill settled over Denis as he observed her costume; he fought with desperate energy against the conclusion that was being thrust upon his mind; it could not—it should not—be as he feared.

"Blanche," said the Sire, in his most flute-like tones, "I have brought a friend to see you, my little girl; turn round and give him your pretty hand. It is good to be devout; but it is necessary to be polite, my niece."

The girl rose to her feet and turned towards the newcomers. She moved all of a piece; and shame and exhaustion were expressed in every line of her fresh young body; and she held her head down and kept her eyes upon the pavement, as she came slowly forward. In the course of her advance, her eyes fell upon Denis de Beaulieu's feet—feet of which he was justly vain, be it remarked, and wore in the most elegant accoutrement even while travelling. She paused—started, as if his yellow boots had conveyed some shocking meaning—and glanced suddenly up into the wearer's countenance. Their eyes met; shame gave place to horror and terror in her looks; the blood left her lips; with a piercing scream she covered her face with her hands and sank upon the chapel floor.

"That is not the man!" she cried. "My uncle, that is not the man!"

The Sire de Malétroit chirped agreeably. "Of course not," he said, " I expected as much. It was so unfortunate you could not remember his name."

"Indeed," she cried, "indeed, I have never seen this person till this moment—I have never so much as set eyes upon him—I never wish to see him again. Sir," she said, turning to Denis, "if you are a gentleman, you will bear me out. Have I ever seen you—have you ever seen me—before this accursed hour?"

"To speak for myself, I have never had that pleasure," answered the young man. "This is the first time, messire, that I have met with your engaging niece."

The old gentleman shrugged his shoulders.

"I am distressed to hear it," he said. "But it is never too late to begin. I had little more acquaintance with my own late lady ere I married her; which proves," he added with a grimace, "that these impromptu marriages may often produce an excellent understanding in the long-run. As the bridegroom is to have a voice in the matter, I will give him two hours to make up for lost time before we proceed with the ceremony." And he turned towards the door, followed by the clergyman.

The girl was on her feet in a moment. "My uncle, you cannot be in earnest," she said. "I declare before God I will stab myself rather than be forced on that young man.

The heart rises at it; God forbids such marriages; you dishonour your white hair. Oh, my uncle, pity me! There is not a woman in all the world but would prefer death to such a nuptial. Is it possible," she added, faltering—"is it possible that you do not believe me—that you still think this"—and she pointed at Denis with a tremor of anger and contempt—"that you still think *this* to be the man?"

"Frankly," said the old gentleman, pausing on the threshold, "I do. But let me explain to you once for all, Blanche de Malétroit, my way of thinking about this affair. When you took it into your head to dishonour my family and the name that I have borne, in peace and war, for more than threescore years, you forfeited, not only the right to question my designs, but that of looking me in the face. If your father had been alive, he would have spat on you and turned you out of doors. His was the hand of iron. You may bless your God you have only to deal with the hand of velvet, mademoiselle. It was my duty to get you married without delay. Out of pure goodwill, I have tried to find your own gallant for you. And I believe I have succeeded. But before God and all the holy angels, Blanche de Malétroit, if I have not, I care not one jack-straw. So let me recommend you to be polite to our young friend; for upon my word, your next groom may be less appetising."

And with that he went out, with the chaplain at his heels; and the arras fell behind the pair.

The girl turned upon Denis with flashing eyes.

"And what, sir," she demanded, "may be the meaning of all this?"

"God knows," returned Denis gloomily. "I am a prisoner in this house, which seems full of mad people. More I know not, and nothing do I understand."

"And pray how came you here?" she asked.

He told her as briefly as he could. "For the rest," he added, "perhaps you will follow my example, and tell me the answer to all these riddles, and what, in God's name, is like to be the end of it."

She stood silent for a little, and he could see her lips tremble and her tearless eyes burn with a feverish lustre. Then she pressed her forehead in both hands.

"Alas, how my head aches!" she said wearily—"to say nothing of my poor heart! But it is due to you to know my story, unmaidenly as it must seem. I am called Blanche de Malétroit; I have been without father or mother for—oh! for as long as I can recollect, and indeed I have been most unhappy all my life. Three months ago a young captain began to stand near me every day in church. I could see that I pleased him; I am much to blame, but I was so glad that any one should love me; and when he passed me a letter, I took it home with me and read it with great pleasure. Since that time he has written many. He was so anxious to speak with me, poor fellow! and kept asking me to leave the door open some evening that we might have two words upon the stair. For he knew how much my uncle trusted me." She gave something like a sob at that, and it was a moment before she could go on. "My uncle is a hard man, but he is very shrewd," she said at last. "He has performed many feats in war, and was a great person at court, and much trusted by Queen Isabeau in old days. How he came to suspect me I cannot tell; but it is hard to keep anything from his knowledge; and this morning, as we came from mass, he took my hand in his, forced it open, and read my little billet, walking by my side all the while. When he had finished, he gave it back to me with great politeness. It contained another request to have the door left open; and this has been the ruin of us all. My uncle kept me strictly in my room until evening, and then ordered me to dress myself as you see me—a hard mockery for a young girl, do you not think so? I suppose, when he could not prevail with me to tell him the young captain's name, he must have laid a trap for him: into which, alas! you have fallen in the anger of God. I looked for much confusion; for how could I tell whether he was willing to take me for his wife on these sharp terms? He might have been trifling with me from the first; or I might have made myself too cheap in his eyes. But truly I had not looked for such a shameful punishment as this! I could not think that God would let a girl be so disgraced before a young man. And now I have told you all; and I can scarcely hope that you will not despise me."

Denis made her a respectful inclination.

"Madam," he said, "you have honoured me by your confidence. It remains for me to prove that I am not unworthy of the honour. Is Messire de Malétroit at hand?"

"I believe he is writing in the salle without," she answered.

"May I lead you thither, madam?" asked Denis, offering his hand with his most courtly bearing.

She accepted it; and the pair passed out of the chapel, Blanche in a very drooping and shamefaced condition, but Denis strutting and ruffling in the consciousness of a mission, and a boyish certainty of accomplishing it with honour.

The Sire de Malétroit rose to meet them with an ironical obeisance.

"Sir," said Denis, with the grandest possible air, "I believe I am to have some say in the matter of this marriage; and let me tell you at once, I will be no party to forcing the inclination of this young lady. Had it been freely offered to me, I should have been proud to accept her hand, for I perceive she is as good as she is beautiful; but as things are, I have now the honour, messire, of refusing."

Blanche looked at him with gratitude in her eyes; but the old gentleman only smiled and smiled, until his smile grew positively sickening to Denis.

"I am afraid," he said, "Monsieur de Beaulieu, that you do not perfectly understand the choice I have to offer you. Follow me, I beseech you, to this window." And he led the way to one of the large windows which stood open on the night. "You observe," he went on, "there is an iron ring in the upper masonry, and reeved through that a very efficacious rope. Now, mark my words: if you should find your disinclination to my niece's person insurmountable, I shall have you hanged out of this window before sunrise. I shall only proceed to such an extremity with the greatest regret, you may believe me. For it is not at all your death that I desire, but my niece's establishment in life. At the same time, it must come to that if you prove obstinate. Your family, Monsieur de Beaulieu, is very well in its way; but if you sprang from Charlemagne, you should not refuse the hand of a Malétroit with impunity—not if she had been as common as the Paris road—not if she were as hideous as the gargoyle over my door. Neither my niece nor you, nor my own private feelings, move me at all in this matter. The honour of my house has been compromised; I believe you to be the guilty person; at least you are now in the secret; and you can hardly wonder if I request you to wipe out the stain. If you will not, your blood be on your own head! It will be no great satisfaction to me to have your interesting relics kicking their heels in the breeze below my windows; but half a loaf is better than no bread, and if I cannot cure the dishonour, I shall at least stop the scandal."

There was a pause.

"I believe there are other ways of settling such imbroglios among gentlemen," said Denis. "You wear a sword, and I hear you have used it with distinction."

The Sire de Malétroit made a signal to the chaplain, who crossed the room with long, silent strides and raised the arras over the third of the three doors. It was only a moment before he let it fall again; but Denis had time to see a dusky passage full of armed men.

"When I was a little younger, I should have been delighted to honour you, Monsieur de Beaulieu," said Sire Alain; "but I am now too old. Faithful retainers are the sinews of age, and I must employ the strength I have. This is one of the hardest things to swallow as a man grows up in years; but with a little patience, even this becomes habitual. You and the lady seem to prefer the salle for what remains of your two hours; and as I have no desire to cross your preference, I shall resign it to your use with all the pleasure in the world. No haste!" he added, holding up his hand, as he saw a dangerous look come into Denis de Beaulieu's face. "If your mind revolts against hanging, it will be time enough two hours hence to throw yourself out of the window or upon the pikes of my retainers. Two hours of life are always two hours. A great many things may turn up in even as little a while as that. And, besides, if I understand her appearance, my niece has still something to say to you. You will not disfigure your last hours by a want of politeness to a lady?"

Denis looked at Blanche, and she made him an imploring gesture.

It is likely that the old gentleman was hugely pleased at this symptom of an understanding; for he smiled on both, and added sweetly: "If you will give me your word of honour, Monsieur de Beaulieu, to await my return at the end of the two hours before attempting anything desperate, I shall withdraw my retainers, and let you speak in greater privacy with mademoiselle."

Denis again glanced at the girl, who seemed to beseech him to agree.

"I give you my word of honour," he said.

Messire de Malétroit bowed, and proceeded to limp about the apartment, clearing his throat the while with that odd musical chirp which had already grown so irritating in the ears of Denis de Beaulieu. He first possessed himself of some papers which lay upon the table; then he went to the mouth of the passage and appeared to give an order to the men behind the arras; and lastly he hobbled out through the door by which Denis had come in, turning upon the threshold to address a last smiling bow to the young couple, and followed by the chaplain with a handlamp.

No sooner were they alone than Blanche advanced towards Denis with her hands extended. Her face was flushed and excited, and her eyes shone with tears.

"You shall not die!" she cried, "you shall marry me after all."

"You seem to think, madam," replied Denis, "that I stand much in fear of death."

"Oh, no, no," she said; "I see you are no poltroon. It is for my own sake—I could not bear to have you slain for such a scruple."

"I am afraid," returned Denis, "that you underrate the difficulty, madam. What you may be too generous to refuse, I may be too proud to accept. In a moment of noble feeling towards me, you forget what you perhaps owe to others."

He had the decency to keep his eyes upon the floor as he said this, and after he had finished, so as not to spy upon her confusion. She stood silent for a moment, then walked suddenly away, and falling on her uncle's chair, fairly burst out sobbing. Denis was in the acme of embarrassment. He looked round, as if to seek for inspiration, and seeing a stool, plumped down upon it for something to do. There he sat, playing with the guard of his rapier, and wishing himself dead a thousand times over, and buried in the nastiest kitchen-heap in France. His eyes wandered round the apartment, but found nothing to arrest them. There were such wide spaces between the furniture, the light fell so baldly and cheerlessly over all, the dark outside air looked in so coldly through the windows, that he thought he had never seen a church so vast nor a tomb so melancholy. The regular sobs of Blanche de Malétroit measured out the time like the ticking of a clock. He read the device upon the shield over and over again, until his eyes became obscured; he stared into shadowy corners until he imagined they were swarming with horrible animals; and every now and again he awoke with a start, to remember that his last two hours were running, and death was on the march.

Oftener and oftener, as the time went on, did his glance settle on the girl herself. Her face was bowed forward and covered with her hands, and she was shaken at intervals by the convulsive hiccup of grief. Even thus she was not an unpleasant object to dwell upon, so plump, and yet so fine, with a warm brown skin, and the most beautiful hair, Denis thought, in the whole world of womankind. Her hands were like her uncle's; but they were more in place at the end of her young arms, and looked infinitely soft and caressing. He remembered how her blue eyes had shone upon him full of anger, pity, and innocence. And the more he dwelt on her perfections, the uglier death looked, and the more deeply was he smitten with penitence at her continued tears. Now he felt that no man could have the courage to leave a world which contained so beautiful a creature; and now he would have given forty minutes of his last hour to have unsaid his cruel speech.

Suddenly a hoarse and ragged peal of cockcrow rose to their ears from the dark valley below the windows. And this shattering noise in the silence of all around was like a light in a dark place, and shook them both out of their reflections.

"Alas, can I do nothing to help you?" she said, looking up.

"Madam," replied Denis, with a fine irrelevancy, "if I have said anything to wound you, believe me it was for your own sake and not for mine."

She thanked him with a tearful look.

"I feel your position cruelly," he went on. "The world has been bitter hard on you. Your uncle is a disgrace to mankind. Believe me, madam, there is no young gentleman in all France but would be glad of my opportunity, to die in doing you a momentary service."

"I know already that you can be very brave and generous," she answered. "What I *want* to know is whether I can serve you—now or afterwards," she added, with a quaver.

"Most certainly," he answered, with a smile. "Let me sit beside you as if I were a friend, instead of a foolish intruder; try to forget how awkwardly we are placed to one another; make my last moments go pleasantly; and you will do me the chief service possible."

"You are very gallant," she added, with a yet deeper sadness; "very gallant—and it somehow pains me. But draw nearer, if you please; and if you find anything to say to me, you will at least make certain of a very friendly listener. Ah! Monsieur de Beaulieu," she broke forth—"ah! Monsieur de Beaulieu, how can I look you in the face?" And she fell to weeping again with a renewed effusion.

"Madam," said Denis, taking her hand in both of his, "reflect on the little time I have before me, and the great bitterness into which I am cast by the sight of your distress. Spare me, in my last moments, the spectacle of what I cannot cure even with the sacrifice of my life."

"I am very selfish," answered Blanche. "I will be braver, Monsieur de Beaulieu, for your sake. But think if I can do you no kindness in the future—if you have no friends to whom I could carry your adieux. Charge me as heavily as you can: every burden will lighten, by so little, the invaluable gratitude I owe you. Put it in my power to do something more for you than weep."

"My mother is married again, and has a young family to care for. My brother Guichard will inherit my fiefs: and if I am not in error, that will content him amply for my death. Life is a little vapour that passeth away, as we are told by those in holy orders. When a man is in a fair way and sees all life open in front of him, he seems to himself to make a very important figure in the world. His horse whinnies to him; the trumpets blow and the girls look out of window as he rides into town before his company; he receives many assurances of trust and regard—sometimes by express in a letter—sometimes face to face, with persons of great consequence falling on his neck. It is not wonderful if his head is turned for a time. But once he is dead, were he as brave as Hercules or as wise as Solomon, he is soon forgotten. It is not ten years since my father fell, with many other knights around him, in a very fierce encounter, and I do not think that any one of them, nor so much as the name of the fight, is now remembered. No, no, madam, the nearer you come to it, you see that death is a dark and dusty corner, where a man gets into his tomb and has the door shut after him till the judgment-day. I have few friends just now, and once I am dead I shall have none."

"Ah, Monsieur de Beaulieu!" she exclaimed, "you forget Blanche de Malétroit."

"You have a sweet nature, madam, and you are pleased to estimate a little service far beyond its worth."

"It is not that," she answered. "You mistake me if you think I am so easily touched by my own concerns. I say so, because you are the noblest man I have ever met; because I recognise in you a spirit that would have made even a common person famous in the land."

"And yet here I die in a mousetrap—with no more noise about it than my own squeaking," answered he.

A look of pain crossed her face, and she was silent for a little while. Then a light came into her eyes, and with a smile she spoke again.

"I cannot have my champion think meanly of himself. Any one who gives his life for another will be met in Paradise by all the heralds and angels of the Lord God. And you have no cause to hang your head. For— Pray, do you think me beautiful?" she asked, with a deep flush.

"Indeed, madam, I do," he said.

"I am glad of that," she answered heartily. "Do you think there are many men in France who have been asked in marriage by a beautiful maiden—with her own lips—and who have refused her to her face? I know you men would half-despise such a triumph; but believe me, we women know more of what is precious in love. There is nothing that should set a person higher in his own esteem; and we women would prize nothing more dearly."

"You are very good," he said; "but you cannot make me forget that I was asked in pity and not for love."

"I am not so sure of that," she replied, holding down her head. "Hear me to an end, Monsieur de Beaulieu. I know how you must despise me; I feel you are right to do so; I am too poor a creature to occupy one thought of your mind, although, alas! you must die for me this morning. But when I asked you to marry me, indeed, and indeed, it was because I respected and admired you, and loved you with my whole soul, from the very moment that you took my part against my uncle. If you had seen yourself, and how noble you looked, you would pity rather than despise me. And now," she went on, hurriedly checking him with her hand, "although I have laid aside all reserve and told you so much, remember that I know your sentiments towards me already. I would not, believe me, being nobly born, weary you with importunities into consent. I too have a pride of my own: and I declare before the holy Mother of God, if you should now go back from your word already given, I would no more marry you than I would marry my uncle's groom."

Denis smiled a little bitterly.

"It is a small love," he said, "that shies at a little pride."

She made no answer, although she probably had her own thoughts.

"Come hither to the window," he said, with a sigh. "Here is the dawn."

And indeed the dawn was already beginning. The hollow of the sky was full of essential daylight, colourless and clean; and the valley underneath was flooded with a grey reflection. A few thin vapours clung in the coves of the forest or lay along the winding course of the river. The scene disengaged a surprising effect of stillness, which was hardly interrupted when the cocks began once more to crow among the steadings. Perhaps the same fellow who had made so horrid a clangour in the darkness not half an hour before now sent up the merriest cheer to greet the coming day. A little wind went bustling and eddying among the tree-tops underneath the windows. And still the daylight kept flooding insensibly out of the east, which was soon to grow incandescent and cast up that red-hot cannon-ball, the rising sun.

Denis looked out over all this with a bit of a shiver. He had taken her hand, and retained it in his almost unconsciously.

"Has the day begun already?" she said; and then, illogically enough: "the night has been so long! Alas! what shall we say to my uncle when he returns?"

"What you will," said Denis, and he pressed her fingers in his.

She was silent.

"Blanche," he said, with a swift, uncertain, passionate utterance, "you have seen whether I fear death. You must know well enough that I would as gladly leap out of that window into the empty air as lay a finger on you without your free and full consent. But if you care for me at all do not let me lose my life in a misapprehension; for I love you better than the whole world; and though I will die for you blithely, it would be like all the joys of Paradise to live on and spend my life in your service."

As he stopped speaking, a bell began to ring loudly in the interior of the house; and a clatter of armour in the corridor showed that the retainers were returning to their post, and the two hours were at an end.

"After all that you have heard?" she whispered, leaning towards him with her lips and eyes.

"I have heard nothing," he replied

"The captain's name was Florimond de Champdivers," she said in his ear.

"I did not hear it," he answered, taking her supple body in his arms and covered her wet face with kisses.

A melodious chirping was audible behind, followed by a beautiful chuckle, and the voice of Messire de Malétroit wished his new nephew a good morning.

The Pavilion on the Links

CHAPTER I

TELLS HOW I CAMPED IN GRADEN SEA-WOOD, AND BEHELD A LIGHT IN THE PAVILION

I WAS A great solitary when I was young. I made it my pride to keep aloof and suffice for my own entertainment; and I may say that I had neither friends nor acquaintances until I met that friend who became my wife and the mother of my children. With one man only was I on private terms: this was R. Northmour, Esquire, of Graden-Easter, in Scotland. We had met at college; and though there was not much liking between us, nor even much intimacy, we were so nearly of a humour that we could associate with ease to both. Misanthropes we believed ourselves to be; but I have thought since that we were only sulky fellows. It was scarcely a companionship, but a co-existence in unsociability. Northmour's exceptional violence of temper made it no easy affair for him to keep the peace with any one but me; and as he respected my silent ways, and let me come and go as I pleased, I could tolerate his presence without concern. I think we called each other friends.

When Northmour took his degree and I decided to leave the University without one, he invited me on a long visit to Graden-Easter; and it was thus that I first became acquainted with the scene of my adventures. The mansion-house of Graden stood in a bleak stretch of country some three miles from the shore of the German Ocean. It was as large as a barrack; and as it had been built of a soft stone, liable to consume in the eager air of the seaside, it was damp and draughty within and half-ruinous without.

It was impossible for two young men to lodge with comfort in such a dwelling. But there stood in the northern part of the estate, in a wilderness of links and blowing sand-hills, and between a plantation and the sea, a small Pavilion or Belvidere, of modern design, which was exactly suited to our wants; and in this hermitage, speaking little, reading much, and rarely associating except at meals, Northmour and I spent four tempestuous winter months. I might have stayed longer; but one March night there sprang up between us a dispute, which rendered my departure necessary. Northmour spoke hotly, I remember, and I suppose I must have made some tart rejoinder. He leaped from his chair and grappled me; I had to fight, without exaggeration, for my life; and it was only with a great effort that I mastered him, for he was near as strong in body as myself, and seemed filled with the devil. The next morning we met on our usual terms; but I judged it more delicate to withdraw; nor did he attempt to dissuade me.

It was nine years before I revisited the neighbourhood. I travelled at that time with a tilt-cart, a tent, and a cookingstove, tramping all day beside the waggon, and at night, whenever it was possible, gipsying in a cove of the hills, or by the side of a wood. I believe I visited in this manner most of the wild and desolate regions both in England and Scotland; and, as I had neither friends nor relations, I was troubled with no correspondence, and had nothing in the nature of headquarters, unless it was the office of my solicitors, from whom I drew my income twice a year. It was a life in which I delighted; and I fully thought to have grown old upon the march, and at last died in a ditch.

It was my whole business to find desolate corners, where I could camp without the fear of interruption; and hence, being in another part of the same shire, I bethought me suddenly of the Pavilion on the Links. No thoroughfare passed within three miles of it. The nearest town, and that was but a fisher village, was at a distance of six or seven. For ten miles of length, and from a depth varying from three miles to half a mile, this belt of barren country lay along the sea. The beach, which was the natural approach, was full of quicksands. Indeed, I may say there is hardly a better place of concealment in the United Kingdom. I determined to pass a week in the Sea-Wood of Graden-Easter, and making a long stage, reached it about sundown on a wild September day.

The country, I have said, was mixed sand-hill and links; *links* being a Scottish name for sand which has ceased drifting and become more or less solidly covered with turf. The pavilion stood on an even space; a little behind it, the wood began in a hedge of elders huddled together by the wind; in front, a few tumbled sand-hills stood between it and the sea. An outcropping of rock had formed a bastion for the sand, so that there was here a promontory in the coast-line between two shallow bays; and just beyond the tides, the rock again cropped out and formed an islet of small dimensions but strikingly designed. The quicksands were of great extent at low water, and had an infamous reputation in the country. Close inshore, between the islet and the promontory, it was said they would swallow a man in four minutes and a half; but there may have been little ground for this precision. The district was alive with rabbits, and haunted by gulls which made a continual piping about the pavilion. On summer days the outlook was bright, and even gladsome; but at sundown in September, with a high wind, and a heavy surf rolling in close along the links, the place told of nothing but dead mariners and sea disaster. A ship beating to windward on the horizon, and a huge truncheon of wreck half-buried in the sands at my feet, completed the innuendo of the scene.

The pavilion—it had been built by the last proprietor, Northmour's uncle, a silly and prodigal virtuoso—presented little signs of age. It was two stories in height, Italian in design, surrounded by a patch of garden in which nothing had prospered but a few coarse flowers, and looked, with its shuttered windows, not like a house that had been deserted, but like one that had never been tenanted by man. Northmour was plainly from home; whether, as usual, sulking in the cabin of his yacht, or in one of his fitful and extravagant appearances in the world of society, I had, of course, no means of guessing. The place had an air of solitude that daunted even a solitary like myself; the wind cried in the chimneys with a strange and wailing note; and it was with a sense of escape, as if I were going indoors, that I turned away and, driving my cart before me, entered the skirts of the wood.

The Sea-Wood of Graden had been planted to shelter

the cultivated fields behind, and check the encroachments of the blowing sand. As you advanced into it from coastward, elders were succeeded by other hardy shrubs; but the timber was all stunted and bushy; it led a life of conflict; the trees were accustomed to swing there all night long in fierce winter tempests; and even in early spring the leaves were already flying, and autumn was beginning, in this exposed plantation. Inland the ground rose into a little hill, which, along with the islet, served as a sailing mark for seamen. When the hill was open of the islet to the north, vessels must bear well to the eastward to clear Graden Ness and the Graden Bullers. In the lower ground, a streamlet ran among the trees, and, being damned with dead leaves and clay of its own carrying, spread out every here and there, and lay in stagnant pools. One or two ruined cottages were dotted about the wood; and, according to Northmour, these were ecclesiastical foundations, and in their time had sheltered pious hermits.

I found a den, or small hollow, where there was a spring of pure water; and there, clearing away the brambles, I pitched the tent, and made a fire to cook my supper. My horse I picketed farther in the wood where there was a patch of sward. The banks of the den not only concealed the light of my fire, but sheltered me from the wind, which was cold as well as high.

The life I was leading made me both hardy and frugal. I never drank but water, and rarely ate anything more costly than oatmeal; and I required so little sleep that, although I rose with the peep of day, I would often lie long awake in the dark or starry watches of the night. Thus in Graden Sea-Wood, although I fell thankfully asleep by eight in the evening, I was awake again before eleven with a full possession of my faculties, and no sense of drowsiness or fatigue. I rose and sat by the fire, watching the trees and clouds tumultuously tossing and fleeing overhead and hearkening to the wind and the rollers along the shore; till at length, growing weary of inaction, I quitted the den, and strolled towards the borders of the wood. A young moon, buried in mist, gave a faint illumination to my steps; and the light grew brighter as I walked forth into the links. The same moment, the wind, smelling salt of the open ocean, and carrying particles of sand, struck me with its full force, so that I had to bow my head.

When I raised it again to look about me, I was aware of a light in the pavilion. It was not stationary; but passed from one window to another as though some one were reviewing the different apartments with a lamp or candle. I watched it for some seconds in great surprise. When I had arrived in the afternoon the house had been plainly deserted; now it was as plainly occupied. It was my first idea that a gang of thieves might have broken in and be now ransacking Northmour's cupboards, which were many and not ill supplied. But what should bring thieves to Graden-Easter? And, again, all the shutters had been thrown open, and it would have been more in the character of such gentry to close them. I dismissed the notion, and fell back upon another: Northmour himself must have arrived, and was now airing and inspecting the pavilion.

I have said that there was no real affection between this man and me; but, had I loved him like a brother, I was then so much more in love with solitude that I should none the less have shunned his company. As it was, I turned and ran for it; and it was with genuine satisfaction that I found myself safely back beside the fire. I had escaped an acquaintance: I should have one more night in comfort. In the morning I might either slip away before Northmour was abroad, or pay him as short a visit as I chose.

But when morning came I thought the situation so diverting that I forgot my shyness. Northmour was at my mercy; I arranged a good practical jest, though I knew well that my neighbour was not the man to jest with in security; and, chuckling beforehand over its success, took my place among the elders at the edge of the wood, whence I could command the door of the pavilion. The shutters were all once more closed, which I remember thinking odd; and the house, with its white walls and green venetians, looked spruce and habitable in the morning light. Hour after hour passed, and still no sign of Northmour. I knew him for a sluggard in the morning; but, as it drew on towards noon, I lost my patience. To say the truth, I had promised myself to break my fast in the pavilion, and hunger began to prick me sharply. It was a pity to let the opportunity go by without some cause for mirth; but the grosser appetite prevailed, and I relinquished my jest with regret, and sallied from the wood.

The appearance of the house affected me, as I drew near, with disquietude. It seemed unchanged since last evening; and I had expected it, I scarce knew why, to wear some external signs of habitation. But no: the windows were all closely shuttered, the chimneys breathed no smoke, and the front door itself was closely padlocked. Northmour therefore had entered by the back; this was the natural, and indeed the necessary, conclusion; and you may judge of my surprise when, on turning the house, I found the backdoor similarly secured.

My mind at once reverted to the original theory of thieves; and I blamed myself sharply for my last night's inaction. I examined all the windows on the lower story, but none of them had been tampered with; I tried the padlocks, but they were both secure. It thus became a problem how the thieves, if thieves they were, had managed to enter the house. They must have got, I reasoned, upon the roof of the outhouse where Northmour used to keep his photographic battery; and from thence, either by the window of the study or that of my old bedroom, completed their burglarious entry.

I followed what I supposed was their example; and, getting on the roof, tried the shutters of each room. Both were secure; but I was not to be beaten; and, with a little force, one of them flew open, grazing, as it did so, the back of my hand. I remember I put the wound to my mouth and stood for perhaps half a minute licking it like a dog, and mechanically gazing behind me over the waste links and the sea; and in that space of time my eye made note of a large schooner yacht some miles to the northeast. Then I threw up the window and climbed in.

I went over the house, and nothing can express my mystification. There was no sign of disorder, but, on the contrary, the rooms were unusually clean and pleasant. I found fires laid ready for lighting; three bedrooms prepared with a luxury quite foreign to Northmour's habits, and with water in the ewers and the beds turned down; a table set for three in the dining-room; and an ample supply of cold meats, game, and vegetables on the pantry shelves. There were guests expected, that was plain; but why guests when Northmour hated society? And, above all, why was the house thus stealthily prepared at dead of night? and why were the shutters closed and the doors padlocked?

I effaced all traces of my visit, and came forth from the window feeling sobered and concerned.

The schooner yacht was still in the same place; and it flashed for a moment through my mind that this might be the *Red Earl* bringing the owner of the pavilion and his guests. But the vessel's head was set the other way.

CHAPTER II

TELLS OF THE NOCTURNAL LANDING FROM THE YACHT

I RETURNED to the den to cook myself a meal, of which I stood in great need, as well as to care for my horse, which I had somewhat neglected in the morning. From time to time I went down to the edge of the wood; but there was no change in the pavilion, and not a human creature was seen all day upon the links. The schooner in the offing was the one touch of life within my range of vision. She, apparently with no set object, stood off and on or lay to, hour after hour; but as the evening deepened she drew steadily nearer. I became more convinced that she carried Northmour and his friends, and that they would probably come ashore after dark; not only because that was of a piece with the secrecy of the preparations, but because the tide would not have flowed sufficiently before eleven to cover Graden Floe and the other sea quags that fortified the shore against invaders.

All day the wind had been going down, and the sea along with it; but there was a return towards sunset of the heavy weather of the day before. The night set in pitch dark. The wind came off the sea in squalls, like the firing of a battery of cannon; now and then there was a flaw of rain and the surf rolled heavier with the rising tide. I was down at my observatory among the elders, when a light was run up to the mast-head of the schooner, and showed she was closer in than when I had last seen her by the dying daylight. I concluded that this must be a signal to Northmour's associates on shore; and, stepping forth into the links, looked around me for something in response.

A small footpath ran along the margin of the wood, and formed the most direct communication between the pavilion and the mansion-house; and as I cast my eyes to that side I saw a spark of light, not a quarter of a mile away, and rapidly approaching. From its uneven course it appeared to be the light of a lantern carried by a person who followed the windings of the path, and was often staggered and taken aback by the more violent squalls. I concealed myself once more among the elders, and waited eagerly for the new-comer's advance. It proved to be a woman; and as she passed within half a rod of my ambush I was able to recognise the features. The deaf and silent old dame who had nursed Northmour in his childhood was his associate in this underhand affair.

I followed her at a little distance, taking advantage of the innumerable heights and hollows, concealed by the darkness, and favoured not only by the nurse's deafness, but by the uproar of the wind and surf. She entered the pavilion, and, going at once to the upper story, opened and set a light in one of the windows that looked towards the sea. Immediately afterwards the light at the schooner's mast-head was run down and extinguished. Its purpose had been attained, and those on board were sure that they were expected. The old woman resumed her preparations; although the other shutters remained closed, I could see a glimmer going to and fro about the house; and a gush of sparks from one chimney after another soon told me that the fires were being kindled.

Northmour and his guests, I was now persuaded, would come ashore as soon as there was water on the floe. It was a wild night for boat service; and I felt some alarm mingle with my curiosity as I reflected on the danger of the landing. My old acquaintance, it was true, was the most eccentric of men; but the present eccentricity was both disquieting and lugubrious to consider. A variety of feelings thus led me towards the beach, where I lay flat on my face in a hollow within six feet of the track that led to the pavilion. Thence, I should have the satisfaction of recognising the arrivals, and, if they should prove to be acquaintances, greeting them as soon as they had landed.

Some time before eleven, while the tide was still dangerously low, a boat's lantern appeared close inshore; and, my attention being thus awakened, I could perceive another still far to seaward, violently tossed, and sometimes hidden by the billows. The weather, which was getting dirtier as the night went on, and the perilous situation of the yacht upon a lee-shore, had probably driven them to attempt a landing at the earliest possible moment.

A little afterwards, four yachtsmen carrying a very heavy chest, and guided by a fifth with a lantern, passed close in front of me as I lay, and were admitted to the pavilion by the nurse. They returned to the beach, and passed me a second time with another chest, larger but apparently not so heavy as the first. A third time they made the transit; and on this occasion one of the yachtsmen carried a leather portmanteau, and the others a lady's trunk and carriage bag. My curiosity was sharply excited. If a woman were among the guests of Northmour, it would show a change in his habits and an apostasy from his pet theories of life, well calculated to fill me with surprise. When he and I dwelt there together, the pavilion had been a temple of misogyny. And now, one of the detested sex was to be installed under its roof. I remembered one or two particulars, a few notes of daintiness and almost of coquetry which had struck me the day before as I surveyed the preparations in the house; their purpose was now clear, and I thought myself dull not to have perceived it from the first.

While I was thus reflecting, a second lantern drew near me from the beach. It was carried by a yachtsman whom I had not yet seen, and who was conducting two other persons to the pavilion. These two persons were unquestionably the guests for whom the house was made ready; and, straining eye and ear, I set myself to watch them as they passed. One was an unusually tall man, in a travelling hat slouched over his eyes, and a highland cape closely buttoned and turned up so as to conceal his face. You could make out no more of him than that he was, as I have said, unusually tall, and walked feebly with a heavy stoop. By his side, and either clinging to him or giving him support—I could not make out which—was a young, tall, and slender figure of a woman. She was extremely pale; but in the light of the lantern her face was so marred by strong and changing shadows that she might equally well have been as ugly as sin or as beautiful as I afterwards found her to be.

When they were just abreast of me, the girl made some remark which was drowned by the noise of the wind.

"Hush!" said her companion; and there was something in the tone with which the word was uttered that thrilled and rather shook my spirits. It seemed to breathe from a bosom labouring under the deadliest terror; I have never heard another syllable so expressive; and I still hear it again when I am feverish at night, and my mind runs upon old times. The man turned towards the girl as he spoke; I had a glimpse of much red beard and a nose which seemed to have been broken in youth; and his light eyes seemed shining in his face with some strong and unpleasant emotion.

But these two passed on and were admitted in their turn to the pavilion.

One by one, or in groups, the seamen returned to the beach. The wind brought me the sound of a rough voice crying, "Shove off!" Then, after a pause, another lantern drew near. It was Northmour alone.

My wife and I, a man and a woman, have often agreed to wonder how a person could be, at the same time, so handsome and so repulsive as Northmour. He had the appearance of a finished gentleman; his face bore every mark of intelligence and courage; but you had only to look at him, even in the most amiable moment, to see that he had the temper of a slaver captain. I never knew a character that was both explosive and revengeful to the same degree; he combined the vivacity of the South with the sustained and deadly hatreds of the North; and both traits were plainly written on his face, which was a sort of danger-signal. In person he was tall, strong, and active; his hair and complexion very dark; his features handsomely designed, but spoiled by a menacing expression.

At that moment he was somewhat paler than by nature; he wore a heavy frown; and his lips worked, and he looked sharply round him as he walked, like a man besieged with apprehensions. And yet I thought he had a look of triumph underlying all, as though he had already done much, and was near the end of an achievement.

Partly from a scruple of delicacy—which I daresay came too late—partly from the pleasure of startling an acquaintance, I desired to make my presence known to him without delay.

I got suddenly to my feet, and stepped forward.

"Northmour!" said I.

I have never had so shocking a surprise in all my days. He leaped on me without a word; something shone in his hand; and he struck for my heart with a dagger. At the same moment I knocked him head over heels. Whether it was my quickness, or his own uncertainty, I know not; but the blade only grazed my shoulder, while the hilt and his fist struck me violently on the mouth.

I fled, but not far. I had often and often observed the capabilities of the sand-hills for protracted ambush or stealthy advances and retreats; and, not ten yards from the scene of the scuffle, plumped down again upon the grass. The lantern had fallen and gone out. But what was my astonishment to see Northmour slip at a bound into the pavilion, and hear him bar the door behind him with a clang of iron!

He had not pursued me. He had run away. Northmour, whom I knew for the most implacable and daring of men, had run away! I could scarcely believe my reason; and yet in this strange business, where all was incredible, there was nothing to make a work about in an incredibility more or less. For why was the pavilion secretly prepared? Why had Northmour landed with his guests at dead of night, in half a gale of wind, and with the floe scarce covered? Why had he sought to kill me? Had he not recognised my voice? I wondered. And, above all, how had he come to have a dagger ready in his hand? A dagger, or even a sharp knife, seemed out of keeping with the age in which we lived; and a gentleman landing from his yacht on the shore of his own estate, even although it was at night and with some mysterious circumstances, does not usually, as a matter of fact, walk thus prepared for deadly onslaught. The more I reflected, the further I felt at sea. I recapitulated the elements of mystery, counting them on my fingers: the pavilion secretly prepared for guests; the guests landed at the risk of their lives and to the imminent peril of the yacht; the guests, or at least one of them, in undisguised and seemingly causeless terror; Northmour with a naked weapon; Northmour stabbing his most intimate acquaintance at a word; last, and not least strange, Northmour fleeing from the man whom he had sought to murder, and barricading himself, like a hunted creature, behind the door of the pavilion. Here were at least six separate causes for extreme surprise; each part and parcel with the others, and forming all together one consistent story. I felt almost ashamed to believe my own senses.

As I thus stood, transfixed with wonder, I began to grow painfully conscious of the injuries I had received in the scuffle; skulked round among the sand-hills; and, by a devious path, regained the shelter of the wood. On the way, the old nurse passed again within several yards of me, still carrying her lantern, on the return journey to the mansion-house of Graden. This made a seventh suspicious feature in the case. Northmour and his guests, it appeared, were to cook and do the cleaning for themselves, while the old woman continued to inhabit the big empty barrack among the policies. There must surely be great cause for secrecy when so many inconveniences were confronted to preserve it.

So thinking, I made my way to the den. For greater security I trod out the embers of the fire, and lit my lantern to examine the wound upon my shoulder. It was a trifling hurt, although it bled somewhat freely, and I dressed it as well as I could (for its position made it difficult to reach) with some rag and cold water from the spring. While I was thus busied I mentally declared war against Northmour and his mystery. I am not an angry man by nature, and I believe there was more curiosity than resentment in my heart. But war I certainly declared; and, by way of preparation, I got out my revolver, and, having drawn the charges, cleaned and reloaded it with scrupulous care. Next I became preoccupied about my horse. It might break loose, or fall to neighing, and so betray my camp in the Sea-Wood. I determined to rid myself of its neighbourhood; and long before dawn I was leading it over the links in the direction of the fisher village.

CHAPTER III

TELLS HOW I BECAME ACQUAINTED WITH MY WIFE

FOR TWO DAYS I skulked round the pavilion, profiting by the uneven surface of the links. I became an adept in the necessary tactics. These low hillocks and shallow dells, running one into another, became a kind of cloak of darkness for my enthralling, but perhaps dishonourable, pursuit. Yet, in spite of this advantage, I could learn but little of Northmour or his guests.

Fresh provisions were brought under cover of darkness by the old woman from the mansion-house. Northmour and the young lady, sometimes together, but more often singly, would walk for an hour or two at a time on the beach beside the quicksand. I could not but conclude that this promenade was chosen with an eye to secrecy; for the spot was open only to the seaward. But it suited me not less excellently; the highest and most accidented of the sand-hills immediately adjoined; and from these, lying flat in a hollow, I could overlook Northmour or the young lady as they walked.

The tall man seemed to have disappeared. Not only did he never cross the threshold, but he never so much as showed face at a window; or, at least, not so far as I could see; for I dared not creep forward beyond a certain distance in the day, since the upper floor commanded the bottoms of the links; and at night, when I could venture farther, the lower windows were barricaded as if to stand a siege. Sometimes I thought the tall man must be confined to bed, for I remembered the feebleness of his gait; and sometimes I thought he must have gone clear away, and that Northmour and the young lady remained alone together in the pavilion. The idea, even then, displeased me.

Whether or not this pair were man and wife, I had seen abundant reason to doubt the friendliness of their relation. Although I could hear nothing of what they said, and rarely so much as glean a decided expression on the face of either, there was a distance, almost a stiffness, in their bearing which showed them to be either unfamiliar or at enmity. The girl walked faster when she was with Northmour than when she was alone; and I conceived that any inclination between a man and a woman would rather delay than accelerate the step. Moreover, she kept a good yard free of him, and trailed her umbrella, as if it were a barrier, on the side between them. Northmour kept sliding closer; and, as the girl retired from his advance, their course lay at a sort of diagonal across the beach, and would have landed them in the surf had it been long enough continued. But when this was imminent, the girl would unostentatiously change sides and put Northmour between her and the sea. I watched these manœuvres, for my part, with high enjoyment and approval, and chuckled to myself at every move.

On the morning of the third day she walked alone for some time, and I perceived, to my great concern, that she was more than once in tears. You will see that my heart was already interested more than I supposed. She had a firm yet airy motion of the body, and carried her head with unimaginable grace; every step was a thing to look at, and she seemed in my eyes to breathe sweetness and distinction.

The day was so agreeable, being calm and sunshiny, with a tranquil sea, and yet with a healthful piquancy and vigour in the air, that, contrary to custom, she was tempted forth a second time to walk. On this occasion she was accompanied by Northmour, and they had been but a short while on the beach, when I saw him take forcible possession of her hand. She struggled, and uttered a cry that was almost a scream. I sprang to my feet, unmindful of my strange position; but, ere I had taken a step, I saw Northmour bareheaded and bowing very low, as if to apologise; and dropped again at once into my ambush. A few words were interchanged; and then, with another bow, he left the beach to return to the pavilion. He passed not far from me, and I could see him, flushed and lowering, and cutting savagely with his cane among the grass. It was not without satisfaction that I recognised my own handiwork in a great cut under his right eye, and a considerable discoloration round the socket.

For some time the girl remained where he had left her, looking out past the islet and over the bright sea. Then with a start, as one who throws off preoccupation and puts energy again upon its mettle, she broke into a rapid and decisive walk. She also was much incensed by what had passed. She had forgotten where she was. And I beheld her walk straight into the borders of the quicksand where it is more abrupt and dangerous. Two or three steps farther and her life would have been in serious jeopardy, when I slid down the face of the sand-hill, which is there precipitous, and, running half-way forward, called to her to stop.

She did so, and turned round. There was not a tremor

of fear in her behaviour, and she marched directly up to me like a queen. I was barefoot, and clad like a common sailor, save for an Egyptian scarf round my waist; and she probably took me at first for some one from the fisher village, straying after bait. As for her, when I thus saw her face to face, her eyes set steadily and imperiously upon mine, I was filled with admiration and astonishment, and thought her even more beautiful than I had looked to find her. Nor could I think enough of one who, acting with so much boldness, yet preserved a maidenly air that was both quaint and engaging; for my wife kept an old-fashioned precision of manner through all her admirable life—an excellent thing in woman, since it sets another value on her sweet familiarities.

"What does this mean?" she asked.

"You were walking," I told her, "directly into Graden Floe."

"You do not belong to these parts," she said again. "You speak like an educated man."

"I believe I have right to that name," said I, "although in this disguise."

But her woman's eye had already detected the sash.

"Oh!" she said; "your sash betrays you."

"You have said the word *betray,*" I resumed. "May I ask you not to betray me? I was obliged to disclose myself in your interest; but if Northmour learned my presence it might be worse than disagreeable for me."

"Do you know," she asked, "to whom you are speaking?"

"Not to Mr. Northmour's wife?" I asked, by way of answer.

She shook her head. All this while she was studying my face with an embarrassing intentness. Then she broke out—

"You have an honest face. Be honest like your face, sir, and tell me what you want and what you are afraid of. Do you think I could hurt you? I believe you have far more power to injure me! And yet you do not look unkind. What do you mean—you, a gentleman—by skulking like a spy about this desolate place? Tell me," she said, "who is it you hate?"

"I hate no one," I answered; "and I fear no one face to face. My name is Cassilis—Frank Cassilis. I lead the life of a vagabond for my own good pleasure. I am one of Northmour's oldest friends; and three nights ago, when I addressed him on these links, he stabbed me in the shoulder with a knife."

"It was you!" she said.

"Why he did so," I continued, disregarding the interruption, "is more than I can guess, and more than I care to know. I have not many friends, nor am I very susceptible to friendship; but no man shall drive me from a place by terror. I had camped in Graden Sea-Wood ere he came; I camp in it still. If you think I mean harm to you or yours, madam, the remedy is in your hand. Tell him that my camp is in the Hemlock Den, and to-night he can stab me in safety while I sleep."

With this I doffed my cap to her, and scrambled up once more among the sand-hills. I do not know why, but I felt a prodigious sense of injustice, and felt like a hero and a martyr; while, as a matter of fact, I had not a word to say in my defence, nor so much as one plausible reason to offer for my conduct. I had stayed at Graden out of a curiosity natural enough, but undignified; and though there was another motive growing in along with the first, it was not one which, at that period, I could have properly explained to the lady of my heart.

Certainly, that night, I thought of no one else; and, though her whole conduct and position seemed suspicious, I could not find it in my heart to entertain a doubt of her integrity. I could have staked my life that she was clear of blame, and, though all was dark at the present, that the explanation of the mystery would show her part in these events to be both right and needful. It was true, let me cudgel my imagination as I pleased, that I could invent no theory of her relations to Northmour; but I felt none the less sure of my conclusion because it was founded on instinct in place of reason, and, as I may say, went to sleep that night with the thought of her under my pillow.

Next day she came out about the same hour alone, and, as soon as the sand-hills concealed her from the pavilion, drew nearer to the edge, and called me by name in guarded tones. I was astonished to observe that she was deadly pale, and seemingly under the influence of strong emotion.

"Mr. Cassilis!" she cried; "Mr. Cassilis!"

I appeared at once, and leaped down upon the beach. A remarkable air of relief overspread her countenance as soon as she saw me.

"Oh!" she cried, with a hoarse sound, like one whose bosom has been lightened of a weight. And then, "Thank God you are still safe!" she added; "I knew, if you were, you would be here." (Was not this strange? So swiftly and wisely does Nature prepare our hearts for these great life-long intimacies, that both my wife and I had been given a presentiment on this the second day of our acquaintance. I had even then hoped that she would seek me; she had felt sure that she would find me.) "Do not," she went on swiftly, "do not stay in this place. Promise me that you will sleep no longer in that wood. You do not know how I suffer; all last night I could not sleep for thinking of your peril."

"Peril?" I repeated. "Peril from whom? From Northmour?"

"Not so," she said. "Did you think I would tell him after what you said?"

"Not from Northmour?" I repeated. "Then how? From whom? I see none to be afraid of."

"You must not ask me," was her reply, "for I am not free to tell you. Only believe me, and go hence—believe me, and go away quickly, quickly, for your life!"

An appeal to his alarm is never a good plan to rid oneself of a spirited young man. My obstinacy was but increased by what she said, and I made it a point of honour to remain. And her solicitude for my safety still more confirmed me in the resolve.

"You must not think me inquisitive, madam," I replied; "but, if Graden is so dangerous a place, you yourself perhaps remain here at some risk."

She only looked at me reproachfully.

"You and your father—" I resumed; but she interrupted me almost with a gasp.

"My father! How do you know that?" she cried.

"I saw you together when you landed," was my answer; and I do not know why, but it seemed satisfactory to both of us, as indeed it was the truth. "But," I continued, "you need have no fear from me. I see you have some reason to be secret, and, you may believe me, your secret is as safe with me as if I were in Graden Floe. I have scarce spoken to any one for years; my horse is my only companion, and even he, poor beast, is not beside me. You see, then, you may count on me for silence. So tell me the truth, my dear young lady, are you not in danger?"

"Mr. Northmour says you are an honourable man," she returned, "and I believe it when I see you. I will tell you so much; you are right; we are in dreadful, dreadful danger, and you share it by remaining where you are."

"Ah!" said I; "you have heard of me from Northmour? And he gives me a good character?"

"I asked him about you last night," was her reply. "I pretended," she hesitated, "I pretended to have met you long ago, and spoken to you of him. It was not true; but I could not help myself without betraying you, and you had put me in a difficulty. He praised you highly."

"And—you may permit me one question—does this danger come from Northmour?" I asked.

"From Mr. Northmour?" she cried. "Oh, no; he stays with us to share it."

"While you propose that I should run away?" I said. "You do not rate me very high."

"Why should you stay?" she asked. "You are no friend of ours."

I know not what came over me, for I had not been conscious of a similar weakness since I was a child, but I was so mortified by this retort that my eyes pricked and filled with tears, as I continued to gaze upon her face.

"No, no," she said, in a changed voice; "I did not mean the words unkindly."

"It was I who offended," I said; and I held out my hand with a look of appeal that somehow touched her, for she gave me hers at once, and even eagerly. I held it for a while in mine, and gazed into her eyes. It was she who first tore her hand away, and, forgetting all about her request and the promise she had sought to extort, ran at the top of her speed, and without turning, till she was out of sight. And then I knew that I loved her, and thought in my glad heart that she—she herself—was not indifferent to my suit. Many a time she has denied it in after days, but it was with a smiling and not a serious denial. For my part, I am sure our hands would not have lain so closely in each other if she had not begun to melt to me already. And, when all is said, it is no great contention, since, by her own avowal, she began to love me on the morrow.

And yet on the morrow very little took place. She

came and called me down as on the day before, upbraided me for lingering at Graden, and, when she found I was still obdurate, began to ask me more particularly as to my arrival. I told her by what series of accidents I had come to witness their disembarkation, and how I had determined to remain, partly from the interest which had been wakened in me by Northmour's guests, and partly because of his own murderous attack. As to the former, I fear I was disingenuous, and led her to regard herself as having been an attraction to me from the first moment that I saw her on the links. It relieves my heart to make this confession even now, when my wife is with God, and already knows all things, and the honesty of my purpose even in this; for while she lived, although it often pricked my conscience, I had never the hardihood to undeceive her. Even a little secret, in such a married life as ours, is like the rose-leaf which kept the Princess from her sleep.

From this the talk branched into other subjects, and I told her much about my lonely and wandering existence; she, for her part, giving ear and saying little. Although we spoke very naturally, and latterly on topics that might seem indifferent, we were both sweetly agitated. Too soon it was time for her to go; and we separated, as if by mutual consent, without shaking hands, for both knew that, between us, it was no idle ceremony.

The next, and that was the fourth day of our acquaintance, we met in the same spot, but early in the morning, with much familiarity and yet much timidity on either side. When she had once more spoken about my danger—and that, I understood, was her excuse for coming—I, who had prepared a great deal of talk during the night, began to tell her how highly I valued her kind interest, and how no one had ever cared to hear about my life, nor had I ever cared to relate it, before yesterday. Suddenly she interrupted me, saying with vehemence—

"And yet, if you knew who I was, you would not so much as speak to me!"

I told her such a thought was madness, and, little as we had met, I counted her already a dear friend; but my protestations seemed only to make her more desperate.

"My father is in hiding!" she cried.

"My dear," I said, forgetting for the first time to add "young lady," "what do I care? If he were in hiding twenty times over, would it make one thought of change in you?"

"Ah, but the cause!" she cried, "the cause! It is—" she faltered for a second—"it is disgraceful to us."

CHAPTER IV

TELLS IN WHAT A STARTLING MANNER I LEARNED THAT I WAS NOT ALONE IN THE GRADEN SEA-WOOD

THIS WAS my wife's story, as I drew it from her among tears and sobs. Her name was Clara Huddlestone: it sounded very beautiful in my ears; but not so beautitul as that other name of Clara Cassilis, which she wore during the longer, and I thank God the happier, portion of her life. Her father, Bernard Huddlestone, had been a private banker in a very large way of business. Many years before, his affairs becoming disordered, he had been led to try dangerous, and at last criminal, expedients to retrieve himself from ruin. All was in vain; he became more and more cruelly involved, and found his honour lost at the same moment with his fortune. About this period Northmour had been courting his daughter with great assiduity, though with small encouragement; and to him, knowing him thus disposed in his favour, Bernard Huddlestone turned for help in his extremity. It was not merely ruin and dishonour, nor merely a legal condemnation, that the unhappy man had brought upon his head. It seems he could have gone to prison with a light heart. What he feared, what kept him awake at night or recalled him from slumber into frenzy, was some secret, sudden, and unlawful attempt upon his life. Hence he desired to bury his existence and escape to one of the islands in the South Pacific, and it was in Northmour's yacht, the *Red Earl*, that he designed to go. The yacht picked them up clandestinely upon the coast of Wales, and had once more deposited them at Graden, till she could be refitted and provisioned for the longer voyage. Nor could Clara doubt that her hand had been stipulated as the price of passage. For, although Northmour was neither unkind nor even discourteous, he had shown himself in several instances somewhat over-bold in speech and manner.

I listened, I need not say, with fixed attention, and put many questions as to the more mysterious part. It was in vain. She had no clear idea of what the blow was, nor of how it was expected to fall. Her father's alarm was unfeigned and physically prostrating, and he had thought more than once of making an unconditional surrender to the police. But the scheme was finally abandoned, for he was convinced that not even the strength of our English prisons could shelter him from his pursuers. He had had many affairs with Italy, and with Italians resident in London, in the later years of his business, and these last, as Clara fancied, were somehow connected with the doom that threatened him. He had shown great terror at the presence of an Italian seaman on board the *Red Earl*, and had bitterly and repeatedly accused Northmour in consequence. The latter had protested that Beppo (that was the seaman's name) was a capital fellow, and could be trusted to the death; but Mr. Huddlestone had continued ever since to declare that all was lost, that it was only a question of days, and that Beppo would be the ruin of him yet.

I regarded the whole story as the hallucination of a mind shaken by calamity. He had suffered heavy loss by his Italian transactions; and hence the sight of an Italian was hateful to him, and the principal part in his nightmare would naturally enough be played by one of that nation.

"What your father wants," I said, "is a good doctor and some calming medicine."

"But Mr. Northmour?" objected your mother. "He is untroubled by losses, and yet he shares in this terror."

I could not help laughing at what I considered her simplicity.

"My dear," said I, "you have told me yourself what reward he has to look for. All is fair in love, you must remember; and if Northmour foments your father's terrors, it is not at all because he is afraid of any Italian man, but simply because he is infatuated with a charming English woman."

She reminded me of his attack upon myself on the night of the disembarkation, and this I was unable to explain. In short, and from one thing to another, it was agreed between us that I should set out at once for the fisher village, Graden-Wester, as it is called, look up all the newspapers I could find, and see for myself if there seemed any basis of fact for these continued alarms. The next morning, at the same hour and place, I was to make my report to Clara. She said no more on that occasion about my departure; nor, indeed, did she make it a secret that she clung to the thought of my proximity as something helpful and pleasant; and, for my part, I could not have left her, if she had gone upon her knees to ask it.

I reached Graden-Wester before ten in the forenoon; for in those days I was an excellent pedestrian, and the distance, as I think I have said, was little over seven miles; fine walking all the way upon the springy turf. The village is one of the bleakest on that coast, which is saying much: there is a church in a hollow; a miserable haven in the rocks, where many boats have been lost as they returned from fishing; two or three score of stone houses arranged along the beach and in two streets, one leading from the harbour, and another striking out from it at right angles; and, at the corner of these two, a very dark and cheerless tavern, by way of principal hotel.

I had dressed myself somewhat more suitably to my station in life, and at once called upon the minister in his little manse beside the graveyard. He knew me, although it was more than nine years since we had met; and when I told him that I had been long upon a walking tour, and was behind with the news, readily lent me an armful of newspapers, dating from a month back to the day before. With these I sought the tavern, and, ordering some breakfast, sat down to study the "Huddlestone Failure."

It had been, it appeared, a very flagrant case. Thousands of persons were reduced to poverty; and one in particular had blown out his brains as soon as payment was suspended. It was strange to myself that, while I read these details, I continued rather to sympathise with Mr. Huddlestone than with his victims; so complete already was the empire of my love for my wife. A price was naturally set upon the banker's head; and, as the case was inexcusable and the public indignation thoroughly aroused, the unusual figure of £750 was offered for his capture. He was reported to have large sums of money in his possession. One day he had been heard of in Spain; the next, there was sure intelligence that he was still lurking between Manchester and Liverpool, or along the border of Wales; and the day after, a telegram would announce his arrival in Cuba or Yucatan. But in all this there was no word of an Italian, nor any sign of mystery.

In the very last paper, however, there was one item not so clear. The accountants who were charged to verify the failure had, it seemed, come upon the traces of a very large number of thousands, which figured for some time in the transactions of the house of Huddlestone; but which came from nowhere, and disappeared in the same mysterious fashion. It was only once referred to by name, and then under the initials "X.X."; but it had plainly been floated for the first time into the business at a period of great depression some six years ago. The name of a distinguished Royal personage had been mentioned by rumour in connection with this sum. "The cowardly desperado"—such, I remember, was the editorial expression—was supposed to have escaped with a large part of this mysterious fund still in his possession.

I was still brooding over the fact, and trying to torture it into some connection with Mr. Huddlestone's danger, when a man entered the tavern and asked for some bread and cheese with a decided foreign accent.

"*Siete Italiano?*" said I.

"*Si, signor*," was his reply.

I said it was unusually far north to find one of his compatriots; at which he shrugged his shoulders, and replied that a man would go anywhere to find work. What work he could hope to find at Graden-Wester, I was totally unable to conceive; and the incident struck so unpleasantly upon my mind that I asked the landlord, while he was counting me some change, whether he had ever before seen an Italian in the village. He said he had once seen some Norwegians, who had been shipwrecked on the other side of Graden Ness and rescued by the lifeboat from Cauldhaven.

"No!" said I; "but an Italian, like the man who had just had bread and cheese."

"What?" cried he, "yon black-avised fellow wi' the teeth? Was he an I-talian? Weel, yon's the first that ever I saw, an' I daresay he's like to be the last."

Even as he was speaking, I raised my eyes, and, casting a glance into the street, beheld three men in earnest conversation together, and not thirty yards away. One of them was my recent companion in the tavern parlour; the other two, by their handsome, sallow features and soft hats, should evidently belong to the same race. A crowd of village children stood around them, gesticulating and talking gibberish in imitation. The trio looked singularly foreign to the bleak dirty street in which they were standing, and the dark grey heaven that overspread them; and I confess my incredulity received at that moment a shock from which it never recovered. I might reason with myself as I pleased, but I could not argue down the effect of what I had seen, and I began to share in the Italian terror.

It was already drawing towards the close of the day before I had returned the newspapers at the manse, and got well forward on to the links on my way home. I shall never forget that walk. It grew very cold and boisterous; the wind sang in the short grass about my feet; thin rain showers came running on the gusts; and an immense mountain range of clouds began to arise out of the bosom of the sea. It would be hard to imagine a more dismal evening; and whether it was from these external influences, or because my nerves were already affected by what I had heard and seen, my thoughts were as gloomy as the weather.

The upper windows of the pavilion commanded a considerable spread of links in the direction of Graden-Wester. To avoid observation, it was necessary to hug the beach until I had gained cover from the higher sand-hills on the little headland, when I might strike across, through the hollows, for the margin of the wood. The sun was about setting; the tide was low, and all the quick-sands uncovered; and I was moving along, lost in unpleasant thought, when I was suddenly thunderstruck to perceive the prints of human feet. They ran parallel to my own course, but low down upon the beach instead of along the border of the turf; and, when I examined them, I saw at once, by the size and coarseness of the impression, that it was a stranger to me and to those in the pavilion who had recently passed that way. Not only so; but from the recklessness of the course which he had followed, steering near to the most formidable portions of the sand, he was as evidently a stranger to the country and to the ill-repute of Graden beach.

Step by step I followed the prints; until, a quarter of a

mile farther, I beheld them die away into the south-eastern boundary of Graden Floe. There, whoever he was, the miserable man had perished. One or two gulls, who had, perhaps, seen him disappear, wheeled over his sepulchre with their usual melancholy piping. The sun had broken through the clouds by a last effort, and coloured the wide level of quicksands with a dusky purple. I stood for some time gazing at the spot, chilled and disheartened by my own reflections, and with a strong and commanding consciousness of death. I remember wondering how long the tragedy had taken, and whether his screams had been audible at the pavilion. And then, making a strong resolution, I was about to tear myself away, when a gust fiercer than usual fell upon this quarter of the beach, and I saw, now whirling high in air, now skimming lightly across the surface of the sands, a soft, black, felt hat, somewhat conical in shape, such as I had remarked already on the heads of the Italians.

I believe, but I am not sure, that I uttered a cry. The wind was driving the hat shoreward, and I ran round the border of the floe to be ready against its arrival. The gust fell, dropping the hat for a while upon the quicksand, and then, once more freshening, landed it a few yards from where I stood. I seized it with the interest you may imagine. It had seen some service; indeed, it was rustier than either of those I had seen that day upon the street. The lining was red, stamped with the name of the maker, which I have forgotten, and that of the place of manufacture, *Venedig*. This (it is not yet forgotten) was the name given by the Austrians to the beautiful city of Venice, then, and for long after, a part of their dominions.

The shock was complete. I saw imaginary Italians upon every side; and, for the first, and, I may say, for the last time in my experience, became overpowered by what is called a panic terror. I knew nothing, that is, to be afraid of, and yet I submit that I was heartily afraid; and it was with a sensible reluctance that I returned to my exposed and solitary camp in the Sea-Wood.

There I ate some cold porridge which had been left over from the night before, for I was disinclined to make a fire; and, feeling strengthened and reassured, dismissed all these fanciful terrors from my mind, and lay down to sleep with composure.

How long I may have slept it is impossible for me to

guess; but I was awakened at last by a sudden, blinding flash of light into my face. It woke me like a blow. In an instant I was upon my knees. But the light had gone as suddenly as it came. The darkness was intense. And, as it was blowing great guns from the sea and pouring with rain, the noises of the storm effectually concealed all others.

It was, I daresay, half a minute before I regained my self-possession. But for two circumstances, I should have thought I had been awakened by some new and vivid form of nightmare. First, the flap of my tent, which I had shut carefully when I retired, was now unfastened; and, second, I could still perceive, with a sharpness that excluded any theory of hallucination, the smell of hot metal and of burning oil. The conclusion was obvious. I had been wakened by some one flashing a bull's-eye lantern in my face. It had been but a flash, and away. He had seen my face, and then gone. I asked myself the object of so strange a proceeding, and the answer came pat. The man, whoever he was, had thought to recognise me, and he had not. There was yet another question unresolved: and to this, I may say, I feared to give an answer; if he had recognised me, what would he have done?

My fears were immediately diverted from myself, for I saw that I had been visited in a mistake; and I became persuaded that some dreadful danger threatened the pavilion. It required some nerve to issue forth into the black and intricate thicket which surrounded and overhung the den; but I groped my way to the links, drenched with rain, beaten upon and deafened by the gusts, and fearing at every step to lay my hand upon some lurking adversary. The darkness was so complete that I might have been surrounded by an army and yet none the wiser, and the uproar of the gale so loud that my hearing was as useless as my sight.

For the rest of that night, which seemed interminably long, I patrolled the vicinity of the pavilion, without seeing a living creature or hearing any noise but the concert of the wind, the sea, and the rain. A light in the upper story filtered through a cranny of the shutter, and kept me company till the approach of dawn.

CHAPTER V

TELLS OF AN INTERVIEW BETWEEN NORTHMOUR, CLARA, AND MYSELF

WITH THE first peep of day, I retired from the open to my old lair among the sand-hills, there to await the coming of my wife. The morning was grey, wild, and melancholy; the wind moderated before sunrise, and then went about, and blew in puffs from the shore; the sea began to go down, but the rain still fell without mercy. Over all the wilderness of links there was not a creature to be seen. Yet I felt sure the neighbourhood was alive with skulking foes. The light had been so suddenly and surprisingly flashed upon my face as I lay sleeping, and the hat that had been blown ashore by the wind from over Graden Floe, were two speaking signals of the peril that environed Clara and the party in the pavilion.

It was perhaps half-past seven, or nearer eight, before I saw the door open, and that dear figure come towards me in the rain. I was waiting for her on the beach before she had crossed the sand-hills.

"I have had such trouble to come!" she cried. "They did not wish me to go walking in the rain."

"Clara," I said, "you are not frightened!"

"No," said she, with a simplicity that filled my heart with confidence. For my wife was the bravest as well as the best of women; in my experience I have not found the two go always together, but with her they did; and she combined the extreme of fortitude with the most endearing and beautiful virtues.

I told her what had happened; and, though her cheek grew visibly paler, she retained perfect control over her senses.

"You see now that I am safe," said I, in conclusion. "They do not mean to harm me; for, had they chosen, I was a dead man last night."

She laid her hand upon my arm.

"And I had no presentiment!" she cried.

Her accent thrilled me with delight. I put my arm about her, and strained her to my side; and before either of us was aware, her hands were on my shoulders, and my lips upon her mouth. Yet up to that moment no word of love had passed between us. To this day I remember the touch of her cheek, which was wet and cold with the rain; and many a time since, when she has been washing her face, I have kissed it again for the sake of that morning on the beach. Now that she is taken from me, and I finish my pilgrimage alone, I recall our old loving-kindnesses and the deep honesty and affection which united us, and my present loss seems but a trifle in comparison.

We may have thus stood for some seconds—for time passes quickly with lovers—before we were startled by a peal of laughter close at hand. It was not natural mirth, but seemed to be affected in order to conceal an angrier feeling. We both turned, though I still kept my left arm about Clara's waist; nor did she seek to withdraw herself; and there, a few paces off upon the beach, stood Northmour, his head lowered, his hands behind his back, his nostrils white with passion.

"Ah! Cassilis!" he said, as I disclosed my face.

"That same," said I; for I was not at all put about.

"And so, Miss Huddlestone," he continued slowly but savagely, "this is how you keep your faith to your father and to me? This is the value you set upon your father's life? And you are so infatuated with this young gentleman that you must brave ruin, and decency, and common human caution—"

"Miss Huddlestone—" I was beginning to interrupt him, when he, in his turn, cut in brutally—

"You hold your tongue," said he; "I am speaking to that girl."

"That girl, as you call her, is my wife," said I; and my wife only leaned a little nearer, so that I knew she had afffirmed my words.

"Your what?" he cried. "You lie!"

"Northmour," I said, "we all know you have a bad temper, and I am the last man to be irritated by words. For all that, I propose that you speak lower, for I am convinced that we are not alone."

He looked round him, and it was plain my remark had in some degree sobered his passion. "What do you mean?" he asked.

I only said one word: "Italians."

He swore a round oath, and looked at us, from one to the other.

"Mr. Cassilis knows all that I know," said my wife.

"What I want to know," he broke out, "is where the devil Mr. Cassilis comes from, and what the devil Mr. Cassilis is doing here. You say you are married; that I do not believe. If you were, Graden Floe would soon divorce you; four minutes and a half, Cassilis. I keep my private cemetery for my friends."

"It took somewhat longer," said I, "for that Italian."

He looked at me for a moment half-daunted, and then, almost civilly, asked me to tell my story. "You have too much the advantage of me, Cassilis," he added. I complied, of course; and he listened, with several ejaculations, while I told him how I had come to Graden: that it was I whom he had tried to murder on the night of landing; and what I had subsequently seen and heard of the Italians.

"Well," said he, when I had done, "it is here at last; there is no mistake about that. And what, may I ask, do you propose to do?"

"I propose to stay with you and lend a hand," said I.

"You are a brave man," he returned, with a peculiar intonation.

"I am not afraid," said I.

"And so," he continued, "I am to understand that you two are married? And you stand up to it before my face, Miss Huddlestone?"

"We are not yet married," said Clara; "but we shall be as soon as we can."

"Bravo!" cried Northmour. "And the bargain? D——n it, you're not a fool, young woman; I may call a spade a spade with you. How about the bargain? You know as well as I do what your father's life depends upon. I have only to put my hands under my coat-tails and walk away, and his throat would be cut before the evening."

"Yes, Mr. Northmour," returned Clara, with great spirit; "but that is what you will never do. You made a bargain that was unworthy of a gentleman; but you are gentleman for all that, and you will never desert a man whom you have begun to help."

"Aha!" said he. "You think I will give my yacht for nothing? You think I will risk my life and liberty for love of the old gentleman; and then, I suppose, be best-man at the wedding, to wind up? Well," he added, wth an odd smile, "perhaps you are not altogether wrong. But ask

Cassilis here. *He* knows me. Am I a man to trust? Am I safe and scrupulous? Am I kind?"

"I know you talk a great deal, and sometimes, I think, very foolishly," replied Clara, "but I know you are a gentleman, and I am not the least afraid."

He looked at her with a peculiar approval and admiration; then, turning to me, "Do you think I would give her up without a struggle, Frank?" said he. "I tell you plainly, you look out. The next time we come to blows—"

"Will make the third," I interrupted, smiling.

"Ay, true; so it will," he said. "I had forgotten. Well, the third time's lucky."

"The third time, you mean, you will have the crew of the *Red Earl* to help," I said.

"Do you hear him?" he asked, turning to my wife.

"I hear two men speaking like cowards," said she. I should despise myself either to think or speak like that. And neither of you believe one word that you are saying, which makes it the more wicked and silly."

"She's a trump!" cried Northmour. "But she's not yet Mrs. Cassills. I say no more. The present is not for me."

Then my wife surprised me.

"I leave you here," she said suddenly. "My father has been too long alone. But remember this: you are to be friends, for you are both good friends to me."

She has since told me her reason for this step. As long as she remained, she declares that we two should have continued to quarrel; and I suppose that she was right, for when she was gone we fell at once into a sort of confidentiality.

Northmour stared after her as she went away over the sand-hill.

"She is the only woman in the world!" he exclaimed, with an oath. "Look at her action."

I, for my part, leaped at this opportunity for a little further light.

"See here, Northmour," said I; "we are all in a tight place, are we not?"

"I believe you, my boy," he answered, looking me in the eyes, and with great emphasis. "We have all hell upon us, that's the truth. You may believe me or not, but I'm afraid of my life."

"Tell me one thing," said I. "What are they after, these Italians? What do they want with Mr. Huddlestone?"

"Don't you know?" he cried. "The black old scamp had *carbonaro* funds on a deposit—two hundred and eighty thousand; and of course he gambled it away on stocks. There was to have been a revolution in the Tridentino, or Parma; but the revolution is off, and the whole wasps' nest is after Huddlestone. We shall all be lucky if we can save our skins."

"The *carbonari!*" I exclaimed; "God help him indeed!"

"Amen!" said Northmour. "And now, look here: I have said that we are in a fix; and, frankly, I shall be glad of your help. If I can't save Huddlestone, I want at least to save the girl. Come and stay in the pavilion; and, there's my hand on it, I shall act as your friend until the old man is either clear or dead. But," he added, "once that is settled, you become my rival once again, and I warn you—mind yourself."

"Done!" said I; and we shook hands.

"And now let us go directly to the fort," said Northmour; and he began to lead the way through the rain.

CHAPTER VI

TELLS OF MY INTRODUCTION TO THE TALL MAN

We were admitted to the pavilion by Clara, and I was surprised by the completeness and security of the defences. A barricade of great strength, and yet easy to displace, supported the door against any violence from without; and the shutters of the dining-room, into which I was led directly, and which was feebly illuminated by a lamp, were even more elaborately fortified. The panels were strengthened by bars and cross-bars; and these, in their turn, were kept in position by a system of braces and struts, some abutting on the floor, some on the roof, and others, in fine, against the opposite wall of the apartment. It was at once a solid and well-designed piece of carpentry; and I did not seek to conceal my admiration.

"I am the engineer," said Northmour. "You remember the planks in the garden? Behold them!"

"I did not know you had so many talents," said I.

"Are you armed?" he continued, pointing to an array of guns and pistols, all in admirable order, which stood in line against the wall or were displayed upon the sideboard.

"Thank you," I returned; "I have gone armed since our last encounter. But, to tell you the truth, I have had nothing to eat since early yesterday evening."

Northmour produced some cold meat, to which I eagerly set myself, and a bottle of good Burgundy, by which, wet as I was, I did not scruple to profit. I have always been an extreme temperance man on principle; but it is useless to push principle to excess, and on this occasion I believe that I finished three-quarters of the bottle. As I ate, I still continued to admire the preparations for defence.

"We could stand a siege," I said at length.

"Ye—es," drawled Northmour; "a very little one, per—haps. It is not so much the strength of the pavilion I misdoubt; it is the double danger that kills me. If we get to shooting, wild as the country is, some one is sure to hear it, and then—why, then it's the same thing, only different, as they say: caged by law, or killed by *carbonari*. There's the choice. It is a devilish bad thing to have the law against you in this world, and so I tell the old gentleman upstairs. He is quite of my way of thinking."

"Speaking of that," said I, "what kind of person is he?"

"Oh, he!" cried the other; "he's a rancid fellow, as far as he goes. I should like to have his neck wrung tomorrow by all the devils in Italy. I am not in this affair for him. You take me? I made a bargain for Missy's hand, and I mean to have it too."

"That by the way," said I. "I understand. But how will Mr. Huddlestone take my intrusion?"

"Leave that to Clara," returned Northmour.

I could have struck him in the face for this coarse familiarity; but I respected the truce, as, I am bound to say, did Northmour, and so long as the danger continued not a cloud arose in our relation. I bear him this testimony with the most unfeigned satisfaction; nor am I without pride when I look back upon my own behaviour. For surely no two men were ever left in a position so invidious and irritating.

As soon as I had done eating, we proceeded to inspect

the lower floor. Window by window we tried the different supports, now and then making an inconsiderable change; and the strokes of the hammer sounded with startling loudness through the house. I proposed, I remember, to make loopholes; but he told me they were already made in the windows of the upper story. It was an anxious business, this inspection, and left me downhearted. There were two doors and five windows to protect, and, counting Clara, only four of us to defend them against an unknown number of foes. I communicated my doubts to Northmour, who assured me, with unmoved composure, that he entirely shared them.

"Before morning," said he, "we shall all be butchered and buried in Graden Floe. For me, that is written."

I could not help shuddering at the mention of the quicksand, but reminded Northmour that our enemies had spared me in the wood.

"Do not flatter yourself," sald he. "Then you were not in the same boat with the old gentleman; now you are. It's the floe for all of us, mark my words."

I trembled for Clara; and just then her dear voice was heard calling us to come upstairs. Northmour showed me the way, and, when he had reached the landing, knocked at the door of what used to be called *My Uncle's Bedroom*, as the founder of the pavilion had designed it especially for himself.

"Come in, Northmour; come in, dear Mr. Cassilis," said a voice from within.

Pushing open the door, Northmour admitted me before him into the apartment. As I came in I could see the daughter slipping out by the side-door into the study, which had been prepared as her bedroom. In the bed, which was drawn back against the wall, instead of standing, as I had last seen it, boldly across the window, sat Bernard Huddlestone, the defaulting banker. Little as I had seen of him by the shifting light of the lantern on the links, I had no difficulty in recognising him for the same. He had a long and sallow countenance, surrounded by a long red beard and side-whiskers. His broken nose and high cheek-bones gave him somewhat the air of a Kalmuck, and his light eyes shone with the excitement of a high fever. He wore a skullcap of black silk; a huge Bible lay open before him on the bed with a pair of gold spectacles in the place, and a pile of other books lay on the stand by his side. The green curtains lent a cadaverous shade to his cheek; and, as he sat propped on pillows, his great stature was painfully hunched, and his head protruded till it overhung his knees. I believe if he had not died otherwise, he must have fallen a victim to consumption in the course of but a very few weeks.

He held out to me a hand, long, thin, and disagreeably hairy.

"Come in, come in, Mr. Cassilis," said he. "Another protector—ahem!—another protector. Always welcome as a friend of my daughter's, Mr. Cassilis. How they have rallied about me, my daughter's friends! May God in Heaven bless and reward them for it!"

I gave him my hand, of course, because I could not help it; but the sympathy I had been prepared to feel for Clara's father was immediately soured by his appearance, and the wheedling, unreal tones in which he spoke.

"Cassilis is a good man," said Northmour; "worth ten."

"So I hear," cried Mr. Huddlestone eagerly; "so my girl tells me. Ah, Mr. Cassilis, my sin has found me out, you see! I am very low, very low; but I hope equally penitent. We must all come to the throne of grace at last, Mr. Cassilis. For my part, I come late indeed; but with unfeigned humility, I trust."

"Fiddle-de-dee!" said Northmour roughly.

"No, no, dear Northmour!" cried the banker. "You must not say that; you must not try to shake me. You forget, my dear, good boy, you forget I may be called this very night before my Maker."

His excitement was pitiful to behold; and I felt myself grow indignant with Northmour, whose infidel opinions I well knew, and heartily derided, as he continued to taunt the poor sinner out of his humour of repentance.

"Pooh, my dear Huddlestone!" said he. "You do yourself injustice. You are a man of the world, inside and out, and were up to all kinds of mischief before I was born. Your conscience is tanned like South American leather—only you forgot to tan your liver, and that, if you will believe me, is the seat of the annoyance."

"Rogue, rogue! bad boy!" said Mr. Huddlestone, shaking his finger, "I am no precisian, if you come to that: I always hated a precisian; but I never lost hold of something better through it all. I have been a bad boy,

Mr. Cassilis; I do not seek to deny that; but it was after my wife's death, and you know, with a widower, it's a different thing: sinful—I won't say no; but there is a gradation, we shall hope. And talking of that— Hark!" he broke out suddenly, his hand raised, his fingers spread, his face racked with interest and terror. "Only the rain, bless God!" he added, after a pause, and with indescribable relief.

For some seconds he lay back among the pillows like a man near to fainting; then he gathered himself together, and, in somewhat tremulous tones, began once more to thank me for the share I was prepared to take in his defence.

"One question, sir," said I, when he had paused. "Is it true that you have money with you?"

He seemed annoyed by the question, but admitted with reluctance that he had a little.

"Well," I continued, "it is their money they are after, is it not? Why not give it up to them?"

"Ah!" replied he, shaking his head, "I have tried that already, Mr. Cassilis; and alas that it should be so! but it is blood they want."

"Huddlestone, that's a little less than fair," said Northmour. "You should mention that what you offered them was upwards of two hundred thousand short. The deficit is worth a reference; it is for what they call a cool sum, Frank. Then, you see, the fellows reason in their clear Italian way; and it seems to them, as indeed it seems to me, that they may just as well have both while they're about it—money and blood together, by George, and no more trouble for the extra pleasure."

"Is it in the pavilion?" I asked.

"It is; and I wish it were in the bottom of the sea instead," said Northmour; and then suddenly—"What are you making faces at me for?" he cried to Mr. Huddlestone, on whom I had unconsciously turned my back. "Do you think Cassilis would sell you?"

Mr. Huddlestone protested that nothing had been further from his mind.

"It is a good thing," retorted Northmour in his ugliest manner. "You might end by wearying us.—What were you going to say?" he added, turning to me.

"I was going to propose an occupation for the afternoon," said I. "Let us carry that money out, piece by piece, and lay it down before the pavilion door. If the *carbonari* come, why, it's theirs at any rate."

"No, no," cried Mr. Huddlestone; "it does not, it cannot belong to them! It should be distributed *pro rata* among all my creditors."

"Come now, Huddlestone," said Northmour, "none of that."

"Well, but my daughter," moaned the wretched man.

"Your daughter will do well enough. Here are two suitors, Cassilis and I, neither of us beggars, between whom she has to choose. And as for yourself, to make an end of arguments, you have no right to a farthing, and, unless I'm much mistaken, you are going to die."

It was certainly very cruelly said; but Mr. Huddlestone was a man who attracted litle sympathy; and, although I saw him wince and shudder, I mentally endorsed the rebuke; nay, I added a contribution of my own.

"Northmour and I," I said, "are willing enough to help you to save your life, but not to escape with stolen property."

He struggled for a while with himself, as though he were on the point of giving way to anger, but prudence had the best of the controversy.

"My dear boys," he said, "do with me or my money what you will. I leave all in your hands. Let me compose myself."

And so we left him, gladly enough I am sure. The last that I saw, he had once more taken up his great Bible, and with tremulous hands was adjusting his spectacles to read.

CHAPTER VII

TELLS HOW A WORD WAS CRIED THROUGH THE PAVILION WINDOW

THE RECOLLECTION of that afternoon will always be graven on my mind. Northmour and I were persuaded that an attack was imminent; and if it had been in our power to alter in any way the order of events, that power would have been used to precipitate rather than delay the critical moment. The worst was to be anticipated; yet we could conceive no extremity so miserable as the suspense we were now suffering. I have never been an eager, though always a great, reader; but I never knew books so insipid as those which I took up and cast aside that afternoon in the pavilion. Even talk became impossible as the hours went on. One or other was always listening for some sound, or peering from an upstairs window over the links. And yet not a sign indicated the presence of our foes.

We debated over and over again my proposal with regard to the money; and had we been in complete possession of our faculties, I am sure we should have condemned it as unwise; but we were flustered with alarm, grasped at a straw, and determined, although it was as much as advertising Mr. Huddlestone's presence in the pavilion, to carry my proposal into effect.

The sum was part in specie, part in bank paper, and part in circular notes payable to the name of James Gregory. We took it out, counted it, enclosed it once more in a despatch-box belonging to Northmour, and prepared a letter in Italian which he tied to the handle. It was signed by both of us under oath, and declared that this was all the money which had escaped the failure of the house of Huddlestone. This was, perhaps, the maddest action ever perpetrated by two persons professing to be sane. Had the despatch-box fallen into other hands than those for which it was intended, we stood criminally convicted on our own written testimony; but as I have said, we were neither of us in a condition to judge soberly, and had a thirst for action that drove us to do something, right or wrong, rather than endure the agony of waiting. Moreover, as we were both convinced that the hollows of the links were alive with hidden spies upon our movements, we hoped that our appearance with the box might lead to a parley, and perhaps a compromise.

It was nearly three when we issued from the pavilion. The rain had taken off; the sun shone quite cheerfully. I have never seen the gulls fly so close about the house or approach so fearlessly to human beings. On the very doorstep one flapped heavily past our heads, and uttered its wild cry in my very ear.

"There is an omen for you," said Northmour, who, like all freethinkers, was much under the influence of superstition. "They think we are already dead."

I made some light rejoinder, but it was with half my heart; for the circumstance had impressed me.

A yard or two before the gate, on a patch of smooth turf, we set down the despatch-box; and Northmour waved a white handkerchief over his head. Nothing replied. We raised our voices, and cried aloud in Italian that we were there as ambassadors to arrange the quarrel; but the stillness remained unbroken save by the sea-gulls and the surf. I had a weight at my heart when we desisted; and I saw that even Northmour was unusually pale. He looked over his shoulder nervously, as though he feared that some one had crept between him and the pavilion door.

"By God," he said in a whisper, "this is too much for me!"

I replied in the same key: "Suppose there should be none, after all?"

"Look there," he returned, nodding with his head, as though he had been afraid to point.

I glanced in the direction indicated; and there, from the northern quarter of the Sea-Wood, beheld a thin column of smoke rising steadily against the now cloudless sky.

"Northmour," I said (we still continued to talk in whispers), "it is not possible to endure this suspense. I prefer death fifty times over. Stay you here to watch the pavilion; I will go forward and make sure, if I have to walk right into their camp."

He looked once again all round him with puckered eyes, and then nodded assentingly to my proposal.

My heart beat like a sledge-hammer as I set out walking rapidly in the direction of the smoke; and, though up to that moment I had felt chill and shivering, I was suddenly conscious of a glow of heat over all my body. The ground in this direction was very uneven; a hundred men might have lain hidden in as many square yards about my path. But I had not practised the business in vain, chose such routes as cut at the very root of concealment, and, by keeping along the most convenient ridges, commanded several hollows at a time. It was not long before I was rewarded for my caution. Coming suddenly on to a mound somewhat more elevated than the surrounding hummocks, I saw, not thirty yards away, a man bent almost double, and running as fast as his attitude permitted along the bottom of a gully. I had dislodged one of the spies from his ambush. As soon as I sighted him, I called loudly both in English and Italian; and he, seeing concealment was no longer possible, straightened himself out, leaped from the gully and made off as straight as an arrow for the borders of the wood.

It was none of my business to pursue; I had learned what I wanted—that we were beleaguered and watched in the pavilion; and I returned at once, and walking as nearly as possible in my old footsteps, to where Northmour awaited me beside the despatch-box. He was even paler than when I had left him, and his voice shook a little.

"Could you see what he was like?" he asked.

"He kept his back turned," I replied.

"Let us get into the house, Frank. I don't think I'm a coward, but I can stand no more of this," he whispered.

All was still and sunshiny about the pavilion as we turned to re-enter it; even the gulls had flown in a wider circuit, and were seen flickering along the beach and sand-hills; and this loneliness terrified me more than a regiment under arms. It was not until the door was barricaded that I could draw a full inspiration and relieve the weight that lay upon my bosom. Northmour and I exchanged a steady glance; and I suppose each made his own reflections on the white and startled aspect of the other.

"You were right," I said. "All is over. Shake hands, old man, for the last time."

"Yes," replied he, "I will shake hands; for, as sure as I am here, I bear no malice. But remember, if, by some impossible accident, we should give the slip to these blackguards, I'll take the upper hand of you by fair or foul."

"Oh," said I, "you weary me."

He seemed hurt, and walked away in silence to the foot of the stairs, where he paused.

"You do not understand," said he. "I am not a swindler, and I guard myself; that is all. It may weary you or not, Mr. Cassilis, I do not care a rush; I speak for my own satisfaction, and not for your amusement. You had better go upstairs and court the girl; for my part, I stay here."

"And I stay with you," I returned. "Do you think I would steal a march, even with your permission?"

"Frank," he said, smiling, "it's a pity you are an ass,

for you have the makings of a man. I think I must be fey to-day; you cannot irritate me even when you try. Do you know," he continued softly, "I think we are the two most miserable men in England, you and I? we have got on to thirty without wife or child, or so much as a shop to look after—poor, pitiful, lost devils, both! And now we clash about a girl! As if there were not several millions in the United Kingdom! Ah, Frank, Frank, the one who loses this throw, be it you or me, he has my pity! It were better for him—how does the Bible say?—that a millstone were hanged about his neck and he were cast into the depth of the sea. Let us take a drink," he concluded suddenly, but without any levity of tone.

I was touched by his words and consented. He sat down on the table in the dining-room, and held up the glass of sherry to his eye.

"If you beat me, Frank," he said, "I shall take to drink. What will you do, if it goes the other way?"

"God knows," I returned.

"Well," said he, "here is a toast in the meantime: '*Italia irredenta!*' "

The remainder of the day was passed in the same dreadful tedium and suspense. I laid the table for dinner, while Northmour and Clara prepared the meal together in the kitchen. I could hear their talk as I went to and fro, and was surprised to find it ran all the time upon myself. Northmour again bracketed us together, and rallied Clara on a choice of husbands; but he continued to speak of me with some feeling, and uttered nothing to my prejudice unless he included himself in the condemnation. This awakened a sense of gratitude in my heart, which combined with the immediateness of our peril to fill my eye with tears. After all, I thought—and perhaps the thought was laughably vain—we were here three very noble human beings to perish in defence of a thieving banker.

Before we sat down to table I looked forth from an upstairs window. The day was beginning to decline; the links were utterly deserted; the despatch-box still lay untouched where we had left it hours before.

Mr. Huddlestone, in a long yellow dressing-gown, took one end of the table, Clara the other; while Northmour and I faced each other from the sides. The lamp was brightly trimmed; the wine was good; the viands, although mostly cold, excellent of their sort. We seemed to have agreed tacitly; all reference to the impending catastrophe was carefully avoided; and, considering our tragic circumstances, we made a merrier party than could have been expected. From time to time, it is true, Northmour or I would rise from table and make a round of the defences; and, on each of these occasions, Mr. Huddlestone was recalled to a sense of his tragic predicament, glanced up with ghastly eyes, and bore for an instant on his countenance the stamp of terror. But he hastened to empty his glass, wiped his forehead with his handkerchief, and joined again in the conversation.

I was astonished at the wit and information he displayed. Mr. Huddlestone's was certainly no ordinary character; he had read and observed for himself; his gifts were sound, and, though I could never have learned to love the man, I began to understand his success in business, and the great respect in which he had been held before his failure. He had, above all, the talent of society; and though I never heard him speak but on this one and most unfavourable occasion, I set him down among the most brilliant conversationalists I ever met.

He was relating with great gusto, and seemingly no feeling of shame, the manœuvres of a scoundrelly commission merchant whom he had known and studied in his youth, and we were all listening with an odd mixture of mirth and embarrassment, when our little party was brought abruptly to an end in the most startling manner.

A noise like that of a wet finger on the window-pane interrupted Mr. Huddlestone's tale; and in an instant we were all four as white as paper, and sat tongue-tied and motionless round the table.

"A snail," I said at last; for I had heard that these animals make a noise somewhat similar in character.

"Snail be d——d!" sald Northmour. "Hush!"

The same sound was repeated twice at regular intervals; and then a formidable voice shouted through the shutters the Italian word "*Traditore!*"

Mr. Huddlestone threw his head in the air; his eyelids quivered; next moment he fell insensible below the table. Northmour and I had each run to the armoury and seized a gun. Clara was on her feet with her hand at her throat.

So we stood waiting, for we thought the hour of attack was certainly come; but second passed after second, and all but the surf remained silent in the neighbourhood of the pavilion.

"Quick," said Northmour; "upstairs with him before they come."

CHAPTER VIII

TELLS THE LAST OF THE TALL MAN

SOMEHOW OR OTHER, by hook and crook, and between the three of us, we got Bernard Huddlestone bundled upstairs and laid upon the bed in *My Uncle's Room.* During the whole process, which was rough enough, he gave no sign of consciousness, and he remained, as we had thrown him, without changing the position of a finger. His daughter opened his shirt and began to wet his head and bosom; while Northmour and I ran to the window. The weather continued clear; the moon, which was now about full, had risen and shed a very clear light upon the links; yet, strain our eyes as we might, we could distinguish nothing moving. A few dark spots, more or less, on the uneven expanse, were not to be identified; they might be crouching men, they might be shadows; it was impossible to be sure.

"Thank God," said Northmour, "Aggie is not coming to-night."

Aggie was the name of the old nurse; he had not thought of her till now; but that he should think of her at all was a trait that surprised me in the man.

We were again reduced to waiting. Northmour went to the fireplace and spread his hands before the red embers, as if he were cold. I followed him mechanically with my eyes, and in so doing turned my back upon the window. At that moment a very faint report was audible from without, and a ball shivered a pane of glass, and buried itself in the shutter two inches from my head. I heard Clara scream; and though I whipped instantly out of range and into a corner, she was there, so to speak, before me, beseeching to know if I were hurt. I felt that I could stand to be shot at every day and all day long, with such marks of solicitude for a reward; and I continued to reassure her, with the tenderest caresses and in complete forgetfulness of our situation, till the voice of Northmour recalled me to myself.

"An air-gun," he said. "They wish to make no noise."

I put Clara aside, and looked at him. He was standing with his back to the fire and his hands clasped behind him; and I knew by the black look on his face that passion was boiling within. I had seen just such a look before he attacked me, that March night, in the adjoining chamber; and, though I could make every allowance for his anger, I confess I trembled for the consequences. He gazed straight before him; but he could see us with the tail of his eye, and his temper kept rising like a gale of wind. With regular battle awaiting us outside, this prospect of an internecine strife within the walls began to daunt me.

Suddenly, as I was thus closely watching his expression and prepared against the worst, I saw a change, a flash, a look of relief, upon his face. He took up the lamp which stood beside him on the table, and turned to us with an air of some excitement.

"There is one point that we must know," said he. "Are they going to butcher the lot of us, or only Huddlestone? Did they take you for him, or fire at you for your own *beaux yeux?*"

"They took me for him, for certain," I replied. "I am near as tall, and my head is fair."

"I am going to make sure," returned Northmour; and he stepped up to the window, holding the lamp above his head, and stood there, quietly affronting death, for half a minute.

Clara sought to rush forward and pull him from the place of danger; but I had the pardonable selfishness to hold her back by force.

"Yes," said Northmour, turning coolly from the window; "It's only Huddlestone they want."

"Oh, Mr. Northmour!" cried Clara; but found no more to add; the temerity she had just witnessed seeming beyond the reach of words.

He, on his part, looked at me, cocking his head, with a fire of triumph in his eyes; and I understood at once that he had thus hazarded his life, merely to attract Clara's notice, and depose me from my position as the hero of the hour. He snapped his fingers.

"The fire is only beginning," said he. "When they warm up to their work they won't be so particular."

A voice was now heard hailing us from the entrance. From the window we could see the figure of a man in the moonlight; he stood motionless, his face uplifted to ours, and a rag of something white on his extended arm; and as we looked right down upon him, though he was a good many yards distant on the links, we could see the moonlight glitter on his eyes.

He opened his lips again, and spoke for some minutes on end, in a key so loud that he might have been heard in every corner of the pavillion, and as far away as the borders of the wood. It was the same voice that had already shouted "*Traditore!*" through the shutters of the dining-room; this time it made a complete and clear statement. If the traitor "Oddlestone" were given up, all others should be spared; if not, no one should escape to tell the tale.

"Well, Huddlestone, what do you say to that?" asked Northmour, turning to the bed.

Up to that moment the banker had given no sign of life, and I, at least, had supposed him to be still lying in a faint; but he replied at once, and in such tones as I have never heard elsewhere, save from a delirious patient, adjured and besought us not to desert him. It was the most hideous and abject performance that my imagination can conceive.

"Enough," cried Northmour; and then he threw open the window, leaned out into the night, and in a tone of exultation, and with a total forgetfulness of what was due to the presence of a lady, poured out upon the ambassador a string of the most abominable raillery both in English and Italian, and bade him be gone where he had come from. I believe that nothing so delighted Northmour at that moment as the thought that we must all infallibly perish before the night was out.

Meantime the Italian put his flag of truce in his pocket, and disappeared, at a leisurely pace, among the sand-hills.

"They make honourable war," said Northmour. "They are all gentlemen and soldiers. For the credit of the thing, I wish we could change sides—you and I, Frank, and you too, Missy my darling—and leave that being on the bed to some one else. Tut! Don't look shocked! We are all going post to what they call eternity, and may as well be above-board while there's time. As far as I'm concerned, if I could first strangle Huddlestone and then get Clara in my arms, I could die with some pride and satisfaction. And as it is, by God, I'll have a kiss!"

Before I could do anything to interfere, he had rudely embraced and repeatedly kissed the resisting girl. Next moment I had pulled him away with fury, and flung him heavily against the wall. He laughed loud and long, and I feared his wits had given way under the strain; for even in the best of days he had been a sparing and a quiet laugher.

"Now, Frank," said he, when his mirth was somewhat appeased, "it's your turn. Here's my hand. Good-bye; farewell!" Then, seeing me stand rigid and indignant, and holding Clara to my side—"Man!" he broke out, "are you angry? Did you think we were going to die with all the airs and graces of society? I took a kiss; I'm glad I had it; and now you can take another if you like, and square accounts."

I turned from him with a feeling of contempt which I did not seek to dissemble.

"As you please," said he. "You've been a prig in life; a prig you'll die."

And with that he sat down on a chair, a rifle over his knee, and amused himself with snapping the lock; but I could see that his ebullition of light spirits (the only one I ever knew him to display) had already come to an end, and was succeeded by a sullen, scowling humour.

All this time our assailants might have been entering the house, and we been none the wiser; we had in truth almost forgotten the danger that so imminently overhung our days. But just then Mr. Huddlestone uttered a cry, and leaped from the bed.

I asked him what was wrong.

"Fire!" he cried. "They have set the house on fire!"

Northmour was on his feet in an instant, and he and I ran through the door of communication with the study. The room was illuminated by a red and angry light. Almost at the moment of our entrance, a tower of flame arose in front of the window, and, with a tingling report, a pane fell inwards on the carpet. They had set fire to the lean-to outhouse, where Northmour used to nurse his negatives.

"Hot work," said Northmour. "Let us try in your old room."

We ran thither in a breath, threw up the casement, and looked forth. Along the whole back wall of the pavilion piles of fuel had been arranged and kindled; and it is probable they had been drenched with mineral oil, for, in spite of the morning's rain, they all burned bravely. The fire had taken a firm hold already on the outhouse, which blazed higher and higher every moment; the back-door was in the centre of a red-hot bonfire; the eaves, we could see, as we looked upward, were already smouldering, for the roof overhung, and was supported by considerable beams of wood. At the same time, hot, pungent, and choking volumes of smoke began to fill the house. There was not a human being to be seen to right or left.

"Ah, well!" said Northmour, "here's the end, thank God."

And we returned to *My Uncle's Room*. Mr. Huddlestone was putting on his boots, still violently trembling, but with an air of determination such as I had not hitherto observed. Clara stood close by him, with her cloak in both hands ready to throw about her shoulders, and a strange look in her eyes, as if she were half-hopeful, half-doubtful of her father.

"Well, boys and girls," said Northmour, "how about a sally? The oven is heating; it is not good to stay here and be baked; and, for my part, I want to come to my hands with them, and be done."

"There is nothing else left," I replied.

And both Clara and Mr. Huddlestone, though with a very different intonation, added, "Nothing."

As we went downstairs the heat was excessive, and the roaring of the fire filled our ears; and we had scarce reached the passage before the stairs window fell in, a branch of flame shot brandishing through the aperture, and the interior of the pavilion became lit up with that dreadful and fluctuating glare. At the same moment we heard the fall of something heavy and inelastic in the upper story. The whole pavilion, it was plain, had gone alight like a box of matches, and now not only flamed sky-high to land and sea, but threatened with every moment to crumble and fall in about our ears.

Northmour and I cocked our revolvers. Mr. Huddlestone, who had already refused a firearm, put us behind him with a manner of command.

"Let Clara open the door," said he. "So, if they fire a

volley, she will be protected. And in the meantime stand behind me. I am the scapegoat; my sins have found me out."

I heard him, as I stood breathless by his shoulder, with my pistol ready, pattering off prayers in a tremulous, rapid whisper; and I confess, horrid as the thought may seem, I despised him for thinking of supplications in a moment so critical and thrilling. In the meantime, Clara, who was dead white, but still possessed her faculties, had displaced the barricade from the front door. Another moment, and she had pulled it open. Firelight and moonlight illuminated the links with confused and changeful lustre, and far away against the sky we could see a long trail of glowing smoke.

Mr. Huddlestone, filled for the moment with a strength greater than his own, struck Northmour and myself a backhander in the chest; and while we were thus for the moment incapacitated from action, lifting his arms above his head like one about to dive, he ran straight forward out of the pavillion.

"Here am I!" he cried—"Huddlestone! Kill me, and spare the others!"

His sudden appearance daunted, I suppose, our hidden enemies; for Northmour and I had time to recover, to seize Clara between us, one by each arm, and to rush forth to his assistance, ere anything further had taken place. But scarce had we passed the threshold when there came near a dozen reports and flashes from every direction among the hollows of the links. Mr. Huddlestone staggered, uttered a weird and freezing cry, threw up his arms over his head, and fell backward on the turf.

"*Traditore! Traditore!*" cried the invisible avengers.

And just then a part of the roof of the pavilion fell in, so rapid was the progress of the fire. A loud, vague, and horrible noise accompanied the collapse, and a vast volume of flame went soaring up to heaven. It must have been visible at that moment from twenty miles out at sea, from the shore at Graden-Wester, and far inland from the peak of Graystiel, the most eastern summit of the Caulder Hills. Bernard Huddlestone, although God knows what were his obsequies, had a fine pyre at the moment of his death.

CHAPTER IX

TELLS HOW NORTHMOUR CARRIED OUT HIS THREAT

I SHOULD HAVE the greatest difficulty to tell you what followed next after this tragic circumstance. It is all to me, as I look back upon it, mixed, strenuous, and ineffectual, like the struggles of a sleeper in a nightmare. Clara, I remember, uttered a broken sigh and would have fallen forward to earth, had not Northmour and I supported her insensible body. I do not think we were attacked; I do not remember even to have seen an assailant; and I believe we deserted Mr. Huddlestone without a glance. I only remember running like a man in a panic, now carrying Clara altogether in my own arms, now sharing her weight with Northmour, now scuffling confusedly for the possession of that dear burden. Why we should have made for my camp in the Hemlock Den, or how we reached it, are points lost for ever to my recollection. The first moment at which I became definitely sure, Clara had been suffered to fall against the outside of my little tent, Northmour and I were tumbling together on the ground, and he, with contained ferocity, was striking for my head with the butt of his revolver. He had already twice wounded me on the scalp; and it is to the subsequent loss of blood that I am tempted to attribute the sudden clearness of my mind.

I caught him by the wrist.

"Northmour," I remember saying, "you can kill me afterwards. Let us first attend to Clara."

He was at that moment uppermost. Scarcely had the words passed my lips, when he had leaped to his feet and ran towards the tent; and the next moment he was straining Clara to his heart and covering her unconscious hands and face with his caresses.

"Shame!" I cried. "Shame to you, Northmour!"

And, giddy though I still was, I struck him repeatedly upon the head and shoulders.

He relinquished his grasp, and faced me in the broken moonlight.

"I had you under, and I let you go," said he; "and now you strike me! Coward!"

"You are the coward," I retorted. "Did she wish your kisses while she was still sensible of what she wanted? Not she! And now she may be dying; and you waste this precious time, and abuse her helplessness. Stand aside, and let me help her."

He confronted me for a moment, white and menacing; then suddenly he stepped aside.

"Help her, then," said he.

I threw myself on my knees beside her, and loosened, as well as I was able, her dress and corset; but while I was thus engaged, a grasp descended on my shoulder.

"Keep your hands off her," sald Northmour fiercely. "Do you think I have no blood in my veins?"

"Northmour," I cried, "if you will neither help her yourself, nor let me do so, do you know that I shall have to kill you?"

"That is better!" he cried. "Let her die also—where's the harm? Step aside from that girl, and stand up to fight!"

"You will observe," said I, half-rising, "that I have not kissed her yet."

"I dare you to," he cried.

I do not know what possessed me; it was one of the things I am most ashamed of in my life, though, as my wife used to say, I knew that my kisses would lie always welcome were she dead or living; down I fell again upon my knees, parted the hair from her forehead, and, with the dearest respect, laid my lips for a moment on that cold brow. It was such a caress as a father might have given; it was such a one as was not unbecoming from a man soon to die to a woman already dead.

"And now," said I, "I am at your service, Mr. Northmour."

But I saw, to my surprise, that he had turned his back upon me.

"Do you hear?" I asked.

"Yes," said he, "I do. If you wish to fight, I am ready. If not, go on and save Clara. All is one to me."

I did not wait to be twice bidden; but, stooping again over Clara, continued my efforts to revive her. She still lay white and lifeless; I began to fear that her sweet spirit had indeed fled beyond recall, and horror and a sense of utter desolation seized upon my heart. I called her by name with the most endearing inflections; I chafed and beat her hands; now I laid her head low, now supported it against my knee; but all seemed to be in vain, and the lids still lay heavy on her eyes.

"Northmour," I said, "there is my hat. For God's sake bring some water from the spring."

Almost in a moment he was by my side with the water.

"I have brought it in my own," he said. "You do not grudge me the privilege?"

"Northmour," I was beginning to say, as I laved her head and breast; but he interrupted me savagely.

"Oh, you hush up!" he said. "The best thing you can do is to say nothing."

I had certainly no desire to talk, my mind being swallowed up in concern for my dear love and her condition; so I continued in silence to do my best towards her recovery, and, when the hat was empty, returned it to him with one word—"More." He had, perhaps, gone several times upon this errand, when Clara reopened her eyes.

"Now," said he, "since she is better, you can spare me, can you not? I wish you a good-night, Mr. Cassilis."

And with that he was gone among the thicket. I made a fire, for I had now no fear of the Italians, who had even spared all the little possessions left in my encampment; and, broken as she was by the excitement and the hideous catastrophe of the evening, I managed, in one way or another—by persuasion, encouragement, warmth, and such simple remedies as I could lay my hand on—to bring her back to some composure of mind and strength of body.

Day had already come, when a sharp "Hist!" sounded from the thicket. I started from the ground; but the voice of Northmour was heard adding, in the most tranquil tones: "Come here, Cassilis, and alone; I want to show you something."

I consulted Clara with my eyes, and, receiving her tacit permission, left her alone, and clambered out of the den. At some distance off I saw Northmour leaning against an elder; and, as soon as he perceived me, he began walking seaward. I had almost overtaken him as he reached the outskirts of the wood.

"Look," said he, pausing.

A couple of steps more brought me out of the foliage. The light of the morning lay cold and clear over that well-known scene. The pavilion was but a blackened wreck; the roof had fallen in, one of the gables had fallen out; and, far and near, the face of the links was cicatrised with little patches of burnt furze. Thick smoke still went straight upwards in the windless air of the morning, and a great pile of ardent cinders filled the bare walls of the house, like coals in an open grate. Close by the islet a schooner yacht lay-to, and a well-manned boat was pulling vigorously for the shore.

"The *Red Earl!*" I cried. "The *Red Earl* twelve hours too late!"

"Feel in your pocket, Frank. Are you armed?" asked Northmour.

I obeyed him, and I think I must have become deadly pale. My revolver had been taken from me.

"You see I have you in my power," he continued. "I disarmed you last night while you were nursing Clara; but this morning—here—take your pistol. No thanks!" he cried, holding up his hand. "I do not like them; that is the only way you can annoy me now."

He began to walk forward across the links to meet the boat, and I followed a step or two behind. In front of the pavilion I paused to see where Mr. Huddlestone had fallen; but there was no sign of him, nor so much as a trace of blood.

"Graden Floe," said Northmour.

He continued to advance till we had come to the head of the beach.

"No farther, please," said he. "Would you like to take her to Graden House?"

"Thank you," I replied; "I shall try to get her to the minister's at Graden-Wester."

The prow of the boat here grated on the beach, and a sailor jumped ashore with a line in his hand.

"Wait a minute, lads!" cried Northmour; and then lower and to my private ear: "You had better say nothing of all this to her," he added.

"On the contrary!" I broke out, "she shall know everything that I can tell."

"You do not understand," he returned, with an air of great dignity. "It will be nothing to her; she expects it of me. Good-bye!" he added, with a nod.

I offered him my hand.

"Excuse me," said he. "It's small, I know; but I can't

push things quite so far as that. I don't wish any sentimental business, to sit by your hearth a white-haired wanderer, and all that. Quite the contrary: I hope to God I shall never again clap eyes on either one of you."

"Well, God bless you, Northmour!" I said heartily.

"Oh, yes," he returned.

He walked down the beach; and the man who was ashore gave him an arm on board, and then shoved off and leaped into the bows himself. Northmour took the tiller; the boat rose to the waves, and the oars between the tholepins sounded crisp and measured in the morning air.

They were not yet half-way to the *Red Earl,* and I was still watching their progress, when the sun rose out of the sea.

One word more, and my story is done. Years after, Northmour was killed fighting under the colours of Garibaldi for the liberation of the Tyrol.

Markheim

"YES," said the dealer, "our windfalls are of various kinds. Some customers are ignorant, and then I touch a dividend on my superior knowledge. Some are dishonest," and here he held up the candle, so that the light fell strongly on his visitor, "and in that case," he continued, "I profit by my virtue."

Markheim had but just entered from the daylight streets, and his eyes had not yet grown familiar with the mingled shine and darkness in the shop. At these pointed words, and before the near presence of the flame, he blinked painfully and looked aside.

The dealer chuckled. "You come to me on Christmas Day," he resumed, "when you know that I am alone in my house, put up my shutters, and make a point of refusing business. Well, you will have to pay for that; you will have to pay for my loss of time, when I should be balancing my books; you will have to pay, besides, for a kind of manner that I remark in you to-day very strongly. I am the essence of discretion, and ask no awkward questions; but when a customer cannot look me in the eye, he has to pay for it." The dealer once more chuckled; and then, changing to his usual business voice, though still with a note of irony, "You can give, as usual, a clear account of how you came into the possession of the object?" he continued. "Still your uncle's cabinet? A remarkable collector, sir!"

And the little pale, round-shouldered dealer stood almost on tip-toe, looking over the top of his gold spectacles, and nodding his head with every mark of disbelief. Markheim returned his gaze with one of infinite pity, and a touch of horror.

"This time," said he, "you are in error. I have not come to sell, but to buy. I have no curios to dispose of; my uncle's cabinet is bare to the wainscot; even were it still intact, I have done well on the Stock Exchange, and should more likely add to it than otherwise, and my errand to-day is simplicity itself. I seek a Christmas present for a lady," he continued, waxing more fluent as he struck into the speech he had prepared; "and certainly I owe you every excuse for thus disturbing you upon so small a matter. But the thing was neglected yesterday; I must produce my little compliment at dinner; and, as you very well know, a rich marriage is not a thing to be neglected."

There followed a pause, during which the dealer seemed to weigh this statement incredulously. The ticking of many clocks among the curious lumber of the shop, and the faint rushing of the cabs in a near thoroughfare, filled up the interval of silence.

"Well, sir," said the dealer, "be it so. You are an old customer after all; and if, as you say, yon have the chance of a good marriage, far be it from me to be an obstacle.—Here is a nice thing for a lady now," he went on, "this hand-glass—fifteenth-century, warranted; comes from a good collection, too; but I reserve the name, in the interests of my customer, who was just like yourself, my dear sir, the nephew and sole heir of a remarkable collector."

The dealer, while he thus ran on in his dry and biting voice, had stooped to take the object from its place; and, as he had done so, a shock had passed through Markheim, a start both of hand and foot, a sudden leap of many tumultuous passions to the face. It passed as swiftly as it came, and left no trace beyond a certain trembling of the hand that now received the glass.

"A glass," he said hoarsely, and then paused, and repeated it more clearly. "A glass? For Christmas? Surely not?"

"And why not?" cried the dealer. "Why not a glass?"

Markheim was looking upon him with an indefinable expression. "You ask me why not?" he sald. "Why, look here—look in it—look at yourself! Do you like to see it? No! nor I—nor any man."

The little man had jumped back when Markheim had so suddenly confronted him with the mirror; but now, perceiving there was nothing worse on hand, he chuckled. "Your future lady, sir, must be pretty hard favoured," said he.

"I ask you," sald Markheim, "for a Christmas present, and you give me this—this damned reminder of years, and sins and follies—this hand-conscience. Did you mean it? Had you a thought in your mind? Tell me. It will be better for you if you do. Come, tell me about yourself. I hazard a guess now, that you are in secret a very charitable man?"

The dealer looked closely at his companion. It was very odd, Markheim did not appear to be laughing; there was something in his face like an eager sparkle of hope, but nothing of mirth.

"What are you driving at?" the dealer asked.

"Not charitable?" returned the other gloomily. "Not charitable? not pious; not scrupulous; unloving, unbeloved; a hand to get money, a safe to keep it. Is that all? Dear God, man, is that all?"

"I will tell you what it is," began the dealer, with some sharpness, and then broke off again into a chuckle. "But I see this is a love-match of yours, and you have been drinking the lady's health."

"Ah!" cried Markheim, with a strange curiosity. "Ah, have you been in love? Tell me about that."

"I," cried the dealer. "I in love! I never had the time, nor have I the time to-day for all this nonsense—Will you take the glass?"

"Where is the hurry?" returned Markheim. "It is very pleasant to stand here talking; and life is so short and insecure that I would not hurry away from any pleasure—no, not even from so mild a one as this. We should rather cling, cling to what little we can get, like a man at a cliff's edge. Every second is a cliff, if you think upon it—a cliff a mile high—high enough, if we fall, to dash us out of every feature of humanity. Hence it is best to talk pleasantly. Let us talk of each other: why should we wear this mask? Let us be confidential. Who knows? —we might become friends."

"I have just one word to say to you," said the dealer. "Either make your purchase, or walk out of my shop!"

"True, true," said Markheim. "Enough fooling. To business. Show me something else."

The dealer stooped once more, this time to replace the glass upon the shelf, his thin blond hair falling over his eyes as he did so. Markheim moved a little nearer, with one hand in the pocket of his greatcoat: he drew himself up and filled his lungs; at the same time many different emotions were depicted together on his face—terror, horror, and resolve, fascination and a physical repulsion; and through a haggard lift of his upper lip his teeth looked out.

"This, perhaps, may suit," observed the dealer: and then, as he began to re-arise, Markheim bounded from behind upon his victim. The long, skewer-like dagger flashed and fell. The dealer struggled like a hen, striking his temple on the shelf, and then tumbled on the floor in a heap.

Time had some score of small voices in that shop, some stately and slow, as was becoming to their great age; others garrulous and hurried. All these told out the seconds in an intricate chorus of tickings. Then the passage of a lad's feet, heavily running on the pavement, broke in upon these smaller voices and startled Markheim into the consciousness of his surroundings. He looked about him awfully. The candle stood on the counter, its flame solemnly wagging in a draught; and by that inconsiderable movement the whole room was filled with noiseless bustle and kept heaving like a sea: the tall shadows nodding, the gross blots of darkness swelling and dwindling as with respiration, the faces of the portraits and the china gods changing and wavering like images in water. The inner door stood ajar, and peered into that leaguer of shadows with a long slit of daylight like a pointing finger.

From these fear-stricken rovings Markheim's eyes returned to the body of his victim, where it lay both humped and sprawling, incredibly small and strangely meaner than in life. In these poor, miserly clothes, in that ungainly attitude, the dealer lay like so much sawdust. Markheim had feared to see it, and, lo! it was nothing. And yet, as he gazed, this bundle of old clothes and pool of blood began to find eloquent voices. There it must lie; there was none to work the cunning hinges or direct the miracle of locomotion—there it must lie till it was found. Found! ay, and then? Then would this dead flesh lift up a cry that would ring over England, and fill the world with the echoes of pursuit. Ay, dead or not, this was still the enemy. "Time was that when the brains were out," he thought; and the first word struck into his mind. Time, now that the deed was accomplished—time, which had closed for the victim, had become instant and momentous for the slayer.

The thought was yet in his mind when, first one and then another, with every variety of pace and voice—one deep as the bell from a cathedral turret, another ringing on its treble notes the prelude of a waltz—the clocks began to strike the hour of three in the afternoon.

The sudden outbreak of so many tongues in that dumb chamber staggered him. He began to bestir himself, going to and fro with the candle, beleaguered by moving shadows, and startled to the soul by chance reflections. In many rich mirrors, some of home design, some from Venice or Amsterdam, he saw his face repeated and repeated, as it were an army of spies; his own eyes met and detected him; and the sound of his own steps, lightly as they fell, vexed the surrounding quiet. And still, as he continued to fill his pockets, his mind accused him, with a sickening iteration, of the thousand faults of his design. He should have chosen a more quiet hour; he should have prepared an alibi; he should not have used a knife; he should have been more cautious, and only bound and gagged the dealer, and not killed him; he should have been more bold, and killed the servant also; he should have done all things otherwise: poignant regrets, weary, incessant toiling of the mind to change what was unchangeable, to plan what was now useless, to be the architect of the irrevocable past. Meanwhile, and behind all this activity, brute terrors, like the scurrying of rats in a deserted attic, filled the more remote chambers of his brain with riot; the hand of the constable would fall heavy on his shoulder, and his nerves would jerk like a hooked fish; or he beheld, in galloping defile, the dock, the prison, the gallows, and the black coffin.

Terror of the people in the street sat down before his mind like a besieging army. It was impossible, he thought, but that some rumour of the struggle must have reached their ears and set on edge their curiosity; and now, in all the neighbouring houses, he divined them sitting motionless and with uplifted ear—solitary people, condemned to spend Christmas dwelling alone on memories of the past, and now startlingly recalled from that tender exercise; happy family parties, struck into silence round the table, the mother still with raised finger: every degree and age and humour, but all, by their own hearths, prying and hearkening and weaving the rope that was to hang him. Sometimes it seemed to him he could not move too softly; the clink of the tall Bohemian goblets rang out loudly like a bell; and alarmed by the bigness of the ticking, he was tempted to stop the clocks. And then, again, with a swift transition of his terrors, the very silence of the place appeared a source of peril, and a thing to strike and freeze the passer-by; and he would step more boldly, and bustle aloud among the contents of the shop, and imitate, with elaborate bravado, the movements of a busy man at ease in his own house.

But he was now so pulled about by different alarms, that, while one portion of his mind was still alert and cunning, another trembled on the brink of lunacy. One hallucination in particular took a strong hold on his credulity. The neighbour hearkening with white face beside his window, the passer-by arrested by a horrible surmise on the pavement—these could at worst suspect, they could not know; through the brick walls and shuttered windows only sounds could penetrate. But here, within the house, was he alone? He knew he was; he had watched the servant set forth sweethearting, in her poor best, "out for the day" written on every ribbon and smile. Yes, he was alone, of course; and yet, in the bulk of empty house above him, he could surely hear a stir of delicate footing—he was surely conscious, inexplicably conscious, of some presence. Ay, surely; to every room and corner of the house his imagination followed it; and now it was a faceless thing, and yet had eyes to see with; and again it was a shadow of himself; and yet again beheld the image of the dead dealer, reinspired with cunning and hatred.

At times, with a strong effort, he would glance at the open door which still seemed to repel his eyes. The house was tall, the skylight small and dirty, the day blind with fog; and the light that filtered down to the ground story was exceedingly faint, and showed dimly on the threshold of the shop. And yet, in that strip of doubtful brightness, did there not hang wavering a shadow?

Suddenly, from the street outside, a very jovial gentleman began to beat with a staff on the shop-door, accompanying his blows with shouts and railleries in which the dealer was continually called upon by name. Markheim, smitten into ice, glanced at the dead man. But no! he lay quite still; he was fled away far beyond ear-shot of these blows and shoutings; he was sunk beneath seas of silence; and his name, which would once have caught his notice above the howling of a storm, had become an empty sound. And presently the jovial gentleman desisted from his knocking and departed.

Here was a broad hint to hurry what remained to be done, to get forth from this accusing neighbourhood, to plunge into a bath of London multitudes, and to reach, on the other side of day, that haven of safety and apparent innocence—his bed. One visitor had come: at any moment another might follow and be more obstinate. To have done the deed, and yet not to reap the profit, would be too abhorrent a failure. The money, that was now Markheim's concern; and as a means to that, the keys.

He glanced over his shoulder at the open door; where the shadow was still lingering and shivering; and with no conscious repugnance of the mind, yet with a tremor of the belly, he drew near the body of his victim. The human character had quite departed. Like a suit half-stuffed with bran, the limbs lay scattered, the trunk doubled, on the floor; and yet the thing repelled him. Although so dingy and inconsiderable to the eye, he feared it might have more significance to the touch. He took the body by the shoulders and turned it on its back. It was strangely light and supple, and the limbs, as if they had been broken, fell into the oddest postures. The face was robbed of all expression; but it was as pale as wax, and shockingly smeared with blood about one temple. That was, for Markheim, the one displeasing circumstance. It carried him back, upon the instant, to a certain fair-day in a fishers' village: a grey day, a piping wind, a crowd upon the street, a blare of brasses, the booming of drums, the nasal voice of a ballad-singer; and a boy going to and fro, buried over-head in the crowd and divided between interest and fear, until, coming out upon the chief place of concourse, he beheld a booth and a great screen with pictures, dismally designed, garishly coloured: Brownrigg with her apprentice; the Mannings with their murdered guest; Weare in the death-grip of Thurtell; and a score besides of famous crimes. The thing was as clear as an illusion; he was once again that little boy; he was looking once again, and with the same sense of physical revolt, at these vile pictures; he was still stunned by the thumping of the drums. A bar of that day's music returned upon his memory; and at that, for the first time, a qualm came over him, a breath of nausea, a sudden weakness of the joints, which he must instantly resist and conquer.

He judged it more prudent to confront than to flee from these considerations; looking the more hardily in the dead face, bending his mind to realise the nature and greatness of his crime. So little a while ago that face had moved with every change of sentiment, that pale mouth had spoken, that body had been all on fire with governable energies; and now, and by his act, that piece of life had been arrested, as the horologist, with interjected finger, arrests the beating of the clock. So he reasoned in vain; he could rise to no more remorseful consciousness; the same heart which had shuddered before the painted effigies of crime looked on the reality unmoved. At lest, he felt a gleam of pity for one who had been endured in rain with all those faculties that can make the world a garden of enchantment, one who had never lived and who was now dead. But of penitence, no, not a tremor.

With that, shaking himself clear of these considerations, he found the keys and advanced towards the open door of the shop. Outside, it had begun to rain smartly; and the sound of the shower upon the roof had banished silence. Like some dripping cavern, the chambers of the house were haunted by an incessant echoing, which filled the ear and mingled with the ticking of the clocks. And, as Markheim approached the door, he seemed to hear, in answer to his own cautious tread, the steps of another foot withdrawing up the stair. The shadow still palpitated loosely on the threshold. He threw a ton's weight of resolve upon his muscles, and drew back the door.

The faint, foggy daylight glimmered dimly on the bare floor and stairs; on the bright suit of armour posted, halbert in hand, upon the landing: and on the dark woodcarvings, and framed pictures that hung against the yellow panels of the wainscot. So loud was the beating of the rain through all the house that, in Markheim's ears, it began to be distinguished into many different sounds.

Footsteps and sighs, the tread of regiments marching in the distance, the chink of money in the counting, and the creaking of doors held stealthily ajar, appeared to mingle with the patter of the drops upon the cupola and the gushing of the water in the pipes. The sense that he was not alone grew upon him to the verge of madness. On every side he was haunted and begirt by presences. He heard them moving in the upper chambers; from the shop he heard the dead man getting to his legs; and as he began with a great effort to mount the stairs, feet fled quietly before him and followed stealthily behind. If he were but deaf, he thought, how tranquilly he would possess his soul! And then again, and hearkening with ever fresh attention, he blessed himself for that unresting sense which held the outposts and stood a trusty sentinel upon his life. His head turned continually on his neck; his eyes, which seemed starting from their orbits, scouted on every side, and on every side were half-rewarded as with the tail of something nameless vanishing. The four-and-twenty steps to the first floor were four-and-twenty agonies.

On that first story, the doors stood ajar, three of them like three ambushes, shaking his nerves like the throats of cannon. He could never again, he felt, be sufficiently immured and fortified from men's observing eyes; he longed to be home, girt in by walls, buried among bedclothes, and invisible to all but God. And at that thought he wondered a little, recollecting tales of other murderers and the fear they were said to entertain of heavenly avengers. It was not so, at least, with him. He feared the laws of nature, lest, in their callous and immutable procedure, they should preserve some damning evidence of his crime. He feared tenfold more, with a slavish, superstitious terror, some scission in the continuity of man's experience, some wilful illegality of nature. He played a game of skill, depending on the rules, calculating consequence from cause; and what if nature, as the defeated tyrant overthrew the chess-board, should break the mould of their succession? The like had befallen Napoleon (so writers said) when the winter changed the time of its appearance. The like might befall Markheim: the solid walls might become transparent and reveal his doings like those of bees in a glass hive; the stout planks might yield under his foot like quicksands and detain him in their clutch; ay, and there were soberer accidents that might destroy him: if, for instance, the house should fall and imprison him beside the body of his victim; or the house next door should fly on fire, and the firemen invade him from all sides. These things he feared; and, in a sense, these things might be called the hands of God reached forth against sin. But about God Himself he was at ease: his act was doubtless exceptional, but so were his excuses, which God knew; it was there, and not among men, that he felt sure of justice.

When he had got safe into the drawing-room, and shut the door behind him, he was aware of a respite from alarms. The room was quite dismantled, uncarpeted besides, and strewn with packing-cases and incongruous furniture; several great pier-glasses, in which he beheld himself at various angles, like an actor on a stage; many pictures, framed and unframed, standing with their faces to the wall; a fine Sheraton sideboard, a cabinet of marquetry, and a great old bed, with tapestry hangings. The windows opened to the floor; but by great good fortune the lower part of the shutters had been closed, and this concealed him from the neighbours. Here, then, Markheim drew in a packing-case before the cabinet, and began to search among the keys. It was a long business, for there were many; and it was irksome besides; for, after all, there might be nothing in the cabinet, and time was on the wing. But the closeness of the occupation sobered him. With the tail of his eye he saw the door—even glanced at it from time to time directly, like a besieged commander, pleased to verify the good estate of his defences. But in truth he was at peace. The rain falling in the street sounded natural and pleasant. Presently, on the other side, the notes of a piano were wakened to the music of a hymn, and the voices of many children took up the air and words. How stately, how comfortable was the melody! How fresh the youthful voices! Markheim gave ear to it smilingly, as he sorted out the keys; and his mind was thronged with answerable ideas and images; church-going children and the pealing of the high organ; children afield, bathers by the brookside, ramblers on the brambly common, kite-flyers in the windy and cloud-navigated sky; and then, at another cadence of the hymn, back again to church, and the somnolence of summer Sundays, and the high genteel voice of the parson (which he smiled a little to recall) and the painted Jacobean tombs, and the dim lettering of the Ten Commandments in the chancel.

And as he sat thus, at once busy and absent, he was startled to his feet. A flash of ice, a flash of fire, a bursting gush of blood went over him, and then he stood transfixed and thrilling. A step mounted the stair slowly and steadily, and presently a hand was laid upon the knob, and the lock clicked, and the door opened.

Fear held Markheim in a vice. What to expect he knew not, whether the dead man walking, or the official ministers of human justice, or some chance witness blindly stumbling in to consign him to the gallows. But when a face was thrust into the aperture, glanced round the room, looked at him, nodded and smiled as if in friendly recognition, and then withdrew again, and the door closed behind it, his fear broke loose from his control in a hoarse cry. At the sound of this the visitant returned.

"Did you call me?" he asked pleasantly, and with that he entered the room and closed the door behind him.

Markheim stood and gazed at him with all his eyes. Perhaps there was a film upon his sight, but the outlines of the new-comer seemed to change and waver like those of the idols in the wavering candlelight of the shop; and at times he thought he knew him; and at times he thought he bore a likeness to himself; and always, like a lump of living terror, there lay in his bosom the conviction that this thing was not of the earth and not of God.

And yet the creature had a strange air of the commonplace, as he stood looking on Markheim with a smile; and when he added: "You are looking for the money, I believe?" it was in the tones of everyday politeness.

Markheim made no answer.

"I should warn you," resumed the other, "that the maid has left her sweetheart earlier than usual and will soon be here. If Mr. Markheim be found in this house, I need not describe to him the consequences."

"You know me?" cried the murderer.

The visitor smiled. "You have long been a favourite of mine," he said; "and I have long observed and often sought to help you."

"What are you?" cried Markheim, "the devil?"

"What I may be," returned the other, "cannot affect the service I propose to render you."

"It can," cried Markheim; "it does! Be helped by you? No, never; not by you! You do not know me yet; thank God, you do not know me!"

"I know you," replied the visitant, with a sort of kind severity, or rather firmness. "I know you to the soul."

"Know me!" cried Markheim. "Who can do so? My life is but a travesty and slander on myself. I have lived to belie my nature. All men do; all men are better than this disguise, that grows about and stifles them. You see each dragged away by life, like one whom bravos have seized and muffled in a cloak. If they had their own control—if you could see their faces, they would be altogether different, they would shine out for heroes and saints! I am worse than most; myself is more overlaid; my excuse is known to me and God. But, had I the time, I could disclose myself."

"To me?" inquired the visitant.

"To you before all," returned the murderer. "I supposed you were intelligent. I thought—since you exist—you would prove a reader of the heart. And yet you would propose to judge me by my acts! Think of it; my acts! I was born and I have lived in a land of giants; giants have dragged me by the wrists since I was born out of my mother—the giants of circumstance. And you would judge me by my acts! But can you not look within? Can you not understand that evil is hateful to me? Can you not see within me the clear writing of conscience, never blurred by any wilful sophistry, although too often disregarded? Can you not read me for a thing that surely must be common as humanity—the unwilling sinner?"

"All this is very feelingly expressed," was the reply, "but it regards me not. These points of consistency are beyond my province, and I care not in the least by what compulsion you may have been dragged away, so as you are but carried in the right direction. But time flies; the servant delays, looking in the faces of the crowd and at the pictures on the hoardings, but still she keeps moving nearer; and remember, it is as if the gallows itself was striding towards you through the Christmas streets! Shall I help you; I, who know all? Shall I tell you where to find the money?"

"For what price?" asked Markheim.

"I offer you the service for a Christmas gift," returned the other.

Markheim could not refrain from smiling with a kind of bitter triumph. "No," said he, "I will take nothing at your hands; if I were dying of thirst, and it was your hand that put the pitcher to my lips, I should find the courage to refuse. It may be credulous, but I will do nothing to commit myself to evil."

"I have no objection to a death-bed repentance," observed the visitant.

"Because you disbelieve their efficacy!" Markheim cried.

"I do not say so," returned the other; "but I look on these things from a different side, and when the life is done my interest falls. The man has lived to serve me, to spread black looks under colour of religion, or to sow tares in the wheat-field, as you do, in a course of weak compliance with desire. Now that he draws so near to his deliverance, he can add but one act of service—to repent, to die smiling, and thus to build up in confidence and hope the more timorous of my surviving followers. I am not so hard a master. Try me. Accept my help. Please yourself in life as you have done hitherto; please yourself more amply, spread your elbows at the board; and when the night begins to fall and the curtains to be drawn, I tell you, for your greater comfort, that you will find it even easy to compound your quarrel with your conscience, and to make a truckling peace with God. I came but now from such a death-bed, and the room was full of sincere mourners, listening to the man's last words: and when I looked into that face, which had been set as a flint against mercy, I found it smiling with hope."

"And do you, then, suppose me such a creature?" asked Markheim. "Do you think I have no more generous aspirations than to sin, and sin, and sin, and, at the last, sneak into heaven? My heart rises at the thought. Is this, then, your experience of mankind? or is it because you find me with red hands that you presume such baseness? and is this crime of murder indeed so impious as to dry up the very springs of good?"

"Murder is to me no special category," replied the other. "All sins are murder, even as all life is war. I behold your race, like starving mariners on a raft, plucking crusts out of the hands of famine and feeding on each other's lives. I follow sins beyond the moment of their acting; I find in all that the last consequence is death; and to my eyes, the pretty maid who thwarts her mother with such taking graces on a question of a ball, drips no less visibly with human gore than such a murderer as yourself. Do I say that I follow sins? I follow virtues also; they differ not by the thickness of a nail, they are both scythes for the reaping angel of Death. Evil, for which I live, consists not in action but in character. The bad man is dear to me; not the bad act, whose fruits, if we could follow them far enough down the hurtling cataract of the ages, might yet be found more blessed than those of the rarest virtues. And it is not because you have killed a dealer, but because you are Markheim, that I offer to forward your escape."

"I will lay my heart open to you," answered Markheim. "This crime on which you find me is my last. On my way to it I have learned many lessons; itself is a lesson, a momentous lesson. Hitherto I have been driven with revolt to what I would not; I was a bond-slave to poverty, driven and scourged. There are robust virtues that can stand in these temptations; mine was not so: I had a thirst of pleasure. But to-day, and out of this deed, I pluck both warning and riches—both the power and a fresh resolve to be myself. I become in all things a free actor in the world; I begin to see myself all changed, these hands the agents of good, this heart at peace. Something comes over me out of the past; something of what I have dreamed on Sabbath evenings to the sound of the church organ, of what I forecast when I shed tears over noble books, or talked, an innocent child, with my mother. There lies my life; I have wandered a few years, but now I see once more my city of destination."

"You are to use this money on the Stock Exchange, I think?" remarked the visitor; "and there, if I mistake not, you have already lost some thousands."

"Ah," said Markheim, "but this time I have a sure thing."

"This time, again, you will lose," replied the visitor quietly.

"Ah, but I will keep back the half!" cried Markheim.

"That also you will lose," said the other.

The sweat started upon Markheim's brow. "Well, then, what matter?" he exclaimed. "Say it be lost, say I am plunged again in poverty, shall one part of me, and that the worse, continue until the end to override the better?

Evil and good run strong in me, haling me both ways. I do not love the one thing, I love all. I can conceive great deeds, renunciations, martyrdoms; and though I be fallen to such a crime as murder, pity is no stranger to my thoughts. I pity the poor; who knows their trials better than myself? I pity and help them; I prize love, I love honest laughter; there is no good thing nor true thing on earth but I love it from my heart. And are my vices only to direct my life and my virtues to lie without effect, like some passive lumber of the mind? Not so; good, also, is the spring of acts."

But the visitant raised his finger. "For six-and-thirty years that you have been in this world," said he, "through many changes of fortune and varieties of humour, I have watched you steadily fall. Fifteen years ago you would have started at a theft. Three years back you would have blenched at the name of murder. Is there any crime, is there any cruelty or meanness, from which you still recoil? —five years from now I shall detect you in the fact! Downward, downward lies your way; nor can anything but death avail to stop you."

"It is true," Markheim said huskily, "I have in some degree complied with evil. But it is so with all: the very saints, in the mere exercise of living, grow less dainty, and take on the tone of their surroundings."

"I will propound to you one simple question," said the other; "and as you answer, I shall read to you your moral horoscope. You have grown in many things more lax; possibly you do right to be so; and at any account, it is the same with all men. But granting that, are you in any one particular, however trifling, more difficult to please with your own conduct, or do you go in all things with a looser rein?"

"In any one?" repeated Markheim, with an anguish of consideration. "No," he added, with despair "in none! I have gone down in all."

"Then," said the visitor, "content yourself with what you are, for you will never change; and the words of your part on this stage are irrevocably written down."

Markheim stood for a long while silent, and indeed it was the visitor who first broke the silence. "That being so," he said, "shall I show you the money?"

"And grace?" cried Markheim.

"Have you not tried it?" returned the other. "Two or

three years ago, did I not see you on the platform of revival meetings, and was not your voice the loudest in the hymn?"

"It is true," said Markheim; "and I see clearly what remains for me by way of duty. I thank you for these lessons from my soul; my eyes are opened, and I behold myself at last for what I am."

At this moment, the sharp note of the door-bell rang through the house; and the visitant, as though this were some concerted signal for which he had been waiting, changed at once in his demeanour.

"The maid!" he cried. "She has returned, as I forewarned you, and there is now before you one more difficult passage. Her master, you must say, is ill; you must let her in, with an assured but rather serious countenance—no smiles, no overacting, and I promise you success! Once the girl within, and the door closed, the same dexterity that has already rid you of the dealer will relieve you of this last danger in your path. Thenceforward you have the whole evening—the whole night, if needful—to ransack the treasures of the house and to make good your safety. This is help that comes to you with the mask of danger. Up!" he cried; "up, friend; your life hangs trembling in the scales: up, and act!"

Markheim steadily regarded his counsellor. "If I be condemned to evil acts," he said, "there is still one door of freedom open—I can cease from action. If my life be an ill thing, I can lay it down. Though I be, as you say truly, at the beck of every small temptation, I can yet, by one decisive gesture, place myself beyond the reach of all. My love of good is damned to barrenness; it may, and let it be! But I have still my hatred of evil; and from that, to your galling disappointment, you shall see that I can draw both energy and courage."

The features of the visitor began to undergo a wonderful and lovely change: they brightened and softened with a tender triumph, and, even as they brightened, faded and dislimned. But Markheim did not pause to watch or understand the transformation. He opened the door and went downstalrs very slowly, thinking to himself. His past went soberly before him; he beheld it as it was, ugly and strenuous like a dream, random as chance-medley—a scene of defeat. Life, as he thus reviewed it, tempted him no longer; but on the farther side he perceived a quiet haven for his bark. He paused in the passage, and looked into the shop, where the candle still burned by the dead body. It was strangely silent. Thoughts of the dealer swarmed into his mind, as he stood gazing. And then the bell once more broke out into impatient clamour.

He confronted the maid upon the threshold with something like a smile.

"You had better go for the police," said he: "I have killed your master."

Olalla

"Now," said the doctor, "my part is done, and, I may say, with some vanity, well done. It remains only to get you out of this cold and poisonous city, and to give you two months of a pure air and an easy conscience. The last is your affair. To the first I think I can help you. It falls indeed rather oddly; it was but the other day the Padre came in from the country, and as he and I are old friends, although of contrary professions, he applied to me in a matter of distress among some of his parishioners. This was a family—but you are ignorant of Spain, and even the names of our grandees are hardly known to you; suffice it, then, that they were once great people, and are now fallen to the brink of destitution. Nothing now belongs to them but the residencia, and certain leagues of desert mountain, in the greater part of which not even a goat could support life. But the house is a fine old place, and stands at a great height among the hills, and most salubriously; and I had no sooner heard my friend's tale than I remembered you. I told him I had a wounded officer, wounded in the good cause, who was now able to make a change; and I proposed that his friends should take you for a lodger. Instantly the Padre's face grew dark, as I had maliciously foreseen it would. It was out of the question, he said. Then let them starve, said I, for I have no sympathy with tatterdemalion pride. There upon we separated, not very content with one another; but yesterday, to my wonder, the Padre returned and made a submission: the difficulty, he said, he had found upon inquiry to be less than he had feared; or, in other words, these proud people had put their pride in their pocket. I closed with the offer; and, subject to your approval, I have taken rooms for you in the residencia. The air of these mountains will renew your blood: and the quiet in which you will there live is worth all the medicines in the world."

"Doctor," said I, "you have been throughout my good angel, and your advice is a command. But tell me, if you please, something of the family with which I am to reside."

"I am coming to that," replied my friend; "and, indeed, there is a difficulty in the way. These beggars are, as I have said, of very high descent, and swollen with the most baseless vanity; they have lived for some generations in a growing isolation, drawing away, on either hand, from the rich who had now become too high for them, and from the poor, whom they still regarded as too low; and even to-day, when poverty forces them to unfasten their door to a guest, they cannot do so without a most ungracious stipulation. You are to remain, they say, a stranger; they will give you attendance, but they refuse from the first the idea of the smallest intimacy."

I will not deny that I was piqued, and perhaps the feeling strengthened my desire to go, for I was confident that I could break down that barrier if I desired. "There is nothing offensive in such a stipulation," said I; "and I even sympathise with the feeling that inspired it."

"It is true they have never seen you," returned the doctor politely; "and if they knew you were the handsomest and the most pleasant man that ever came from England (where I am told that handsome men are common, but pleasant ones not so much so), they would doubtless make you welcome with a better grace. But since you take the thing so well, it matters not. To me, indeed, it seems discourteous. But you will find yourself the gainer. The family will not much tempt you. A mother, a son, and a daughter; an old woman said to be half-witted, a country lout, and a country girl, who stands very high with her confessor, and is, therefore," chuckled the physician, "most likely plain; there is not much in that to attract the fancy of a dashing officer."

"And yet you say they are high-born," I objected.

"Well, as to that, I should distinguish," returned the doctor. "The mother is; not so the children. The mother was the last representative of a princely stock, degenerate both in parts and fortune. Her father was not only poor, he was mad: and the girl ran wild about the residencia till his death. Then, much of the fortune having died with him, and the family being quite extinct, the girl ran wilder than ever, until at last she married, Heaven knows whom, a muleteer some say, others a smuggler; while there are some who uphold there was no marriage at all, and that Felipe and Olalla are bastards. The union, such as it was, was tragically dissolved some years ago; but they live in such seclusion, and the country at that time was in so much disorder, that the precise manner of the man's end is known ony to the priest—if even to him."

"I begin to think I shall have strange experiences," said I.

"I would not romance, if I were you," replied the doctor; "you will find, I fear, a very grovelling and commonplace reality. Felipe, for instance, I have seen. And what am I to say? He is very rustic, very cunning, very loutish, and, I should say, an innocent; the others are probably to match. No, no, señor commandante, you must seek congenial society among the great sights of our mountains; and in these at least, if you are at all a lover of the works of nature, I promise you will not be disappointed."

The next day Felipe came for me in a rough country cart, drawn by a mule; and a little before the stroke of noon, after I had said farewell to the doctor, the innkeeper, and different good souls who had befriended me during my sickness, we set forth out of the city by the eastern gate, and began to ascend into the Sierra. I had been so long a prisoner, since I was left behind for dying after the loss of the convoy, that the mere smell of the earth set me smiling. The country through which we went was wild and rocky, partially covered with rough woods, now of the cork-tree, and now of the great Spanish chestnut, and frequently intersected by the beds of mountain torrents. The sun shone, the wind rustled joyously; and we had advanced some miles, and the city had already shrunk into an inconsiderable knoll upon the plain behind us, before my attention began to be diverted to the companion of my drive. To the eye, he seemed but a diminutive, loutish, well-made country lad, such as the doctor had described, mighty quick and active, but devoid of any culture; and this first impression was with most observers final. What began to strike me was his familiar, chattering talk; so strangely inconsistent with the terms on which I was to be received; and partly from his imperfect enunciation, partly from the sprightly incoherence of the matter, so very difficult to follow clearly without an effort of the mind. It is true I had before talked with persons of a similar mental constitution; persons who seemed to live (as he did) by the senses, taken and possessed by the visual object of the moment and unable to discharge their minds of that impression. His seemed to me (as I sat, distantly giving ear) a kind of conversation proper to drivers, who pass much of their time in a great vacancy of the intellect and threading the sights of a familiar country. But this was not the case of Felipe; by his own account, he was a home-keeper; "I wish I was there now," he said; and then, spying a tree by the wayside, he broke off to tell me that he had once seen a crow among its branches.

"A crow?" I repeated, struck by the ineptitude of the remark, and thinking I had heard imperfectly.

But by this time he was already filled with a new idea; hearkening with a rapt intentness, his head on one side, his face puckered; and he struck me rudely, to make me hold my peace. Then he smiled and shook his head.

"What did you hear?" I asked.

"Oh, it is all right," he said; and began encouraging his mule with cries that echoed unhumanly up the mountain walls.

I looked at him more closely. He was superlatively well-built, light, and lithe and strong; he was well-featured; his yellow eyes were very large, though, perhaps, not very expressive; take him altogether, he was a pleasant-looking lad, and I had no fault to find with him, beyond that he was of a dusky hue, and inclined to hairiness; two characteristics that I disliked. It was his mind that puzzled, and yet attracted me. The doctor's phrase—an innocent—came back to me; and I was wondering if that were, after all, the true description, when the road began to go down into the narrow and naked chasm of a torrent. The waters thundered tumultuously in the bottom; and the ravine was filled full of the sound, the thin spray, and the claps of wind, that accompanied their descent. The scene was certainly impressive; but the road was in that part very securely walled in; the mule went steadily forward; and I was astonished to perceive the paleness of terror in the face of my companion. The voice of that wild river was inconstant, now sinking lower as if in weariness, now doubling its hoarse tones; momentary freshets seemed to swell its volume, sweeping down the gorge, raving and booming against the barrier walls; and

I observed it was at each of these accessions to the clamour that my driver more particularly winced and blanched. Some thoughts of Scottish superstition and the river-kelpie passed across my mind; I wondered if perchance the like were prevalent in that part of Spain; and turning to Felipe, sought to draw him out.

"What is the matter?" I asked.

"Oh, I am afraid," he replied.

"Of what are you afraid?" I returned. "This seems one of the safest places on this very dangerous road."

"It makes a noise," he said, with a simplicity of awe that set my doubts at rest.

The lad was but a child in intellect; his mind was like his body, active and swift, but stunted in development; and I began from that time forth to regard him with a measure of pity, and to listen at first with indulgence, and at last even with pleasure, to his disjointed babble.

By about four in the afternoon we had crossed the summit of the mountain line, said farewell to the western sunshine, and began to go down upon the other side, skirting the edge of many ravines and moving through the shadow of dusky woods. There rose upon all sides the voice of falling water, not condensed and formidable as in the gorge of the river, but scattered and sounding gaily and musically from glen to glen. Here, too, the spirits of my driver mended, and he began to sing aloud in a falsetto voice, and with a singular bluntness of musical perception, never true either to melody or key, but wandering at will, and yet somehow with an effect that was natural and pleasing, like that of the song of birds. As the dusk increased, I fell more and more under the spell of this artless warbling, listening and waiting for some articulate air, and still disappointed; and when at last I asked him what it was he sang—"Oh," cried he, "I am just singing!" Above all, I was taken with a trick he had of unweariedly repeating the same note at little intervals; it was not so monotonous as you would think, or, at least, not disagreeable; and it seemed to breathe a wonderful contentment with what is, such as we love to fancy in the attitude of trees, or the quiescence of a pool.

Night had fallen dark before we came out upon a plateau, and drew up a little after, before a certain lump of superior blackness which I could only conjecture to be the residencia. Here my guide, getting down from the cart, hooted and whistled for a long time in vain; until at last an old peasant man came towards us from somewhere in the surrounding dark, carrying a candle in his hand. By the light of this I was able to perceive a great arched doorway of a Moorish character: it was closed by iron-studded gates, in one of the leaves of which Felipe opened a wicket. The peasant carried off the cart to some out-building; but my guide and I passed through the wicket, which was closed again behind us; and, by the glimmer of the candle, passed through a court, up a stone stair, along a section of an open gallery, and up more stairs again, until we came at last to the door of a great and somewhat bare apartment. This room, which I understood was to be mine, was pierced by three windows, lined with some lustrous wood disposed in panels, and carpeted with the skins of many savage animals. A bright fire burned in the chimney, and shed abroad a changeful flicker; close up to the blaze there was drawn a table, laid for supper; and in the far end a bed stood ready. I was pleased by these preparations, and said so to Felipe; and he, with the same simplicity of disposition that I had already remarked in him, warmly re-echoed my praises. "A fine room." he said; "a very fine room. And fire, too; fire is good; it melts out the pleasure in your bones. And the bed," he continued, carrying over the candle in that direction—"see what fine sheets—how soft, how smooth, smooth"; and he passed his hand again and again over their texture, and then laid down his head and rubbed his cheeks among them with a grossness of content that somehow offended me. I took the candle from his hand (for I feared he would set the bed on fire) and walked back to the supper-table, where, perceiving a measure of wine, I poured out a cup and called to him to come and drink of it. He started to his feet at once and ran to me with a strong expression of hope; but when he saw the wine he visibly shuddered.

"Oh, no," he said, "not that; that is for you. I hate it."

"Very well, Señor," said I; "then I will drink to your good health, and to the prosperity of your house and family. Speaking of which," I added, after I had drunk, "shall I not have the pleasure of laying my salutations in person at the feet of the Señora, your mother?"

But at these words all the childishness passed out of his face, and was succeeded by a look of indescribable cunning and secrecy. He backed away from me at the same time, as though I were an animal about to leap or some dangerous fellow with a weapon, and when he had got near the door, glowered at me sullenly with contracted pupils. "No," he said at last, and the next moment was gone noiselessly out of the room; and I heard his footing die away downstairs as light as rainfall, and silence closed over the house.

After I had supped I drew up the table nearer to the bed and began to prepare for rest; but in the new position of the light, I was struck by a picture on the wall. It represented a woman, still young. To judge by her costume and the mellow unity which reigned over the canvas, she had long been dead; to judge by the vivacity of the attitude, the eyes and the features, I might have been beholding in a mirror the image of life. Her figure was very slim and strong, and of a just proportion; red tresses lay like a crown over her brow; her eyes, of a very golden brown, held mine with a look; and her face, which was perfectly shaped, was yet marred by a cruel, sullen, and sensual expression. Something in both face and figure, something exquisitely intangible, like the echo of an echo, suggested the features and bearing of my guide; and I stood a while unpleasantly attracted and wondering at the oddity of the resemblance. The common, carnal stock of that race, which had been originally designed for such high dames as the one now looking on me from the canvas, had fallen to baser uses, wearing country clothes, sitting on the shaft and holding the reins of a mule cart, to bring home a lodger. Perhaps an actual link subsisted; perhaps some scruple of the delicate flesh that was once clothed upon with the satin and brocade of the dead lady, now winced at the rude contact of Felipe's frieze.

The first light of the morning shone full upon the portrait, and, as I lay awake, my eyes continued to dwell upon it with growing complacency; its beauty crept about my heart insidiously, silencing my scruples one after another; and while I knew that to love such a woman were to sign and seal one's own sentence of degeneration, I still knew that, if she were alive, I should love her. Day after day the double knowledge of her wickedness and of my weakness grew clearer. She came to be the heroine of many day-dreams, in which her eyes led on to, and sufficiently rewarded, crimes. She cast a dark shadow on my fancy, and when I was out in the free air of heaven, taking vigorous exercise and healthily renewing the current of my blood, it was often a glad thought to me that my enchantress was safe in the grave, her wand of beauty broken, her lips closed in silence, her philtre spilt. And yet I had a half-lingering terror that she might not be dead after all, but re-arisen in the body of some descendant.

Felipe served my meals in my own apartment; and his resemblance to the portrait haunted me. At times it was not; at times, upon some change of attitude or flash of expression, it would leap out upon me like a ghost. It was above all in his ill tempers that the likeness triumphed. He certainly liked me; he was proud of my notice, which he sought to engage by many simple and childlike devices; he loved to sit close before my fire, talking his broken talk or singing his odd, endless, wordless, songs, and sometimes drawing his hand over my clothes with an affectionate manner of caressing that never failed to cause in me an embarrassment of which I was ashamed. But for all that, he was capable of flashes of causeless anger and fits of sturdy sullenness. At a word of reproof, I have seen him upset the dish of which I was about to eat, and this not surreptitiously, but with defiance; and similarly at a hint of inquisition. I was not unnaturally curious, being in a strange place and surrounded by strange people; but at the shadow of a question he shrank back, lowering and dangerous. Then it was that, for a fraction of a second, this rough lad might have been the brother of the lady in the frame. But these humours were swift to pass; and the resemblance died along with them.

In these first days I saw nothing of any one but Felipe, unless the portrait is to be counted; and since the lad was plainly of weak mind, and had moments of passion, it may be wondered that I bore his dangerous neighbourhood with equanimity. As a matter of fact, it was for some time irksome; but it happened before long that I obtained over him so complete a mastery as set my disquietude at rest.

It fell in this way. He was by nature slothful, and much of a vagabond, and yet he kept by the house, and not only waited upon my wants, but laboured every day in the garden or small farm to the south of the residencia. Here he would be joined by the peasant whom I had seen on the night of my arrival, and who dwelt at the far end of the enclosure, about half a mile away, in a rude out-house; but it was plain to me that of these two, it was Felipe who did most; and though I would sometimes see him throw down his spade and go to sleep among the very plants he had been digging, his constancy and energy were admirable in themselves, and still more so since I was well assured they were foreign to his disposition, and the fruit of an ungrateful effort. But while I admired, I wondered what had called forth in a lad so shuttle-witted this enduring sense of duty. How was it sustained? I asked myself, and to what length did it prevail over his instincts? The priest was possibly his inspirer; but the priest came one day to the residencia. I saw him both come and go after an interval of close upon an hour, from a knoll where I was sketching, and all that time Felipe continued to labour undisturbed in the garden.

At last, in a very unworthy spirit, I determined to debauch the lad from his good resolutions, and, waylaying him at the gate, easily persuaded him to join me in a ramble. It was a fine day, and the woods to which I led him were green and pleasant and sweet-smelling, and alive with the hum of insects. Here he discovered himself in a fresh character, mounting up to heights of gaiety that abashed me, and displaying an energy and grace of movement that delighted the eye. He leaped, he ran round me in mere glee; he would stop, and look and listen, and seem to drink in the world like a cordial; and then he would suddenly spring into a tree with one bound, and hang and gambol there like one at home. Little as he said to me, and that of not much import, I have rarely enjoyed more stirring company; the sight of his delight was a continual feast; the speed and accuracy of his movements pleased me to the heart; and I might have been so thoughtlessly unkind as to make a habit of these walks, had not chance prepared a very rude conclusion to my pleasure. By some swiftness or dexterity the lad captured a squirrel in a tree top. He was then some way ahead of me, but I saw him drop to the ground and crouch there, crying aloud for pleasure like a child. The sound stirred my sympathies, it was so fresh and innocent; but as I bettered my pace to draw near, the cry of the squirrel knocked upon my heart. I have heard and seen much of the cruelty of lads, and above all, of peasants; but what I now beheld struck me into a passion of anger. I thrust the fellow aside, plucked the poor brute out of his hands, and with swift mercy killed it. Then I turned upon the torturer, spoke to him long out of the heat of my indignation, calling him names at which he seemed to wither; and at length, pointing towards the residencia, bade him begone and leave me, for I chose to walk with men, not with vermin. He fell upon his knees, and, the words coming to him with more clearness than usual, poured out a stream of the most touching supplications, begging me in mercy to forgive him, to forget what he had done, to look to the future. "Oh, I try so hard," he said. "Oh, commandante, bear with Felipe this once; he will never be a brute again!" Thereupon, much more affected than I cared to show, I suffered myself to be persuaded, and at last shook hands with him and made it up. But the squirrel, by way of penance, I made him bury; speaking of the poor thing's beauty, telling him what pains it had suffered, and how base a thing was the abuse of strength. "See, Felipe," said I, "you are strong indeed; but in my hands you are as helpless as that poor thing of the trees. Give me your hand in mine. You cannot remove it. Now suppose that I were cruel like you, and took a pleasure in pain. I only tighten my hold, and see how you suffer." He screamed aloud, his face stricken ashy and dotted with needle-points of sweat; and when I set him free, he fell to the earth and nursed his hand and moaned over it like a baby. But he took the lesson in good part; and whether from that, or from what I had said to him, or the higher notion he now had of my bodily strength, his original affection was changed into a dog-like, adoring fidelity.

Meanwhile I gained rapidly in health. The residencia stood on the crown of a stony plateau; on every side the mountains hemmed it about; only from the roof, where was a bartizan, there might be seen, between two peaks, a small segment of plain, blue with extreme distance. The air in these altitudes moved freely and largely; great clouds congregated there, and were broken up by the wind and left in tatters on the hill-tops; a hoarse and yet faint rumbling of torrents rose from all round; and one could there study all the ruder and more ancient characters of nature in something of their pristine force. I delighted from the first in the vigorous scenery and changeful weather; nor less in the antique and dilapidated mansion where I dwelt. This was a large oblong, flanked at two opposite corners by bastion-like projections, one of which commanded the door, while both were loopholed for musketry. The lower story was, besides, naked of windows, so that the building, if garrisoned, could not be carried without artillery. It enclosed an open court planted with pomegranate trees. From this a broad flight of marble stairs ascended to an open gallery, running all round and resting, towards the court, on slender pillars. Thence, again, several enclosed stairs led to the upper stories of the house, which were thus broken up into distinct divisions. The windows, both within and without, were closely shuttered; some of the stonework in the upper parts had fallen; the roof, in one place, had been wrecked in one of the flurries of wind which were common in these mountains; and the whole house, in the strong, beating sunlight, and standing out above a grove of stunted cork-trees, thickly laden and discoloured with dust, looked like the sleeping palace of the legend. The court, in particular, seemed the very home of slumber. A hoarse cooing of doves haunted about the eaves; the winds were excluded, but when they blew outside, the mountaln dust fell here as thick as rain, and veiled the red bloom of the pomegranates; shuttered windows and the closed doors of numerous cellars, and the vacant arches of the gallery, enclosed it; and all day long the sun made broken profiles on the four sides, and paraded the shadow of the pillars on the gallery floor. At the ground level there was, however, a certain pillared recess, which bore the marks of human habitation. Though it was open in front upon the court, it was yet provided with a chimney, where a wood fire would be always prettily blazing; and the tile floor was littered with the skins of animals.

It was in this place that I first saw my hostess. She had drawn one of the skins forward and sat in the sun, leaning against a pillar. It was her dress that struck me first of all, for it was rich and brightly coloured, and shone out in that dusty courtyard with something of the same relief as the flowers of the pomegranates. At a second look it was her beauty of person that took hold of me. As she sat back—watching me, I thought, though with invisible eyes—and wearing at the same time an expression of almost imbecile good-humour and contentment, she showed a perfectness of feature and a quiet nobility of attitude that were beyond a statue's. I took off my hat to her in passing, and her face puckered with suspicion as swiftly and lightly as a pool ruffles in the breeze; but she paid no heed to my courtesy. I went forth on my customary walk a trifle daunted, her idol-like impassivity haunting me; and when I returned, although she was still in much the same posture, I was half surprised to see that she had moved as far as the next pillar, following the sunshine. This time, however, she addressed me wlth some trivial salutation, civilly enough conceived, and uttered in the same deep-chested, and yet indistinct and lisping tones, that had already baffled the utmost niceness of my hearing from her son. I answered rather at a venture; for not only did I fail to take her meaning with precision, but the sudden disclosure of her eyes disturbed me. They were unusually large, the iris golden like Felipe's, but the pupil at that moment so distended that they seemed almost black; and what affected me was not so much their size as (what was perhaps its consequence) the singular insignificance of their regard. A look more blankly stupid I have never met. My eyes dropped before it even as I spoke, and I went on my way upstairs to my own room, at once baffled and embarrassed. Yet when I came there and saw the face of the portrait, I was again reminded of the miracle of family descent. My hostess was, indeed, both older and fuller in person; her eyes were of a different colour; her face, besides, was not only free from the ill-significance that offended and attracted me in the painting; it was devoid of either good or bad—a moral blank expressing literally naught. And yet there was a likeness, not so much speaking as immanent, not so much in any particular feature as upon the whole. It should seem, I thought, as if when the master set his signature to that grave canvas, he had not only caught the image of one smiling and false-eyed woman, but stamped the essential quality of a race.

From that day forth, whether I came or went, I was sure to find the Señora seated in the sun against a pillar, or stretched on a rug before the fire; only at times she would shift her station to the top round of the stone stair-case, where she lay with the same nonchalance right across my path. In all these days, I never knew her to display the least spark of energy beyond what she expended in brushing and re-brushing her copious copper-coloured hair, or in lisping out, in the rich and broken hoarseness of her voice, her customary idle salutations to myself. These, I think, were her two chief pleasures, beyond that of mere quiescence. She seemed always proud of her remarks, as though they had been witticisms: and, indeed, though they were empty enough, like the conversation of many respectable persons, and turned on a very narrow range of subjects, they were never meaningless or incoherent; nay, they had a certain beauty of their own, breathing, as they did, of her entire contentment. Now she would speak of the warmth, in which (like her son) she greatly delighted; now of the flowers of the pomegranate trees, and now of the white doves and long-winged swallows that fanned the air of the court. The birds excited her. As they raked the eaves in their swift flight, or skimmed sidelong past her with a rush of wind, she would sometimes stir, and sit a little up, and seem to awaken from her doze of satisfaction. But for the rest of her days she lay luxuriously folded on herself and sunk in sloth and pleasure. Her invincible content at first annoyed me, but I came gradually to find repose in the spectacle, until at last it grew to be my habit to sit down beside her four times in the day, both coming and going, and to talk with her sleepily, I scarce knew of what. I had come to like her dull, almost animal neighbourhood; her beauty and her stupidity soothed and amused me. I began to find a kind of transcendental good sense in her remarks, and her unfathomable good-nature moved me to admiration and envy. The liking was returned; she enjoyed my presence half-unconsciously, as a man in deep meditation may enjoy the babbling of a brook. I can scarce say she brightened when I came, for satisfaction was written on her face eternally, as on some foolish statue's; but I was made conscious of her pleasure by some more intimate communication than the sight. And one day, as I sat within reach of her on the marble step, she suddenly shot forth one of her hands and patted mine. The thing was done, and she was back in her accustomed attitude, before my mind had received intelligence of the caress; and when I turned to look her in the face I could perceive no answerable sentiment. It was plain she attached no moment to the act, and I blamed myself for my own more uneasy consciousness.

The sight and (if I may so call it) the acquaintance of the mother confirmed the view I had already taken of the son. The family blood had been impoverished, perhaps by long inbreeding, which I knew to be a common error among the proud and the exclusive. No decline, indeed, was to be traced in the body, which had been handed down unimpaired in shapeliness and strength; and the faces of to-day were struck as sharply from the mint as the face of two centuries ago that smiled upon me from the portrait. But the intelligence (that more precious heirloom) was degenerate; the treasure of ancestral memory ran low; and it had required the potent, plebeian crossing of a muleteer or mountain *contrabandista* to raise what approached hebetude in the mother into the active oddity of the son. Yet of the two, it was the mother I preferred. Of Felipe, vengeful and placable, full of starts and shyings, inconstant as a hare, I could even conceive as a creature possibly noxious. Of the mother I had no thoughts but those of kindness. And indeed, as spectators are apt ignorantly to take sides, I grew something of a partisan in the enmity which I perceived to smoulder between them. True, it seemed mostly on the mother's part. She would sometimes draw in her breath as he came near, and the pupils of her vacant eyes would contract as if with horror or fear. Her emotions, such as they were, were much upon the surface and readily shared; and this latent repulsion occupied my mind, and kept me wondering on what grounds it rested, and whether the son was certainly in fault.

I had been about ten days in the residencia, when there sprang up a high and harsh wind, carrying clouds of dust. It came out of malarious lowlands, and over several snowy sierras. The nerves of those on whom it blew were strung and jangled; their eyes smarted with the dust; their legs ached under the burthen of their body; and the touch of one hand upon another grew to be odious. The wind, besides, came down the gullies of the hills and stormed about the house with a great, hollow buzzing and whistling that was wearisome to the ear and dismally depressing to the mind. It did not so much blow in gusts as with the steady sweep of a waterfall, so that there was no remission of discomfort while it blew. But higher up on the mountain it was probably of a more variable strength, with accesses of fury; for there came down at times a far-off wailing, infinitely grievous to hear; and at times, on one of the high shelves or terraces, there would start up, and then disperse, a tower of dust, like the smoke of an explosion.

I no sooner awoke in bed than I was conscious of the nervous tension and depression of the weather, and the effect grew stronger as the day proceeded. It was in vain that I resisted; in vain that I set forth upon my customary morning's walk; the irrational, unchanging fury of the storm had soon beat down my strength and wrecked my temper; and I returned to the residencia, glowing with dry heat, and foul and gritty with dust. The court had a forlorn appearance; now and then a glimmer of sun fled over it; now and then the wind swooped down upon the pomegranates, and scattered the blossoms, and set the window shutter clapping on the wall. In the recess the Señora was pacing to and fro with a flushed countenance and bright eyes; I thought, too, she was speaking to herself, like one in anger. But when I addressed her with my customary salutation, she only replied by a sharp gesture and continued her walk. The weather had distempered even this impassive creature; and as I went on upstairs I was the less ashamed of my own discomposure.

All day the wind continued; and I sat in my room and made a feint of reading, or walked up and down, and listened to the riot overhead. Night fell, and I had not so much as a candle. I began to long for some society, and stole down to the court. It was now plunged in the blue of the first darkness; but the recess was redly lighted by the fire. The wood had been piled high, and was crowned by a shock of flames, which the draught of the chimney brandished to and fro. In this strong and shaken brightness the Señora continued pacing from wall to wall with disconnected gestures, clasping her hands, stretching forth her arms, throwing back her head as in appeal to heaven. In these disordered movements the beauty and grace of the woman showed more clearly; but there was a light in her eye that struck on me unpleasantly; and when I had looked on a while in silence, and seemingly unobserved, I turned tail as I had come, and groped my way back again to my own chamber.

By the time Felipe brought my supper and lights, my nerve was utterly gone; and, had the lad been such as I was used to seeing him, I should have kept him (even by force, had that been necessary) to take off the edge from my distasteful solitude. But on Felipe, also, the wind had exercised its influence. He had been feverish all day; now that the night had come he was fallen into a low and tremulous humour that reacted on my own. The sight of his scared face, his starts and pallors and sudden hearkenings, unstrung me; and when he dropped and broke a dish, I fairly leaped out of my seat.

"I think we are all mad to-day," said I, affecting to laugh.

"It is the black wind," he replied dolefully. "You feel as if you must do something, and you don't know what it is."

I noted the aptness of the description; but, indeed, Felipe had sometimes a strange felicity in rendering into words the sensations of the body. "And your mother, too," said I; "she seems to feel this weather much. Do you not fear she may be unwell?"

He stared at me a little, and then said, "No," almost defiantly; and the next moment, carrying his hand to his brow, cried out lamentably on the wind and the noise that made his head go round like a millwheel. "Who can be well?" he cried; and, indeed, I could only echo his question, for I was disturbed enough myself.

I went to bed early, wearied with day-long restlessness; but the poisonous nature of the wind, and its ungodly and unintermittent uproar, would not suffer me to sleep. I lay there and tossed, my nerves and senses on the stretch. At times I would doze, dream horribly, and wake again; and these snatches of oblivion confused me as to time. But it must have been late on in the night, when I was suddenly startled by an outbreak of pitiable and hateful cries. I leaped from my bed, supposing I had dreamed; but the cries still continued to fill the house, cries of pain, I thought, but certainly of rage also, and so savage and discordant that they shocked the heart. It was no illusion; some living thing, some lunatic or some wild animal was being foully tortured. The thought of Felipe and the squirrel flashed into my mind, and I ran to the door; but it had been locked from the outside, and I might shake it as I pleased, I was a fast prisoner. Still the cries continued. Now they would dwindle down into a moaning that seemed to be articulate, and at these times I made sure they must be human; and again they would break forth and fill the house with ravings worthy of hell. I stood at the door and gave ear to them, till at last they died away. Long after that, I still lingered and still continued to hear them mingle in fancy wih the storming of the wind; and when at last I crept to my bed, it was with a deadly sickness and a blackness of horror on my heart.

It was little wonder if I slept no more. Why had I been locked in? What had passed? Who was the author of these indescribable and shocking cries? A human being? It was inconceivable. A beast? The cries were scarce quite bestial; and what animal, short of a lion or a tiger, could thus shake the solid walls of the residencia? And while I was thus turning over the elements of the mystery, it came into my mind that I had not yet set eyes upon the daughter of the house. What was more probable than that the daughter of the Señora, and the sister of Felipe, should be herself insane? Or, what more likely than that these ignorant and half-witted people should seek to manage an afflicted kinswoman by violence? Here was a solution; and yet when I called to mind the cries (which I never did without a shuddering chill) it seemed altogether insufficient: not even cruelty could wring such cries from madness. But of one thing I was sure: I could not live in a house where such a thing was half conceivable, and not probe the matter home and, if necessary, interfere.

The next day came, the wind had blown itself out, and there was nothing to remind me of the business of the night. Felipe came to my bedside with obvious cheerfulness; as I passed through the court the Señora was sunning herself with her accustomed immobility; and when I issued from the gateway I found the whole face of nature austerely smiling, the heavens of a cold blue, and sown with great cloud islands, and the mountainsides mapped forth into provinces of light and shadow. A short walk restored me to myself, and renewed within me the resolve to plumb this mystery; and when, from the vantage of my knoll, I had seen Felipe pass forth to his labours in the garden, I returned at once to the residencia to put my design in practice. The Señora appeared plunged in slumber; I stood a while and marked her, but she did not stir; even if my design were indiscreet, I had little to fear from such a guardian; and turning away, I mounted to the gallery and began my exploration of the house.

All morning I went from one door to another, and entered spacious and faded chambers, some rudely shuttered, some receiving their full charge of daylight, all empty and unhomely. It was a rich house, on which Time had breathed its tarnish and dust had scattered disillusion. The spider swung there; the bloated tarantula scampered on the cornices; ants had their crowded highways on the floor of halls of audience; the big and foul fly, that lives on carrion and is often the messenger of death, had set up his nest in the rotten woodwork, and buzzed heavily about the rooms. Here and there a stool or two, a couch, a bed, or a great carved chair remained behind, like islets on the bare floors, to testify of man's bygone habitation; and everywhere the walls were set with the portraits of the dead. I could judge by these decaying effigies, in the house of what a great and a handsome race I was then wandering. Many of the men wore orders on their breasts and had the port of noble offices; the women were all richly attired; the canvases, most of them, by famous hands. But it was not so much these evidences of greatness that took hold upon my mind, even contrasted, as they were, with the present depopulation and decay of that great house. It was rather the parable of family life that I read in this succession of fair faces and shapely bodies. Never before had I so realised the miracle of the continued race, the creation and re-creation, the weaving and changing and handing down of fleshly elements. That a child should be born of its mother, that it should grow and clothe itself (we know not how) with humanity, and put on inherited looks, and turn its head with the manner of one ascendant, and offer its hand with the gesture of another, are wonders dulled for us by repetition. But in the singular unity of look, in the common features and common bearing, of all these painted generations on the walls of the residencia, the miracle started out and looked me in the face. And an ancient mirror falling opportunely in my way, I stood and read my own features a long while, tracing out on either hand the filaments of descent and the bonds that knit me with my family.

At last, in the course of these investigations, I opened the door of a chamber that bore the marks of habitation. It was of large proportions and faced to the north, where the mountains were most wildly figured. The embers of a fire smouldered and smoked upon the hearth, to which a chair had been drawn close. And yet the aspect of the chamber was ascetic to the degree of sternness; the chair was uncushioned; the floor and walls were naked; and beyond the books which lay here and there in some confusion, there was no instrument of either work or pleasure. The sight of books in the house of such a family exceedingly amazed me; and I began with a great hurry, and in momentary fear of interruption, to go from one to another and hastily inspect their character. They were of all sorts, devotional, historical, and scientific, but mostly of a great age and in the Latin tongue. Some I could see to bear the marks of constant study; others had been torn across and tossed aside as if in petulance or disapproval. Lastly, as I cruised about that empty chamber, I espied some papers written upon with pencil on a table near the window. An unthinking curiosity led me to take one up. It bore a copy of verses, very roughly metred in the original Spanish, and which I may render somewhat thus—

"Pleasure approached with pain and shame,
Grief with a wreath of lilies came.
Pleasure showed the lovely sun;
Jesu dear, how sweet it shone!
Grief with her worn hand pointed on,
Jesu dear, to Thee!"

Shame and confusion at once fell on me; and, laying down the paper, I beat an immediate retreat from the apartment. Neither Felipe nor his mother could have read the books nor written these rough but feeling verses. It was plain I had stumbled with sacrilegious feet into the room of the daughter of the house. God knows, my own heart most sharply punished me for my indiscretion. The thought that I had thus secretly pushed my way into the confidence of a girl so strangely situated, and the fear that she might somehow come to hear of it, oppressed me like guilt. I blamed myself besides for my suspicions of the night before; wondered that I should ever have attributed those shocking cries to one of whom I now conceived as of a saint, spectral of mien, wasted with maceration, bound up in the practices of a mechanical devotion, and dwelling in a great isolation of soul with her incongruous relatives; and as I leaned on the balustrade of the gallery and looked down into the bright close of pomegranates and at the gaily dressed and somnolent woman, who just then stretched herself and delicately licked her lips as in the very sensuality of sloth, my mind swiftly compared the scene with the cold chamber looking northward on the mountains, where the daughter dwelt.

That same afternoon, as I sat upon my knoll, I saw the Padre enter the gates of the residencia. The revelation of the daughter's character had struck home to my fancy, and almost blotted out the horrors of the night before; but at sight of this worthy man the memory revived. I descended, then, from the knoll, and making a circuit among the woods, posted myself by the wayside to await his passage. As soon as he appeared I stepped forth and introduced myself as the lodger of the residencia. He had a very strong, honest countenance, on which it was easy to read the mingled emotions with which he regarded me, as a foreigner, a heretic, and yet one who had been wounded for the good cause. Of the family at the residencia he spoke with reserve, and yet with respect. I mentioned that I had not yet seen the daughter, whereupon he remarked that that was as it should be, and looked at me a little askance. Lastly, I plucked up courage to refer to the cries that had disturbed me in the night. He heard me out in silence, and then stopped and partly turned about, as though to mark beyond doubt that he was dismissing me.

"Do you take tobacco-powder?" said he, offering his snuff-box; and then, when I had refused, "I am an old man," he added, "and I may be allowed to remind you that you are a guest."

"I have, then, your authority," I returned, firmly enough, although I flushed at the implied reproof, "to let things take their course, and not to interfere?"

He said "Yes," and with a somewhat uneasy salute turned and left me where I was. But he had done two things: he had set my conscience at rest, and he had awakened my delicacy. I made a great effort, once more dismissed the recollections of the night, and fell once more to brooding on my saintly poetess. At the same time, I could not quite forget that I had been locked in, and that night when Felipe brought me my supper I attacked him warily on both points of interest.

"I never see your sister," said I casually.

"Oh, no," said he; "she is a good, good girl," and his mind instantly veered to something else.

"Your sister is pious, I suppose?" I asked in the next pause.

"Oh!" he cried, joining his hands with extreme fervour, "a saint; it is she that keeps me up."

"You are very fortunate," said I, "for the most of us, I am afraid, and myself among the number, are better at going down."

"Señor," said Felipe earnestly, "I would not say that. You should not tempt your angel. If one goes down, where is he to stop?"

"Why, Felipe," said I, "I had no guess you were a preacher, and I may say a good one; but I suppose that is your sister's doing?"

He nodded at me with round eyes.

"Well, then," I continued, "she has doubtless reproved you for your sin of cruelty?"

"Twelve times!" he cried; for this was the phrase by which the odd creature expressed the sense of frequency. "And I told her you had done so—I remembered that," he added proudly—"and she was pleased."

"Then, Felipe," said I, "what were those cries that I heard last night? for surely they were cries of some creature in suffering."

"The wind," returned Felipe, looking in the fire.

I took his hand in mine, at which, thinking it to be a caress, he smiled with a brightness of pleasure that came near disarming my resolve. But I trod the weakness down. "The wind," I repeated; "and yet I think it was this hand," holding it up, "that had first locked me in." The lad shook visibly, but answered never a word. "Well," said I, "I am a stranger and a guest. It is not my part either to meddle or to judge in your affairs; in these you shall take your sister's counsel, which I cannot doubt to be excellent. But in so far as concerns my own I will be no man's prisoner, and I demand that key." Half an hour later my door was suddenly thrown open, and the key tossed ringing on the floor.

A day or two after I came in from a walk a little before the point of noon. The Señora was lying lapped in slumber on the threshold of the recess; the pigeons dozed below the eaves like snowdrifts; the house was under a deep spell of noontide quiet; and only a wandering and gentle wind from the mountain stole round the galleries, rustled among the pomegranates, and pleasantly stirred the shadows. Something in the stillness moved me to imitation, and I went very lightly across the court and up the marble staircase. My foot was on the topmost round, when a door opened, and I found myself face to face with Olalla. Surprise transfixed me; her loveliness struck to my heart; she glowed in the deep shadow of the gallery, a gem of colour; her eyes took hold upon mine and clung there, and bound us together like the joining of hands; and the moments we thus stood face to face, drinking each other in, were sacramental and the wedding of souls. I know not how long it was before I awoke out of a deep trance, and, hastily bowing, passed on into the upper stair. She did not move, but followed me with her great, thirsting eyes; and as I passed out of sight it seemed to me as if she paled and faded.

In my own room, I opened the window and looked out, and could not think what change had come upon that austere field of mountains that it should thus sing and shine under the lofty heaven. I had seen her—Olalla! And the stone crags answered, Olalla! and the dumb, unfathomable azure answered, Olalla! The pale saint of my dreams had vanished for ever; and in her place I beheld this maiden on whom God had lavished the richest colours and the most exuberant energies of life, whom He had made active as a deer, slender as a reed, and in whose great eyes He had lighted the torches of the soul. The thrill of her young life, strung like a wild animal's, had entered into me; the force of soul that had looked out from her eyes and conquered mine, mantled about my heart and sprang to my lips in singing. She passed through my veins: she was one with me.

I will not say that this enthusiasm declined; rather my soul held out in its ecstasy as in a strong castle, and was there besieged by cold and sorrowful considerations. I could not doubt but that I loved her at first sight, and already with a quivering ardour that was strange to my experience. What then was to follow? She was the child of an afflicted house, the Señora's daughter, the sister of Felipe; she bore it even in her beauty. She had the lightness and swiftness of the one, swift as an arrow, light as dew; like the other, she shone on the pale background of the world with the brilliancy of flowers. I could not call by the name of brother that half-witted lad, nor by the name of mother that immovable and lovely thing of flesh, whose silly eyes and perpetual simper now recurred to my mind like something hateful. And if I could not marry, what then? She was helplessly unprotected; her eyes, in that single and long glance, which had been all our intercourse, had confessed a weakness equal to my own; but in my heart I knew her for the student of the cold northern chamber, and the writer of the sorrowful lines; and this was a knowledge to disarm a brute. To flee was more than I could find courage for; but I registered a vow of unsleeping circumspection.

As I turned from the window, my eyes alighted on the portrait. It had fallen dead, like a candle after sunrise; it followed me with eyes of paint. I knew it to be like, and marvelled at the tenacity of type in that declining race; but the likeness was swallowed up in difference. I remembered how it had seemed to me a thing unapproachable in the life, a creature rather of the painter's craft than of the modesty of nature, and I marvelled at the thought, and exulted in the image of Olalla. Beauty I had seen before, and not been charmed, and I had been often drawn to women, who were not beautiful except to me; but in Olalla all that I desired and had not dared to imagine was united.

I did not see her the next day, and my heart ached and my eyes longed for her, as men long for morning. But the day after, when I returned, about my usual hour, she was once more on the gallery, and our looks once more met and embraced. I would have spoken, I would have drawn near to her; but strongly as she plucked at my heart, drawing me like a magnet, something yet more imperious withheld me; and I could only bow and pass by; and she, leaving my salutation unanswered, only followed me with her noble eyes.

I had now her image by rote, and as I conned the traits in memory it seemed as if I read her very heart. She was dressed with something of her mother's coquetry and love of positive colour. Her robe, which I knew she must have made with her own hands, clung about her with a cunning grace. After the fashion of that country, besides, her bodice stood open in the middle, in a long slit, and here, in spite of the poverty of the house, a gold coin, hanging by a ribbon, lay on her brown bosom. These were proofs, had any been needed, of her inborn delight in life and her own loveliness. On the other hand, in her eyes that hung upon mine, I could read depth beyond depth of passion and sadness, lights of poetry and hope, blacknesses of despair, and thoughts that were above the earth. It was a lovely body, but the inmate, the soul, was more than worthy of that lodging. Should I leave this incomparable flower to wither unseen on these rough mountains? Should I despise the great gift offered me in the eloquent silence of her eyes? Here was a soul immured; should I not burst its prison? All side considerations fell off from me; were she the child of Herod I swore I should make her mine; and that very evening I set myself, with a mingled sense of treachery and disgrace, to captivate the brother. Perhaps I read him with more favourable eyes, perhaps the thought of his sister always summoned up the better qualities of that imperfect soul; but he had never seemed to me so amiable, and his very likeness to Olalla, while it annoyed, yet softened me.

A third day passed in vain—an empty desert of hours. I would not lose a chance, and loitered all afternoon in the court, where (to give myself a countenance) I spoke more than usual with the Señora. God knows it was with a most tender and sincere interest that I now studied her; and even as for Felipe, so now for the mother, I was conscious of a growing warmth of toleration. And yet I wondered. Even while I spoke with her, she would doze off into a little sleep, and presently awake again without embarrassment; and this composure staggered me. And again, as I marked her make infinitesimal changes in her posture, savouring and lingering on the bodily pleasure of the movement, I was driven to wonder at this depth of passive sensuality. She lived in her body; and her consciousness was all sunk into and disseminated through her members, where it luxuriously dwelt. Lastly, I could not grow accustomed to her eyes. Each time she turned on me those great beautiful and meaningless orbs, wide open to the day, but closed against human inquiry—each time I had occasion to observe the lively changes of her pupils which expanded and contracted in a breath—I know not what it was came over me, I can find no name for the mingled feeling of disappointment, annoyance, and distaste that jarred along my nerves. I tried her on a variety of subjects, equally in vain; and at last led the talk to her daughter. But even there she proved indifferent; said she was pretty, which (as with children) was her highest word of commendation, but was plainly incapable of any higher thought; and when I remarked that Olalla seemed silent, merely yawned in my face and replied that speech was of no great use when you had nothing to say. "People speak much, very much," she added, looking at me with expanded pupils; and then again yawned, and again showed me a mouth that was as dainty as a toy. This time I took the hint, and, leaving her to her repose, went up into my own chamber to sit by the open window, looking on the hills and not beholding them, sunk in lustrous and deep dreams, and hearkening in fancy to the note of a voice that I had never heard.

I awoke on the fifth morning with a brightness of anticipation that seemed to challenge fate. I was sure of myself, light of heart and foot, and resolved to put my love incontinently to the touch of knowledge. It should lie no longer under the bonds of silence, a dumb thing, living by the eye only, like the love of beasts; but should now put on the spirit, and enter upon the joys of the complete human intimacy. I thought of it with wild hopes, like a voyager to El Dorado; into that unknown and lovely country of her soul, I no longer trembled to adventure. Yet when I did indeed encounter her, the same force of passion descended on me and at once submerged my mind; speech seemed to drop away from me like a childish habit; and I but drew near to her as the giddy man draws near to the margin of a gulf. She drew back from me a little as I came; but her eyes did not waver from mine, and these lured me forward. At last, when I was already within reach of her, I stopped. Words were denied me; if I advanced I could but clasp her to my heart in silence; and all that was sane in me, all that was still unconquered, revolted against the thought of such an accost. So we stood for a second, all our life in our eyes, exchanging salvos of attraction and yet each resisting; and then, with a great effort of the will, and conscious at the same time of a sudden bitterness of disappointment, I turned and went away in the same silence.

What power lay upon me that I could not speak? And she, why was she also silent? Why did she draw away before me dumbly, with fascinated eyes? Was this love? or was it a mere brute attraction, mindless and inevitable, like that of the magnet for the steel? We had never spoken, we were wholly strangers; and yet an influence, strong as the grasp of a giant, swept us silently together. On my side, it filled me with impatience; and yet I was sure that she was worthy; I had seen her books, read her verses, and thus, in a sense, divined the soul of my mistress. But on her side, it struck me almost cold. Of me, she knew nothing but my bodily favour; she was drawn to me as stones fall to the earth; the laws that rule the earth conducted her, unconsenting, to my arms; and I drew back at the thought of such a bridal, and began to be jealous for myself. It was not thus that I desired to be loved. And then I began to fall into a great pity for the girl herself. I thought how sharp must be her mortification, that she, the student, the recluse, Felipe's saintly monitress, should have thus confessed an overweening weakness for a man with whom she had never exchanged a word. And at the coming of pity, all other thoughts were swallowed up; and I longed only to find and console and reassure her; to tell her how wholly her love was returned on my side, and how her choice, even if blindly made, was not unworthy.

The next day it was glorious weather; depth upon depth of blue over-canopied the mountains; the sun shone wide; and the wind in the trees and the many fallen torrents in the mountains filled the air with delicate and haunting music. Yet I was prostrated with sadness. My heart wept for the sight of Olalla, as a child weeps for its mother. I sat down on a boulder on the verge of the low cliffs that bound the plateau to the north. Thence I looked down into the wooded valley of a stream, where no foot came. In the mood I was in, it was even touching to behold the place untenanted; it lacked Olalla; and I thought of the delight and glory of a life passed wholly with her in that strong air, and among these rugged and lovely surroundings, at first with a whimpering sentiment, and then again with such a fiery joy that I seemed to grow in strength and stature, like a Samson.

And then suddenly I was aware of Olalla drawing near. She appeared out of a grove of cork-trees, and came straight towards me; and I stood up and waited. She seemed in her walking a creature of such life and fire and lightness as amazed me; yet she came quietly and slowly. Her energy was in the slowness; but for inimitable strength,

I felt she would have run, she would have flown to me. Still, as she approached, she kept her eyes lowered to the ground; and when she had drawn quite near, it was without one glance that she addressed me. At the first note of her voice I started. It was for this I had been waiting; this was the last test of my love. And lo, her enunciation was precise and clear, not lisping and incomplete like that of her family; and the voice, though deeper than usual with women, was still both youthful and womanly. She spoke in a rich chord; golden contralto strains mingled with hoarseness, as the red threads were mingled with the brown among her tresses. It was not only a voice that spoke to my heart directly; but it spoke to me of her. And yet her words immediately plunged me back upon despair.

"You will go away," she said, "to-day."

Her example broke the bonds of my speech; I felt as lightened of a weight, or as if a spell had been dissolved. I know not in what words I answered; but, standing before her on the cliffs, I poured out the whole ardour of my love, telling her that I lived upon the thought of her, slept only to dream of her loveliness, and would gladly forswear my country, my language, and my friends, to live for ever by her side. And then, strongly commanding myself, I changed the note; I reassured, I comforted her; I told her I had divined in her a pious and heroic spirit, with which I was worthy to sympathise, and which I longed to share and lighten. "Nature," I told her, "was the voice of God, which men disobey at peril; and if we were thus dumbly drawn together, ay, even as by a miracle of love, it must imply a divine fitness in our souls; we must be made" I said—"made for one another. We should be mad rebels," I cried out—"mad rebels against God, not to obey this instinct."

She shook her head. "You will go to-day," she repeated, and then with a gesture, and in a sudden, sharp note—"no, not to-day," she cried, "to-morrow!"

But at this sign of relenting, power came in upon me in a tide. I stretched out my arms and called upon her name; and she leaped to me and clung to me. The hills rocked about us, the earth quailed; a shock as of a blow went through me and left me blind and dizzy. And the next moment she had thrust me back, broken rudely from my arms, and fled with the speed of a deer among the cork-trees.

I stood and shouted to the mountains; I turned and went back towards the residencia, walking upon air. She sent me away, and yet I had but to call upon her name and she came to me. These were but the weaknesses of girls, from which even she, the strangest of her sex, was not exempted. Go? Not I, Olalla—Oh, not I, Olalla, my Olalla! A bird sang near by; and in that season birds were rare. It bade me be of good cheer. And once more the whole countenance of nature, from the ponderous and stable mountains down to the lightest leaf and the smallest darting fly in the shadow of the groves, began to stir before me and to put on the lineaments of life and wear a face of awful joy. The sunshine struck upon the hills, strong as a hammer on the anvil, and the hills shook; the earth, under that vigorous insolation, yielded up heady scents; the woods smouldered in the blaze. I felt the thrill of travail and delight run through the earth. Something elemental, something rude, violent, and savage, in the love that sang in my heart, was like a key to nature's secrets; and the very stones that rattled under my feet appeared alive and friendly. Olalla! Her touch had quickened, and renewed, and strung me up to the old pitch of concert with the rugged earth, to a swelling of the soul that men learn to forget in their polite assemblies. Love burned in me like rage; tenderness waxed fierce; I hated, I adored, I pitied, I revered her with ecstasy. She seemed the link that bound me in with dead things on the one hand, and with our pure and pitying God upon the other: a thing brutal and divine, and akin at once to the innocence and to the unbridled forces of the earth.

My head thus reeling, I came into the courtyard of the residencia, and the sight of the mother struck me like a revelation. She sat there, all sloth and contentment, blinking under the strong sunshine, branded with a passive enjoyment, a creature set quite apart, before whom my ardour fell away like a thing ashamed. I stopped a moment, and, commanding such shaken tones as I was able, said a word or two. She looked at me with her unfathomable kindness; her voice in reply sounded vaguely out of the realm of peace in which she slumbered, and there fell on my mind, for the first time, a sense of respect for one so uniformly innocent and happy, and I passed on in a kind of wonder at myself that I should be so much disquieted.

On my table there lay a piece of the same yellow paper I had seen in the north room; it was written on with pencil in the same hand, Olalla's hand, and I picked it up with a sudden sinking of alarm, and read, "If you have any kindness for Olalla, if you have any chivalry for a creature sorely wrought, go from here to-day; in pity, in honour, for the sake of Him who died, I supplicate that you shall go." I looked at this a while in mere stupidity, then I began to awaken to a weariness and horror of life; the sunshine darkened outside on the bare hills, and I began to shake like a man in terror. The vacancy thus suddenly opened in my life unmanned me like a physical void. It was not my heart, it was not my happiness, it was life itself that was involved. I could not lose her. I said so, and stood repeating it. And then, like one in a dream, I moved to the window, put forth my hand to open the casement, and thrust it through the pane. The blood spurted from my wrist; and with an instantaneous quietude and command of myself, I pressed my thumb on the little leaping fountain, and reflected what to do. In that empty room there was nothing to my purpose; I felt, besides, that I required assistance. There shot into my mind a hope that Olalla herself might be my helper, and I turned and went downstairs, still keeping my thumb upon the wound.

There was no sign of either Olalla or Felipe, and I addressed myself to the recess, whither the Señora had now drawn quite back and sat dozing close before the fire, for no degree of heat appeared too much for her.

"Pardon me," said I, "if I disturb you, but I must apply to you for help."

She looked up sleepily and asked me what it was, and with the very words I thought she drew in her breath with a widening of the nostrils and seemed to come suddenly and fully alive.

"I have cut myself," I said, "and rather badly. See!" And I held out my two hands, from which the blood was oozing and dripplng.

Her great eyes opened wide, the pupils shrank into points; a veil seemed to fall from her face, and leave it sharply expressive and yet inscrutable. And as I still stood, marvelling a little at her disturbance, she came swiftly up to me, and stooped and caught me by the hand; and the next moment my hand was at her mouth, and she had bitten me to the bone. The pang of the bite, the sudden spurting of blood, and the monstrous horror of the act, flashed through me all in one, and I beat her back; and she sprang at me again and again, with bestial cries, cries that I recognised, such cries as had awakened me on the night of the high wind. Her strength was like that of madness; mine was rapidly ebbing with the loss of blood; my mind besides was whirling with the abhorrent strangeness of the onslaught, and I was already forced against the wall, when Olalla ran betwixt us, and Felipe, following at a bound, pinned down his mother on the floor.

A trance-like weakness fell upon me; I saw, heard, and felt, but I was incapable of movement. I heard the struggle roll to and fro upon the floor, the yells of the catamount ringing up to heaven as she strove to reach me. I felt Olalla clasp me in her arms, her hair falling on my face, and, with the strength of a man, raise and half drag, half carry me upstairs into my own room, where she cast me down upon the bed. Then I saw her hasten to the door and lock it, and stand an instant listening to the savage cries that shook the residencia. And then, swift and light as a thought, she was again beside me, binding up my hand, laying it in her bosom, moaning and mourning over it, with dove-like sounds. They were not words that came to her, they were sounds more beautiful than speech, infinitely touching, infinitely tender; and yet as I lay there, a thought stung to my heart, a thought wounded me like a sword, a thought, like a worm in a flower, profaned the holiness of my love. Yes, they were beautiful sounds, and they were inspired by human tenderness; but was their beauty human?

All day I lay there. For a long time the cries of that nameless female thing, as she struggled with her half-witted whelp, resounded through the house, and pierced me with despairing sorrow and disgust. They were the death-cry of my love; my love was murdered; it was not only dead, but an offence to me; and yet, think as I pleased, feel as I must, it still swelled within me like a storm of sweetness, and my heart melted at her looks and touch. This horror that had sprung out, this doubt upon

Olalla, this savage and bestial strain that ran not only through the whole behaviour of her family, but found a place in the very foundations and story of our love—though it appalled, though it shocked and sickened me, was yet not of power to break the knot of my infatuation.

When the cries had ceased, there came a scraping at the door, by which I knew Felipe was without; and Olalla went and spoke to him—I know not what. With that exception, she stayed close beside me, now kneeling by my bed and fervently praying, now sitting with her eyes upon mine. So then, for these six hours I drank in her beauty, and silently perused the story in her face. I saw the golden coin hover on her breaths; I saw her eyes darken and brighten, and still speak no language but that of an unfathomable kindness; I saw the faultless face, and, through the robe, the lines of the faultless body. Night came at last, and in the growing darkness of the chamber the sight of her slowly melted; but even then the touch of her smooth hand lingered in mine and talked with me. To lie thus in deadly weakness and drink in the traits of the beloved, is to re-awake to love from whatever shock of disillusion. I reasoned with myself; and I shut my eyes on horrors, and again I was very bold to accept the worst. What mattered it, if that imperious sentiment survived; if her eyes still beckoned and attached me; if now, even as before, every fibre of my dull body yearned and turned to her? Late on in the night some strength revived in me, and I spoke:—

"Olalla," I said, "nothing matters; I ask nothing; I am content; I love you."

She knelt down a while and prayed, and I devoutly respected her devotions. The moon had begun to shine in upon one side of each of the three windows, and make a misty clearness in the room, by which I saw her indistinctly. When she re-arose she made the sign of the cross.

"It is for me to speak," she said, "and for you to listen. I know; you can but guess. I prayed, how I prayed for you to leave this place. I begged it of you, and I know you would have granted me even this; or if not, oh let me think so!"

"I love you," I said.

"And yet you have lived in the world," she said; after a pause, "you are a man and wise; and I am but a child. Forgive me, if I seem to teach, who am as ignorant as the trees of the mountain; but those who learn much do but skim the face of knowledge; they seize the laws, they conceive the dignity of the design—the horror of the living fact fades from their memory. It is we who sit at home with evil, who remember, I think, and are warned and pity. Go, rather, go now, and keep me in mind. So I shall have a life in the cherished places of your memory; a life as much my own as that which I lead in this body."

"I love you," I said once more; and reaching out my weak hand, took hers, and carried it to my lips, and kissed it. Nor did she resist, but winced a little; and I could see her look upon me with a frown that was not unkindly, only sad and baffled. And then it seemed she made a call upon her resolution; plucked my hand towards her, herself at the same time leaning somewhat forward, and laid it on the beating of her heart. "There," she cried, "you feel the very footfall of my life. It only moves for you; it is yours. But is it even mine? It is mine indeed to offer you, as I might take the coin from my neck, as I might break a live branch from a tree, and give it you. And yet not mine! I dwell, or I think I dwell (if I exist at all), somewhere apart, an impotent prisoner, and carried about and deafened by a mob that I disown. This capsule, such as throbs against the sides of animals, knows you at a touch for its master; ay, it loves you! But my soul, does my soul? I think not; I know not, fearing to ask. Yet when you spoke to me, your words were of the soul; it is of the soul that you ask—it is only from the soul that you would take me."

"Olalla," I said, "the soul and the body are one, and mostly so in love. What the body chooses, the soul loves; where the body clings, the soul cleaves; body for body, soul to soul, they come together at God's signal; and the lower part (if we can call aught low) is only the footstool and foundation of the highest."

"Have you," she said, "seen the portraits in the house of my fathers? Have you looked at my mother or at Felipe? Have your eyes never rested on that picture that hangs by your bed? She who sat for it died ages ago; and she did evil in her life. But, look again: there is my hand to the least line, there are my eyes and my hair. What is mine, then, and what am I? If not a curve in this poor body of mine (which you love, and for the sake of which you dotingly dream that you love me), not a gesture that

I can frame, not a tone of my voice, not any look from my eyes, no, not even now when I speak to him I love, but has belonged to others? Others, ages dead, have wooed other men with my eyes; other men have heard the pleading of the same voice that now sounds in your ears. The hands of the dead are in my bosom; they move me, they pluck me, they guide me; I am a puppet at their command; and I but re-inform features and attributes that have long been laid aside from evil in the quiet of the grave. Is it me you love, friend? or the race that made me? The girl who does not know and cannot answer for the least portion of herself? or the stream of which she is a transitory eddy, the tree of which she is the passing fruit? The race exists; it is old, it is ever young, it carries its eternal destiny in its bosom; upon it, like waves upon the sea, individual succeeds to individual, mocked with a semblance of self-control, but they are nothing. We speak of the soul, but the soul is in the race."

"You fret against the common law," I said. "You rebel against the voice of God, which He has made so winning to convince, so imperious to command. Hear it, and how it speaks between us! Your hand clings to mine, your heart leaps at my touch, the unknown elements of which we are compounded awake and run together at a look; the clay of the earth remembers its independent life and yearns to join us; we are drawn together as the stars are turned about in space, or as the tides ebb and flow; by things older and greater than we ourselves."

"Alas!" she said, "what can I say to you? My fathers, eight hundred years ago, ruled all this province: they were wise, great, cunning, and cruel; they were a picked race of the Spanish; their flags led in war; the king called them his cousin; the people, when the rope was slung for them or when they returned and found their hovels smoking, blasphemed their name. Presently a change began. Man has risen; if he has sprung from the brutes, he can descend again to the same level. The breath of weariness blew on their humanity and the cords relaxed; they began to go down; their minds fell on sleep, their passions awoke in gusts, heady and senseless like the wind in the gutters of the mountains; beauty was still handed down, but no longer the guiding wit nor the human heart; the seed passed on, it was wrapped in flesh, the flesh covered the bones, but they were the bones and the flesh of brutes, and their mind was as the mind of flies. I speak to you as I dare; but you have seen for yourself how the wheel has gone backward with my doomed race. I stand, as it were, upon a little rising ground in this desperate descent, and see both before and behind, both what we have lost and to what we are condemned to go farther downward. And shall I—I that dwell apart in the house of the dead, my body, loathing its ways—shall I repeat the spell? Shall I bind another spirit, reluctant as my own, into this bewitched and tempest-broken tenement that I now suffer in? Shall I hand down this cursed vessel of humanity, charge it with fresh life as with fresh poison, and dash it, like a fire, in the faces of posterity? But my vow has been given; the race shall cease from off the earth. At this hour my brother is making ready; his foot will soon be on the stair; and you will go with him and pass out of my sight for ever. Think of me sometimes as one to whom the lesson of life was very harshly told, but who heard it with courage; as one who loved you indeed, but who hated herself so deeply that her love was hateful to her; as one who sent you away and yet would have longed to keep you for ever: who had no dearer hope than to forget you, and no greater fear than to be forgotten."

She had drawn towards the door as she spoke, her rich voice sounding softer and farther away; and with the last word she was gone, and I lay alone in the moonlit chamber. What I might have done had not I lain bound by my extreme weakness, I know not; but as it was, there fell upon me a great and blank despair. It was not long before there shone in at the door the ruddy glimmer of a lantern, and Felipe, coming, charged me without a word upon his shoulders, and carried me down to the great gate, where the cart was waiting. In the moonlight the hills stood out sharply, as if they were of cardboard; on the glimmering surface of the plateau, and from among the low trees which swung together and sparkled in the wind, the great black cube of the residencia stood out bulkily, its mass only broken by three dimly lighted windows in the northern front above the gate. They were Olalla's windows, and as the cart jolted onwards I kept my eyes fixed upon them till, where the road dipped into a valley, they were lost to my view for ever. Felipe walked in silence beside the shafts, but from time to time he would check the mule and seem to look back upon me; and at length drew quite near and laid his hand upon my head. There was such kindness in the touch, and such a simplicity, as of the brutes, that tears broke from me like the bursting of an artery.

"Felipe," I said, "take me where they will ask no questions."

He said never a word, but he turned his mule about, end for end, retraced some part of the way we had gone, and, striking into another path, led me to the mountain village, which was, as we say in Scotland, the kirk-town of that thinly peopled district. Some broken memories dwell in my mind of the day breaking over the plain, of the cart stopping, of arms that helped me down, of a bare room into which I was carried, and of a swoon that fell upon me like sleep.

The next day and the days following, the old priest was often at my side with his snuff-box and prayer-book, and after a while, when I began to pick up strength, he told me that I was now on a fair way to recovery, and must as soon as possible hurry my departure; whereupon, without naming any reason, he took snuff and looked at me sideways. I did not affect ignorance; I knew he must have seen Olalla. "Sir," said I, "you know that I do not ask in wantonness. What of that family?"

He said they were very unfortunate; that it seemed a declining race, and that they were very poor and had been much neglected.

"But she has not," I said. "Thanks, doubtless, to yourself, she is instructed and wise beyond the use of women."

"Yes," he said, "the Señorita is well-informed. But the family has been neglected."

"The mother?" I queried.

"Yes, the mother too," said the Padre, taking snuff. "But Felipe is a well-intentioned lad."

"The mother is odd?" I asked.

"Very odd," replied the priest.

"I think, sir, we beat about the bush," said I. "You must know more of my affairs than you allow. You must know my curiosity to be justified on many grounds. Will you not be frank with me?"

"My son," said the old gentleman, "I will be very frank with you on matters within my competence; on those of which I know nothing it does not require much discretion to be silent. I will not fence with you, I take your meaning perfectly; and what can I say, but that we are all in God's hands, and that His ways are not our ways? I have even advised with my superiors in the Church, but they, too, were dumb. It is a great mystery."

"Is she mad?" I asked.

"I will answer you according to my belief. She is not," returned the Padre, "or she was not. When she was young—God help me, I fear I neglected that wild lamb—she was surely sane; and yet, although it did not run to such heights, the same strain was already notable; it had been so before her in her father, ay, and before him, and this inclined me, perhaps, to think too lightly of it. But these things go on growing, not only in the individual but in the race."

"When she was young," I began, and my voice failed me for a moment, and it was only with a great effort that I was able to add, "was she like Olalla?"

"Now God forbid!" exclaimed the Padre. "God forbid that any man should think so slightingly of my favourite penitent. No, no; the Señorita (but for her beauty, which I wish most honestly she had less of) has not a hair's resemblance to what her mother was at the same age. I could not bear to have you think so; though, heaven knows, it were, perhaps, better that you should."

At this I raised myself in bed, and opened my heart to the old man; telling him of our love and of her decision; owning my own horrors, my own passing fancies, but telling him that these were at an end; and with something more than a purely formal submission, appealing to his judgment.

He heard me very patiently and without surprise; and when I had done he sat for some time silent. Then he began: "The Church," and instantly broke off again to apologise. "I had forgotten, my child, that you were not a Christian," said he. "And indeed, upon a point so highly unusual, even the Church can scarce be said to have decided. But would you have my opinion? The Señorita is, in a matter of this kind, the best judge; I would accept her judgment."

On the back of that he went away, nor was he thenceforward so assiduous in his visits; indeed, even when I began to get about again, he plainly feared and deprecated my society, not as in distaste, but much as a man might be disposed to flee from the riddling sphinx. The villagers, too, avoided me; they were unwilling to be my guides upon the mountain. I thought they looked at me askance, and I made sure that the more superstitious crossed themselves on my approach. At first I set this down to my heretical opinions; but it began at length to dawn upon me that if I was thus redoubted it was because I had stayed at the residencia. All men despise the savage notions of such peasantry; and yet I was conscious of a chill shadow that seemed to fall and dwell upon my love. It did not conquer, but I may not deny that it restrained, my ardour.

Some miles westward of the village there was a gap in the sierra, from which the eye plunged direct upon the residencia; and thither it became my daily habit to repair. A wood crowned the summit; and just where the pathway issued from its fringes, it was overhung by a considerable shelf of rock, and that, in its turn, was surmounted by a crucifix of the size of life and more than usually painful in design. This was my perch; thence, day after day, I looked down upon the plateau, and the great old house, and could see Felipe, no bigger than a fly, going to and fro about the garden. Sometimes mists would draw across the view, and be broken up again by mountain winds; sometimes the plain slumbered below me in unbroken sunshine; it would sometimes be all blotted out by rain. This distant post, these interrupted sights of the place where my life had been so strangely changed, suited the indecision of my humour. I passed whole days there, debating with myself the various elements of our position, now leaning to the suggestions of love, now giving an ear to prudence, and in the end halting irresolute between the two.

One day, as I was sitting on my rock, there came by that way a somewhat gaunt peasant wrapped in a mantle. He was a stranger, and plainly did not know me even by repute; for, instead of keeping the other side, he drew near and sat down beside me, and we had soon fallen in talk. Among other things, he told me he had been a muleteer, and in former years had much frequented these mountains; later on, he had followed the army with his mules, had realised a competence, and was now living retired with his family.

"Do you know that house?" I inquired at last, pointing to the residencia, for I readily wearied of any talk that kept me from the thought of Olalla.

He looked it me darkly and crossed himself.

"Too well," he said, "it was there that one of my comrades sold himself to Satan; the Virgin shield us from temptations! He has paid the price; he is now burning in the reddest place in hell!"

A fear came upon me; I could answer nothing; and presently the man resumed, as if to himself: "Yes," he said, "O yes, I know it. I have passed its doors. There was snow upon the pass, the wind was driving it; sure enough there was death that night upon the mountains, but there was worse beside the hearth. I took him by the arm, Señor, and dragged him to the gate; I conjured him, by all he loved and respected, to go forth with me; I went on my knees before him in the snow; and I could see he was moved by my entreaty. And just then she came out on the gallery, and called him by his name; and he turned, and there was she, standing with a lamp in her hand and smiling on him to come back. I cried out aloud to God, and threw my arms about him, but he put me by, and left me alone. He had made his choice; God help us. I would pray for him, but to what end? there are sins that not even the Pope can loose."

"And your friend," I asked, "what became of him?"

"Nay, God knows," said the muleteer. "If all be true that we hear, his end was like his sin, a thing to raise the hair."

"Do you mean that he was killed?" I asked.

"Sure enough, he was killed," returned the man. "But how? Ah, how? But these are things that it is sin to speak of."

"The people of that house . . ." I began.

But he interrupted me with a savage outburst. "The people?" he cried. "What people? There are neither men nor women in that house of Satan's! What? have you lived here so long, and never heard?" And here he put his mouth to my ear and whispered, as if even the fowls of the mountain might have overheard and been stricken with horror.

What he told me was not true, nor was it even original; being, indeed, but a new edition, vamped up again by village ignorance and superstition, of stories nearly as ancient as the race of man. It was rather the application that appalled me. In the old days, he said, the Church would have burned out that nest of basilisks; but the arm of the Church was now shortened; his friend Miguel had been unpunished by the hands of men, and left to the more awful judgment of an offended God. This was wrong; but it should be so no more. The Padre was sunk in age; he was even bewitched himself; but the eyes of his flock were now awake to their own danger; and some day—ay, and before long—the smoke of that house should go up to heaven.

He left me filled with horror and fear. Which way to turn I knew not; whether first to warn the Padre, or to carry my ill news direct to the threatened inhabitants of the residencia. Fate was to decide for me; for, while I was still hesitating, I beheld the veiled figure of a woman drawing near to me up the pathway. No veil could deceive my penetration; by every line and every movement I recognised Olalla; and keeping hidden behind a corner of the rock, I suffered her to gain the summit. Then I came forward. She knew me and paused, but did not speak; I, too, remained silent; and we continued for some time to gaze upon each other wlth a passionate sadness.

"I thought you had gone," she said at length. "It is all that you can do for me—to go. It is all I ever asked of you. And you still stay. But do you know, that every day heaps up the peril of death, not only on your head, but on ours? A report has gone about the mountain; it is thought you love me, and the people will not suffer it."

I saw she was already informed of her danger, and I rejoiced at it. "Olalla," I said, "I am ready to go this day, this very hour, but not alone."

She stepped aside and knelt down before the crucifix to pray, and I stood by and looked now at her and now at the object of her adoration, now at the living figure of the penitent, and now at the ghastly, daubed countenance, the painted wounds, and the projected ribs of the image. The silence was only broken by the wailing of some large birds that circled sidelong, as if in surprise or alarm, about the summit of the hills. Presently Olalla rose again, turned towards me, raised her veil, and, still leaning with one hand on the shaft of the crucifix, looked upon me with a pale and sorrowful countenance.

"I have laid my hand upon the cross," she said. "The Padre says you are no Christian; but look up for a moment with my eyes, and behold the face of the Man of Sorrows. We are all such as He was—the inheritors of sin; we must all bear and expiate a past which was not ours; there is in all of us—ay, even in me—a sparkle of the divine. Like Him, we must endure for a little while, until morning returns, bringing peace. Suffer me to pass on upon my way alone; it is thus that I shall be least lonely, counting for my friend Him who is the friend of all the distressed; it is thus that I shall be the most happy, having taken my farewell of earthly happiness, and willingly accepted sorrow for my portion."

I looked at the face of the crucifix, and, though I was no friend to images, and despised that imitative and grimacing art of which it was a rude example, some sense of what the thing implied was carried home to my intelligence. The face looked down upon me with a painful and deadly contraction; but the rays of a glory encircled it, and reminded me that the sacrifice was voluntary. It stood there, crowning the rock, as it still stands on so many highway sides, vainly preaching to passers-by, an emblem of sad and noble truths; that pleasure is not an end, but an accident; that pain is the choice of the magnanimous; that it is best to suffer all things and do well. I turned and went down the mountain in silence; and when I looked back for the last time before the wood closed about my path, I saw Olalla still leaning on the crucifix.

The Bottle Imp

THERE WAS a man of the island of Hawaii, whom I shall call Keawe; for the truth is, he still lives, and his name must be kept secret; but the place of his birth was not far from Honaunau, where the bones of Keawe the Great lie hidden in a cave. This man was poor, brave, and active; he could read and write like a schoolmaster; he was a first-rate mariner besides, sailed for some time in the island steamers, and steered a whaleboat on the Hamakua coast. At length it came in Keawe's mind to have a sight of the great world and foreign cities, and he shipped on a vessel bound to San Francisco.

This is a fine town, with a fine harbour, and rich people uncountable; and, in particular, there is one hill which is covered with palaces. Upon this hill Keawe was one day taking a walk with his pocket full of money, viewing great houses upon either hand with pleasure. "What fine houses these are!" he was thinking, "and how happy must those people be who dwell in them, and take no care for the morrow!" The thought was in his mind when he came abreast of a house that was smaller than some others, but all finished and beautified like a toy; the steps of that house shone like silver, and the borders of the garden bloomed like garlands, and the windows were bright like diamonds; and Keawe stopped and wondered at the excellence of all he saw. So stopping, he was aware of a man that looked forth upon him through a window so clear that Keawe could see him as you see a fish in a pool upon the reef. The man was elderly, with a bald head and a black beard; and his face was heavy with sorrow, and he bitterly sighed. And the truth of it is, that as Keawe looked in upon the man, and the man looked out upon Keawe, each envied the other.

All of a sudden the man smiled and nodded, and

beckoned Keawe to enter, and met him at the door of the house.

"This is a fine house of mine," said the man, and bitterly sighed. "Would you not care to view the chambers?"

So he led Keawe all over it, from the cellar to the roof, and there was nothing there that was not perfect of its kind, and Keawe was astonished.

"Truly," said Keawe, "this is a beautiful house; if I lived in the like of it I should be laughing all day long. How comes it, then, that you should be sighing?"

"There is no reason," said the man, "why you should not have a house in all points similar to this, and finer, if you wish. You have some money, I suppose?"

"I have fifty dollars," said Keawe; "but a house like this will cost more than fifty dollars."

The man made a computation. "I am sorry you have no more," said he, "for it may raise you trouble in the future; but it shall be yours at fifty dollars."

"The house?" asked Keawe.

"No, not the house," replied the man; "but the bottle. For, I must tell you, although I appear to you so rich and fortunate, all my fortune, and this house itself and its garden, came out of a bottle not much bigger than a pint. This is it."

And he opened a lockfast place, and took out a round-bellied bottle with a long neck; the glass of it was white like milk, with changing rainbow colours in the grain. Withinsides something obscurely moved, like a shadow and a fire.

"This is the bottle," said the man; and when Keawe laughed, "You do not believe me?" he added. "Try, then, for yourself. See if you can break it."

So Keawe took the bottle up and dashed it on the floor till he was weary; but it jumped on the floor like a child's ball, and was not injured.

"This is a strange thing," said Keawe. "For by the touch of it, as well as by the look, the bottle should be of glass."

"Of glass it is," replied the man, sighing more heavily than ever; "but the glass of it was tempered in the flames of hell. An imp lives in it, and that is the shadow we behold there moving; or so I suppose. If any man buy this bottle the imp is at his command; all that he desires—

love, fame, money, houses like this house, ay, or a city like this city—all are his at the word uttered. Napoleon had this bottle, and by it he grew to be the king of the world; but he sold it at the last, and fell. Captain Cook had this bottle, and by it he found his way to so many islands; but he, too, sold it, and was slain upon Hawaii. For, once it is sold, the power goes and the protection; and unless a man remain content with what he has, ill will befall him."

"And yet you talk of selling it yourself?" Keawe said.

"I have all I wish, and I am growing elderly," replied the man. "There is one thing the imp cannot do—he cannot prolong life; and, it would not be fair to conceal from you, there is a drawback to the bottle; for if a man die before he sells it, he must burn in hell for ever."

"To be sure, that is a drawback and no mistake," cried Keawe. "I would not meddle with the thing. I can do without a house, thank God; but there is one thing I could not be doing with one particle, and that is to be damned."

"Dear me, you must not run away with things," returned the man. "All you have to do is to use the power of the imp in moderation, and then sell it to someone else, as I do to you, and finish your life in comfort."

"Well, I observe two things," said Keawe. "All the time you keep sighing like a maid in love, that is one; and, for the other, you sell this bottle very cheap."

"I have told you already why I sigh," said the man. "It is because I fear my health is breaking up; and, as you said yourself, to die and go to the devil is a pity for anyone. As for why I sell so cheap, I must explain to you there is a peculiarity about the bottle. Long ago, when the devil brought it first upon earth, it was extremely expensive, and was sold first of all to Prester John for many millions of dollars; but it cannot be sold at all, unless sold at a loss. If you sell it for as much as you paid for it, back it comes to you again like a homing pigeon. It follows that the price has kept falling in these centuries, and the bottle is now remarkably cheap. I bought it myself from one of my great neighbours on this hill, and the price I paid was only ninety dollars. I could sell it for as high as eighty-nine dollars and ninety-nine cents, but not a penny dearer, or back the thing must come to me. Now, about this there are two bothers. First, when you offer a bottle so singular for eighty odd dollars, people suppose you to be jesting. And second—but there is no hurry about that—and I need not go into it. Only remember it must be coined money that you sell it for."

"How am I to know that this is all true?" asked Keawe.

"Some of it you can try at once," replied the man. "Give me your fifty dollars, take the bottle, and wish your fifty dollars back into your pocket. If that does not happen, I pledge you my honour I will cry off the bargain and restore your money."

"You are not deceiving me?" said Keawe.

The man bound himself with a great oath.

"Well, I will risk that much," said Keawe, "for that can do no harm." And he paid over his money to the man, and the man handed him the bottle.

"Imp of the bottle," said Keawe, "I want my fifty dollars back." And sure enough he had scarce said the word before his pocket was as heavy as ever.

"To be sure this is a wonderful bottle," said Keawe.

"And now good-morning to you, my fine fellow, and the devil go with you for me!" said the man.

"Hold on," said Keawe, "I don't want any more of this fun. Here, take your bottle back."

"You have bought it for less than I paid for it," replied the man, rubbing his hands. "It is yours now; and, for my part, I am only concerned to see the back of you." And with that he rang for his Chinese servant, and had Keawe shown out of the house.

Now, when Keawe was in the street, with the bottle under his arm, he began to think. "If all is true about this bottle, I may have made a losing bargain," thinks he. "But perhaps the man was only fooling me." The first thing he did was to count his money; the sum was exact—forty-nine dollars American money, and one Chili piece. "That looks like the truth," said Keawe. "Now I will try another part."

The streets in that part of the city were as clean as a ship's decks, and though it was noon, there were no passengers. Keawe set the bottle in the gutter and walked away. Twice he looked back, and there was the milky, round-bellied bottle where he left it. A third time he looked back, and turned a corner; but he had scarce done so, when something knocked upon his elbow, and behold! it was the long neck sticking up; and as for the round belly, it was jammed into the pocket of his pilot-coat.

"And that looks like the truth," said Keawe.

The next thing he did was to buy a corkscrew in a shop, and go apart into a secret place in the fields. And there he tried to draw the cork, but as often as he put the screw in, out it came again, and the cork as whole as ever.

"This is some new sort of cork," said Keawe, and all at once he began to shake and sweat, for he was afraid of that bottle.

On his way back to the port-side he saw a shop where a man sold shells and clubs from the wild islands, old heathen deities, old coined money, pictures from China and Japan, and all manner of things that sailors bring in their seachests. And here he had an idea. So he went in and offered the bottle for a hundred dollars. The man of the shop laughed at him at the first, and offered him five; but, indeed, it was a curious bottle—such glass was never blown in any human glass-works, so prettily the colours shone under the milky white, and so strangely the shadow hovered in the midst; so, after he had disputed a while after the manner of his kind, the shopman gave Keawe sixty silver dollars for the thing, and set it on a shelf in the midst of his window.

"Now," said Keawe, "I have sold that for sixty which I bought for fifty—or, to say truth, a little less, because one of my dollars was from Chili. Now I shall know the truth upon another point."

So he went back on board his ship, and, when he opened his chest, there was the bottle, and had come more quickly than himself. Now Keawe had a mate on board whose name was Lopaka.

"What ails you," said Lopaka, "that you stare in your chest?"

They were alone in the ship's forecastle, and Keawe bound him to secrecy, and told all.

"This is a very strange affair," said Lopaka; "and I fear you will be in trouble about this bottle. But there is one point very clear—that you are sure of the trouble, and you had better have the profit in the bargain. Make up your mind what you want with it; give the order, and if it is done as you desire, I will buy the bottle myself; for

I have an idea of my own to get a schooner, and go trading through the islands."

"That is not my idea," said Keawe; "but to have a beautiful house and garden on the Kona Coast, where I was born, the sun shining in at the door, flowers in the garden, glass in the windows, pictures on the walls, and toys and fine carpets on the tables, for all the world like the house I was in this day—only a story higher, and with balconies all about like the King's palace; and to live there without care and make merry with my friends and relatives."

"Well," said Lopaka, "let us carry it back with us to Hawaii; and if all comes true, as you suppose, I will buy the bottle, as I said, and ask a schooner."

Upon that they were agreed, and it was not long before the ship returned to Honolulu, carrying Keawe and Lopaka, and the bottle. They were scarce come ashore when they met a friend upon the beach, who began at once to condole with Keawe.

"I do not know what I am to be condoled about," said Keawe.

"Is it possible you have not heard," said the friend, "your uncle—that good old man—is dead, and your cousin—that beautiful boy—was drowned at sea?"

Keawe was filled with sorrow, and, beginning to weep and to lament, he forgot about the bottle. But Lopaka was thinking to himself, and presently, when Keawe's grief was a little abated, "I have been thinking," said Lopaka. "Had not your uncle lands in Hawaii, in the district of Kaü?"

"No," said Keawe, "not in Kaü; they are on the mountain-side—a little way south of Hookena."

"These lands will now be yours?" asked Lopaka.

"And so they will," says Keawe, and began again to lament for his relatives.

"No," said Lopaka, "do not lament at present. I have a thought in my mind. How if this should be the doing of the bottle? For here is the place ready for your house."

"If this be so," cried Keawe, "it is a very ill way to serve me by killing my relatives. But it may be, indeed; for it was in just such a station that I saw the house with my mind's eye."

"The house, however, is not yet built," said Lopaka.

"No, nor like to be!" said Keawe; "for though my

uncle has some coffee and ava and bananas, it will not be more than will keep me in comfort; and the rest of that land is the black lava."

"Let us go to the lawyer," said Lopaka; "I have still this idea in my mind."

Now, when they came to the lawyer's, it appeared Keawe's uncle had grown monstrous rich in the last days, and there was a fund of money.

"And here is the money for the house!" cried Lopaka.

"If you are thinking of a new house," said the lawyer. "here is the card of a new architect, of whom they tell me great things."

"Better and better!" cried Lopaka. "Here is all made plain for us. Let us continue to obey orders."

So they went to the architect, and he had drawings of houses on his table.

"You want something out of the way," said the architect. "How do you like this?" and he handed a drawing to Keawe.

Now, when Keawe set eyes on the drawing, he cried out aloud, for it was the picture of his thought exactly drawn.

"I am in for this house," thought he. "Little as I like the way it comes to me, I am in for it now, and I may as well take the good along with the evil."

So he told the architect all that he wished, and how he would have that house furnished, and about the pictures on the wall and the knick-knacks on the tables; and he asked the man plainly for how much he would undertake the whole affair.

The architect put many questions, and took his pen and made a computation; and when he had done he named the very sum that Keawe had inherited.

Lopaka and Keawe looked at one another and nodded.

"It is quite clear," thought Keawe, "that I am to have this house, whether or no. It comes from the devil, and I fear I will get little good by that; and of one thing I am sure, I will make no more wishes as long as I have this bottle. But with the house I am saddled, and I may as well take the good along with the evil."

So he made his terms with the architect, and they signed a paper; and Keawe and Lopaka took ship again and sailed to Australia; for it was concluded between them they should not interfere at all but leave the architect and the bottle imp to build and to adorn that house at their own pleasure.

The voyage was a good voyage, only all the time Keawe was holding in his breath, for he had sworn he would utter no more wishes, and take no more favours from the devil. The time was up when they got back. The architect told them that the house was ready, and Keawe and Lopaka took a passage in the *Hall*, and went down Kona way to view the house, and see if all had been done fitly according to the thought that was in Keawe's mind.

Now, the house stood on the mountain side, visible to ships. Above, the forest ran up into the clouds of rain; below, the black lava fell in cliffs, where the kings of old lay buried. A garden bloomed about that house with every hue of flowers; and there was an orchard of papaia on the one hand and an orchard of bread-fruit on the other, and right in front, toward the sea, a ship's mast had been rigged up and bore a flag. As for the house, it was three stories high, with great chambers and broad balconies on each. The windows were of glass, so excellent that it was as clear as water and as bright as day. All manner of furniture adorned the chambers. Pictures hung upon the wall in golden frames: pictures of ships, and men fighting, and of the most beautiful women, and of singular places; nowhere in the world are there pictures of so bright a colour as those Keawe found hanging in his house. As for the knick-knacks, they were extraordinary fine; chiming clocks and musical boxes, little men with nodding heads, books filled wlth pictures, weapons of price from all quarters of the world, and the most elegant puzzles to entertain the leisure of a solitary man. And as no one would care to live in such chambers, only to walk through and view them, the balconies were made so broad that a whole town might have lived upon them in delight; and Keawe knew not which to prefer, whether the back porch, where you got the land-breeze, and looked upon the orchards and the flowers, or the front balcony, where you could drink the wind of the sea, and look down the steep wall of the mountain and see the *Hall* going by once a week or so between Hookena and the hills of Pele, or the schooners plying up the coast for wood and ava and bananas.

When they had viewed all, Keawe and Lopaka sat on the porch.

"Well," asked Lopaka, "is it all as you designed?"

"Words cannot utter it," said Keawe. "It is better than I dreamed, and I am sick with satisfaction."

"There is but one thing to consider," said Lopaka; "all this may be quite natural, and the bottle imp have nothing whatever to say to it. If I were to buy the bottle, and got no schooner after all, I should have put my hand in the fire for nothing. I gave you my word, I know; but yet I think you would not grudge me one more proof."

"I have sworn I would take no more favours," said Keawe. "I have gone already deep enough."

"This is no favour I am thinking of," replied Lopaka. "It is only to see the imp himself. There is nothing to be gained by that, and so nothing to be ashamed of; and yet, if I once saw him, I should be sure of the whole matter. So indulge me so far, and let me see the imp; and, after that, here is the money in my hand, and I will buy it."

"There is only one thing I am afraid of," said Keawe. "The imp may be very ugly to view: and if you once set eyes upon him you might be very undesirous of the bottle."

"I am a man of my word," said Lopaka. "And here is the money betwixt us."

"Very well," replied Keawe. "I have a curiosity myself.—So come, let us have one look at you, Mr. Imp."

Now as soon as that was said the imp looked out of the bottle, and in again, swift as a lizard; and there sat Keawe and Lopaka turned to stone. The night had quite come, before either found a thought to say or voice to say it with; and then Lopaka pushed the money over and took the bottle.

"I am a man of any word," said he, "and had need to be so, or I would not touch this bottle with my foot. Well, I shall get my schooner and a dollar or two for my pocket; and then I will be rid of this devil as fast as I can. For to tell you the plain truth, the look of him has cast me down."

"Lopaka," said Keawe, "do not you think any worse of me than you can help; I know it is night, and the roads bad, and the pass by the tombs an ill place to go by so late, but I declare since I have seen that little face, I cannot eat or sleep or pray till it is gone from me. I will give you a lantern, and a basket to put the bottle in, and any picture or fine thing in all my house that takes your fancy;—and be gone at once, and go sleep at Hookena with Nahinu."

"Keawe," said Lopaka, "many a man would take this ill; above all, when I am doing you a turn so friendly as to keep my word and buy the bottle; and for that matter, the night, and the dark, and the way by the tombs, must be all tenfold more dangerous to a man with such a sin upon his conscience, and such a bottle under his arm. But for my part, I am so extremely terrified myself I have not the heart to blame you. Here I go then; and I pray God you may be happy in your house, and I fortunate with my schooner, and both get to heaven in the end in spite of the devil and his bottle."

So Lopaka went down the mountain; and Keawe stood in his front balcony, and listened to the clink of the horse's shoes, and watched the lantern go shining down the path, and along the cliff of caves where the old dead are buried; and all the time he trembled and clasped his hands, and prayed for his friend, and gave glory to God that he himself was escaped out of that trouble.

But the next day came very brightly, and that new house of his was so delightful to behold that he forgot his terrors. One day followed another, and Keawe dwelt there in perpetual joy. He had his place on the back porch; it was there he ate and lived, and read the stories in the Honolulu newspapers; but when anyone came by they would go in and view the chambers and the pictures. And the fame of the house went far and wide; it was called *Ka-Hale-Nui*—the Great House—in all Kona; and sometimes the Bright House, for Keawe kept a Chinaman, who was all day dusting and furbishing; and the glass, and the gilt, and the fine stuffs, and the pictures, shone as bright as the morning. As for Keawe himself, he could not walk in the chambers without singing, his heart was so enlarged; and when ships sailed by upon the sea, he would fly his colours on the mast.

So time went by, until one day Keawe went upon a visit as far as Kailua to certain of his friends. There he was well feasted; and left as soon as he could the next morning, and drove hard, for he was impatient to behold his beautiful house; and, besides, the night then coming on was the night in which the dead of old days go abroad in the sides of Kona; and having already meddled with the devil, he was the more chary of meeting with the dead. A little beyond Honaunau, looking far ahead, he was aware of a woman bathing in the edge of the sea; and she seemed a well-grown girl, but he thought no more of it. Then he saw her white shift flutter as she put it on, and then her red holoku; and by the time he came abreast of her she was done with her toilet, and had come up from the sea, and stood by the track side in her red holoku, and she was all freshened with the bath, and her eyes shone and were kind. Now Keawe no sooner beheld her than he drew rein.

"I thought I knew everyone in this country," said he. "How comes it that I do not know you?"

"I am Kokua, daughter of Kiano," said the girl, "and I have just returned from Oahu. Who are you?"

"I will tell you who I am in a little," said Keawe, dismounting from his horse, "but not now. For I have a thought in my mind, and if you knew who I was, you might have heard of me, and would not give me a true answer. But tell me, first of all, one thing: Are you married?"

At this Kokua laughed out aloud. "It is you who ask questions," she said. "Are you married yourself?"

"Indeed, Kokua, I am not," replied Keawe, "and never thought to be until this hour. But here is the plain truth. I have met you here at the roadside, and I saw your eyes, which are like the stars, and my heart went to you as swift as a bird. And so now, if you want none of me, say so, and I will go on to my own place; but if you think me no worse than any other young man, say so, too, and I will turn aside to your father's for the night, and to-morrow I will talk with the good man."

Kokua said never a word, but she looked at the sea and laughed.

"Kokua," said Keawe, "if you say nothing, I will take that for the good answer; so let us be stepping to your father's door."

She went on ahead of him, still without speech; only sometimes she glanced back and glanced away again, and she kept the strings of her hat in her mouth.

Now, when they had come to the door, Kiano came out on his verandah, and cried out and welcomed Keawe by name. At that the girl looked over, for the fame of the great house had come to her ears; and, to be sure, it was a great temptation. All that evening they were very merry together; and the girl was as bold as brass under the eyes of her parents, and made a mock of Keawe, for she had a quick wit. The next day he had a word with Kiano, and found the girl alone.

"Kokua," said he, "you made a mock of me all the evening; and it is still time to bid me go. I would not tell you who I was, because I have so fine a house, and I feared you would think too much of that house and too little of the man who loves you. Now you know all, and if you wish to have seen the last of me, say so at once."

"No," said Kokua; but this time she did not laugh, nor did Keawe ask for more.

This was the wooing of Keawe; things had gone quickly; but so an arrow goes, and the ball of a rifle swifter still, and yet both may strike the target. Things had gone fast, but they had gone far also, and the thought of Keawe rang in the maiden's head; she heard his voice in the breach of the surf upon the lava, and for this young man that she had seen but twice she would have left father and mother and her native islands. As for Keawe himself, his horse flew up the path of the mountain under the cliff of tombs, and the sound of the hoofs, and the sound of Keawe singing to himself for pleasure, echoed in the caverns of the dead. He came to the Bright House, and still he was singing. He sat and ate in the broad balcony, and the Chinaman wondered at his master, to hear how he sang between the mouthfuls. The sun went down into the sea, and the night came; and Keawe walked the balconies by lamplight, high on the mountains, and the voice of his singing startled men on ships.

"Here am I now upon my high place," he said to himself. "Life may be no better; this is the mountain top: and all shelves about me toward the worse. For the first time I will light up the chambers, and bathe in my fine bath with the hot water and the cold, and sleep alone in the bed of my bridal chamber."

So the Chinaman had word, and he must rise from sleep and light the furnaces; and as he wrought below, beside the boilers, he heard his master singing and rejoicing above him in the lighted chambers. When the water began to be hot the Chinaman cried to his master; and Keawe went into the bathroom; and the Chinaman heard him sing as he filled the marble basin; and heard him sing, and the singing broken, as he undressed; until of a sudden the song ceased. The Chinaman listened, and listened; he called up the house to Keawe to ask if all were well, and Keawe answered him "Yes," and bade him go to bed; but there was no more singing in the Bright House; and all night long the Chinaman heard his master's feet go round and round the balconies without repose.

Now the truth of it was this: as Keawe undressed for his bath, he spied upon his flesh a patch like a patch of lichen on a rock, and it was then that he stopped singing. For he knew the likeness of that patch, and knew that he was fallen in the Chinese Evil.*

Now, it is a sad thing for any man to fall into this sickness. And it would be a sad thing for anyone to leave a house so beautiful and so commodious, and depart from all his friends to the north coast of Molokai between the mighty cliff and the sea-breakers. But what was that to the case of the man Keawe, he who had met his love but yesterday, and won her but that morning, and now saw all his hopes break, in a moment, like a piece of glass?

A while he sat upon the edge of the bath; then sprang, with a cry, and ran outside; and to and fro, to and fro, along the balcony, like one despairing.

"Very willingly could I leave Hawaii, the home of my fathers," Keawe was thinking. "Very lightly could I leave my house, the high-placed, the many-windowed, here upon the mountains. Very bravely could I go to Molokai, to Kalaupapa by the cliffs, to live with the smitten and to sleep there, far from my fathers. But what wrong have I done, what sin lies upon my soul, that I should have encountered Kokua coming cool from the sea-water in the evening? Kokua, the soul ensnarer! Kokua, the light of my life! Her may I never wed, her may I look upon no longer, her may I no more handle with my loving hand; and it is for this, it is for you, O Kokua! that I pour my lamentations!"

Now you are to observe what sort of a man Keawe was, for he might have dwelt there in the Bright House for years, and no one been the wiser of his sickness; but he reckoned nothing of that, if he must lose Kokua. And again, he might have wed Kokua even as he was; and so

* Leprosy.

many would have done, because they have the souls of pigs; but Keawe loved the maid manfully, and he would do her no hurt and bring her in no danger.

A little beyond the midst of the night, there came in his mind the recollection of that bottle. He went round to the back porch, and called to memory the day when the devil had looked forth; and at the thought ice ran in his veins.

"A dreadful thing is the bottle," thought Keawe, "and dreadful is the imp, and it is a dreadful thing to risk the flames of hell. But what other hope have I to cure my sickness or to wed Kokua? What!" he thought, "would I beard the devil once, only to get me a house, and not face him again to win Kokua?"

Thereupon he called to mind it was the next day the *Hall* went by on her return to Honolulu. "There must I go first," he thought, "and see Lopaka. For the best hope that I have now is to find that same bottle I was so pleased to be rid of."

Never a wink could he sleep; the food stuck in his throat; but he sent a letter to Kiano, and, about the time when the steamer would be coming, rode down beside the cliff of the tombs. It rained; his horse went heavily; he looked up at the black mouths of the caves, and he envied the dead that slept there and were done with trouble; and called to mind how he had galloped by the day before, and was astonished. So he came down to Hookena, and there was all the country gathered for the steamer as usual. In the shed before the store they sat and jested and passed the news; but there was no matter of speech in Keawe's bosom, and he sat in their midst and looked without on the rain falling on the houses, and the surf beating among the rocks, and the sighs arose in his throat.

"Keawe of the Bright House is out of spirits," said one to another. Indeed, and so he was, and little wonder.

Then the *Hall* came, and the whale-boat carried him on board. The after-part of the ship was full of Haoles* who had been to visit the volcano, as their custom is; and the midst was crowded with Kanakas, and the fore-part with wild bulls from Hilo and horses from Kaü; but Keawe sat apart from all in his sorrow, and watched for

* Whites.

the house of Kiano. There it sat, low upon the shore in the black rocks, and shaded by the cocoa-palms, and there by the door was a red holoku, no greater than a fly, and going to and fro with a fly's busyness. "Ah, queen of my heart," he cried, "I'll venture my dear soul to win you!"

Soon after, darkness fell, and the cabins were lit up, and the Haoles sat and played at the cards and drank whisky as their custom is; but Keawe walked the deck all night; and all the next day, as they steamed under the lee of Maui or of Molokai, he was still pacing to and fro like a wild animal in a menagerie.

Towards evening they passed Diamond Head, and came to the pier of Honolulu. Keawe stepped out among the crowd and began to ask for Lopaka. It seemed he had become the owner of a schooner—none better in the islands—and was gone upon an adventure as far as Pola-Pola or Kahiki; so there was no help to be looked for from Lopaka. Keawe called to mind a friend of his, a lawyer in the town (I must not tell his name), and inquired of him. They said he was grown suddenly rich, and had a fine new house upon Waikiki shore; and this put a thought in Keawe's head, and he called a hack and drove to the lawyer's house.

The house was all brand new, and the trees in the garden no greater than walking-sticks, and the lawyer, when he came, had the air of a man well pleased.

"What can I do to serve you?" said the lawyer.

"You are a friend of Lopaka's," replied Keawe," and Lopaka purchased from me a certain piece of goods that I thought you might enable me to trace."

The lawyer's face became very dark. "I do not profess to misunderstand you, Mr. Keawe," said he, "though this is an ugly business to be stirring in. You may be sure I know nothing, but yet I have a guess, and if you would apply in a certain quarter I think you might have news."

And he named the name of a man, which, again, I had better not repeat. So it was for days, and Keawe went from one to another, finding everywhere new clothes and carriages, and fine new houses, and men everywhere in great contentment, although, to be sure, when he hinted at his business their faces would cloud over.

"No doubt I am upon the track," thought Keawe. "These new clothes and carriages are all the gifts of the little imp, and these glad faces are the faces of men who have taken their profit and got rid of the accursed thing in safety. When I see pale cheeks and hear sighing, I shall know that I am near the bottle."

So it befell at last that he was recommended to a Haole in Beritania Street. When he came to the door, about the hour of the evening meal, there were the usual marks of the new house, and the young garden, and the electric light shining in the windows; but when the owner came, a shock of hope and fear ran through Keawe; for here was a young man, white as a corpse, and black about the eyes, the hair shedding from his head, and such a look in his countenance as a man may have when he is waiting for the gallows.

"Here it is, to be sure," thought Keawe, and so with this man he noways veiled his errand. "I am come to buy the bottle," said he.

At the word, the young Haole of Beritania Street reeled against the wall.

"The bottle!" he gasped. "To buy the bottle!" Then he seemed to choke, and seizing Keawe by the arm carried him into a room and poured out wine in two glasses.

"Here is my respects," said Keawe, who had been much about with Haoles in his time. "Yes," he added, "I am come to buy the bottle. What is the price by now?"

At that word the young man let his glass slip through his fingers, and looked upon Keawe like a ghost.

"The price," says he; "the price! You do not know the price?"

"It is for that I am asking you," returned Keawe. "But why are you so much concerned? Is there anything wrong about the price?"

"It has dropped a great deal in value since your time, Mr. Keawe," said the young man, stammering.

"Well, well, I shall have the less to pay for it," says Keawe. "How much did it cost you?"

The young man was as white as a sheet. "Two cents," said he.

"What!" cried Keawe, "two cents? Why, then, you can only sell it for one. And he who buys it—" The words died upon Keawe's tongue; he who bought it could never sell it again, the bottle and the bottle imp must abide with him until he died, and when he died must carry him to the red end of hell.

The young man of Beritania Street fell upon his knees. "For God's sake, buy it!" he cried. "You can have all my fortune in the bargain. I was mad when I bought it at that price. I had embezzled money at my store; I was lost else: I must have gone to gaol."

"Poor creature," said Keawe, "you would risk your soul upon so desperate an adventure, and to avoid the proper punishment of your own disgrace; and you think I could hesitate with love in front of me. Give me the bottle and the change which I make sure you have all ready. Here is a five-cent piece."

It was as Keawe supposed; the young man had the change ready in a drawer; the bottle changed hands, and Keawe's fingers were no sooner clasped upon the stalk than he had breathed his wish to be a clean man. And, sure enough, when he got home to his room, and stripped himself before a glass, his flesh was whole like an infant's. And here was the strange thing: he had no sooner seen this miracle than his mind was changed within him, and he cared naught for the Chinese Evil, and little enough for Kokua; and had but the one thought, that here he was bound to the bottle imp for time and for eternity, and had no better hope but to be a cinder for ever in the flames of hell. Away ahead of him he saw them blaze with his mind's eye, and his soul shrank, and darkness fell upon the light.

When Keawe came to himself a little, he was aware it was the night when the band played at the hotel. Thither he went, because he feared to be alone; and there, among happy faces, walked to and fro, and heard the tunes go up and down, and saw Berger beat the measure, and all the while he heard the flames crackle, and saw the red fire burning in the bottomless pit. Of a sudden the band played *Hiki-ao-ao;* that was a song that he had sung with Kokua, and at the strain courage returned to him.

"It is done now," he thought, "and once more let me take the good along with the evil."

So it befell that he returned to Hawaii by the first steamer, and as soon as it could be managed he was wedded to Kokua, and carried her up the mountain side to the Bright House.

Now it was so with these two, that when they were together, Keawe's heart was stilled; but so soon as he was alone he fell into a brooding horror, and heard the flames crackle, and saw the red fire burn in the bottomless pit. The girl, indeed, had come to him wholly; her heart leapt in her side at sight of him, her hand clung to his; and she was so fashioned from the hair upon her head to the nails upon her toes that none could see her without joy. She was pleasant in her nature. She had the good word always. Full of song she was, and went to and fro in the Bright House, the brightest thing in its three stories, carolling like the birds. And Keawe beheld and heard her with delight, and then must shrink upon one side, and weep and groan to think upon the price that he had paid for her; and then he must dry his eyes, and wash his face, and go and sit with her on the broad balconies, joining in her songs, and, with a sick spirit, answering her smiles.

There came a day when her feet began to be heavy and her songs more rare; and now it was not Keawe only that would weep apart, but each would sunder from the other and sit in opposite balconies with the whole width of the Bright House betwixt. Keawe was so sunk in his despair he scarce observed the change, and was only glad he had more hours to sit alone and brood upon his destiny, and was not so frequently condemned to pull a smiling face on a sick heart. But one day, coming softly through the house, he heard the sound of a child sobbing, and there was Kokua rolling her face upon the balcony floor, and weeping like the lost.

"You do well to weep in this house, Kokua," he said. "And yet I would give the head off my body that you (at least) might have been happy."

"Happy!" she cried. "Keawe, when you lived alone in your Bright House, you were the word of the island for a happy man; laughter and song were in your mouth, and your face was as bright as the sunrise. Then you wedded poor Kokua; and the good God knows what is amiss in her—but from that day you have not smiled. O!" she cried, "what ails me? I thought I was pretty, and I knew I loved him. What ails me that I throw this cloud upon my husband?"

"Poor Kokua," said Keawe. He sat down by her side, and sought to take her hand; but that she plucked away. "Poor Kokua!" he said again. "My poor child—my pretty. And I had thought all this while to spare you! Well, you shall know all. Then at least, you will pity poor Keawe;

then you will understand how much he loved you in the past—that he dared hell for your possession—and how much he loves you still (the poor condemned one), that he can yet call up a smile when he beholds you."

With that he told her all, even from the beginning.

"You have done this for me?" she cried. "Ah, well, then what do I care!"—and she clasped and wept upon him.

"Ah, child!" said Keawe, "and yet, when I consider of the fire of hell, I care a good deal!"

"Never tell me," said she; "no man can be lost because he loved Kokua, and no other fault. I tell you, Keawe, I shall save you with these hands, or perish in your company. What! you loved me, and gave your soul, and you think I will not die to save you in return?"

"Ah, my dear! you might die a hundred times, and what difference would that make?" he cried, "except to leave me lonely till the time comes of my damnation?"

"You know nothing," said she. "I was educated in a school in Honolulu; I am no common girl. And I tell you, I shall save my lover. What is this you say about a cent? But all the world is not American. In England they have a piece they call a farthing, which is about half a cent. Ah! sorrow!" she cried, "that makes it scarcely better, for the buyer must be lost, and we shall find none so brave as my Keawe! But then, there is France: they have a small coin there which they call a centime, and these go five to the cent, or thereabout. We could not do better. Come, Keawe, let us go to the French islands; let us go to Tahiti as fast as ships can bear us. There we have four centimes, three centimes, two centimes, one centime; four possible sales to come and go on; and two of us to push the bargain. Come, my Keawe! kiss me, and banish care. Kokua will defend you."

"Gift of God!" he cried. "I cannot think that God will punish me for desiring aught so good! Be it as you will, then; take me where you please: I put my life and my salvation in your hands."

Early the next day Kokua was about her preparations. She took Keawe's chest that he went with sailoring; and first she put the bottle in a corner; and then packed it with the richest of their clothes and the bravest of the knick-knacks in the house. "For," said she, "we must seem to be rich folks, or who will believe in the bottle?"

All the time of her preparation she was as gay as a bird; only when she looked upon Keawe the tears would spring in her eye, and she must run and kiss him. As for Keawe, a weight was off his soul; now that he had his secret shared, and some hope in front of him, he seemed like a new man, his feet went lightly on the earth, and his breath was good to him again. Yet was terror still at his elbow; and ever and again, as the wind blows out a taper, hope died in him, and he saw the flames toss and the red fire burn in hell.

It was given out in the country they were gone pleasuring to the States, which was thought a strange thing, and yet not so strange as the truth, if any could have guessed it. So they went to Honolulu in the *Hall,* and thence in the *Umatilla* to San Francisco with a crowd of Haoles, and at San Francisco took their passage by the mail brigantine, the *Tropic Bird,* for Papeete, the chief place of the French in the south islands. Thither they came, after a pleasant voyage, on a fair day of the trade wind, and saw the reef with the surf breaking, and Motuiti with its palms, and the schooner riding withinside, and the white houses of the town low down along the shore among green trees, and overhead the mountains and the clouds of Tahiti, the wise island.

It was judged the most wise to hire a house, which they did accordingly, opposite the British Consul's, to make a great parade of money, and themselves conspicuous with carriages and horses. This it was very easy to do, so long as they had the bottle in their possession; for Kokua was more bold than Keawe, and, whenever she had a mind, called on the imp for twenty or a hundred dollars. At this rate they soon grew to be remarked in the town; and the strangers from Hawaii, their riding and their driving, the fine holokus and the rich lace of Kokua, became the matter of much talk.

They got on well after the first with the Tahitian language, which is indeed like to the Hawaiian, with a change of certain letters: and as soon as they had any freedom of speech, began to push the bottle. You are to consider it was not an easy subject to introduce; it was not easy to persuade people you were in earnest, when you offered to sell them for four centimes the spring of health and riches inexhaustlble. It was necessary besides to explain the dangers of the bottle; and either people disbelieved the whole thing and laughed, or they thought the more of the darker part, became overcast with gravity, and drew away from Keawe and Kokua, as from persons who had dealings with the devil. So far from gaining ground, these two began to find they were avoided in the town; the children ran away from them screaming, a thing intolerable to Kokua; Catholics crossed themselves as they went by; and all persons began with one accord to disengage themselves from their advances.

Depression fell upon their spirits. They would sit at night in their new house, after a day's weariness, and not exchange one word, or the silence would be broken by Kokua bursting suddenly into sobs. Sometimes they would pray together; sometimes they would have the bottle out upon the floor, and sit all evening watching how the shadow hovered in the midst. At such times they would be afraid to go to rest. It was long ere slumber came to them, and, if either dozed off, it would be to wake and find the other silently weeping in the dark, or, perhaps, to wake alone, the other having fled from the house and the neighbourhood of that bottle, to pace under the bananas in the little garden, or to wander on the beach by moonlight.

One night it was so when Kokua awoke. Keawe was gone. She felt in the bed, and his place was cold. Then fear fell upon her, and she sat up in bed. A little moonshine filtered through the shutters. The room was bright, and she could spy that bottle on the floor. Outside it blew high, the great trees of the avenue cried aloud, and the fallen leaves rattled in the verandah. In the midst of this Kokua was aware of another sound; whether of a beast or of a man she could scarce tell, but it was as sad as death, and cut her to the soul. Softly she arose, set the door ajar, and looked forth into the moonlit yard. There, under the bananas, lay Keawe, his mouth in the dust, and as he lay he moaned.

It was Kokua's first thought to run forward and console him; her second potently withheld her. Keawe had borne himself before his wife like a brave man; it became her little in the hour of weakness to intrude upon his shame. With the thought she drew back into the house.

"Heaven!" she thought, "how careless have I been—how weak! It is he, not I, that stands in this eternal peril; it was he, not I, that took the curse upon his soul. It is for my sake, and for the love of a creature of so little worth and such poor help, that he now beholds so close to him the flames of hell—ay, and smells the smoke of it, lying without there in the wind and moonlight. Am I so dull of spirit that never till now I have surmised my duty, or have I seen it before and turned aside? But now, at least, I take up my soul in both the hands of my affection; now I say farewell to the white steps of heaven and the waiting faces of my friends. A love for a love, and let mine be equalled with Keawe's! A soul for a soul, and be it mine to perish!"

She was a deft woman with her hands, and was soon apparelled. She took in her hands the change—the precious centimes they kept ever at their side; for this coin is little used, and they had made provision at a government office. When she was forth in the avenue clouds came on the wind, and the moon was blackened. The town slept, and she knew not whither to turn till she heard one coughing in the shadow of the trees.

"Old man," said Kokua, "what do you here abroad in the cold night?"

The old man could scarce express himself for coughing, but she made out that he was old and poor, and a stranger in the island.

"Will you do me a service?" said Kokua. "As one stranger to another, and as an old man to a young woman, will you help a daughter of Hawaii?"

"Ah," said the old man. "So you are the witch from the Eight Islands, and even my old soul you seek to entangle. But I have heard of you, and defy your wickedness."

"Sit down here," said Kokua, "and let me tell you a tale." And she told him the story of Keawe from the beginning to the end.

"And now," said she, "I am his wife, whom he bought with his soul's welfare. And what should I do? If I went to him myself and offered to buy it, he would refuse. But if you go, he will sell it eagerly; I will await you here; you will buy it for four centimes, and I will buy it again for three. And the Lord strengthen a poor girl!"

"If you meant falsely," said the old man, "I think God would strike you dead."

"He would!' cried Kokua. "Be sure He would. I could not be so treacherous—God would not suffer it."

"Give me the four centimes and await me here," said the old man.

Now, when Kokua stood alone in the street her spirit died. The wind roared in the trees, and it seemed to her rushing of the flames of hell; the shadows tossed in the light of the street lamp, and they seemed to her the snatching hands of the evil ones. If she had had the strength, she must have run away, and if she had had the breath she must have screamed aloud; but in truth she could do neither, and stood and trembled in the avenue, like an affrighted child.

Then she saw the old man returning, and he had the bottle in his hand.

"I have done your bidding," said he. "I left your husband weeping like a child; to-night he will sleep easy." And he held the bottle forth.

"Before you give it me," Kokua panted, "take the good with the evil—ask to be delivered from your cough."

"I am an old man," replied the other, "and too near the gate of the grave to take a favour from the devil. —But what is this? Why do you not take the bottle? Do you hesitate?"

"Not hesitate!" cried Kokua. "I am only weak. Give me a moment. It is my hand resists, my flesh shrinks back from the accursed thing. One moment only!"

The old man looked upon Kokua kindly. "Poor child!" said he, "you fear; your soul misgives you. Well, let me keep it. I am old, and can never more be happy in this world, and as for the next—"

"Give it me!" gasped Kokua. "There is your money. Do you think I am so base as that? Give me the bottle."

"God bless you, child," said the old man.

Kokua concealed the bottle under her holoku, said farewell to the old man, and walked off along the avenue, she cared not whither. For all roads were now the same to her, and led equally to hell. Sometimes she walked, and sometimes ran; sometimes she screamed out loud in the night, and sometimes lay by the wayside in the dust and wept. All that she had heard of hell came back to her; she saw the flames blaze, and she smelt the smoke, and her flesh withered on the coals.

Near day she came to her mind again, and returned to the house. It was even as the old man said—Keawe slumbered like a child. Kokua stood and gazed upon his face.

"Now, my husband," said she, "it is your turn to sleep. When you wake it will be your turn to sing and laugh. But for poor Kokua, alas! that meant no evil—for poor Kokua no more sleep, no more singing, no more delight, whether in earth or heaven."

With that she lay down in the bed by his side, and her misery was so extreme that she fell in a deep slumber instantly.

Late in the morning her husband woke her and gave her the good news. It seemed he was silly with delight, for he paid no heed to her distress, ill though she dissembled it. The words stuck in her mouth, it mattered not; Keawe did the speaking. She ate not a bite, but who was to observe it? for Keawe cleared the dish. Kokua saw and heard him, like some strange thing in a dream; there were times when she forgot or doubted, and put her hands to her brow; to know herself doomed and hear her husband babble seemed so monstrous.

All the while Keawe was eating and talking, and planning the time of their return, and thanking her for saving him, and fondling her, and calling her the true helper after all. He laughed at the old man that was fool enough to buy that bottle.

"A worthy old man he seemed," Keawe said. "But no one can judge by appearances. For why did the old reprobate require the bottle?"

"My husband," said Kokua humbly, "his purpose may have been good."

Keawe laughed like an angry man.

"Fiddle-de-dee!" cried Keawe. "An old rogue, I tell you, and an old ass to boot. For the bottle was hard enough to sell at four centimes; and at three it will be quite impossible. The margin is not broad enough, the thing begins to smell of scorching—brrr!" said he, and shuddered. "It is true I bought it myself at a cent, when I knew not there were smaller coins. I was a fool for my pains; there will never be found another: and whoever has that bottle now will carry it to the pit."

"O my husband!" said Kokua. "Is it not a terrible thing to save oneself by the eternal ruin of another? It seems to me I could not laugh. I would be humbled.

I would be filled with melancholy. I would pray for the poor holder."

Then Keawe, because he felt the truth of what she said, grew the more angry. "Heighty-teighty!" cried he. "You may be filled with melancholy if you please. It is not the mind of a good wife. If you thought at all of me you would sit shamed."

Thereupon he went out, and Kokua was alone.

What chance had she to sell that bottle at two centimes? None, she perceived. And if she had any there was her husband hurrying her away to a country where there was nothing lower than a cent. And here—on the morrow of her sacrifice—was her husband leaving her and blaming her.

She would not even try to profit by what time she had, but sat in the house, and now had the bottle out and viewed it with unutterable fear, and now, with loathing, hid it out of sight.

By and by Keawe came back, and would have her take a drive.

"My husband, I am ill," she said. "I am out of heart. Excuse me, I can take no pleasure."

Then was Keawe more wroth than ever. With her, because he thought she was brooding over the case of the old man; and with himself, because he thought she was right, and was ashamed to be so happy.

"This is your truth," cried he, "and this your affection! Your husband is just saved from eternal ruin, which he encountered for the love of you—and you can take no pleasure! Kokua, you have a disloyal heart."

He went forth again furious, and wandered in the town all day. He met friends, and drank with them; they hired a carriage and drove into the country, and there drank again. All the time Keawe was ill at ease, because he was taking this pastime while his wife was sad, and because he knew in his heart that she was more right than he; and the knowledge made him drink the deeper.

Now there was an old brutal Haole drinking with him, one that had been a boatswain of a whaler, a runaway, a digger in gold mines, a convict in prisons. He had a low mind and a foul mouth; he loved to drink and to see others drunken; and he pressed the glass upon Keawe. Soon there was no more money in the company.

"Here you!" says the boatswain, "you are rich, you

have been always saying. You have a bottle or some foolishness."

"Yes," says Keawe, "I am rich; I will go back and get some money from my wife, who keeps it."

"That's a bad idea, mate," said the boatswain. "Never you trust a petticoat with dollars. They're all as false as water; you keep an eye on her."

Now this word stuck in Keawe's mind; for he was muddled with what he had been drinking.

"I should not wonder but she was false, indeed," thought he. "Why else should she be so cast down at my release? But I will show her I am not the man to be fooled. I will catch her in the act."

Accordingly, when they were back in town, Keawe bade the boatswain wait for him at the corner, by the old calaboose, and went forward up the avenue alone to the door of his house. The night had come again; there was a light within, but never a sound; and Keawe crept about the corner, opened the back-door softly, and looked in.

There was Kokua on the floor, the lamp at her side; before her was a milk-white bottle, with a round belly and a long neck; and as she viewed it, Kokua wrung her hands.

A long time Keawe stood and looked in the doorway. At first he was struck stupid; and then fear fell upon him that the bargain had been made amiss, and the bottle had come back to him as it came at San Francisco; and at that his knees were loosened, and the fumes of the wine departed from his head like mists off a river in the morning. And then he had another thought; and it was a strange one, that made his cheeks to burn.

"I must make sure of this," thought he.

So he closed the door, and went softly round the corner again, and then came noisily in, as though he were but now returned. And, lo! by the time he opened the front door no bottle was to be seen; and Kokua sat in a chair and started up like one awakened out of sleep.

"I have been drinking all day and making merry," said Keawe. "I have been with good companions, and now I only come back for money, and return to drink and carouse with them again."

Both his face and voice were as stern as judgment, but Kokua was too troubled to observe.

"You do well to use your own, my husband," said she, and her words trembled.

"O, I do well in all things," said Keawe, and he went straight to the chest and took out money. But he looked besides in the corner where they kept the bottle and there was no bottle there.

At that the chest heaved upon the floor like a sea-billow, and the house span about him like a wreath of smoke, for he saw he was lost now, and there was no escape. "It is what I feared," he thought. "It is she who has bought it."

And then he came to himself a little and rose up; but the sweat streamed on his face as thick as the rain and as cold as the well-water.

"Kokua," said he, "I said to you to-day what ill became me. Now I return to carouse with my jolly companions," and at that he laughed a little quietly. "I will take more pleasure in the cup if you forgive me."

She clasped his knees in a moment; she kissed his knees with flowing tears.

"O," she cried, "I asked but a kind word!"

"Let us never one think hardly of the other," said Keawe, and was gone out of the house.

Now, the money that Keawe had taken was only some of that store of centime pieces they had laid in at their arrival. It was very sure he had no mind to be drinking. His wife had given her soul for him, now he must give his for hers; no other thought was in the world with him.

At the corner, by the old calaboose, there was the boatswain waiting.

"My wife has the bottle," said Keawe, "and, unless you help me to recover it, there can be no more money and no more liquor to-night."

"You do not mean to say you are serious about that bottle?" cried the boatswain.

"There is the lamp," said Keawe. "Do I look as if I was jesting?"

"That is so," said the boatswain. "You look as serious as a ghost."

"Well, then," said Keawe, "here are two centimes; you must go to my wife in the house, and offer her these for the bottle, which (if I am not much mistaken) she will give you instantly. Bring it to me here, and I will buy it back from you for one; for that is the law with this bottle, that it still must be sold for a less sum. But whatever you do, never breathe a word to her that you have come from me."

"Mate, I wonder are you making a fool of me?" asked the boatswain.

"It will do you no harm if I am," returned Keawe.

"That is so, mate," said the boatswain.

"And if you doubt me," added Keawe, "you can try. As soon as you are clear of the house, wish to have your pocket full of money, or a bottle of the best rum, or what you please, and you will see the virtue of the thing."

"Very well, Kanaka," says the boatswain. "I will try; but if you are having your fun out of me, I will take my fun out of you with a belaying-pin."

So the whaler-man went off up the avenue; and Keawe stood and waited. It was near the same spot where Kokua had waited the night before; but Keawe was more resolved, and never faltered in his purpose; only his soul was bitter with despair.

It seemed a long time he had to wait before he heard a voice singing in the darkness of the avenue. He knew the voice to be the boatswain's; but it was strange how drunken it appeared upon a sudden.

Next, the man himself came stumbling into the light of the lamp. He had the devil's bottle buttoned in his coat; another bottle was in his hand; and even as he came in view he raised it to his mouth and drank.

"You have it," said Keawe. "I see that."

"Hands off!" cried the boatswain, jumping back. "Take a step near me and I'll smash your mouth. You thought you could make a cat's-paw of me, did you?"

"What do you mean?" cried Keawe.

"Mean?" cried the boatswain. "This is a pretty good bottle, this is; that's what I mean. How I got it for two centimes I can't make out; but I'm sure you shan't have it for one."

"You mean you won't sell it?" gasped Keawe.

"No, *sir!*" cried the boatswain. "But I'll give you a drink of the rum, if you like."

"I tell you," said Keawe, "the man who has that bottle goes to hell."

"I reckon I'm going anyway," returned the sailor; "and this bottle's the best thing to go with I've struck yet. No, sir!" he cried again, "this is my bottle now, and you can go and fish for another."

"Can this be true?" Keawe cried. "For your own sake, I beseech you, sell it me!"

"I don't value any of your talk," replied the boatswain. "You thought I was a flat; now you see I'm not; and there's an end. If you won't have a swallow of the rum I'll have one myself. Here's your health, and good-night to you!"

So off he went down the avenue towards town, and there goes the bottle out of the story.

But Keawe ran to Kokua light as the wind; and great was their joy that night; and great, since then, has been the peace of all their days in the Bright House.

The Beach of Falesá

CHAPTER I

A SOUTH SEA BRIDAL

I SAW THAT island first when it was neither night nor morning. The moon was to the west, setting, but still broad and bright. To the east, and right amidships of the dawn, which was all pink, the day-star sparkled like a diamond. The land breeze blew in our faces, and smelt strong of wild lime and vanilla: other things besides, but these were the most plain; and the chill of it set me sneezing. I should say I had been for years on a low island near the line, living for the most part solitary among natives. Here was a fresh experience: even the tongue would be quite strange to me; and the look of these woods and mountains, and the rare smell of them, renewed my blood.

The captain blew out the binnacle lamp.

"There!" said he, "there goes a bit of smoke, Mr. Wiltshire, behind the break of the reef. That's Falesá, where your station is, the last village to the east; nobody lives to windward—I don't know why. Take my glass, and you can make the houses out."

I took the glass; and the shores leaped nearer, and I saw the tangle of the woods and the breach of the surf, and the brown roofs and the black insides of houses peeped among the trees.

"Do you catch a bit of white there to the east'ard?" the captain continued. "That's your house. Coral built, stands high, verandah you could walk on three abreast; best station in the South Pacific. When old Adams saw it, he took and shook me by the hand. 'I've dropped into a soft thing here,' says he. 'So you have,' says I, 'and time too!' Poor Johnny! I never saw him again but the once, and then he had changed his tune—couldn't get on with the natives, or the whites, or something; and the next time we came round there he was dead and buried. I took and put up a bit of stick to him: 'John Adams, *obit* eighteen and sixty-eight. Go thou and do likewise.' I missed that man. I never could see much harm in Johnny."

"What did he die of?" I inquired.

"Some kind of sickness," says the captain. "It appears it took him sudden. Seems he got up in the night, and filled up on Pain-Killer and Kennedy's Discovery. No go: he was booked beyond Kennedy. Then he had tried to open a case of gin. No go again: not strong enough. Then he must have turned to and run out on the verandah, and capsized over the rail. When they found him, the next day, he was clean crazy—carried on all the time about somebody watering his copra. Poor John!"

"Was it thought to be the island?" I asked.

"Well, it was thought to be the island, or the trouble, or something," he replied. "I never could hear but what it was a healthy place. Our last man, Vigours, never turned a hair. He left because of the beach—said he was afraid of Black Jack and Case and Whistling Jimmie, who was still alive at the time, but got drowned soon afterward when drunk. As for old Captain Randall, he's been here any time since eighteen-forty, forty-five. I never could see much harm in Billy, nor much change. Seems as if he might live to be Old Kafoozleum. No, I guess it's healthy."

"There's a boat coming now," said I. "She's right in the pass; looks to be a sixteen-foot whale; two white men in the stern-sheets."

"That's the boat that drowned Whistling Jimmie!" cried the captain; "let's see the glass. Yes, that's Case, sure enough, and the darkie. They've got a gallows bad reputation, but you know what a place the beach is for talking. My belief, that Whistling Jimmie was the worst of the trouble; and he's gone to glory, you see. What'll you bet they ain't after gin? Lay you five to two they take six cases."

When these two traders came aboard I was pleased with the looks of them at once, or, rather, with the looks of both, and the speech of one. I was sick for white neighbours after my four years at the line, which I always counted years of prison; getting tabooed, and going down to the Speak House to see and get it taken off; buying gin and going on a break, and then repenting; sitting in the house at night with the lamp for company; or walking on the beach and wondering what kind of a fool to call myself for being where I was. There were no other whites upon my island, and when I sailed to the next, rough customers made the most of the society. Now to see these two when they came aboard was a pleasure. One was a negro, to be sure; but they were both rigged out smart in striped pyjamas and straw hats, and Case would have passed muster in a city. He was yellow and smallish, had a hawk's nose to his face, pale eyes, and his beard trimmed with scissors. No man knew his country, beyond he was of English speech; and it was clear he came of a good family and was splendidly educated. He was accomplished too; played the accordion first-rate; and give him a piece of string or a cork or a pack of cards, and he could show you tricks equal to any professional. He could speak, when he chose, fit for a drawing-room; and when he chose he could blaspheme worse than a Yankee boatswain, and talk smart to sicken a Kanaka. The way he thought would pay best at the moment, that was Case's way, and it always seemed to come natural, and like as if he was born to it. He had the courage of a lion and the cunning of a rat; and if he's not in hell to-day, there's no such place. I know but one good point to the man: that he was fond of his wife, and kind to her. She was a Samoa woman, and dyed her hair red, Samoa style; and when he came to die (as I have to tell of) they found one strange thing—that he had made a will, like a Christian, and the widow got the lot: all his, they said, and all Black Jack's, and the most of Billy Randall's in the bargain, for it was Case that kept the books. So she went off home in the schooner *Manu'a,* and does the lady to this day in her own place.

But of all this on that first morning I knew no more than a fly. Case used me like a gentleman and like a friend, made me welcome to Falesá, and put his services at my disposal, which was the more helpful from my ignorance of the native. All the better part of the day we sat drinking better acquaintance in the cabin, and I never heard a man talk more to the point. There was *no* smarter trader, and none dodgier, in the islands. I thought Falesá seemed to be the right kind of a place; and the more I drank the lighter my heart. Our last trader had fled the place at half an hour's notice, taking a chance passage in a labour ship from up west. The captain, when he came, had found the station closed, the keys left with the native pastor, and a letter from the runaway, confessing he was fairly frightened of his life. Since then the firm had not been represented, and of course there was no cargo. The wind, besides, was fair, the captain hoped he could make his next island by dawn, with a good tide, and the business of landing my trade was gone about lively. There was no call for me to fool with it, Case said; nobody would touch my things, every one was honest in Falesá, only about chickens or an odd knife or an odd stick of tobacco; and the best I could do was to sit quiet till the vessel left, then come straight to his house, see old Captain Randall, the father of the beach, take pot-luck, and go home to sleep when it got dark. So it was high noon, and the schooner was under way, before I set my foot on shore at Falesá.

I had a glass or two on board; I was just off a long cruise, and the ground heaved under me like a ship's deck. The world was like all new painted; my foot went along to music; Falesá might have been Fiddler's Green, if there is such a place, and more's the pity if there isn't! It was good to foot the grass, to look aloft at the green mountains, to see the men with their green wreaths and the women in their bright dresses, red and blue. On we went, in the strong sun and the cool shadow, liking both; and all the children in the town came trotting after with their shaven heads and their brown bodies, and raising a thin kind of a cheer in our wake, like crowing poultry.

"By the by," says Case, "we must get you a wife."

"That's so," said I; "I had forgotten."

There was a crowd of girls about us, and I pulled myself up and looked among them like a Bashaw. They were all dressed out for the sake of the ship being in; and the women of Falesá are a handsome lot to see. If they have a fault, they are a trifle broad in the beam; and I was just thinking so when Case touched me.

"That's pretty," says he.

I saw one coming on the other side alone. She had been fishing; all she wore was a chemise, and it was wetted through. She was young and very slender for an island maid, with a long face, a high forehead, and a shy, strange, blindish look, between a cat's and a baby's.

"Who's she?" said I. "She'll do."

"That's Uma," said Case, and he called her up and spoke to her in the native. I didn't know what he said; but when he was in the midst she looked up at me quick and timid, like a child dodging a blow, then down again, and presently smiled. She had a wide mouth, the lips and the chin cut like any statue's; and the smile came out for a moment and was gone. Then she stood with her head bent, and heard Case to an end, spoke back in the pretty Polynesian voice, looking him full in the face, heard him again in answer, and then with an obeisance started off. I had just a share of the bow, but never another shot of her eye, and there was no more word of smiling.

"I guess it's all right," said Case. "I guess you can have her. I'll make it square with the old lady. You can have your pick of the lot for a plug of tobacco," he added, sneering.

I suppose it was the smile stuck in my memory, for I spoke back sharp. "She doesn't look that sort," I cried.

"I don't know that she is," said Case. "I believe she's as right as the mail. Keeps to herself, don't go round with the gang, and that. O no, don't you misunderstand me—Uma's on the square." He spoke eager, I thought, and that surprised and pleased me. "Indeed," he went on, "I shouldn't make so sure of getting her, only she cottoned to the cut of your jib. All you have to do is to keep dark and let me work the mother my own way; and I'll bring the girl round to the captain's for the marriage."

I didn't care for the word marriage, and I said so.

"O, there's nothing to hurt in the marriage," says he. "Black Jack's the chaplain."

By this time we had come in view of the house of these three white men; for a negro is counted a white man, and so is a Chinese! a strange idea, but common in the islands. It was a board house with a strip of rickety verandah. The store was to the front, with a counter, scales, and the poorest possible display of trade: a case or two of tinned meats, a barrel of hard bread, a few bolts of cotton stuff, not to be compared with mine; the only thing well represented being the contraband, firearms and liquor. "If these are my only rivals," thinks I, "I should do well in Falesá." Indeed, there was only the one way they could touch me, and that was with the guns and drink.

In the back room was old Captain Randall, squatting

on the floor native fashion, fat and pale, naked to the waist, grey as a badger, and his eyes set with drink. His body was covered with grey hair and crawled over by flies; one was in the corner of his eye—he never heeded; and the mosquitoes hummed about the man like bees. Any clean-minded man would have had the creature out at once and buried him; and to see him, and think he was seventy, and remember he had once commanded a ship, and come ashore in his smart togs, and talked big in bars and consulates, and sat in club verandahs, turned me sick and sober.

He tried to get up when I came in, but that was hopeless; so he reached me a hand instead, and stumbled out some salutation.

"Papa's pretty full this morning," observed Case. "We've had an epidemic here; and Captain Randall takes gin for a prophylactic—don't you, Papa?"

"Never took such a thing in my life!" cried the captain indignantly. "Take gin for my health's sake, Mr. Wha's-ever-your-name—'s a precautionary measure."

"That's all right, Papa," said Case. "But you'll have to brace up. There's going to be a marriage—Mr. Wiltshire here is going to get spliced."

The old man asked to whom.

"To Uma," said Case.

"Uma!" cried the captain. "Wha's he want Uma for? 's he come here for his health, anyway? Wha' 'n hell's he want Uma for?"

"Dry up, Papa," said Case. " 'Tain't you that's to marry her. I guess you're not her godfather and godmother. I guess Mr. Wiltshire's going to please himself."

With that he made an excuse to me that he must move about the marriage and left me alone with the poor wretch that was his partner and (to speak truth) his gull. Trade and station belonged both to Randall; Case and the negro were parasites; they crawled and fed upon him like the flies, he none the wiser. Indeed, I have no harm to say of Billy Randall beyond the fact that my gorge rose at him, and the time I now passed in his company was like a nightmare.

The room was stifling hot and full of flies; for the house was dirty and low and small, and stood in a bad place, behind the village, in the borders of the bush, and sheltered from the trade. The three men's beds were on the floor, and a litter of pans and dishes. There was no standing furniture; Randall, when he was violent, tearing it to laths. There I sat and had a meal which was served us by Case's wife; and there I was entertained all day by that remains of man, his tongue stumbling among low old jokes and long old stories, and his own wheezy laughter always ready, so that he had no sense of my depression. He was nipping gin all the while. Sometimes he fell asleep, and awoke again, whimpering and shivering, and every now and again he would ask me why I wanted to marry Uma. "My friend," I was telling myself all day, "you must not come to be an old gentleman like this."

It might be four in the afternoon, perhaps, when the back door was thrust slowly open, and a strange old native woman crawled into the house almost on her belly. She was swathed in black stuff to her heels; her hair was grey in swatches; her face was tattooed, which was not the practice in that island; her eyes big and bright and crazy. These she fixed upon me with a rapt expression that I saw to be part acting. She said no plain words, but smacked and mumbled with her lips, and hummed aloud, like a child over its Christmas pudding. She came straight across the house, heading for me, and, as soon as she was alongside, caught up my hand and purred and crooned over it like a great cat. From this she slipped into a kind of song.

"Who the devil's this?" cried I, for the thing startled me.

"It's Fa'avao," says Randall; and I saw he had hitched along the floor into the farthest corner.

"You ain't afraid of her?" I cried.

"Me 'fraid!" cried the captain. "My dear friend, I defy her! I don't let her put her foot in here, only I suppose 's different to-day, for the marriage. 's Uma's mother."

"Well, suppose it is; what's she carrying on about?" I asked, more irritated, perhaps more frightened, than I cared to show; and the captain told me she was making up a quantity of poetry in my praise because I was to marry Uma. "All right, old lady," says I, with rather a failure of a laugh, "anything to oblige. But when you're done with my hand, you might let me know."

She did as though she understood; the song rose into a cry, and stopped; the woman crouched out of the house the same way that she came in, and must have plunged straight into the bush, for when I followed her to the door she had already vanished.

"These are rum manners," said I.

" 's a rum crowd," said the captain, and, to my surprise, he made the sign of the cross on his bare bosom.

"Hillo!" says I, "are you a Papist?"

He repudiated the idea with contempt. "Hard-shell Baptis'," said he. "But, my dear friend, the Papists got some good ideas too; and tha' 's one of 'em. You take my advice, and whenever you come across Uma or Fa'avao or Vigours, or any of that crowd, you take a leaf out o' the priests, and do what I do. Savvy," says he, repeated the sign, and winked his dim eye at me. "No, *sir!*" he broke out again, "no Papists here!" and for a long time entertained me with his religious opinions.

I must have been taken with Uma from the first, or I should certainly have fled from that house, and got into the clean air, and the clean sea, or some convenient river—though, it's true, I was committed to Case; and, besides, I could never have held my head up in that island if I had run from a girl upon my wedding-night.

The sun was down, the sky all on fire, and the lamp had been some time lighted, when Case came back with Uma and the negro. She was dressed and scented; her kilt was of fine tapa, looking richer in the folds than any silk; her bust, which was of the colour of dark honey, she wore bare only for some half a dozen necklaces of seeds and flowers; and behind her ears and in her hair she had the scarlet flowers of the hibiscus. She showed the best bearing for a bride conceivable, serious and still; and I thought shame to stand up with her in that mean house and before that grinning negro. I thought shame, I say; for the mountebank was dressed with a big paper collar, the book he made believe to read from was an odd volume of a novel, and the words of his service not fit to be set down. My conscience smote me when we joined hands; and when she got her certificate I was tempted to throw up the bargain and confess. Here is the document. It was Case that wrote it, signatures and all, in a leaf out of the ledger:—

> This is to certify that Uma, daughter of Fa'avao of Falesá, island of——, is illegally married to Mr. John

Wiltshire for one week, and Mr. John Wiltshire is at liberty to send her to hell when he pleases.*

JOHN BLACKAMOAR,
Chaplain to the Hulks.

Extracted from the Register
by William T. Randall,
Master Mariner.

A nice paper to put in a girl's hand and see her hide away like gold. A man might easily feel cheap for less. But it was the practice in these parts, and (as I told myself) not the least the fault of us white men, but of the missionaries. If they had let the natives be, I had never needed this deception, but taken all the wives I wished, and left them when I pleased, with a clear conscience.

The more ashamed I was, the more hurry I was in to be gone; and our desires thus jumping together, I made the less remark of a change in the traders. Case had been all eagerness to keep me; now, as though he had attained a purpose, he seemed all eagerness to have me go. Uma, he said, could show me to my house, and the three bade us farewell indoors.

The night was nearly come; the village smelt of trees and flowers and the sea and breadfruit-cooking; there came a fine roll of sea from the reef, and from a distance, among the woods and houses many pretty sounds of men and children. It did me good to breathe free air; it did me good to be done with the captain and see, instead, the creature at my side. I felt for all the world as though she were some girl at home in the Old Country, and, forgetting myself for the minute, took her hand to walk with. Her fingers nestled into mine, I heard her breathe deep and quick, and all at once she caught my hand to her face and pressed it there. "You good!" she cried, and ran ahead of me, and stopped and looked back and smiled, and ran ahead of me again, thus guiding me through the edge of the bush, and by a quiet way to my own house.

The truth is, Case had done the courting for me in style—told her I was mad to have her, and cared nothing for the consequence; and the poor soul, knowing that which I was still ignorant of, believed it, every word, and

*Subsequent editions have restored what Stevenson originally wrote: "is illegally married to Mr. John Wiltshire for one night, and Mr. John Wiltshire is at liberty to send her to hell the next morning."

had her head nigh turned with vanity and gratitude. Now, of all this I had no guess; I was one of those most opposed to any nonsense about native women, having seen so many whites eaten up by their wives' relatives, and made fools of in the bargain; and I told myself I must make a stand at once, and bring her to her bearings. But she looked so quaint and pretty as she ran away and then awaited me, and the thing was done so like a child or a kind dog, that the best I could do was just to follow her whenever she went on, to listen for the fall of her bare feet, and to watch in the dusk for the shining of her body. And there was another thought came in my head. She played kitten with me now when we were alone; but in the house she had carried it the way a countess might, so proud and humble. And what with her dress—for all there was so little of it, and that native enough—what with her fine tapa and fine scents, and her red flowers and seeds, that were quite as bright as jewels, only larger—it came over me she was a kind of countess really, dressed to hear great singers at a concert, and no even mate for a poor trader like myself.

She was the first in the house; and while I was still without I saw a match flash and the lamplight kindle in the windows. The station was a wonderful fine place, coral built, with quite a wide verandah, and the main room high and wide. My chests and cases had been piled in, and made rather of a mess; and there, in the thick of the confusion, stood Uma by the table, awaiting me. Her shadow went all the way up behind her into the hollow of the iron roof; she stood against it bright, the lamplight shining on her skin. I stopped in the door, and she looked at me, not speaking, with eyes that were eager and yet daunted; then she touched herself on the bosom.

"Me—your wife," she said. It had never taken me like that before; but the want of her took and shook all through me, like the wind in the luff of a sail.

I could not speak if I had wanted; and if I could, I would not. I was ashamed to be so much moved about a native, ashamed of the marriage too, and the certificate she had treasured in her kilt; and I turned aside and made believe to rummage among my cases. The first thing I lighted on was a case of gin, the only one that I had brought; and, partly for the girl's sake, and partly for horror of the recollections of old Randall, took a sudden resolve. I prised the lid off. One by one I drew the bottles with a pocket corkscrew, and sent Uma out to pour the stuff from the verandah.

She came back after the last, and looked at me puzzled like.

"No good," said I, for I was now a little better master of my tongue. "Man he drink, he no good."

She agreed with this, but kept considering. "Why you bring him?" she asked presently. "Suppose you no want drink, you no bring him, I think."

"That's all right," said I. "One time I want drink too much; now no want. You see, I no savvy I get one little wifie. Suppose I drink gin, my little wifie be 'fraid."

To speak to her kindly was about more than I was fit for; I had made my vow I would never let on to weakness with a native, and I had nothing for it but to stop.

She stood looking gravely down at me where I sat by the open case. "I think you good man," she said. And suddenly she had fallen before me on the floor. "I belong you all-e-same pig!" she cried.

CHAPTER II

THE BAN

I CAME ON the verandah just before the sun rose on the morrow. My house was the last on the east; there was a cape of woods and cliffs behind that hid the sunrise. To the west, a swift cold river ran down, and beyond was the green of the village, dotted with cocoa-palms and bread-fruits and houses. The shutters were some of them down and some open; I saw the mosquito bars still stretched, with shadows of people new-awakened sitting up inside; and all over the green others were stalking silent, wrapped in their many-coloured sleeping clothes like Bedouins in Bible pictures. It was mortal still and solemn and chilly, and the light of the dawn on the lagoon was like the shining of a fire.

But the thing that troubled me was nearer hand. Some dozen young men and children made a piece of a half-circle, flanking my house: the river divided them, some were on the near side, some on the far, and one on a boulder in the midst; and they all sat silent, wrapped in their sheets, and stared at me and my house as straight as pointer dogs. I thought it strange as I went out. When I had bathed and come back again, and found them all there, and two or three more along with them, I thought it stranger still. What could they see to gaze at in my house, I wondered, and went in.

But the thought of these starers stuck in my mind, and presently I came out again. The sun was now up, but it was still behind the cape of woods. Say a quarter of an hour had come and gone. The crowd was greatly increased, the far bank of the river was lined for quite a way—perhaps thirty grown folk, and of children twice as many, some standing, some squatted on the ground, and all staring at my house. I have seen a house in the South Sea village thus surrounded, but then a trader was thrashing his wife inside, and she singing out. Here was nothing: the stove was alight, the smoke going up in a Christian manner; all was shipshape and Bristol fashion. To be sure, there was a stranger come, but they had a chance to see that stranger yesterday, and took it quiet enough. What ailed them now? I leaned my arms on the rail and stared back. Devil a wink they had in them! Now and then I could see the children chatter, but they spoke so low not even the hum of their speaking came my length. The rest were like graven images: they stared at me, dumb and sorrowful, with their bright eyes; and it came upon me things would look not much different if I were on the platform of the gallows, and these good folk had come to see me hanged.

I felt I was getting daunted, and began to be afraid I looked it, which would never do. Up I stood, made believe to stretch myself, came down the verandah stair, and strolled towards the river. There went a short buzz from one to the other, like what you hear in theatres when the curtain goes up; and some of the nearest gave back the matter of a pace. I saw a girl lay one hand on a young man and make a gesture upward with the other; at the same time she said something in the native with a gasping voice. Three little boys sat beside my path, where I must pass within three feet of them. Wrapped in their sheets, with their shaved heads and bits of top-knots, and queer faces, they looked like figures on a chimney-piece. A while they sat their ground, solemn as judges. I came up hand over fist, doing my five knots, like a man that meant business; and I thought I saw a sort of wink and a gulp in the three faces. Then one jumped up (he was the farthest off) and ran for his mammy. The other two, trying to follow suit, got foul, came to ground together bawling, wriggled right out of their sheets mother-naked, and in a moment there were all three of them scampering for their lives and singing out like pigs. The natives, who would never let a joke slip, even at a burial, laughed and let up, as short as a dog's bark.

They say it scares a man to be alone. No such thing. What scares him in the dark or the high bush is that he can't make sure, and there might be an army at his elbow. What scares him worst is to be right in the midst of a crowd, and have no guess of what they're driving at. When that laugh stopped, I stopped too. The boys had not yet made their offing, they were still on the full stretch going the one way, when I had already gone about ship and was sheering off the other. Like a fool I had come out, doing my five knots; like a fool I went back again. It must have been the funniest thing to see, and, what knocked me silly, this time no one laughed; only one old woman gave a kind of pious moan, the way you have heard Dissenters in their chapels at the sermon.

"I never saw such fools of Kanakas as your people here," I said once to Uma, glancing out of the window at the starers.

"Savvy nothing," says Uma, with a kind of disgusted air that she was good at.

And that was all the talk we had upon the matter, for I was put out, and Uma took the thing so much as a matter of course that I was fairly ashamed.

All day, off and on, now fewer and now more, the fools sat about the west end of my house and across the river, waiting for the show, whatever that was—fire to come down from heaven, I suppose, and consume me, bones and baggage. But by evening, like real islanders, they had wearied of the business, and got away, and had a dance instead in the big house of the village, where I heard them singing and clapping hands till, maybe, ten at night, and the next day it seemed they had forgotten I existed. If fire had come down from heaven or the earth opened and swallowed me, there would have been no-body to see the sport or take the lesson, or whatever you like to call it. But I was to find that they hadn't forgot either, and kept an eye lifting for phenomena over my way.

I was hard at it both these days getting my trade in order and taking stock of what Vigours had left. This was a job that made me pretty sick, and kept me from thinking on much else. Ben had taken stock the trip before—I knew I could trust Ben—but it was plain somebody had been making free in the meantime. I found I was out by what might easily cover six months' salary and profit, and I could have kicked myself all round the village to have been such a blamed ass, sitting boozing with that Case instead of attending to my own affairs and taking stock.

However, there's no use crying over spilt milk. It was done now, and couldn't be undone. All I could do was to get what was left of it, and my new stuff (my own choice) in order, to go round and get after the rats and cockroaches, and to fix up that store regular Sydney style. A fine show I made of it; and the third morning when I had lit my pipe and stood in the doorway and looked in, and turned and looked far up the mountain and saw the cocoa-nuts waving and posted up the tons of copra, and over the village green and saw the island dandies and reckoned up the yards of print they wanted for their kilts and dresses, I felt as if I was in the right place to make a fortune, and go home again and start a public-house. There was I, sitting in that verandah, in as handsome a piece of scenery as you could find, a splendid sun, and a fine, fresh, healthy trade that stirred up a man's blood like sea-bathing; and the whole thing was clean gone from me, and I was dreaming England, which is, after all, a nasty, cold, muddy hole, with not enough light to see to read by; and dreaming the looks of my public, by a cant of a broad high-road like an avenue, and with the sign on a green tree.

So much for the morning; but the day passed and the devil any one looked near me, and from all I knew of natives in other islands I thought this strange. People laughed a little at our firm and their fine stations, and at this station of Falesá in particular; all the copra in the district wouldn't pay for it (I had heard them say) in fifty years, which I supposed was an exaggeration. But when the day went, and no business came at all, I began to get downhearted; and, about three in the afternoon, I went out for a stroll to cheer me up. On the green I saw a white man coming with a cassock on, by which and by the face of him I knew he was a priest. He was a good-natured old soul to look at, gone a little grizzled, and so dirty you could have written with him on a piece of paper.

"Good day, sir," said I.

He answered me eagerly in native.

"Don't you speak any English?" said I.

"French," says he.

"Well," said I, "I'm sorry, but I can't do anything there."

He tried me a while in the French, and then again in native, which he seemed to think was the best chance. I made out he was after more than passing the time of day with me, but had something to communicate, and I listened the harder. I heard the names of Adams and Case and of Randall—Randall the oftenest—and the word "poison," or something like it, and a native word that he said very often. I went home, repeating it to myself.

"What does fussy-ocky mean?" I asked of Uma, for that was as near as I could come to it.

"Make dead," said she.

"The devil it does!" says I. "Did you ever hear that Case had poisoned Johnny Adams?"

"Every man he savvy that," says Uma, scornful-like. "Give him white sand—bad sand. He got the bottle still. Suppose he give you gin, you no take him."

Now I had heard much the same sort of story in other islands, and the same white powder always to the front, which made me think the less of it. For all that, I went over to Randall's place to see what I could pick up, and found Case on the doorstep, cleaning a gun.

"Good shooting here?" says I.

"A1," says he. "The bush is full of all kinds of birds. I wish copra was as plenty," says he—I thought, slyly—"but there don't seem anything doing."

I could see Black Jack in the store, serving a customer.

"That looks like business, though," said I.

"That's the first sale we've made in three weeks," said he.

"You don't tell me?" says I. "Three weeks? Well, well."

"If you don't believe me," he cries, a little hot, "you can go and look at the copra-house. It's half empty to this blessed hour."

"I shouldn't be much the better for that, you see," says I. "For all I can tell, it might have been whole empty yesterday."

"That's so," says he, with a bit of a laugh.

"By the by," I said, "what sort of a party is that priest? Seems rather a friendly sort."

At this Case laughed right out loud. "Ah!" says he, "I see what ails you now. Galuchet's been at you." *Father Galoshes* was the name he went by most, but Case always gave it the French quirk, which was another reason we had for thinking him above the common.

"Yes, I have seen him," I says. "I made out he didn't think much of your Captain Randall."

"That he don't!" says Case. "It was the trouble about poor Adams. The last day, when he lay dying, there was young Buncombe round. Ever met Buncombe?"

I told him no.

"He's a cure, is Buncombe!" laughs Case. "Well, Buncombe took it in his head that, as there was no other clergyman about, bar Kanaka pastors, we ought to call in Father Galuchet, and have the old man administered and take the sacrament. It was all the same to me, you may suppose; but I said I thought Adams was the fellow to consult. He was jawing away about watered copra and a sight of foolery. 'Look here,' I said, 'you're pretty sick. Would you like to see Galoshes?' He sat right up on his elbow. 'Get the priest,' says he, 'get the priest; don't let me die here like a dog!' He spoke kind of fierce and eager, but sensible enough. There was nothing to say against that, so we sent and asked Galuchet if he would come. You bet he would. He jumped in his dirty linen at the thought of it. But we had reckoned without Papa. He's a hard-shell Baptist, is Papa; no Papists need apply. And he took and locked the door. Buncombe told him he was bigoted, and I thought he would have had a fit. 'Bigoted!' he says. 'Me bigoted? Have I lived to hear it from a jackanapes like you?' And he made for Buncombe, and I had to hold them apart; and there was Adams in the middle, gone luny again, and carrying on about copra like a born fool. It was good as the play, and I was about knocked out of time with laughing, when all of a sudden Adams sat up, clapped his hands to his chest, and went into horrors. He died hard, did John Adams," says Case, with a kind of a sudden sternness.

"And what became of the priest?" I asked.

"The priest?" says Case. "O! he was hammering on the door outside, and crying on the natives to come and beat it in, and singing out it was a soul he wished to save, and that. He was in a rare taking, was the priest. But what would you have? Johnny had slipped his cable: no more Johnny in the market; and the administration racket clean played out. Next thing, word came to Randall the priest was praying upon Johnny's grave. Papa was pretty full, and got a club, and lit out straight for the place, and there was Galoshes on his knees, and a lot of natives looking on. You wouldn't think Papa cared that much about anything, unless it was liquor; but he and the priest stuck to it two hours, slanging each other in native, and every time Galoshes tried to kneel down Papa went for him with the club. There never were such larks in Falesá. The end of it was that Captain Randall was knocked over with some kind of a fit or stroke, and the priest got in his goods after all. But he was the angriest priest you ever heard of, and complained to the chiefs about the outrage, as he called it. That was no account, for our chiefs are Protestant here; and, anyway, he had been making trouble about the drum for morning school, and they were glad to give him a wipe. Now he swears old Randall gave Adams poison or something, and when the two meet they grin at each other like baboons."

He told the story as natural as could be, and like a man that enjoyed the fun; though, now I come to think of it after so long, it seems rather a sickening yarn. However, Case never set up to be soft, only to be square and hearty, and a man all round; and, to tell the truth, he puzzled me entirely.

I went home and asked Uma if she were a Popey, which I had made out to be the native word for Catholics.

"*E le ai!*" says she. She always used the native when she meant "no" more than usually strong, and, indeed, there's more of it. "No good Popey," she added.

Then I asked her about Adams and the priest, and she told me much the same yarn in her own way. So that I was left not much further on, but inclined, upon the whole, to think the bottom of the matter was the row about the sacrament, and the poisoning only talk.

The next day was a Sunday, when there was no business to be looked for. Uma asked me in the morning if I was going to "pray"; I told her she bet not, and she stopped home herself with no more words. I thought this seemed unlike a native, and a native woman, and a woman that had new clothes to show off; however, it suited me to the ground, and I made the less of it. The queer thing was that I came next door to going to church after all, a thing I'm little likely to forget. I had turned out for a stroll, and heard the hymn tune up. You know how it is. If you hear folk singing, it seems to draw you: and pretty soon I found myself alongside the church. It was a little, long, low place, coral built, rounded off at both ends like a whale-boat, a big native roof on the top of it, windows without sashes and doorways without doors. I stuck my head into one of the windows, and the sight was so new to me—for things went quite different in the islands I was acquainted with—that I stayed and looked on. The congregation sat on the floor on mats, the women on one side, the men on the other, all rigged out to kill—the women with dresses and trade hats, the men in white jackets and shirts. The hymn was over; the pastor, a big buck Kanaka, was in the pulpit, preaching for his life; and by the way he wagged his hand, and worked his voice, and made his points, and seemed to argue with the folk, I made out he was a gun at the business. Well, he looked up suddenly and caught my eye, and I give you my word he staggered in the pulpit; his eyes bulged out of his head, his hand rose and pointed at me like as if against his will, and the sermon stopped right there.

It isn't a fine thing to say for yourself, but I ran away; and if the same kind of a shock was given me, I should run away again to-morrow. To see that palavering Kanaka struck all of a heap at the mere sight of me gave me a feeling as if the bottom had dropped out of the world. I went right home, and stayed there, and said nothing. You might think I would tell Uma, but that was against my system. You might have thought I would have gone over and consulted Case; but the truth was I was ashamed to speak of such a thing, I thought every one would blurt out laughing in my face. So I held my tongue, and thought all the more; and the more I thought, the less I liked the business.

By Monday night I got it clearly in my head I must be tabooed. A new store to stand open two days in a village and not a man or woman come to see the trade was past believing.

"Uma," said I, "I think I am tabooed."

"I think so," said she.

I thought a while whether I should ask her more, but it's a bad idea to set natives up with any notion of consulting them, so I went to Case. It was dark, and he was sitting alone, as he did mostly, smoking on the stairs.

"Case," said I, "here's a queer thing. I'm tabooed."

"O, fudge!" says he, " 'tain't the practice in these islands."

"That may be, or it mayn't," said I. "It's the practice where I was before. You can bet I know what it's like; and I tell it you for a fact, I'm tabooed."

"Well," said he, "what have you been doing?"

"That's what I want to find out," said I.

"O, you can't be," said he; "it ain't possible. However, I'll tell you what I'll do. Just to put your mind at rest, I'll go round and find out for sure. Just you waltz in and talk to Papa."

"Thank you," I said, "I'd rather stay right out here on the verandah. Your house is so close."

"I'll call Papa out here, then," says he.

"My dear fellow," I says, "I wish you wouldn't. The fact is, I don't take to Mr. Randall."

Case laughed, took a lantern from the store, and set out into the village. He was gone perhaps a quarter of an hour, and he looked mighty serious when he came back.

"Well," said he, clapping down the lantern on the verandah steps. "I would never have believed it. I don't know where the impudence of these Kanakas 'll go next; they seem to have lost all idea of respect for whites. What we want is a man-o-war—a German, if we could—they know how to manage Kanakas."

"I *am* tabooed, then?" I cried.

"Something of the sort," said he. "It's the worst thing of the kind I've heard of yet. But I'll stand by you, Wiltshire, man to man. You come round here to-morrow about nine, and we'll have it out with the chiefs. They're afraid of me, or they used to be; but their heads are so big by now, I don't know what to think. Understand me, Wiltshire; I don't count this your quarrel," he went on, with a great deal of resolution, "I count it all of our quarrel, I count it the White Man's Quarrel, and I'll stand to it through thick and thin, and there's my hand on it."

"Have you found out what's the reason?" I asked.

"Not yet," said Case. "But we'll fix them down to-morrow."

Altogether I was pretty well pleased with his attitude, and almost more the next day, when we met to go before the chiefs, to see him so stern and resolved. The chiefs awaited us in one of their big oval houses, which was marked out to us from a long way off by the crowd about the eaves, a hundred strong if there was one—men, women, and children. Many of the men were on their way to work and wore green wreaths, and it put me in thoughts of the 1st of May at home. This crowd opened and buzzed about the pair of us as we went in, with a sudden angry animation. Five chiefs were there; four mighty stately men, the fifth old and puckered. They sat on mats in their white kilts and jackets; they had fans in their hands, like fine ladies; and two of the younger ones wore Catholic medals, which gave me matter of reflection. Our place was set, and the mats laid for us over against these grandees, on the near side of the house; the midst was empty; the crowd, close at our backs, murmured, and craned, and jostled to look on, and the shadows of them tossed in front of us on the clean pebbles of the floor. I was just a hair put out by the excitement of the commons, but the quiet, civil appearance of the chiefs reassured me, all the more when their spokesman began and made a long speech in a low tone of voice, sometimes waving his hand towards Case, sometimes towards me and sometimes knocking with his knuckles on the mat. One thing was clear: there was no sign of anger in the chiefs.

"What's he been saying?" I asked, when he had done.

"O, just that they're glad to see you, and they understand by me you wish to make some kind of complaint, and you're to fire away, and they'll do the square thing."

"It took a precious long time to say that," said I.

"O, the rest was sawder and *bonjour* and that," said Case. "You know what Kanakas are."

"Well, they don't get much *bonjour* out of me," said I. "You tell them who I am. I'm a white man, and a British subject, and no end of a big chief at home; and I've come here to do them good, and bring them civilisation; and no sooner have I got my trade sorted out than they go and taboo me, and no one dare come near my place!

Tell them I don't mean to fly in the face of anything legal; and if what they want's a present, I'll do what's fair. I don't blame any man looking out for himself, tell them, for that's human nature; but if they think they're going to come any of their native ideas over me, they'll find themselves mistaken. And tell them plain that I demand the reason of this treatment as a white man and a British subject."

That was my speech. I know how to deal with Kanakas: give them plain sense and fair dealing, and—I'll do them that much justice—they knuckle under every time. They haven't any real government or any real law, that's what you've got to knock into their heads; and even if they had, it would be a good joke if it was to apply to a white man. It would be a strange thing if we came all this way and couldn't do what we pleased. The mere idea has always put my monkey up, and I rapped my speech out pretty big. Then Case translated it—or made believe to, rather—and the first chief replied, and then a second, and a third, all in the same style, easy and genteel, but solemn underneath. Once a question was put to Case, and he answered it, and all hands (both chiefs and commons) laughed out aloud, and looked at me. Last of all, the puckered old fellow and the big young chief that spoke first started in to put Case through a kind of catechism. Sometimes I made out that Case was trying to fence and stuck to him like hounds, and the sweat ran down his face, which was no very pleasant sight to me, and at some of his answers the crowd moaned and murmured, which was worse a hearing. It's a cruel shame I knew no native, for (as I now believe) they were asking Case about my marriage, and must have had a tough job of it to clear his feet. But leave Case alone; he had the brains to run a parliament.

"Well, is that all?" I asked, when a pause came.

"Come along," says he, mopping his face; "I'll tell you outside."

"Do you mean they won't take the taboo off?" I cried.

"It's something queer," said he. "I'll tell you outside. Better come away."

"I won't take it at their hands," cried I. "I ain't that kind of a man. You don't find me turn my back on a parcel of Kanakas."

"You'd better," said Case.

He looked at me with a signal in his eye; and the five chiefs looked at me civilly enough, but kind of pointed; and the people looked at me, and craned and jostled. I remembered the folks that watched my house, and how the pastor had jumped in his pulpit at the bare sight of me; and the whole business seemed so out of the way that I rose and followed Case. The crowd opened again to let us through, but wider than before, the children on the skirts running and singing out, and as we two white men walked away they all stood and watched us.

"And now," said I, "what is all this about?"

"The truth is, I can't rightly make it out myself. They have a down on you," says Case.

"Taboo a man because they have a down on him!" I cried. "I never heard the like."

"It's worse than that, you see," said Case. "You ain't tabooed—I told you that couldn't be. The people won't go near you, Wiltshire, and there's where it is."

"They won't go near me? What do you mean by that? Why won't they go near me?" I cried.

Case hesitated. "Seems they're frightened," says he in a low voice.

I stopped dead short. "Frightened?" I repeated. "Are you gone crazy, Case? What are they frightened of?"

"I wish I could make out," Case answered, shaking his head. "Appears like one of their tomfool superstitions. That's what I don't cotton to," he said. "It's like the business about Vigours."

"I'd like to know what you mean by that, and I'll trouble you to tell me," says I.

"Well, you know, Vigours lit out and left all standing," said he. "It was some superstition business—I never got the hang of it; but it began to look bad before the end."

"I've heard a different story about that," said I, "and I had better tell you so. I heard he ran away because of you."

"O! well, I suppose he was ashamed to tell the truth," says Case; "I guess he thought it silly. And it's a fact that I packed him off. 'What would you do, old man?' says he.—'Get,' says I, 'and not think twice about it.' I was the gladdest kind of man to see him clear away. It ain't my notion to turn my back on a mate when he's in a tight place, but there was that much trouble in the village that I couldn't see where it might likely end. I was a fool to be so much about with Vigours. They cast it up to me to-day. Didn't you hear Maea—that's the young chief, the big one—ripping out about 'Vika'? That was him they were after. They don't seem to forget it, somehow."

"This is all very well," said I, "but it don't tell me what's wrong; it don't tell me what they're afraid of—what their idea is."

"Well, I wish I knew," said Case. "I can't say fairer than that."

"You might have asked, I think," says I.

"And so I did," says he. "But you must have seen for yourself, unless you're blind, that the asking got the other way. I'll go as far as I dare for another white man; but when I find I'm in the scrape myself, I think first of my own bacon. The loss of me is I'm too good-natured. And I'll take the freedom of telling you you show a queer kind of gratitude to a man who's got into all this mess along of your affairs."

"There's a thing I am thinking of," said I. "You were a fool to be so much about with Vigours. One comfort, you haven't been much about with me. I notice you've never been inside my house. Own up now; you had word of this before?"

"It's a fact I haven't been," said he. "It was an oversight, and I am sorry for it, Wiltshire. But about coming now, I'll be quite plain."

"You mean you won't?" I asked.

"Awfully sorry, old man, but that's the size of it," says Case.

"In short, you're afraid?" says I.

"In short, I'm afraid," says he.

"And I'm still to be tabooed for nothing?" I asked.

"I tell you you're not tabooed," said he. "The Kanakas won't go near you, that's all. And who's to make 'em? We traders have a lot of gall, I must say; we make these poor Kanakas take back their laws, and take up their taboos, and that whenever it happens to suit us. But you don't mean to say you expect a law-obliging people to deal in your store whether they want to or not? You don't mean to tell me you've got the gall for that? And if you had, it would be a queer thing to propose to me. I would just like to point out to you, Wiltshire, that I'm a trader myself."

"I don't think I would talk of gall if I was you," said I.

"Here's about what it comes to, as well as I can make out: None of the people are to trade with me, and they're all to trade with you. You're to have the copra, and I'm to go to the devil and shake myself. And I don't know any native, and you're the only man here worth mention that speaks English, and you have the gall to up and hint to me my life's in danger, and all you've got to tell me is you don't know why!"

"Well, it *is* all I have to tell you," said he. "I don't know—I wish I did."

"And so you turn your back and leave me to myself. Is that the position?" says I.

"If you like to put it nasty," says he. "I don't put it so. I say merely, 'I'm going to keep clear of you; or, if I don't, I'll get in danger for myself.' "

"Well," says I, "you're a nice kind of white man!"

"O, I understand; you're riled," said he. "I would be, myself. I can make excuses."

"All right," I said, "go and make excuses somewhere else. Here's my way, there's yours!"

With that we parted, and I went straight home, in a hot temper, and found Uma trying on a lot of trade goods like a baby.

"Here," I said, "you quit that foolery! Here's a pretty mess to have made, as if I wasn't bothered enough anyway! And I thought I told you to get dinner!"

And then I believe I gave her a bit of the rough side of my tongue, as she deserved. She stood up at once, like a sentry to his officer; for I must say she was always well brought up, and had a great respect for whites.

"And now," says I, "you belong round here, you're bound to understand this. What am I tabooed for, anyway? Or, if I ain't tabooed, what makes the folks afraid of me?"

She stood and looked at me with eyes like saucers.

"You no savvy?" she gasps at last.

"No," said I. "How would you expect me to? We don't have any such craziness where I come from."

"Ese no tell you?" she asked again.

(*Ese* was the name the natives had for Case; it may mean foreign, or extraordinary; or it might mean a mummy apple; but most like it was only his own name misheard and put in a Kanaka spelling.)

"Not much," said I.

"Damn Ese!" she cried.

You might think it funny to hear this Kanaka girl come out with a big swear. No such thing. There was no swearing in her—no, nor anger; she was beyond anger, and meant the word simple and serious. She stood there straight as she said it. I cannot justly say that I ever saw a woman look like that before or after, and it struck me mum. Then she made a kind of an obeisance, but it was the proudest kind, and threw her hands out open.

"I 'shamed," she said. "I think you savvy. Ese he tell me you savvy, he tell me you no mind, tell me you love me too much. Taboo belong me," she said, touching herself on the bosom, as she had done upon our wedding-night. "Now I go 'way, taboo he go 'way too. Then you get too much copra. You like more better, I think. *Tofâ, alii,*" says she in the native—"Farewell, chief!"

"Hold on!" I cried. "Don't be in such a hurry."

She looked at me sidelong with a smile. "You see you get copra," she said, the same as you might offer candies to a child.

"Uma," said I, "hear reason. I didn't know, and that's a fact; and Case seems to have played it pretty mean upon the pair of us. But I do know now, and I don't mind; I love you too much. You no go 'way, you no leave me, I too much sorry."

"You no love me," she cried, "you talk me bad words!" And she threw herself in a corner of the floor, and began to cry.

Well, I'm no scholar, but I wasn't born yesterday, and I thought the worst of that trouble was over. However, there she lay—her back turned, her face to the wall—and shook with sobbing like a little child, so that her feet jumped with it. It's strange how it hits a man when he's in love; for there's no use mincing things—Kanaka and all, I was in love with her, or just as good. I tried to take her hand, but she would none of that. "Uma," I said, "there's no sense in carrying on like this. I want you stop here, I want my little wifie, I tell you true."

"No tell me true," she sobbed.

"All right," says I, "I'll wait till you're through with this." And I sat right down beside her on the floor, and set to smooth her hair with my hand. At first she wriggled away when I touched her; then she seemed to notice me no more; then her sobs grew gradually less, and presently stopped; and the next thing I knew, she raised her face to mine.

"You tell me true? You like me stop?" she asked.

"Uma," I said, "I would rather have you than all the copra in the South Seas," which was a very big expression, and the strangest thing was that I meant it.

She threw her arms about me, sprang close up, and pressed her face to mine in the island way of kissing, so that I was all wetted with her tears, and my heart went out to her wholly. I never had anything so near me as this little brown bit of a girl. Many things went together, and all helped to turn my head. She was pretty enough to eat; it seemed she was my only friend in that queer place; I was ashamed that I had spoken rough to her: and she was a woman, and my wife, and a kind of a baby besides that I was sorry for; and the salt of her tears was in my mouth. And I forgot Case and the natives; and I forgot that I knew nothing of the story, or only remembered it to banish the remembrance; and I forgot that I was to get no copra, and so could make no livelihood; and I forgot my employers, and the strange kind of service I was doing them, when I preferred my fancy to their business; and I forgot even that Uma was no true wife of mine, but just a maid beguiled, and that in a pretty shabby style. But that is to look too far on. I will come to that part of it next.

It was late before we thought of getting dinner. The stove was out, and gone stone-cold; but we fired up after a while, and cooked each a dish, helping and hindering each other, and making a play of it like children. I was so greedy of her nearness that I sat down to dinner with my lass upon my knee, made sure of her with one hand, and ate with the other. Ay, and more than that. She was the worst cook, I suppose, God made; the things she set her hand to, it would have sickened an honest horse to eat of; yet I made my meal that day on Uma's cookery, and can never call to mind to have been better pleased.

I didn't pretend to myself, and I didn't pretend to her. I saw that I was clean gone; and if she was to make a fool of me, she must. And I suppose it was this that set her talking, for now she made sure that we were friends. A lot she told me, sitting in my lap and eating my dish, as I ate hers, from foolery—a lot about herself and her mother and Case, all which would be very tedious, and fill sheets if I set it down in Beach de Mar, but which I must give a hint of in plain English, and one thing about myself, which had a very big effect on my concerns, as you are soon to hear.

It seems she was born in one of the Line Islands; had been only two or three years in these parts, where she had come with a white man, who was married to her mother and then died; and only the one year in Falesá. Before that they had been a good deal on the move, trekking about after the white man, who was one of those rolling stones that keep going round after a soft job. They talk about looking for gold at the end of a rainbow; if a man wants an employment that'll last him till he dies, let him start out on the soft-job hunt. There's meat and drink in it too, and beer and skittles, for you never hear of them starving, and rarely see them sober; and as for steady sport, cock-fighting isn't in the same county with it. Anyway, this beachcomber carried the woman and her daughter all over the shop, but mostly to out-of-the-way islands, where there were no police, and he thought, perhaps, the soft job hung out. I've my own view of this old party; but I was just as glad he had kept Uma clear of Apia and Papeete and these flash towns. At last he struck Fale-alii on this island, got some trade—the Lord knows how!—muddled it all away in the usual style, and died worth next to nothing, bar a bit of land at Falesá that he had got for a bad debt, which was what put it in the minds of the mother and daughter to come there and live. It seems Case encouraged them all he could, and helped to get their house built. He was very kind those days, and gave Uma trade, and there is no doubt he had his eye on her from the beginning. However, they had scarce settled, when up turned a young man, a native, and wanted to marry her. He was a small chief, and had some fine mats and old songs in his family, and was "very pretty," Uma said; and, altogether, it was an extraordinary match for a penniless girl and an out-islander.

At the first word of this I got downright sick with jealousy.

"And you mean to say you would have married him?" I cried.

"*Ioe*, yes," said she. "I like too much!"

"Well!" I said. "And suppose I had come round after?"

"I like you more better now," said she. "But, suppose I marry Ioane, I one good wife. I no common Kanaka. Good girl!" says she.

Well, I had to be pleased with that; but I promise you I didn't care about the business one little bit. And I liked the end of that yarn no better than the beginning. For it seems this proposal of marriage was the start of all the trouble. It seems, before that, Uma and her mother had been looked down upon, of course, for kinless folk and out-islanders, but nothing to hurt; and, even when Ioane came forward, there was less trouble at first than might have been looked for. And then, all of a sudden, about six months before my coming, Ioane backed out and left that part of the island, and from that day to this Uma and her mother had found themselves alone. None called at their house, none spoke to them on the roads. If they went to church, the other women drew their mats away and left them in a clear place by themselves. It was a regular excommunication, like what you read of in the Middle Ages, and the cause or sense of it beyond guessing. It was some *tala pepelo,* Uma said, some lie, some calumny; and all she knew of it was that the girls who had been jealous of her luck with Ioane used to twit her with his desertion, and cry out, when they met her alone in the woods, that she would never be married. "They tell me no man he marry me. He too much 'fraid," she said.

The only soul that came about them after this desertion was Master Case. Even he was chary of showing himself, and turned up mostly by night; and pretty soon he began to table his cards and make up to Uma. I was still sore about Ioane, and when Case turned up in the same line of business I cut up downright rough.

"Well," I said, sneering, "and I suppose you thought Case 'very pretty' and 'liked too much'?"

"Now you talk silly," said she. "White man, he come here, I marry him all-e-same Kanaka; very well, then he marry me all-e-same white woman. Suppose he no marry, he go 'way, woman he stop. All-e-same thief, empty hand, Tonga-heart—no can love! Now you come marry me. You big heart—you no 'shamed island-girl. That thing I love you for too much. I proud."

I don't know that ever I felt sicker all the days of my life. I laid down my fork, and I put away "the island-girl";

I didn't seem somehow to have any use for either, and I went and walked up and down in the house, and Uma followed me with her eyes, for she was troubled, and small wonder! But troubled was no word for it with me. I so wanted, and so feared, to make a clean breast of the sweep that I had been.

And just then there came a sound of singing out of the sea; it sprang up suddenly clear and near, as the boat turned the headland, and Uma, running to the window, cried out it was "Misi" come upon his rounds.

I thought it was a strange thing I should be glad to have a missionary; but, if it was strange, it was still true.

"Uma," said I, "you stop here in this room, and don't budge a foot out of it till I come back."

CHAPTER III

THE MISSIONARY

As I CAME out on the verandah, the mission-boat was shooting for the mouth of the river. She was a long whale-boat painted white; a bit of an awning astern; a native pastor crouched on the wedge of the poop, steering; some four-and-twenty paddles flashing and dipping, true to the boat-song; and the missionary under the awning, in his white clothes, reading in a book, and set him up! It was pretty to see and hear; there's no smarter sight in the islands than a missionary boat with a good crew and a good pipe to them; and I considered it for half a minute, with a bit of envy perhaps, and then strolled down towards the river.

From the opposite side there was another man aiming for the same place, but he ran and got there first. It was Case; doubtless his idea was to keep me apart from the missionary, who might serve me as interpreter; but my mind was upon other things. I was thinking how he had jockeyed us about the marriage, and tried his hand on Uma before, and at the sight of him rage flew into my nostrils.

"Get out of that, you low swindling thief!" I cried.

"What's that you say?" says he.

I gave him the word again, and rammed it down with a

good oath. "And if ever I catch you within six fathoms of my house," I cried, "I'll clap a bullet in your measly carcase."

"You must do as you like about your house," said he, "where I told you I have no thought of going; but this is a public place."

"It's a place where I have private business," said I. "I have no idea of a hound like you eavesdropping, and I give you notice to clear out."

"I don't take it, though," says Case.

"I'll show you, then," said I.

"We'll have to see about that," said he.

He was quick with his hands, but he had neither the height nor the weight, being a flimsy creature alongside a man like me, and, besides, I was blazing to that height of wrath that I could have bit into a chisel. I gave him first the one and then the other, so that I could hear his head rattle and crack, and he went down straight.

"Have you had enough?" cried I. But he only looked up white and blank, and the blood spread up on his face like wine upon a napkin. "Have you had enough?" I cried again. "Speak up, and don't be malingering there, or I'll take my feet to you."

He sat up at that, and held his head—by the look of him you could see it was spinning—and the blood poured on his pyjamas.

"I've had enough for this time," says he, and he got up staggering, and went off by the way that he had come.

The boat was close in; I saw the missionary had laid his book to one side, and I smiled to myself. "He'll know I'm a man, anyway," thinks I.

This was the first time, in all my years in the Pacific, I had ever exchanged two words with any missionary, let alone asked for a favour. I didn't like the lot—no trader does; they look down upon us, and make no concealment; and, besides, they're partly Kanakaised, and suck up with natives instead of with other white men like themselves. I had on a rig of clean striped pyjamas—for, of course, I had dressed decent to go before the chiefs; but when I saw the missionary step out of this boat in the regular uniform, white duck clothes, pith helmet, white shirt and tie, and yellow boots to his feet, I could have bunged stones at him. As he came nearer, queering me pretty curious (because of the fight, I suppose), I saw he looked mortal sick, for the truth was he had a fever on, and had just had a chill in the boat.

"Mr. Tarleton, I believe?" says I, for I had got his name.

"And you, I suppose, are the new trader?" says he.

"I want to tell you first that I don't hold with missions," I went on, "and that I think you and the likes of you do a sight of harm, filling up the natives with old wives' tales and bumptiousness."

"You are perfectly entitled to your opinions," says he, looking a bit ugly, "but I have no call to hear them."

"It so happens that you've got to hear them," I said. "I'm no missionary, nor missionary lover; I'm no Kanaka, nor favourer of Kanakas—I'm just a trader; I'm just a common, low-down, God-damned white man and British subject, the sort you would like to wipe your boots on. I hope that's plain!"

"Yes, my man," said he. "It's more plain than creditable. When you are sober, you'll be sorry for this."

He tried to pass on, but I stopped him with my hand. The Kanakas were beginning to growl. Guess they didn't like my tone, for I spoke to that man as free as I would to you.

"Now, you can't say I've deceived you," said I, "and I can go on. I want a service—I want two services, in fact—and, if you care to give me them, I'll perhaps take more stock in what you call your Christianity."

He was silent for a moment. Then he smiled. "You are rather a strange sort of man," says he.

"I'm the sort of man God made me," says I. "I don't set up to be a gentleman," I said.

"I am not quite so sure," said he. "And what can I do for you, Mr.——?"

"Wiltshire," I says, "though I'm mostly called Welsher; but Wiltshire is the way it's spelt, if the people on the beach could only get their tongues about it. And what do I want? Well I'll tell you the first thing. I'm what you call a sinner—what I call a sweep—and I want you to help me make it up to a person I've deceived."

He turned and spoke to his crew in the native. "And now I am at your service," said he, "but only for the time my crew are dining. I must be much farther down the coast before night. I was delayed at Papa-malulu till this morning, and I have an engagement in Fale-alii tomorrow night."

I led the way to my house in silence, and rather pleased with myself for the way I had managed the talk, for I like a man to keep his self-respect.

"I was sorry to see you fighting," says he.

"O, that's part of the yarn I want to tell you," I said. "That's service number two. After you've heard it you'll let me know whether you're sorry or not."

We walked right in through the store, and I was surprised to find Uma had cleared away the dinner things. This was so unlike her ways that I saw she had done it out of gratitude, and liked her the better. She and Mr. Tarleton called each other by name, and he was very civil to her seemingly. But I thought little of that; they can always find civility for a Kanaka, it's us white men they lord it over. Besides, I didn't want much Tarleton just then. I was going to do my pitch.

"Uma," said I, "give us your marriage certificate." She looked put out. "Come," said I, "you can trust me. Hand it up."

She had it about her person, as usual, I believe she thought it was a pass to heaven, and if she died without having it handy she would go to hell. I couldn't see where she put it the first time, I couldn't see now where she took it from; it seemed to jump into her hand like that Blavatsky business in the papers. But it's the same way with all island women, and I guess they're taught it when young.

"Now," said I, with the certificate in my hand, "I was married to this girl by Black Jack the negro. The certificate was wrote by Case, and it's a dandy piece of literature, I promise you. Since then I've found that there's a kind of cry in the place against this wife of mine, and so long as I keep her I cannot trade. Now, what would any man do in my place, if he was a man?" I said. "The first thing he would do is this, I guess." And I took and tore up the certificate and bunged the pieces on the floor.

"*Aué!*"* cried Uma, and began to clap her hands; but I caught one of them in mine.

"And the sccond thing that he would do," said I, "if he was what I would call a man and you would call a man, Mr. Tarleton, is to bring the girl right before you or any other missionary, and to up and say: 'I was wrong mar-

* Alas!

ried to this wife of mine, but I think a heap of her, and now I want to be married to her right.' Fire away, Mr. Tarleton. And I guess you'd better do it in native; it'll please the old lady," I said, giving her the proper name of a man's wife upon the spot.

So we had in two of the crew for to witness, and were spliced in our own house; and the parson prayed a good bit, I must say—but not so long as some—and shook hands with the pair of us.

"Mr. Wiltshire," he says, when he had made out the lines and packed off the witnesses, "I have to thank you for a very lively pleasure. I have rarely performed the marriage ceremony with more grateful emotions."

That was what you would call talking. He was going on, besides, with more of it, and I was ready for as much taffy as he had in stock, for I felt good. But Uma had been taken up with something half through the marriage, and cut straight in.

"How your hand he get hurt?" she asked.

"You ask Case's head, old lady," says I.

She jumped with joy, and sang out.

"You haven't made much of a Christian of this one," says I to Mr. Tarleton.

"We didn't think her one of our worst," says he, "when she was at Fale-alii; and if Uma bears malice I shall be tempted to fancy she has good cause."

"Well, there we are at service number two," said I. "I want to tell you our yarn, and see if you can let daylight in."

"Is it long?" he asked.

"Yes," I cried; "it's a goodish bit of a yarn!"

"Well, I'll give you all the time I can spare," says he, looking at his watch. "But I must tell you fairly, I haven't eaten since five this morning, and, unless you can let me have something, I am not likely to eat again before seven or eight to-night."

"By God, we'll give you dinner!" I cried.

I was a little caught up at my swearing, just when all was going straight; and so was the missionary, I suppose, but he made believe to look out of the window, and thanked us.

So we ran him up a bit of a meal. I was bound to let the old lady have a hand in it, to show off, so I deputised her to brew the tea. I don't think I ever met such tea as she turned out. But that was not the worst for she got round with the salt-box, which she considered an extra European touch, and turned my stew into sea-water. Altogether, Mr. Tarleton had a devil of a dinner of it; but he had plenty entertainment by the way, for all the while that we were cooking, and afterwards, when he was making believe to eat, I kept posting him up on Master Case and the beach of Falesá, and he putting questions that showed he was following close.

"Well," said he at last, "I am afraid you have a dangerous enemy. This man Case is very clever, and seems really wicked. I must tell you I have had my eye on him for nearly a year, and have rather had the worst of our encounters. About the time when the last representative of your firm ran so suddenly away, I had a letter from Namu, the native pastor, begging me to come to Falesá at my earliest convenience, as his flock were all 'adopting Catholic practices.' I had great confidence in Namu; I fear it only shows how easily we are deceived. No one could hear him preach and not be persuaded he was a man of extraordinary parts. All our islanders easily acquire a kind of eloquence, and can roll out and illustrate, with a great deal of vigour and fancy, second-hand sermons; but Namu's sermons are his own, and I cannot deny that I have found them means of grace. Moreover, he has a keen curiosity in secular things, does not fear work, is clever at carpentering and has made himself so much respected among the neighbouring pastors that we call him, in a jest which is half serious, the Bishop of the East. In short, I was proud of the man; all the more puzzled by his letter, and took an occasion to come this way. The morning before my arrival, Vigours had been sent on board the *Lion,* and Namu was perfectly at his ease, apparently ashamed of his letter, and quite unwilling to explain it. This, of course, I could not allow, and he ended by confessing that he had been much concerned to find his people using the sign of the cross, but since he had learned the explanation his mind was satisfied. For Vigours had the Evil Eye, a common thing in a country of Europe called Italy, where men were often struck dead by that kind of devil, and it appeared the sign of the cross was a charm against its power.

" 'And I explain it, Misi' said Namu, 'in this way: The country in Europe is a Popey country, and the devil of the Evil Eye may be a Catholic devil, or, at least, used to Catholic ways. So then I reasoned thus: If this sign of the cross were used in a Popey manner it would be sinful, but when it is used only to protect men from a devil, which is a thing harmless in itself, the sign too must be, as a bottle is neither good nor bad, harmless. For the sign is neither good nor bad. But if the bottle be full of gin, the gin is bad; and if the sign be made in idolatry bad, so is the idolatry.' And, very like a native pastor, he had a text apposite about the casting out of devils.

" 'And who has been telling you about the Evil Eye?' I asked.

"He admitted it was Case. Now, I am afraid you will think me very narrow, Mr. Wiltshire, but I must tell you I was displeased, and cannot think a trader at all a good man to advise or have an influence upon my pastors. And, besides, there had been some flying talk in the country of old Adams and his being poisoned, to which I had paid no great heed; but it came back to me at the moment.

" 'And is this Case a man of a sanctified life?' I asked.

"He admitted he was not; for, though he did not drink, he was profligate with women, and had no religion.

" 'Then,' said I, 'I think the less you have to do with him the better.'

"But it is not easy to have the last word with a man like Namu. He was ready in a moment with an illustration. 'Misi,' said he, 'you have told me there were wise men, not pastors, not even holy, who knew many things useful to be taught—about trees, for instance, and beasts, and to print books, and about the stones that are burned to make knives of. Such men teach you in your college, and you learn from them, but take care not to learn to be unholy. Misi, Case is my college.'

"I knew not what to say. Mr. Vigours had evidently been driven out of Falesá by the machinations of Case, and with something not very unlike the collusion of my pastor. I called to mind it was Namu who had reassured me about Adams and traced the rumour to the ill-will of the priest. And I saw I must inform myself more thoroughly from an impartial source. There is an old rascal of a chief here, Faiaso, whom I daresay you saw to-day at the council; he has been all his life turbulent and sly, a great fomentor of rebellions, and a thorn in the side of the mission and the island. For all that he is very shrewd, and, except in politics or about his own misdemeanours, a teller of the truth. I went to his house, told him what I had heard, and besought him to be frank. I do not think I had ever a more painful interview. Perhaps you will understand me, Mr. Wiltshire, if I tell you that I am perfectly serious in these old wives' tales with which you reproached me, and as anxious to do well for these islands as you can be to please and to protect your pretty wife. And you are to remember that I thought Namu a paragon, and was proud of the man as one of the first ripe fruits of the mission. And now I was informed that he had fallen in a sort of dependence upon Case. The beginning of it was not corrupt; it began, doubtless, in fear and respect, produced by trickery and pretence; but I was shocked to find that another element had been lately added, that Namu helped himself in the store, and was believed to be deep in Case's debt. Whatever the trader said, that Namu believed with trembling. He was not alone in this; many in the village lived in a similar subjection; but Namu's case was the most influential, it was through Namu Case had wrought most evil; and with a certain following among the chiefs, and the pastor in his pocket, the man was as good as master of the village. You know something of Vigours and Adams, but perhaps you have never heard of old Underhill, Adams' predecessor. He was a quiet, mild old fellow, I remember, and we were told he had died suddenly: white men die very suddenly in Falesá. The truth, as I now heard it, made my blood run cold. It seems he was struck with a general palsy, all of him dead but one eye, which he continually winked. Word was started that the helpless old man was now a devil, and this vile fellow Case worked upon the natives' fears, which he professed to share, and pretended he durst not go into the house alone. At last a grave was dug, and the living body buried at the far end of the village. Namu, my pastor, whom I had helped to educate, offered up a prayer at the hateful scene.

"I felt myself in a very difficult position. Perhaps it was my duty to have denounced Namu and had him deposed. Perhaps I think so now, but at the time it seemed less clear. He had a great influence, it might prove greater than mine. The natives are prone to superstition; perhaps by stirring them up I might but ingrain and spread these dangerous fancies. And Namu besides, apart from this novel and accursed influence, was a good pastor, an able man, and spiritually minded. Where should I look for a better? How was I to find as good? At that moment, with Namu's failure fresh in my view, the work of my life appeared a mockery; hope was dead in me. I would rather repair such tools as I had than go abroad in quest of others that must certainly prove worse; and a scandal is, at the best, a thing to be avoided when humanly possible. Right or wrong, then, I determined on a quiet course. All that night I denounced and reasoned with the erring pastor, twitted him with his ignorance and want of faith, twitted him with his wretched attitude, making clean the outside of the cup and platter, callously helping at a murder, childishly flying in excitement about a few childish, unnecessary, and inconvenient gestures; and long before day I had him on his knees and bathed in the tears of what seemed a genuine repentance. On Sunday I took the pulpit in the morning, and preached from First Kings, nineteenth, on the fire, the earthquake, and the voice, distinguishing the true spiritual power, and referring with such plainness as I dared to recent events in Falesá. The effect produced was great, and it was much increased when Namu rose in his turn and confessed that he had been wanting in faith and conduct, and was convinced of sin. So far, then, all was well; but there was one unfortunate circumstance. It was nearing the time of our 'May' in the island, when the native contributions to the missions are received; it fell in my duty to make a notification on the subject, and this gave my enemy his chance, by which he was not slow to profit.

"News of the whole proceedings must have been carried to Case as soon as church was over, and the same afternoon he made an occasion to meet me in the midst of the village. He came up with so much intentness and animosity that I felt it would be damaging to avoid him.

" 'So,' says he, in native, 'here is the holy man. He has been preaching against me, but that was not in his heart. He has been preaching upon the love of God; but that was not in his heart, it was between his teeth. Will you know what was in his heart?' cries he. 'I will show it you!' And, making a snatch at my head he made believe to pluck out a dollar, and held it in the air.

"There went that rumour through the crowd with which Polynesians receive a prodigy. As for myself, I stood amazed. The thing was a common conjuring trick which I have seen performed at home a score of times; but how was I to convince the villagers of that? I wished I had learned legerdemain instead of Hebrew, that I might have paid the fellow out with his own coin. But there I was; I could not stand there silent, and the best I could find to say was weak.

" 'I will trouble you not to lay hands on me again,' said I.

" 'I have no such thought,' said he, 'nor will I deprive you of your dollar. Here it is,' he said, and flung it at my feet. I am told it lay where it fell three days."

"I must say it was well played," said I.

"O! he is clever," said Mr. Tarleton, "and you can now see for yourself how dangerous. He was a party to the horrid death of the paralytic; he is accused of poisoning Adams; he drove Vigours out of the place by lies that might have led to murder; and there is no question but he has now made up his mind to rid himself of you. How he means to try we have no guess; only be sure it's something new. There is no end to his readiness and invention."

"He gives himself a sight of trouble," says I. "And, after all, what for?"

"Why, how many tons of copra may they make in this district?" asked the missionary.

"I daresay as much as sixty tons," says I.

"And what is the profit to the local trader?" he asked.

"You may call it three pounds," said I.

"Then you can reckon for yourself how much he does it for," said Mr. Tarleton. "But the more important thing is to defeat him. It is clear he spread some report against Uma, in order to isolate and have his wicked will of her. Failing of that, and seeing a new rival come upon the scene, he used her in a different way. Now, the first point to find out is about Namu. Uma, when people began to leave you and your mother alone, what did Namu do?"

"Stop away all-e-same," says Uma.

"I fear the dog has returned to his vomit," said Mr. Tarleton. "And now what am I to do for you? I will speak to Namu, I will warn him he is observed; it will be strange if he allow anything to go on amiss when he is put upon his guard. At the same time, this precaution may fail, and then you must turn elsewhere. You have two people at hand to whom you might apply. There is, first of all, the priest, who might protect you by the Catholic interest; they are a wretchedly small body, but they count two chiefs. And then there is old Faiaso. Ah! if it had been some years ago you would have needed no one else; but his influence is much reduced; it has gone into Maea's hands, and Maea, I fear, is one of Case's jackals. In fine, if the worst comes to the worst, you must send up or come yourself to Fale-alii, and, though I am not due at this end of the island for a month, I will just see what can be done."

So Mr. Tarleton said farewell; and half an hour later the crew were singing and the paddles flashing in the missionary boat.

CHAPTER IV

DEVIL-WORK

NEAR A MONTH went by without much doing. The same night of our marriage Galoshes called round, and made himself mighty civil, and got into a habit of dropping in about dark and smoking his pipe with the family. He could talk to Uma, of course, and started to teach me native and French at the same time. He was a kind old buffer, though the dirtiest you would wish to see, and he muddled me up with foreign languages worse than the tower of Babel.

That was one employment we had, and it made me feel less lonesome; but there was no profit in the thing, for though the priest came and sat and yarned, none of his folks could be enticed into my store; and if it hadn't been for the other occupation I struck out there wouldn't have been a pound of copra in the house. This was the idea: Fa'avao (Uma's mother) had a score of bearing trees. Of course we could get no labour, being all as good as tabooed, and the two women and I turned to and made copra with our own hands. It was copra to make your mouth water when it was done—I never understood how much the natives cheated me till I had made that four hundred pounds of my own hand—and it weighed so light I felt inclined to take and water it myself.

When we were at the job a good many Kanakas used to put in the best of the day looking on, and once that nigger turned up. He stood back with the natives and laughed and did the big don and the funny dog till I began to get riled.

"Here you nigger!" says I.

"I don't address myself to you, Sah," says the nigger. "Only speak to gen'le'um."

"I know," says I, "but it happens I was addressing myself to you, Mr. Black Jack. And all I want to know is just this: did you see Case's figure-head about a week ago?"

"No, Sah," says he.

"That's all right, then," says I; "for I'll show you the own brother to it, only black, in the inside of about two minutes."

And I began to walk towards him, quite slow, and my hands down; only there was trouble in my eye, if anybody took the pains to look.

"You're a low, obstropulous fellow, Sah," says he.

"You bet!" says I.

By that time he thought I was about as near as convenient, and lit out so it would have done your heart good to see him travel. And that was all I saw of that precious gang until what I am about to tell you.

It was one of my chief employments these days to go pot-hunting in the woods, which I found (as Case had told me) very rich in game. I have spoken of the cape which shut up the village and my station from the east. A path went about the end of it, and led into the next bay. A strong wind blew here daily, and as the line of the barrier reef stopped at the end of the cape, a heavy surf ran on the shores of the bay. A little cliffy hill cut the valley in two parts, and stood close on the beach; and at high water the sea broke right on the face of it, so that all passage was stopped. Woody mountains hemmed the place all round; the barrier to the east was particularly steep and leafy, the lower parts of it, along the sea, falling in sheer black cliffs streaked with cinnabar; the upper part lumpy with the tops of the great trees. Some of the trees were bright green, and some red, and the sand of the beach as black as your shoes. Many birds hovered round the bay, some of them snow-white; and the flying-fox (or vampire) flew there in broad daylight, gnashing its teeth.

For a long while I came as far as this shooting, and went no farther. There was no sign of any path beyond, and the cocoa-palms in the front of the foot of the valley were the last this way. For the whole "eye" of the island, as natives call the windward end, lay desert. From Falesá round about to Papa-malulu, there was neither house, nor man, nor planted fruit-tree; and the reef being mostly absent, and the shores bluff, the sea beat direct among crags, and there was scarce a landing-place.

I should tell you that after I began to go in the woods, although no one offered to come near my store, I found people willing enough to pass the time of day with me where nobody could see them; and as I had begun to pick up native, and most of them had a word or two of English, I began to hold little odds and ends of conversation, not to much purpose to be sure, but they took off the worst of the feeling, for it's a miserable thing to be made a leper of.

It chanced one day towards the end of the month, that I was sitting in this bay in the edge of the bush, looking east, with a Kanaka. I had given him a fill of tobacco, and we were making out to talk as best we could; indeed, he had more English than most.

I asked him if there was no road going eastward.

"One time one road," said he. "Now he dead."

"Nobody he go there?" I asked.

"No good," said he. "Too much devil he stop there."

"Oho!" says I, "got-um plenty devil, that bush?"

"Man devil, woman devil; too much devil," said my friend. "Stop here all-e-time. Man he go there, no come back."

I thought if this fellow was so well posted on devils and spoke of them so free, which is not common, I had better fish for a little information about myself and Uma.

"You think me one devil?" I asked.

"No think devil," said he soothingly. "Think all-e-same fool."

"Uma, she devil?" I asked again.

"No, no; no devil. Devil stop bush," said the young man.

I was looking in front of me across the bay, and I saw the hanging front of the woods pushed suddenly open, and Case, with a gun in his hand, step forth into the sunshine on the black beach. He was got up in light pyjamas, near white, his gun sparkled, he looked mighty conspicuous; and the sand-crabs scuttled from all round him to their holes.

"Hullo, my friend!" says I, "you no talk all-e-same true. Ese he go, he come back."

"Ese no all-e-same; Ese *Tiapolo,*" says my friend; and, with a "Good-bye," slunk off among the trees.

I watched Case all round the beach, where the tide was low; and let him pass me on the homeward way to Falesá. He was in deep thought, and the birds seemed to know it, trotting quite near him on the sand, or wheeling and calling in his ears. When he passed me I could see by the working of his lips that he was talking to himself, and, what pleased me mightily, he had still my trade mark on his brow. I tell you the plain truth: I had a mind to give him a gunful in his ugly mug, but I thought better of it.

All this time, and all the time I was following home, I kept repeating that native word, which I remembered by "Polly, put the kettle on and make us all some tea," tea-a-pollo.

"Uma," says I, when I got back, "what does *Tiapolo* mean?"

"Devil," says she.

"I thought *aitu* was the word for that," I said.

"*Aitu* 'nother kind of devil," said she; "stop bush, eat Kanaka. Tiapolo big chief devil, stop home; all-e-same Christian devil."

"Well then," said I, "I'm no farther forward. How can Case be Tiapolo?"

"No all-e-same," said she. "Ese belong Tiapolo; Tiapolo too much like; Ese all-e-same his son. Suppose Ese he wish something, Tiapolo he make him."

"That's mighty convenient for Ese," says I. "And what kind of things does he make for him?"

Well, out came a rigmarole of all sorts of stories, many of which (like the dollar he took from Mr. Tarleton's head) were plain enough to me, but others I could make nothing of; and the thing that most surprised the Kanakas was what surprised me least—namely, that he would go in the desert among all the *aitus*. Some of the boldest, however, had accompanied him, and had heard him speak with the dead and give them orders, and, safe in his protection, had returned unscathed. Some said he had a church there, where he worshipped Tiapolo, and Tiapolo appeared to him; others swore that there was no sorcery at all, that he performed his miracles by the power of prayer, and the church was no church, but a prison, in which he had confined a dangerous *aitu*. Namu had been in the bush with him once, and returned glorifying God for these wonders. Altogether, I began to have a glimmer of the man's position, and the means by which he had acquired it, and, though I saw he was a tough nut to crack, I was noways cast down.

"Very well," said I, "I'll have a look at Master Case's place of worship myself, and we'll see about the glorifying."

At this Uma fell in a terrible taking; if I went in the high bush I should never return; none could go there but by the protection of Tiapolo.

"I'll chance it on God's," said I. "I'm a good sort of fellow, Uma, as fellows go, and I guess God'll con me through."

She was silent for a while. "I think," said she, mighty solemn—and then, presently—"Victoreea, he big chief?"

"You bet!" said I.

"He like you too much?" she asked again.

I told her, with a grin, I believed the old lady was rather partial to me.

"All right," said she. "Victoreea he big chief, like you too much. No can help you here in Falesá; no can do—too far off. Maea he small chief—stop here. Suppose he like you—make you all right. All-e-same God and Tiapolo. God he big chief—got too much work. Tiapolo he small chief—he like too much make-see, work very hard."

"I'll have to hand you over to Mr. Tarleton," said I. "Your theology's out of its bearings, Uma."

However, we stuck to this business all the evening, and, with the stories she told me of the desert and its dangers, she came near frightening herself into a fit. I don't remember half a quarter of them, of course, for I paid little heed; but two come back to me kind of clear.

About six miles up the coast there is a sheltered cove they call *Fanga-anaana*—"the haven full of caves." I've seen it from the sea myself, as near as I could get my boys to venture in; and it's a little strip of yellow sand. Black cliffs overhang it, full of the black mouths of caves;

great trees overhang the cliffs, and dangle-down lianas; and in one place, about the middle, a big brook pours over in a cascade. Well, there was a boat going by here, with six young men of Falesá, "all very pretty," Uma said, which was the loss of them. It blew strong, there was a heavy head sea, and by the time they opened Fanga-anaana, and saw the white cascade and the shady beach, they were all tired and thirsty, and their water had run out. One proposed to land and get a drink, and, being reckless fellows, they were all of the same mind except the youngest. Lotu was his name; he was a very good young gentleman, and very wise; and he held out that they were crazy, telling them the place was given over to spirits and devils and the dead, and there were no living folk nearer than six miles the one way, and maybe twelve the other. But they laughed at his words, and, being five to one, pulled in, beached the boat, and landed. It was a wonderful pleasant place, Lotu said, and the water excellent. They walked round the beach, but could see nowhere any way to mount the cliffs, which made them easier in their mind; and at last they sat down to make a meal on the food they had brought with them. They were scarce set, when there came out of the mouth of one of the black caves six of the most beautiful ladies ever seen: they had flowers in their hair, and the most beautiful breasts, and necklaces of scarlet seeds; and began to jest with these young gentlemen, and the young gentlemen to jest back with them, all but Lotu. As for Lotu, he saw there could be no living woman in such a place, and ran, and flung himself in the bottom of the boat, and covered his face, and prayed. All the time the business lasted Lotu made one clean break of prayer, and that was all he knew of it, until his friends came back, and made him sit up, and they put to sea again out of the bay, which was now quite deserted, and no word of the six ladies. But, what frightened Lotu most, not one of the five remembered anything of what had passed, but they were all like drunken men, and sang and laughed in the boat, and skylarked. The wind freshened and came squally, and the sea rose extraordinary high; it was such weather as any man in the islands would have turned his back to and fled home to Falesá; but these five were like crazy folk, and cracked on all sail and drove their boat into the seas. Lotu went to the bailing, none of the others thought to help him, but sang and skylarked and carried on, and spoke singular things beyond a man's comprehension, and laughed out loud when they said them. So the rest of the day Lotu bailed for his life in the bottom of the boat, and was all drenched with sweat and cold sea-water; and none heeded him. Against all expectation, they came safe in a dreadful tempest to Papamalulu, where the palms were singing out, and the cocoa-nuts flying like cannon-balls about the village green; and the same night the five young gentlemen sickened, and spoke never a reasonable word until they died.

"And do you mean to tell me you can swallow a yarn like that?" I asked.

She told me the thing was well known, and with handsome young men alone it was even common; but this was the only case where five had been slain the same day and in a company by the love of the women-devils; and it had made a great stir in the island, and she would be crazy if she doubted.

"Well, anyway," says I, "you needn't be frightened about me. I've no use for the women-devils. You're all the women I want, and all the devil too, old lady."

To this she answered there were other sorts, and she had seen one with her own eyes. She had gone one day alone to the next bay, and, perhaps, got too near the margin of the bad place. The boughs of the high bush overshadowed her from the cant of the hills, but she herself was outside on a flat place, very stony, and growing full of young mummy-apples four and five feet high. It was a dark day in the rainy season, and now there came squalls that tore off the leaves and sent them flying, and now it was all still as in a house. It was in one of these still times that a whole gang of birds and flying foxes came pegging out of the bush like creatures frightened. Presently after she heard a rustle nearer hand, and saw, coming out of the margin of the trees, among the mummy-apples, the appearance of a lean grey old boar. It seemed to think as it came, like a person; and all of a sudden, as she looked at it coming, she was aware it was no boar, but a thing that was a man with a man's thoughts. At that she ran, and the pig after her, and as the pig ran it holla'd aloud, so that the place rang with it.

"I wish I had been there with my gun," said I. "I guess that pig would have holla'd so as to surprise himself."

But she told me a gun was of no use with the like of these, which were the spirits of the dead.

Well, this kind of talk put in the evening, which was the best of it; but of course it didn't change my notion, and the next day, with my gun and a good knife, I set off upon a voyage of discovery. I made, as near as I could, for the place where I had seen Case come out; for if it was true he had some kind of establishment in the bush I reckoned I should find a path. The beginning of the desert was marked off by a wall to call it so, for it was more of a long mound of stones. They say it reaches right across the island, but how they know it is another question, for I doubt if anyone has made the journey in a hundred years, the natives sticking chiefly to the sea, and their little colonies along the coast, and that part being mortal high and steep and full of cliffs. Up to the west side of the wall the ground has been cleared, and there are cocoa-palms and mummy-apples and guavas, and lots of sensitive. Just across, the bush begins outright; high bush at that, trees going up like the masts of ships, and ropes of liana hanging down like a ship's rigging, and nasty orchids growing in the forks like funguses. The ground where there was no underwood looked to be a heap of boulders. I saw many green pigeons which I might have shot, only I was there with a different idea. A number of butterflies flopped up and down along the ground like dead leaves; sometimes I would hear a bird calling, sometimes the wind overhead, and always the sea along the coast.

But the queerness of the place it's more difficult to tell of, unless to one who has been alone in the high bush himself. The brightest kind of a day it is always dim down there. A man can see to the end of nothing; whichever way he looks the wood shuts up, one bough folding with another like the fingers of your hand; and whenever he listens he hears always something new—men talking, children laughing, the strokes of an axe a far way ahead of him, and sometimes a sort of a quick, stealthy scurry near at hand that makes him jump and look to his weapons. It's all very well for him to tell himself that he's alone, bar trees and birds; he can't make out to believe it; whichever way he turns the whole place seems to be alive and looking on. Don't think it was Uma's yarns that put me out; I don't value native talk a fourpenny-piece; it's a thing that's natural in the bush, and that's the end of it.

As I got near the top of the hill, for the ground of the wood goes up in this place steep as a ladder, the wind began to sound straight on, and the leaves to toss and switch open and let in the sun. This suited me better; it was the same noise all the time, and nothing to startle. Well, I had got to a place where there was an underwood of what they call wild cocoa-nut—mighty pretty with its scarlet fruit—when there came a sound of singing in the wind that I thought I had never heard the like of. It was all very fine to tell myself it was the branches; I knew better. It was all very fine to tell myself it was a bird; I knew never a bird that sang like that. It rose and swelled, and died away and swelled again; and now I thought it was like someone weeping, only prettier; and now I thought it was like harps; and there was one thing I made sure of, it was a sight too sweet to be wholesome in a place like that. You may laugh if you like; but I declare I called to mind the six young ladies that came, with their scarlet necklaces, out of the cave at Fanga-alana, and wondered if they sang like that. We laugh at the natives and their superstitions; but see how many traders take them up, splendidly educated white men that have been bookkeepers (some of them) and clerks in the old country. It's my belief a superstition grows up in a place like the different kind of weeds; and as I stood there and listened to that wailing I twittered in my shoes.

You may call me a coward to be frightened; I thought myself brave enough to go on ahead. But I went mighty carefully, with my gun cocked, spying all about me like a hunter, fully expecting to see a handsome young woman sitting somewhere in the bush, and fully determined (if I did) to try her with a charge of duck-shot. And sure enough, I had not gone far when I met with a queer thing. The wind came on the top of the wood in a strong puff, the leaves in front of me burst open, and I saw for a second something hanging in a tree. It was gone in a wink, the puff blowing by and the leaves closing. I tell you the truth: I had made up my mind to see an *aitu*; and if the thing had looked like a pig or a woman, it wouldn't have given me the same turn. The trouble was that it seemed kind of square, and the idea of a square thing that was alive and sang knocked me sick and silly. I must have stood quite a while; and I made pretty certain it was right out of the same tree that the singing came. Then I began to come to myself a bit.

"Well," says I, "if this is really so, if this is a place where there are square things that sing, I'm gone up anyway. Let's have my fun for my money."

But I thought I might as well take the off-chance of a prayer being any good; so I plumped on my knees and prayed out loud; and all the time I was praying the strange sounds came out of the tree, and went up and down, and changed, for all the world like music, only you could see it wasn't human—there was nothing there that you could whistle.

As soon as I had made an end in proper style, I laid down my gun, stuck my knife between my teeth, walked right up to that tree, and began to climb. I tell you my heart was like ice. But presently, as I went up, I caught another glimpse of the thing, and that relieved me, for I thought it seemed like a box; and when I had got right up to it I near fell out of the tree with laughing.

A box it was, sure enough, and a candle-box at that, with the brand upon the side of it; and it had banjo-strings stretched so as to sound when the wind blew. I believe they call the thing a Tyrolean* harp, whatever that may mean.

"Well, Mr. Case," said I, "you've frightened me once, but I defy you to frighten me again," I says, and slipped down the tree, and set out again to find my enemy's head office, which I guessed would not be far away.

The undergrowth was thick in this part; I couldn't see before my nose, and must burst my way through by main force and ply the knife as I went, slicing the cords of the lianas and slashing down whole trees at a blow. I call them trees for the bigness, but in truth they were just big weeds, and sappy to cut through like carrot. From all this crowd and kind of vegetation, I was just thinking to myself, the place might have once been cleared, when I came on my nose over a pile of stones, and saw in a moment it was some kind of a work of man. The Lord knows when it was made or when deserted, for this part of the island has lain undisturbed since long before the whites came. A few steps beyond I hit into the path I had been always looking for. It was narrow, but well beaten, and I saw that Case had plenty of disciples. It seems, indeed, it was a piece of fashionable boldness to venture

* Æolian.

up here with the trader, and a young man scarce reckoned himself grown till he had got his breech tattooed, for one thing and seen Case's devils for another. This is mighty like Kanakas; but, if you look at it another way, it's mighty like white folks too.

A bit along the path I was brought to a clear stand, and had to rub my eyes. There was a wall in front of me, the path passing it by a gap; it was tumble-down, and plainly very old, but built of big stones very well laid; and there is no native alive to-day upon that island that could dream of such a piece of building. Along all the top of it was a line of queer figures, idols or scarecrows, or what not. They had carved and painted faces, ugly to view, their eyes and teeth were of shell, their hair and their bright clothes blew in the wind, and some of them worked with the tugging. There are islands up west where they make these kind of figures till to-day; but if ever they were made in this island, the practice and the very recollection of it are now long forgotten. And the singular thing was that all these bogies were as fresh as toys out of a shop.

Then it came in my mind that Case had let out to me the first day that he was a good forger of island curiosities, a thing by which so many traders turn an honest penny. And with that I saw the whole business, and how this display served the man a double purpose, first of all, to season his curiosities, and then to frighten those that came to visit him.

But I should tell you (what made the thing more curious) that all the time the Tyrolean harps were harping round me in the trees, and even while I looked, a green-and-yellow bird (that, I suppose, was building) began to tear the hair off the head of one of the figures.

A little farther on I found the best curiosity of the museum. The first I saw of it was a longish mound of earth with a twist to it. Digging off the earth with my hands, I found underneath tarpaulin stretched on boards, so that this was plainly the roof of a cellar. It stood right on the top of the hill, and the entrance was on the far side, between two rocks, like the entrance to a cave. I went as far in as the bend, and, looking round the corner, saw a shining face. It was big and ugly, like a pantomime mask, and the brightness of it waxed and dwindled, and at times it smoked.

"Oho!" says I, "luminous paint!"

And I must say I rather admired the man's ingenuity. With a box of tools and a few mighty simple contrivances he had made out to have a devil of a temple. Any poor Kanaka brought up here in the dark, with the harps whining all round him, and shown that smoking face in the bottom of a hole, would make no kind of doubt but he had seen and heard enough devils for a lifetime. It's easy to find out what Kanakas think. Just go back to yourself any way round from ten to fifteen years old, and there's an average Kanaka. There are some pious, just as there are pious boys; and the most of them, like the boys again, are middling honest, and yet think it rather larks to steal, and are easy scared, and rather like to be so. I remember a boy I was at school with at home who played the Case business. He didn't know anything, that boy; he couldn't do anything; he had no luminous paint and no Tyrolean harps; he just boldly said he was a sorcerer, and frightened us out of our boots, and we loved it. And then it came in my mind how the master had once flogged that boy, and the surprise we were all in to see the sorcerer catch it and bum like anybody else. Thinks I to myself, "I must find some way of fixing it so for Master Case." And the next moment I had my idea.

I went back by the path, which, when once you had found it, was quite plain and easy walking; and when I stepped out on the black sands, who should I see but Master Case himself! I cocked my gun and held it handy, and we marched up and passed without a word, each keeping the tail of his eye on the other; and no sooner had we passed than we each wheeled round like fellows drilling, and stood face to face. We had each taken the same notion in his head, you see, that the other fellow might give him the load of his gun in the stern.

"You've shot nothing," says Case.

"I'm not on the shoot to-day," said I.

"Well, the devil go with you for me," says he.

"The same to you," says I.

But we stuck just the way we were; no fear of either of us moving.

Case laughed. "We can't stop here all day, though," said he.

"Don't let me detain you," says I.

He laughed again. "Look here, Wiltshire, do you think me a fool?" he asked.

"More of a knave, if you want to know," says I.

"Well, do you think it would better me to shoot you here, on this open beach?" said he. "Because I don't. Folks come fishing every day. There may be a score of them up the valley now, making copra; there might be half a dozen on the hill behind you, after pigeons; they might be watching us this minute, and I shouldn't wonder. I give you my word I don't want to shoot you. Why should I? You don't hinder me any. You haven't got one pound of copra but what you made with your own hands, like a negro slave. You're vegetating—that's what I call it—and I don't care where you vegetate, nor yet how long. Give me your word you don't mean to shoot me, and I'll give you a lead and walk away."

"Well," said I, "you're frank and pleasant, ain't you? And I'll be the same. I don't mean to shoot you to-day. Why should I? This business is beginning; it ain't done yet, Mr. Case. I've given you one turn already; I can see the marks of my knuckles on your head to this blooming hour, and I've more cooking for you. I'm not a paralee, like Underhill. My name ain't Adams, and it ain't Vigours; and I mean to show you that you've met your match."

"This is a silly way to talk," said he. "This is not the talk to make me move on with."

"All right," said I, "stay where you are. I ain't in any hurry, and you know it. I can put in a day on this beach and never mind. I ain't got any copra to bother with. I ain't got any luminous paint to see to."

I was sorry I said that last, but it whipped out before I knew. I could see it took the wind out of his sails, and he stood and stared at me with his brow drawn up. Then I suppose he made up his mind he must get to the bottom of this.

"I take you at your word," says he, and turned his back and walked right into the devil's bush.

I let him go, of course, for I had passed my word. But I watched him as long as he was in sight, and after he was gone lit out for cover as lively as you would want to see, and went the rest of the way home under the bush, for I didn't trust him sixpence-worth. One thing I saw, I had been ass enough to give him warning, and that which I meant to do I must do at once.

You would think I had had about enough excitement for one morning, but there was another turn waiting me. As soon as I got far enough round the cape to see my house I made out there were strangers there; a little farther, and no doubt about it. There was a couple of armed sentinels squatting at my door. I could only suppose the trouble about Uma must have come to a head, and the station been seized. For aught I could think, Uma was taken up already, and these armed men were waiting to do the like with me.

However, as I came nearer which I did at top speed, I saw there was a third native sitting on the verandah like a guest, and Uma was talking with him like a hostess. Nearer still I made out it was the big young chief, Maea, and that he was smiling away and smoking. And what was he smoking? None of your European cigarettes fit for a cat, not even the genuine big, knock-me-down native article that a fellow can really put in the time with if his pipe is broke—but a cigar, and one of my Mexicans at that, that I could swear to. At sight of this my heart started beating, and I took a wild hope in my head that the trouble was over, and Maea had come round.

Uma pointed me out to him as I came up, and he met me at the head of my own stairs like a thorough gentleman.

"Vilivili," said he, which was the best they could make of my name, "I pleased."

There is no doubt when an island chief wants to be civil he can do it. I saw the way things were from the word-go. There was no call for Uma to say to me: "He no 'fraid Ese now, come bring copra." I tell you I shook hands with that Kanaka like as if he was the best white man in Europe.

The fact was, Case and he had got after the same girl; or Maea suspected it, and concluded to make hay of the trader on the chance. He had dressed himself up, got a couple of his retainers cleaned and armed to kind of make the thing more public, and, just waiting till Case was clear of the village, came round to put the whole of his business my way. He was rich as well as powerful. I suppose that man was worth fifty thousand nuts per annum. I gave him the price of the beach and a quarter cent better, and as for credit, I would have advanced him the inside of the store and the fittings besides, I was so pleased to see him. I must say he bought like a gentleman:

rice and tins and biscuits enough for a week's feast, and stuffs by the bolt. He was agreeable besides; he had plenty fun to him; and we cracked jests together, mostly through the interpreter, because he had mighty little English, and my native was still off colour. One thing I made out: he could never really have thought much harm of Uma; he could never have been really frightened, and must just have made believe from dodginess, and because he thought Case had a strong pull in the village and could help him on.

This set me thinking that both he and I were in a tightish place. What he had done was to fly in the face of the whole village, and the thing might cost him his authority. More than that, after my talk with Case on the beach, I thought it might very well cost me my life. Case had as good as said he would pot me if ever I got any copra; he would come home to find the best business in the village had changed hands; and the best thing I thought I could do was to get in first with the potting.

"See here, Uma," says I, "tell him I'm sorry I made him wait, but I was up looking at Case's Tiapolo store in the bush."

"He want savvy if you no 'fraid?" translated Uma.

I laughed out. "Not much!" says I. "Tell him the place is a blooming toy-shop! Tell him in England we give these things to the kids to play with."

"He want savvy if you hear devil sing?" she asked next.

"Look here," I said, "I can't do it now because I've got no banjo-strings in stock; but the next time the ship comes round I'll have one of these same contraptions right here in my verandah, and he can see for himself how much devil there is to it. Tell him, as soon as I can get the strings I'll make one for his picaninnies. The name of the concern is a Tyrolean harp; and you can tell him the name means in English that nobody but dam-fools give a cent for it."

This time he was so pleased he had to try his English again: "You talk true?" says he.

"Rather!" said I. "Talk all-e-same Bible.—Bring out a Bible here, Uma, if you've got such a thing, and I'll kiss it. Or, I'll tell you what's better still," says I, taking a header, "ask him if he's afraid to go up there himself by day."

It appeared he wasn't; he could venture as far as that by day and in company.

"That's the ticket, then!" said I. "Tell him the man's a fraud and the place foolishness, and if he'll go up there to-morrow he'll see all that's left of it. But tell him this, Uma, and mind he understands it: If he gets talking, it's bound to come to Case, and I'm a dead man! I'm playing his game, tell him, and if he says one word my blood will be at his door and be the damnation of him here and after."

She told him, and he shook hands with me up to the hilt, and says he: "No talk. Go up to-mollow. You my friend?"

"No, sir," says I, "no such foolishness.—I've come here to trade, tell him, and not to make friends. But as to Case, I'll send that man to glory!"

So off Maea went, pretty well pleased, as I could see.

CHAPTER V

NIGHT IN THE BUSH

WELL, I was committed now; Tiapolo had to be smashed up before next day, and my hands were pretty full, not only with preparations, but with argument. My house was like a mechanics' debating society: Uma was so made up that I shouldn't go into the bush by night, or that, if I did, I was never to come back again. You know her style of arguing: you've had a specimen about Queen Victoria and the devil; and I leave you to fancy if I was tired of it before dark.

At last I had a good idea. What was the use of casting my pearls before her? I thought; some of her own chopped hay would be likelier to do the business.

"I'll tell you what, then," said I. "You fish out your Bible, and I'll take that up along with me. That'll make me right."

She swore a Bible was no use.

"That's just your Kanaka ignorance," sald I. "Bring the Bible out."

She brought it, and I turned to the title-page, where I thought there would likely be some English, and so there was. "There!" said I. "Look at that! '*London: Printed for the British and Foreign Bible Society, Blackfriars,*' and the date, which I can't read, owing to its being in these X's. There's no devil in hell can look near the Bible Society, Blackfriars. Why, you silly!" I said, "how do you suppose we get along with our own *aitus* at home? All Bible Society!"

"I think you no got any," said she. "White man, he tell me you no got."

"Sounds likely, don't it?" I asked. "Why would these islands all be chock full of them and none in Europe?"

"Well, you no got bread-fruit," said she.

I could have torn my hair. "Now, look here, old lady," said I, "you dry up, for I'm tired of you. I'll take the Bible, which'll put me as straight as the mail, and that's the last word I've got to say."

The night fell extraordinary dark, clouds coming up with sundown and overspreading all; not a star showed; there was only an end of a moon, and that not due before the small hours. Round the village, what with the lights and the fires in the open houses, and the torches of many fishers moving on the reef, it kept as gay as an illumination; but the sea and the mountains and woods were all clean gone. I suppose it might be eight o'clock when I took the road, laden like a donkey. First there was that Bible, a book as big as your head, which I had let myself in for by my own tomfoolery. Then there was my gun, and knife, and lantern, and patent matches, all necessary. And then there was the real plant of the affair in hand, a mortal weight of gunpowder, a pair of dynamite fishing bombs, and two or three pieces of slow match that I had hauled out of the tin cases and spliced together the best way I could; for the match was only trade stuff, and a man would be crazy that trusted it. Altogether, you see, I had the materials of a pretty good blow-up! Expense was nothing to me; I wanted that thing done right.

As long as I was in the open, and had the lamp in my house to steer by, I did well. But when I got to the path, it fell so dark I could make no headway, walking into trees and swearing there, like a man looking for the matches in his bedroom. I knew it was risky to light up, for my lantern would be visible all the way to the point of the cape, and as no one went there after dark, it would be talked about, and come to Case's ears. But what was I to do? I had either to give the business over and lose caste with Maea, or light up, take my chance, and get through the thing the smartest I was able.

As long as I was on the path I walked hard, but when I came to the black beach I had to run. For the tide was now nearly flowed; and to get through with my powder dry between the surf and the steep hill, took all the quickness I possessed. As it was, even, the wash caught me to the knees, and I came near falling on a stone. All this time the hurry I was in, and the free air and smell of the sea, kept my spirits lively; but when I was once in the bush and began to climb the path I took it easier. The fearsomeness of the wood had been a good bit rubbed off for me by Master Case's banjo-strings and graven images, yet I thought it was a dreary walk, and guessed, when the disciples went up there, they must be badly scared. The light of the lantern, striking among all these trunks and forked branches and twisted rope-ends of lianas, made the whole place, or all that you could see of it, a kind of a puzzle of turning shadows. They came to meet you, solid and quick like giants, and then span off and vanished; they hove up over your head like clubs, and flew away into the night like birds. The floor of the bush glimmered with dead wood, the way the match-box used to shine after you had struck a lucifer. Big, cold drops fell on me from the branches overhead like sweat. There was no wind to mention; only a little icy breath of a land-breeze that stirred nothing; and the harps were silent.

The first landfall I made was when I got through the bush of wild cocoa-nuts, and came in view of the bogies on the wall. Mighty queer they looked by the shining of the lantern, with their painted faces and shell eyes, and their clothes and their hair hanging. One after another I pulled them all up and piled them in a bundle on the cellar roof, so as they might go to glory with the rest. Then I chose a place behind one of the big stones at the entrance, buried my powder and the two shells, and arranged my match along the passage. And then I had a look at the smoking head, just for good-bye. It was doing fine.

"Cheer up," says I. "You're booked."

It was my first idea to light up and be getting homeward; for the darkness and the glimmer of the dead wood and the shadows of the lantern made me lonely. But I knew where one of the harps hung; it seemed a pity it shouldn't go with the rest; and at the same time I couldn't help letting on to myself that I was mortal tired of my employment, and would like best to be at home and have the door shut. I stepped out of the cellar and argued it fore and back. There was a sound of the sea far down below me on the coast; nearer hand not a leaf stirred; I might have been the only living creature this side of Cape Horn. Well, as I stood there thinking, it seemed the bush woke and became full of little noises. Little noises they were, and nothing to hurt—a bit of a crackle, a bit of a rush—but the breath jumped right out of me and my throat went as dry as a biscuit. It wasn't Case I was afraid of, which would have been common-sense; I never thought of Case; what took me, as sharp as the colic, was the old wives' tales, the devil-women and the man-pigs. It was the toss of a penny whether I should run: but I got a purchase on myself, and stepped out, and held up the lantern (like a fool) and looked all round.

In the direction of the village and the path there was nothing to be seen; but when I turned inland it's a wonder to me I didn't drop. There, coming right up out of the desert and the bad bush—there, sure enough, was a devil-woman, just as the way I had figured she would look. I saw the light shine on her bare arms and her bright eyes, and there went out of me a yell so big that I thought it was my death.

"Ah! No sing out!" says the devil-woman, in a kind of a high whisper. "Why you talk big voice? Put out light! Ese he come."

"My God Almighty, Uma, is that you?" says I.

*"Ioe,"** says she. "I come quick. Ese here soon."

"You come alone?" I asked. "You no 'fraid?"

"Ah, too much 'fraid!" she whispered, clutching me. "I think die."

"Well," says I, with a kind of a weak grin, "I'm not the one to laugh at you, Mrs. Wiltshire, for I'm about the worst scared man in the South Pacific myself."

She told me in two words what brought her. I was scarce gone, it seems, when Fa'avao came in, and the old woman had met Black Jack running as hard as he was fit from our house to Case's. Uma neither spoke nor stopped, but lit right out to come and warn me. She was so close

*Yes.

at my heels that the lantern was her guide across the beach, and afterwards, by the glimmer of it in the trees, she got her line up hill. It was only when I had got to the top or was in the cellar that she wandered Lord knows where! and lost a sight of precious time, afraid to call out lest Case was at the heels of her, and falling in the bush, so that she was all knocked and bruised. That must have been when she got too far to the southward, and how she came to take me in the flank at last and frighten me beyond what I've got the words to tell of.

Well, anything was better than a devil-woman, but I thought her yarn serious enough. Black Jack had no call to be about my house, unless he was set there to watch; and it looked to me as if my tomfool word about the paint, and perhaps some chatter of Maea's had got us all in a clove hitch. One thing was clear: Uma and I were here for the night; we daren't try to go home before day, and even then it would be safer to strike round up the mountain and come in by the back of the village, or we might walk into an ambuscade. It was plain, too, that the mine should be sprung immediately, or Case might be in time to stop it.

I marched into the tunnel, Uma keeping tight hold of me, opened my lantern, and lit the match. The first length of it burned like a spill of paper, and I stood stupid, watching it burn, and thinking we were going aloft with Tiapolo, which was none of my views. The second took to a better rate, though faster than I cared about; and at that I got my wits again, hauled Uma clear of the passage, blew out and dropped the lantern, and the pair of us groped our way into the bush until I thought it might be safe, and lay down together by a tree.

"Old lady," I said, "I won't forget this night. You're a trump, and that's what's wrong with you."

She humped herself close up to me. She had run out the way she was, with nothing on her but her kilt; and she was all wet with the dews and the sea on the black beach, and shook straight on with cold and the terror of the dark and the devils.

"Too much 'fraid," was all she said.

The far side of Case's hill goes down near as steep as a precipice into the next valley. We were on the very edge of it, and I could see the dead wood shine and hear the sea sound far below. I didn't care about the position, which left me no retreat, but I was afraid to change. Then I saw I had made a worse mistake about the lantern, which I should have left lighted, so that I could have had a crack at Case when he stepped into the shine of it. And even if I hadn't had the wit to do that, it seemed a senseless thing to leave the good lantern to blow up with the graven images. The thing belonged to me, after all, and was worth money, and might come in handy. If I could have trusted the match, I might have run in still and rescued it. But who was going to trust the match? You know what trade is. The stuff was good enough for Kanakas to go fishing with, where they've got to look lively anyway, and the most they risk is only to have their hand blown off. But for any one that wanted to fool around a blow-up like mine that match was rubbish.

Altogether, the best I could do was to lie still, see my shot-gun handy, and wait for the explosion. But it was a solemn kind of a business. The blackness of the night was like solid; the only thing you could see was the nasty bogy glimmer of the dead wood, and that showed you nothing but itself; and as for sounds, I stretched my ears till I thought I could have heard the match burn in the tunnel, and that bush was as silent as a coffin. Now and then there was a bit of a crack; but whether it was near or far, whether it was Case stubbing his toes within a few yards of me, or a tree breaking miles away, I knew no more than the babe unborn.

And then, all of a sudden, Vesuvius went off. It was a long time coming; but when it came (though I say it that shouldn't) no man could ask to see a better. At first it was just a son of a gun of a row, and a spout of fire, and the wood lighted up so that you could see to read. And then the trouble began. Uma and I were half buried under a wagonful of earth, and glad it was no worse, for one of the rocks at the entrance of the tunnel was fired clean into the air, fell within a couple of fathoms of where we lay, and bounded over the edge of the hill, and went pounding down into the next valley. I saw I had rather under-calculated our distance, or overdone the dynamite and powder, which you please.

And presently I saw I had made another slip. The noise of the thing began to die off, shaking the island; the dazzle was over; and yet the night didn't come back the way I expected. For the whole wood was scattered with red coals and brands from the explosion; they were all round me on the flat; some had fallen below in the valley, and some stuck and flared in the tree-tops. I had no fear of fire, for these forests are too wet to kindle. But the trouble was that the place was all lit up—not very bright, but good enough to get a shot by; and the way the coals were scattered, it was just as likely Case might have the advantage as myself. I looked all round for his white face, you may be sure; but there was not a sign of him. As for Uma, the life seemed to have been knocked right out of her by the bang and blaze of it.

There was one bad point in my game. One of the blessed graven images had come down all afire, hair and clothes and body, not four yards away from me. I cast a mighty noticing glance all round; there was still no Case, and I made up my mind I must get rid of that burning stick before he came, or I should be shot there like a dog.

It was my first idea to have crawled, and then I thought speed was the main thing, and stood half up to make a rush. The same moment from somewhere between me and the sea there came a flash and a report, and a rifle bullet screeched in my ear. I swung straight round and up with my gun, but the brute had a Winchester, and before I could as much as see him his second shot knocked me over like a nine-pin. I seemed to fly in the air, then came down by the run and lay half a minute, silly; and then I found my hands empty, and my gun had flown over my head as I fell. It makes a man mighty wide awake to be in the kind of box that I was in. I scarcely knew where I was hurt, or whether I was hurt or not, but turned right over on my face to crawl after my weapon. Unless you have tried to get about with a smashed leg you don't know what pain is, and I let out a howl like a bullock's.

This was the unluckiest noise that ever I made in my life. Up to then Uma had stuck to her tree like a sensible woman, knowing she would be only in the way; but as soon as she heard me sing out she ran forward. The Winchester cracked again and down she went.

I had sat up, leg and all, to stop her; but when I saw her tumble I clapped down again where I was, lay still, and felt the handle of my knife. I had been scurried and put out before. No more of that for me. He had knocked over my girl, I had got to fix him for it; and I lay there and gritted my teeth, and footed up the chances. My leg was broke, my gun was gone. Case had still ten shots in his Winchester. It looked a kind of hopeless business. But I never despaired nor thought upon despairing: that man had got to go.

For a goodish bit not one of us let on. Then I heard Case begin to move nearer in the bush, but mighty careful. The image had burned out; there were only a few coals left here and there, and the wood was main dark, but had a kind of a low glow in it like a fire on its last legs. It was by this that I made out Case's head looking at me over a big tuft of ferns, and at the same time the brute saw me and shouldered his Winchester. I lay quite still, and as good as looked into the barrel: it was my last chance, but I thought my heart would have come right out of its bearings. Then he fired. Lucky for me it was no shotgun, for the bullet struck within an inch of me and knocked the dirt in my eyes.

Just you try and see if you can lie quiet, and let a man take a sitting shot at you and miss you by a hair. But I did, and lucky too. A while Case stood with the Winchester at the port-arms; then he gave a little laugh to himself and stepped round the ferns.

"Laugh!" thought I. "If you had the wit of a louse you would be praying!"

I was all as taut as a ship's hawser or the spring of a watch, and as soon as he came within reach of me I had him by the ankle, plucked the feet right out from under him, laid him out, and was upon the top of him, broken leg and all, before he breathed. His Winchester had gone the same road as my shot-gun; it was nothing to me—I defied him now. I'm a pretty strong man anyway, but I never knew what strength was till I got hold of Case. He was knocked out of time by the rattle he came down with, and threw up his hands together, more like a frightened woman, so that I caught both of them with my left. This wakened him up, and he fastened his teeth in my forearm like a weasel. Much I cared. My leg gave me all the pain I had any use for, and I drew my knife and got it in the place.

"Now," said I, "I've got you; and you're gone up, and a good job too! Do you feel the point of that? That's for Underhill! And there's for Adams! And now here's for Uma, and that's going to knock your blooming soul right out of you!"

With that I gave him the cold steel for all I was worth. His body kicked under me like a spring sofa; he gave a dreadful kind of a long moan, and lay still.

"I wonder if you're dead? I hope so!" I thought, for my head was swimming. But I wasn't going to take chances; I had his own example too close before me for that; and I tried to draw the knife out to give it him again. The blood came over my hands, I remember, hot as tea; and with that I fainted clean away, and fell with my head on the man's mouth.

When I came to myself it was pitch dark; the cinders had burned out; there was nothing to be seen but the shine of the dead wood, and I couldn't remember where I was nor why I was in such pain, nor what I was all wetted with. Then it came back, and the first thing I attended to was to give him the knife again a half a dozen times up to the handle. I believe he was dead already, but it did him no harm, and did me good.

"I bet you're dead now," I said, and then I called to Uma.

Nothing answered, and I made a move to go and grope for her, fouled my broken leg, and fainted again.

When I came to myself the second time the clouds had all cleared away, except a few that sailed there, white as cotton. The moon was up—a tropic moon. The moon at home turns a wood black, but even this old butt end of a one showed up that forest as green as by day. The night birds—or, rather, they're a kind of early morning bird—sang out with their long, falling notes like nightingales. And I could see the dead man, that I was still half resting on, looking right up into the sky with his open eyes, no paler than when he was alive; and a little way off Uma tumbled on her side. I got over to her the best way I was able, and when I got there she was broad awake, and crying and sobbing to herself with no more noise than an insect. It appears she was afraid to cry out loud, because of the *aitus*. Altogether she was not much hurt, but scared beyond belief; she had come to her senses a long while ago, cried out to me, heard nothing in reply, made out we were both dead, and had lain there ever since, afraid to budge a finger. The ball had ploughed up her shoulder and she had lost a main quantity of blood; but I soon had that tied up the way it ought to be with the tail of my shirt and a scarf I had on, got her head on my sound knee and my back against a trunk, and settled down to wait for morning. Uma was for neither use nor ornament, and could only clutch hold of me and shake and cry. I don't suppose there was ever anybody worse scared, and, to do her justice, she had had a lively night of it. As for me, I was in a good bit of pain and fever, but not so bad when I sat still; and every time I looked over to Case I could have sung and whistled. Talk about meat and drink! To see that man lying there dead as a herring filled me full.

The night birds stopped after a while; and then the light began to change, the east came orange, the whole wood began to whirr with singing like a musical box, and there was the broad day.

I didn't expect Maea for a long while yet; and indeed I thought there was an off-chance he might go back on the whole idea and not come at all. I was the better pleased when, about an hour after daylight, I heard sticks smashing and a lot of Kanakas laughing and singing out to keep their courage up.

Uma sat up quite brisk at the first word of it; and presently we saw a party come stringing out of the path, Maea in front, and behind him a white man in a pith helmet. It was Mr. Tarleton, who had turned up late last night in Falesá, having left his boat and walked the last stage with a lantern.

They buried Case upon the field of glory, right in the hole where he had kept the smoking head. I waited till the thing was done; and Mr. Tarleton prayed, which I thought tomfoolery, but I'm bound to say he gave a pretty sick view of the dear departed's prospects, and seemed to have his own ideas of hell. I had it out with him afterwards, told him he had scamped his duty, and what he had ought to have done was to up like a man and tell the Kanakas plainly Case was damned, and a good riddance; but I never could get him to see it my way. Then they made me a litter of poles and carried me down to the station. Mr. Tarleton set my leg, and made a regular missionary splice of it, so that I limp to this day. That done, he took down my evidence, and Uma's, and Maea's, wrote it all out fine, and had us sign it; and then he got the chiefs and marched over to Papa Randall's to seize Case's papers.

All they found was a bit of a diary, kept for a good many years, and all about the price of copra, and chickens being stolen, and that; and the books of the business and the will I told you of in the beginning, by both of which the whole thing (stock, lock, and barrel) appeared to belong to the Samoa woman. It was I that bought her out at a mighty reasonable figure, for she was in a hurry to get home. As for Randall and the black, they had to tramp; got into some kind of a station on the Papa-malulu side; did very bad business, for the truth is neither of the pair was fit for it, and lived mostly on fish, which was the means of Randall's death. It seems there was a nice shoal in one day, and Papa went after them with the dynamite; either the match burned too fast, or Papa was full, or both, but the shell went off (in the usual way) before he threw it, and where was Papa's hand? Well, there's nothing to hurt in that; the islands up north are all full of one-handed men, like the parties in the "Arabian Nights"; but either Randall was too old, or he drank too much, and the short and the long of it was that he died. Pretty soon after, the nigger was turned out of the island for stealing from white men, and went off to the west, where he found men of his own colour, in case he liked that, and the men of his own colour took and ate him at some kind of a corroborree, and I'm sure I hope he was to their fancy!

So there was I, left alone in my glory at Falesá; and when the schooner came round I filled her up, and gave her a deck-cargo half as high as the house. I must say Mr. Tarleton did the right thing by us; but he took a meanish kind of a revenge.

"Now, Mr. Wiltshire," said he, "I've put you all square with everybody here. It wasn't difficult to do, Case being gone; but I have done it, and given my pledge besides that you will deal fairly with the natives. I must ask you to keep my word."

Well, so I did. I used to be bothered about my balances, but I reasoned it out this way: We all have queerish balances, and the natives all know it, and water their copra in a proportion so that it's fair all round; but the truth is, it did use to bother me, and, though I did well in Falesá, I was half glad when the firm moved me on to another station, where I was under no kind of a pledge and could look my balances in the face.

As for the old lady, you know her as well as I do. She's only the one fault. If you don't keep your eye lifting she would give away the roof off the station. Well, it seems it's natural in Kanakas. She's turned a powerful big woman now, and could throw a London bobby over her shoulder. But that's natural in Kanakas too, and there's no manner of doubt that she's an A1 wife.

Mr. Tarleton's gone home, his trick being over. He was the best missionary I ever struck, and now, it seems, he's parsonising down Somerset way. Well, that's best for him; he'll have no Kanakas there to get luny over.

My public-house? Not a bit of it, nor ever likely. I'm stuck here, I fancy. I don't like to leave the kids, you see: and—there's no use talking—they're better here than what they would be in a white man's country, though Ben took the eldest up to Auckland, where he's being schooled with the best. But what bothers me is the girls. They're only half-castes, of course; I know that as well as you do, and there's nobody thinks less of half-castes than I do; but they're mine, and about all I've got. I can't reconcile my mind to their taking up with Kanakas, and I'd like to know where I'm to find the whites?

Weir of Hermiston

INTRODUCTORY

IN THE WILD end of a moorland parish, far out of the sight of any house, there stands a cairn among the heather, and a little by east of it, in the going down of the braeside, a monument with some verses half defaced. It was here that Claverhouse shot with his own hand the Praying Weaver of Balweary, and the chisel of Old Mortality has clinked on that lonely gravestone. Public and domestic history have thus marked with a bloody finger this hollow among the hills; and since the Cameronian gave his life there, two hundred years ago, in a glorious folly, and without comprehension or regret, the silence of the moss has been broken once again by the report of firearms and the cry of the dying.

The Deil's Hags was the old name. But the place is now called Francie's Cairn. For a while it was told that Francie walked. Aggie Hogg met him in the gloaming by the cairnside, and he spoke to her, with chattering teeth, so that his words were lost. He pursued Rob Todd (if any one could have believed Robbie) for the space of half a mile with pitiful entreaties. But the age is one of incredulity; these superstitious decorations speedily fell off; and the facts of the story itself, like the bones of a giant buried there and half dug up, survived, naked and imperfect, in the memory of the scattered neighbours. To this day, of winter nights, when the sleet is on the window and the cattle are quiet in the byre, there will be told again, amid the silence of the young and the additions and corrections of the old, the tale of the Justice-Clerk and of his son, young Hermiston, that vanished from men's knowledge; of the two Kirsties and the four Black Brothers of the Cauldstaneslap; and of Frank Innes, "the young fool advocate," that came into these moorland parts to find his destiny.

CHAPTER I

LIFE AND DEATH OF MRS. WEIR

THE Lord Justice-Clerk was a stranger in that part of the country; but his lady wife was known there from a child, as her race had been before her. The old "riding Rutherfords of Hermiston," of whom she was the last descendant, had been famous men of yore, ill neighbours, ill subjects, and ill husbands to their wives, though not their properties. Tales of them were rife for twenty miles about; and their name was even printed in the page of our Scots histories, not always to their credit. One bit the dust at Flodden; one was hanged at his peel door by James the Fifth; another fell dead in a carouse with Tom Dalyell; while a fourth (and that was Jean's own father) died presiding at a Hell-Fire Club, of which he was the founder. There were many heads shaken in Crossmichael at that judgment; the more so as the man had a villainous reputation among high and low, and both with the godly and the worldly. At that very hour of his demise he had ten going pleas before the Session, eight of them oppressive. And the same doom extended even to his agents; his grieve, that had been his right hand in many a left-hand business, being cast from his horse one night and drowned in a peat-hag on the Kye-skairs; and his very doer (although lawyers have long spoons) surviving him not long, and dying on a sudden in a bloody flux.

In all these generations, while a male Rutherford was in the saddle with his lads, or brawling in a change-house, there would be always a white-faced wife immured at home in the old peel or the later mansion-house. It seemed this succession of martyrs bided long, but took their vengeance in the end, and that was in the person of the last descendant, Jean. She bore the name of the Rutherfords, but she was the daughter of their trembling wives. At the first she was not wholly without charm. Neighbours recalled in her, as a child, a strain of elfin wilfulness, gentle little mutinies, sad little gaieties, even a morning gleam of beauty that was not to be fulfilled. She withered in the growing, and (whether it was the sins of her sires or the sorrows of her mothers) came to her maturity depressed, and, as it were, defaced; no blood of life in her, no grasp or gaiety; pious, anxious, tender, tearful, and incompetent.

It was a wonder to many that she had married—seeming so wholly of the stuff that makes old maids. But chance cast her in the path of Adam Weir, then the new Lord Advocate, a recognised, risen man, the conqueror of many obstacles, and thus late in the day beginning to think upon a wife. He was one who looked rather to obedience than beauty, yet it would seem he was struck with her at the first look. "Wha's she?" he said, turning to his host; and, when he had been told, "Ay," says he, "she looks menseful. She minds me—"; and then, after a pause (which some have been daring enough to set down to sentimental recollections), "Is she releegious?" he asked, and was shortly after, at his own request, presented. The acquaintance, which it seems profane to call a courtship, was pursued with Mr. Weir's accustomed industry, and was long a legend, or rather a source of legends, in the Parliament House. He was described coming, rosy with much port, into the drawing-room, walking direct up to the lady, and assailing her with pleasantries to which the embarrassed fair one responded, in what seemed a kind of agony, "Eh, Mr. Weir!" or "O, Mr. Weir!" or "Keep me, Mr. Weir!" On the very eve of their engagement, it was related that one had drawn near to the tender couple, and had overheard the lady cry out, with the tones of one who talked for the sake of talking, "Keep me, Mr. Weir, and what became of him?" and the profound accents of the suitor reply, "Haangit, mem, haangit." The motives upon either side were much debated. Mr. Weir must have supposed his bride to be somewhat suitable; perhaps he belonged to that class of men who think a weak head the ornament of women—an opinion invariably punished in this life. Her descent and her estate were beyond question. Her wayfaring ancestors and her litigious father had done well by Jean. There was ready money and there were broad acres, ready to fall to the husband, to lend dignity to his descendants, and to himself a title, when he should be called upon the Bench. On the side of Jean, there was perhaps some fascination of curiosity as to this unknown male animal that approached her with the roughness of a ploughman and the *aplomb* of an advocate. Being so trenchantly opposed to all she knew, loved, or understood, he may well have seemed to her the extreme, if scarcely the ideal, of his sex. And besides, he was an ill man to refuse. A little over forty at the period of his marriage, he looked already older, and to the force of manhood added the senatorial dignity of years; it was, perhaps, with an unreverend awe, but he was awful. The Bench, the Bar, and the most experienced and reluctant witness bowed to his authority—and why not Jeannie Rutherford?

The heresy about foolish women is always punished, I have said, and Lord Hermiston began to pay the penalty at once. His house in George Square was wretchedly ill-guided; nothing answerable to the expense of maintenance but the cellar, which was his own private care. When things went wrong at dinner, as they continually did, my lord would look up the table at his wife: "I think these broth would be better to sweem in than to sup." Or else to the butler: "Here, M'Killop, awa' wi' this Raadical gigot—tak' it to the French, man, and bring me some puddocks! It seems rather a sore kind of business that I should be all day in Court haanging Radicals, and get nawthing to my denner." Of course this was but a manner of speaking, and he had never hanged a man for being a Radical in his life; the law, of which he was the faithful minister, directing otherwise. And of course these growls were in the nature of pleasantry, but it was of a recondite sort; and uttered as they were in his resounding voice, and commented on by that expression which they called in the Parliament House "Hermiston's hanging face"—they struck mere dismay into the wife. She sat before him speechless and fluttering; at each dish, as at a fresh ordeal, her eye hovered toward my lord's countenance and fell again; if he but ate in silence, unspeakable relief was her portion; if there were complaint, the world was darkened. She would seek out the cook, who was always her *sister in the Lord.* "O, my dear, this is the most dreidful thing that my lord can never be contented in his own house!" she would begin; and weep and pray with the cook; and then the cook would pray with Mrs. Weir; and the next day's meal would never be a penny the better—and the next cook (when she came) would be worse, if anything, but just as pious. It was often wondered that Lord Hermiston bore it as he did; indeed, he was a stoical old voluptuary, contented with sound wine and plenty of it. But there were moments when he overflowed. Perhaps half a dozen times in the history of his married life—"Here! tak' it awa', and bring me a piece of bread and kebbuck!" he had exclaimed, with an appalling explosion of his voice and rare gestures. None thought to dispute or to make excuses; the service was arrested; Mrs. Weir sat at the head of the table whimpering without disguise; and his lordship opposite munched his bread and cheese in ostentatious disregard. Once only Mrs. Weir had ventured to appeal. He was passing her chair on his way into the study.

"O, Edom!" she wailed, in a voice tragic with tears, and reaching out to him both hands, in one of which she held a sopping pocket-handkerchief.

He paused and looked upon her with a face of wrath, into which there stole, as he looked, a twinkle of humour.

"Noansense!" he said. "You and your noansense! What do I want with a Christian faim'ly? I want Christian broth! Get me a lass that can plain-boil a potato, if she was a whüre off the streets." And with these words, which echoed in her tender ears like blasphemy, he had passed on to his study and shut the door behind him.

Such was the housewifery in George Square. It was better at Hermiston, where Kirstie Elliott, the sister of a neighbouring bonnet-laird, and an eighteenth cousin of the lady's, bore the charge of all, and kept a trim house and a good country table. Kirstie was a woman in a thousand, clean, capable, notable; once a moorland Helen, and still comely as a blood horse and healthy as the hill wind. High in flesh and voice and colour, she ran the house with her whole intemperate soul, in a bustle, not without buffets. Scarce more pious than decency in those days required, she was the cause of many an anxious thought and many a tearful prayer to Mrs. Weir. Housekeeper and mistress renewed the parts of Martha and Mary; and though with a pricking conscience, Mary reposed on Martha's strength as on a rock. Even Lord Hermiston held Kirstie in a particular regard. There were few with whom he unbent so gladly, few whom he favoured with so many pleasantries. "Kirstie and me maun have our joke," he would declare, in high good-humour, as he buttered Kirstie's scones, and she waited at table. A man who had no need either of love or of popularity, a keen reader of men and of events, there was perhaps only one truth for which he was quite unprepared: he would have been quite unprepared to learn that Kirstie hated him. He thought maid and master were well matched; hard, handy, healthy, broad Scots folk, without a hair of nonsense to the pair of them. And the fact was that she made a goddess and an only child of the effete and tearful lady; and even as she waited at table her hands would sometimes itch for my lord's ears.

Thus, at least, when the family were at Hermiston, not only my lord, but Mrs. Weir too, enjoyed a holiday. Free from the dreadful looking-for of the miscarried dinner, she would mind her seam, read her piety books, and take her walk (which was my lord's orders), sometimes by herself, sometimes with Archie, the only child of that scarce natural union. The child was her next bond to life. Her frosted sentiment bloomed again, she breathed deep of life, she let loose her heart, in that society. The miracle of her motherhood was ever new to her. The sight of the little man at her skirt intoxicated her with the sense of power, and froze her with the consciousness of her responsibility. She looked forward, and, seeing him in fancy grow up and play his diverse part on the world's theatre, caught in her breath and lifted up her courage with a lively effort. It was only with the child that she forgot herself and was at moments natural; yet it was only with the child that she had conceived and managed to pursue a scheme of conduct. Archie was to be a great man and a good; a minister if possible, a saint for certain. She tried to engage his mind upon her favourite books, Rutherford's "Letters," Scougal's "Grace Abounding," and the like. It was a common practice of hers (and strange to remember now) that she would carry the child to the Deil's Hags, sit with him on the Praying Weaver's Stone, and talk of the Covenanters till their tears ran down. Her view of history was wholly artless, a design in snow and ink; upon the one side, tender innocents with psalms upon their lips; upon the other, the persecutors, booted, bloody-minded, flushed with wine: a suffering Christ, a raging Beelzebub. *Persecutor* was a word that knocked upon the woman's heart; it was her highest thought of wickedness, and the mark of it was on her house. Her great-great-grandfather had drawn the sword against the Lord's anointed on the field of Rullion Green, and breathed his last (tradition said) in the arms of the detestable Dalyell. Nor could she blind herself to this, that had they lived in those old days, Hermiston himself would have been numbered alongside of Bloody Mackenzie and the politic Lauderdale and Rothes, in the band of God's immediate enemies. The sense of this moved her to the more fervour; she had a voice for that name of *persecutor* that thrilled in the child's marrow; and when one day the mob hooted and hissed them all in my lord's travelling carriage, and cried, "Down with the persecutor! down with Hanging Hermiston!" and mamma covered her eyes and wept, and papa let down the glass and looked out upon the rabble with his droll formidable face, bitter and smiling, as they said he sometimes looked when he gave sentence, Archie was for the moment too much amazed to be alarmed, but he had scarce got his mother by herself before his shrill voice was raised demanding an explanation: why had they called papa a persecutor?

"Keep me, my precious!" she exclaimed. "Keep me, my dear! this is poleetical. Ye must never ask me anything poleetical, Erchie. Your faither is a great man, my dear, and it's no for me or you to be judging him. It would be telling us all, if we behaved ourselves in our several stations the way your faither does in his high office; and let me hear no more of any such disrespectful and undutiful questions! No that you meant to be undutiful, my lamb; your mother kens that—she kens it well, dearie!" And so slid off to safer topics, and left on the mind of the child an obscure but ineradicable sense of something wrong.

Mrs. Weir's philosophy of life was summed in one expression—tenderness. In her view of the universe, which was all lighted up with a glow out of the doors of hell, good people must walk there in a kind of ecstasy of tenderness. The beasts and plants had no souls; they were here but for a day, and let their day pass gently! And as for the immortal men, on what black, downward path were many of them wending, and to what a horror of an immortality! "Are not two sparrows," "Whosoever shall smite thee," "God sendeth His rain," "Judge not, that ye be not judged"—these texts made her body of divinity; she put them on in the morning with her clothes and lay down to sleep with them at night; they haunted her like a favourite air, they clung about her like a favourite perfume. Their minister was a marrowy expounder of the law, and my lord sat under him with relish; but Mrs. Weir respected him from far off; heard him (like the cannon of a beleaguered city) usefully booming outside on the dogmatic ramparts; and meanwhile, within and out of shot, dwelt in her private garden which she watered with grateful tears. It seems strange to say of this colourless and ineffectual woman, but she was a true enthusiast, and might have made the sunshine and the glory of a cloister. Perhaps none but Archie knew she could be eloquent; perhaps none but he had seen her—her colour raised, her hands clasped or quivering—glow with gentle ardour. There is a corner of the policy of Hermiston, where you come suddenly in view of the summit of Black Fell, sometimes like the mere grass top of a hill, sometimes (and this is her own expression) like a precious jewel in the heavens. On such days, upon the sudden view of it, her hand would tighten on the child's fingers, her voice rise like a song. *"I to the hills!"* she would repeat. "And O,' Erchie, arena these like the hills of Naphtali?" and her tears would flow.

Upon an impressionable child the effect of this continual and pretty accompaniment to life was deep. The woman's quietism and piety passed on to his different nature undiminished; but whereas in her it was a native sentiment, in him it was only an implanted dogma. Nature and the child's pugnacity at times revolted. A cad from the Potterrow once struck him in the mouth; he struck back, the pair fought it out in the back stable lane towards the Meadows, and Archie returned with a considerable decline in the number of his front teeth, and unregenerately boasting of the losses of the foe. It was a sore day for Mrs. Weir; she wept and prayed over the infant backslider until my lord was due from Court, and she must resume that air of tremulous composure with which she always greeted him. The judge was that day in an observant mood, and remarked upon the absent teeth.

"I am afraid Erchie will have been fechting with some of thae blagyard lads," said Mrs. Weir.

My lord's voice rang out as it did seldom in the privacy of his own house. "I'll have nonn of that, sir!" he cried "Do you hear me?—nonn of that! No son of mine shall be speldering in the glaur with any dirty raibble."

The anxious mother was grateful for so much support; she had even feared the contrary. And that night when she put the child to bed—"Now, my dear, ye see!" she said, "I told you what your faither would think of it, if he heard ye had fallen into this dreidful sin; and let you and me pray to God that ye may be keepit from the like temptation or stren'thened to resist it!"

The womanly falsity of this was thrown away. Ice and iron cannot be welded; and the points of view of the Justice-Clerk and Mrs. Weir were not less unassimilable. The character and position of his father had long been a stumbling-block to Archie, and with every year of his age the difficulty grew more instant. The man was mostly silent; when he spoke at all, it was to speak of the things of the world, always in a worldly spirit, often in language that the child had been schooled to think coarse, and sometimes with words that he knew to be sins in themselves. Tenderness was the first duty, and my lord was invariably harsh. God was love; the name of my lord (to all who knew him) was fear. In the world, as schematised for Archie by his mother, the place was marked for such a creature. There were some whom it was good to pity and well (though very likely useless) to pray for; they were named reprobates, goats, God's enemies, brands for the burning; and Archie tallied every mark of identification, and drew the inevitable private inference that the Lord Justice-Clerk was the chief of sinners.

The mother's honesty was scarce complete. There was one influence she feared for the child and still secretly combated; that was my lord's; and half unconsciously, half in a wilful blindness, she continued to undermine her husband with his son. As long as Archie remained silent, she did so ruthlessly, with a single eye to heaven and the child's salvation; but the day came when Archie spoke. It was 1801, and Archie was seven, and beyond his years for curiosity and logic, when he brought the case up openly. If judging were sinful and forbidden, how came papa to be a judge? to have that sin for a trade? to bear the name of it for a distinction?

"I can't see it," said the little Rabbi, and wagged his head.

Mrs. Weir abounded in commonplace replies.

"No, I canna see it," reiterated Archie. "And I'll tell you what, mamma, I don't think you and me's justifeed in staying with him."

The woman awoke to remorse; she saw herself disloyal

to her man, her sovereign and bread-winner, in whom (with what she had of worldliness) she took a certain subdued pride. She expatiated in reply on my lord's honour and greatness; his useful services in this world of sorrow and wrong, and the place in which he stood, far above where babes and innocents could hope to see or criticise. But she had builded too well—Archie had his answers pat: Were not babes and innocents the type of the kingdom of heaven? Were not honour and greatness the badges of the world? And at any rate, how about the mob that had once seethed about the carriage?

"It's all very fine," he concluded, "but in my opinion, papa has no right to be it. And it seems that's not the worst yet of it. It seems he's called 'the Hanging Judge'—it seems he's crooool. I'll tell you what it is, mamma, there's a tex' borne in upon me: It were better for that man if a milestone were bound upon his back and him flung into the deepestmost pairts of the sea."

"O my lamb, ye must never say the like of that!" she cried. "Ye're to honour faither and mother, dear, that your days may be long in the land. It's Atheists that cry out against him—French Atheists, Erchie! Ye would never surely even yourself down to be saying the same thing as French Atheists? It would break my heart to think that of you. And O, Erchie, here arena *you* setting up to *judge?* And have ye no forgot God's plain command—the First with Promise, dear? Mind you upon the beam and the mote!"

Having thus carried the war into the enemy's camp, the terrified lady breathed again. And no doubt it is easy thus to circumvent a child with catchwords, but it may be questioned how far it is effectual. An instinct in his breast detects the quibble, and a voice condemns it. He will instantly submit, privately hold the same opinion. For even in this simple and antique relation of the mother and the child, hypocrisies are multiplied.

When the Court rose that year and the family returned to Hermiston, it was a common remark in all the country that the lady was sore failed. She seemed to lose and seize again her touch with life, now sitting inert in a sort of durable bewilderment, anon waking to feverish and weak activity. She dawdled about the lasses at their work, looking stupidly on; she fell to rummaging in old cabinets and presses, and desisted when half through; she would begin remarks with an air of animation and drop them without a struggle. Her common appearance was of one who has forgotten something and is trying to remember; and when she overhauled, one after another, the worthless and touching mementoes of her youth, she might have been seeking the clue to that lost thought. During this period she gave many gifts to the neighbours and house lasses, giving them with a manner of regret that embarrassed the recipients.

The last night of all she was busy on some female work, and toiled upon it with so manifest and painful a devotion that my lord (who was not often curious) inquired as to its nature.

She blushed to the eyes. "O, Edom, it's for you!" she said. "It's slippers. I—I hae never made ye any."

"Ye daft auld wife!" returned his lordship. "A bonny figure I would be, palmering about in bauchles!"

The next day, at the hour of her walk, Kirstie interfered. Kirstie took this decay of her mistress very hard; bore her a grudge, quarrelled with and railed upon her, the anxiety of a genuine love wearing the disguise of temper. This day of all days she insisted disrespectfully, with rustic fury, that Mrs. Weir should stay at home. But, "No, no," she said, "it's my lord's orders," and set forth as usual. Archie was visible in the acre bog, engaged upon some childish enterprise, the instrument of which was mire; and she stood and looked at him a while like one about to call; then thought otherwise, sighed, and shook her head, and proceeded on her rounds alone. The house lasses were at the burn-side washing, and saw her pass with her loose, weary, dowdy gait.

"She's a terrible feckless wife the mistress!" said the one.

"Tut," said the other, "the wumman's seeck."

"Weel, I canna see nae differ in her," returned the first. "A füshionless quean, a feckless carline."

The poor creature thus discussed rambled a while in the grounds without a purpose. Tides in her mind ebbed and flowed, and carried her to and fro like seaweed. She tried a path, paused, returned, and tried another; questing, forgetting her quest; the spirit of choice extinct in her bosom, or devoid of sequency. On a sudden, it appeared as though she had remembered, or had formed a resolution, wheeled about, returned with hurried steps, and appeared in the dining-room, where Kirstie was at the cleaning, like one charged with an important errand.

"Kirstie!" she began, and paused; and then with conviction, "Mr. Weir isna speeritually minded, but he has been a good man to me."

It was perhaps the first time since her husband's elevation that she had forgotten the handle to his name, of which the tender, inconsistent woman was not a little proud. And when Kirstie looked up at the speaker's face, she was aware of a change.

"Godsake, what's the maitter wi' ye, mem?" cried the housekeeper, starting from the rug.

"I do not ken," answered her mistress, shaking her head. "But he is not speeritually minded, my dear."

"Here, sit down with ye! Godsake, what ails the wife?" cried Kirstie, and helped and forced her into my lord's own chair by the cheek of the hearth.

"Keep me, what's this?" she gasped. "Kirstie, what's this? I'm frich'ened."

They were her last words.

It was the lowering nightfall when my lord returned. He had the sunset in his back, all clouds and glory; and before him, by the wayside, spied Kirstie Elliott waiting. She was dissolved in tears, and addressed him in the high, false note of barbarous mourning, such as still lingers modified among Scots heather.

"The Lord peety ye, Hermiston! the Lord prepare ye!" she keened out. "Weary upon me, that I should have to tell it!"

He reined in his horse and looked upon her with the hanging face.

"Has the French landit?" cried he.

"Man, man," she said, "is that a' ye can think of? The Lord prepare ye: the Lord comfort and support ye!"

"Is onybody deid?" says his lordship. "It's no Erchie?"

"Bethankit, no!" exclaimed the woman, startled into a more natural tone. "Na, na, it's no sae bad as that. It's the mistress, my lord; she just fair flittit before my e'en. She just gi'ed a sab and was by wi' it. Eh, my bonny Miss Jeannie, that I mind sae weel!" And forth again upon that pouring tide of lamentation in which women of her class excel and over-abound.

Lord Hermiston sat in the saddle beholding her. Then he seemed to recover command upon himself.

"Weel, it's something of the suddenest," said he. "But she was a dwaibly body from the first."

And he rode home at a precipitate amble with Kirstie at his horse's heels.

Dressed as she was for her last walk, they had laid the dead lady on her bed. She was never interesting in life; in death she was not impressive; and as her husband stood before her, with his hands crossed behind his powerful back, that which he looked upon was the very image of the insignificant.

"Her and me were never cut out for one another," he remarked at last. "It was a daft-like marriage." And then, with a most unusual gentleness of tone, "Puir bitch," said he, "puir bitch !" Then suddenly: "Where's Erchie?"

Kirstie had decoyed him to her room and given him "a jeely-piece."

"Ye have some kind of gumption, too," observed the judge, and considered his housekeeper grimly. "When all's said," he added, "I micht have done waur—I micht have been marriet upon a skirling Jezebel like you!"

"There's naebody thinking of you, Hermiston!" cried the offended woman. "We think of her that's out of her sorrows. And could *she* have done waur? Tell me that, Hermiston—tell me that before her clay-cauld corp!"

"Weel, there's some of them gey an' ill to please," observed his lordship.

CHAPTER II

FATHER AND SON

My Lord Justice-Clerk was known to many; the man Adam Weir perhaps to none. He had nothing to explain or to conceal; he sufficed wholly and silently to himself; and that part of our nature which goes out (too often with false coin) to acquire glory or love, seemed in him to be omitted. He did not try to be loved, he did not care to be; it is probable the very thought of it was a stranger to his mind. He was an admired lawyer, a highly unpopular judge; and he looked down upon those who were his inferiors in either distinction, who were lawyers of less grasp or judges not so much detested. In all the rest of his days and doings, not one trace of vanity appeared; and he went on through life with a mechanical movement, as of the unconscious, that was almost august.

He saw little of his son. In the childish maladies with which the boy was troubled, he would make daily inquiries and daily pay him a visit, entering the sick-room with a facetious and appalling countenance, letting off a few perfunctory jests, and going again swiftly, to the patient's relief. Once, a Court holiday falling opportunely, my lord had his carriage, and drove the child himself to Hermiston, the customary place of convalescence. It is conceivable he had been more than usually anxious, for that journey always remained in Archie's memory as a thing apart, his father having related to him from beginning to end, and with much detail, three authentic murder cases. Archie went the usual round of other Edinburgh boys, the High School and the College; and Hermiston looked on, or rather looked away, with scarce an affectation of interest in his progress. Daily, indeed, upon a signal after dinner, he was brought in, given nuts and a glass of port, regarded sardonically, sarcastically questioned. "Well, sir, and what have you donn with your book to-day?" my lord might begin, and set him posers in law Latin. To a child just stumbling into Corderius, Papinian and Paul proved quite invincible. But papa had memory of no other. He was not harsh to the little scholar, having a vast fund of patience learned upon the Bench, and was at no pains whether to conceal or to express his disappointment. "Well, ye have a long jaunt before ye yet!" he might observe, yawning, and fall back on his own thoughts (as like as not) until the time came for separation, and my lord would take the decanter and the glass, and be off to the back chamber looking on the Meadows, where he toiled on his cases till the hours were small. There was no "fuller man" on the Bench; his memory was marvellous, though wholly legal; if he had to "advise" extempore, none did it better; yet there was none who more earnestly prepared. As he thus watched in the night, or sat at table and forgot the presence of his son, no doubt but he tasted deeply of recondite pleasures. To be wholly devoted to some intellectual exercise is to have succeeded in life; and perhaps only in law and the higher mathematics may this devotion be maintained, suffice to itself without reaction, and find continual rewards without excitement. This atmosphere of his father's sterling industry was the best of Archie's education. Assuredly it did not attract him; assuredly it rather rebutted and depressed. Yet it was still present, unobserved like the ticking of a clock, an arid ideal, a tasteless stimulant in the boy's life.

But Hermiston was not all of one piece. He was, besides, a mighty toper; he could sit at wine until the day dawned, and pass directly from the table to the Bench with a steady hand and a clear head. Beyond the third bottle, he showed the plebeian in a larger print; the low, gross accent, the low, foul mirth, grew broader and commoner; he became less formidable, and infinitely more disgusting. Now, the boy had inherited from Jean Rutherford a shivering delicacy, unequally mated with potential violence. In the playing-fields, and amongst his own companions, he repaid a coarse expression with a blow; at his father's table (when the time came for him to join these revels) he turned pale and sickened in silence. Of all the guests whom he there encountered, he had toleration for only one: David Keith Carnegie, Lord Glenalmond. Lord Glenalmond was tall and emaciated, with long features and long delicate hands. He was often compared with the statue of Forbes of Culloden in the Parliament House; and his blue eye, at more than sixty, preserved some of the fire of youth. His exquisite disparity with any of his fellow-guests, his appearance as of an artist and an aristocrat stranded in rude company, riveted the boy's attention; and as curiosity and interest are the things in the world that are the most immediately and certainly rewarded, Lord Glenalmond was attracted by the boy.

"And so this is your son, Hermiston?" he asked, laying his hand on Archie's shoulder. "He's getting a big lad."

"Hout!" said the gracious father, "just his mother over again—daurna say boo to a goose!"

But the stranger retained the boy, talked to him, drew him out, found in him a taste for letters, and a fine, ardent, modest, youthful soul; and encouraged him to be a visitor on Sunday evenings in his bare, cold, lonely dining-room, where he sat and read in the isolation of a bachelor grown old in refinement. The beautiful gentleness and grace of the old judge, and the delicacy of his person, thoughts, and language, spoke to Archie's heart in its own tongue. He conceived the ambition to be such another; and, when the day came for him to choose a profession, it was in emulation of Lord Glenalmond, not of Lord Hermiston, that he chose the Bar. Hermiston looked on at this friendship with some secret pride, but openly with the intolerance of scorn. He scarce lost an opportunity to put them down with a rough jape; and, to say truth, it was not difficult, for they were neither of them quick. He had a word of contempt for the whole crowd of poets, painters, fiddlers, and their admirers, the bastard race of amateurs, which was continually on his lips. "Signor Feedle-eerie!" he would say. "O, for Goad's sake, no more of the Signor!"

"You and my father are great friends, are you not?" asked Archie once.

"There is no man that I more respect, Archie," replied Lord Glenalmond. "He is two things of price: he is a great lawyer, and he is upright as the day."

"You and he are so different," said the boy, his eyes dwelling on those of his old friend, like a lover's on his mistress's.

"Indeed so," replied the judge; "very different. And so I fear are you and he. Yet I would like it very ill if my young friend were to misjudge his father. He has all the Roman virtues: Cato and Brutus were such; I think a son's heart might well be proud of such an ancestry of one."

"And I would sooner he were a plaided herd," cried Archie, with sudden bitterness.

"And that is neither very wise, nor I believe entirely true," returned Glenalmond. "Before you are done you will find some of these expressions rise on you like a remorse. They are merely literary and decorative; they do not aptly express your thought, nor is your thought clearly apprehended, and no doubt your father (if he were here) would say, 'Signor Feedle-eerie!' "

With the infinitely delicate sense of youth, Archie avoided the subject from that hour. It was perhaps a pity. Had he but talked—talked freely—let himself gush out in words (the way youth loves to do, and should), there might have been no tale to write upon the Weirs of Hermiston. But the shadow of a threat of ridicule sufficed; in the slight tartness of these words he read a prohibition; and it is likely that Glenalmond meant it so.

Besides the veteran, the boy was without confidant or friend. Serious and eager, he came through school and college, and moved among a crowd of the indifferent, in the seclusion of his shyness. He grew up handsome, with an open, speaking countenance, with graceful, youthful ways; he was clever, he took prizes, he shone in the Speculative Society. It should seem he must become the centre of a crowd of friends; but something that was in part the delicacy of his mother, in part the austerity of his father, held him aloof from all. It is a fact, and a strange one, that among his contemporaries Hermiston's son was thought to be a chip of the old block. "You're a friend of Archie Weir's?" said one to Frank Innes; and Innes replied, with his usual flippancy and more than his usual insight: "I know Weir, but I never met Archie." No one had met Archie, a malady most incident to only sons. He flew his private signal, and none heeded it; it seemed he was abroad in a world from which the very hope of intimacy was banished; and he looked round about him on the concourse of his fellow-students, and forward to the trivial days and acquaintances that were to come, without hope or interest.

As time went on, the tough and rough old sinner felt himself drawn to the son of his loins and sole continuator of his new family, with softnesses of sentiment that he could hardly credit and was wholly impotent to express. With a face, voice, and manner trained through forty years to terrify and repel, Rhadamanthus may be great, but he will scarce be engaging. It is a fact that he tried to propitiate Archie, but a fact that cannot be too lightly taken; the attempt was so unconspicuously made, the failure so stoically supported. Sympathy is not due to these steadfast iron natures. If he failed to gain his son's friendship, or even his son's toleration, on he went up the great, bare staircase of his duty, uncheered and undepressed. There might have been more pleasure in his relations with Archie, so much he may have recognised at moments; but pleasure was a by-product of the singular chemistry of life, which only fools expected.

An idea of Archie's attitude, since we are all grown up and have forgotten the days of our youth, it is more difficult to convey. He made no attempt whatsoever to understand the man with whom he dined and breakfasted. Parsimony of pain, glut of pleasure, these are the two alternating ends of youth; and Archie was of the parsimonious. The wind blew cold out of a certain quarter—he turned his back upon it; stayed as little as was possible in his father's presence; and when there, averted his eyes as much as was decent from his father's face. The lamp shone for many hundred days upon these two at table—my lord ruddy, gloomy, and unreverend; Archie with a potential brightness that was always dimmed and veiled in that society; and there were not, perhaps, in Christendom two men more radically strangers. The father, with a grand simplicity, either spoke of what interested himself, or maintained an unaffected silence. The son turned in his head for some topic that should be quite safe, that would spare him fresh evidences either of my lord's inherent grossness or of the innocence of his inhumanity; treading gingerly the ways of intercourse, like a lady gathering up her skirts in a by-path. If he made a mistake, and my lord began to abound in matter of offence, Archie drew himself up, his brow grew dark, his share of the talk expired; but my lord would faithfully and cheerfully continue to pour out the worst of himself before his silent and offended son.

" Well, it's a poor hert that never rejoices!" he would say, at the conclusion of such a nightmare interview. "But I must get to my plew-stilts." And he would seclude himself as usual in the back room, and Archie go forth into the night and the city quivering with animosity and scorn.

CHAPTER III

IN THE MATTER OF THE HANGING OF DUNCAN JOPP

IT CHANCED in the year 1813 that Archie strayed one day into the Justiciary Court. The macer made room for the son of the presiding judge. In the dock, the centre of men's eyes, there stood a whey-coloured, misbegotten caitiff, Duncan Jopp, on trial for his life. His story, as it was raked out before him in that public scene, was one of disgrace and vice and cowardice, the very nakedness of crime; and the creature heard, and it seemed at times as though he understood—as if at times he forgot the horror of the place he stood in, and remembered the shame of what had brought him there. He kept his head bowed and his hands clutched upon the rail; his hair dropped in his eyes and at times he flung it back; and now he glanced about the audience in a sudden fellness of terror, and now looked in the face of his judge and gulped. There was pinned about his throat a piece of dingy flannel; and this it was perhaps that turned the scale in Archie's mind between disgust and pity. The creature stood in a vanishing point; yet a little while, and he was still a man, and had eyes and apprehension; yet a little longer, and with a last sordid piece of pageantry, he would cease to be. And here, in the meantime, with a trait of human nature that caught at the beholder's breath, he was tending a sore throat.

Over against him, my Lord Hermiston occupied the Bench in the red robes of criminal jurisdiction, his face framed in the white wig. Honest all through, he did not affect the virtue of impartiality; this was no case for refinement; there was a man to be hanged, he would have said, and he was hanging him. Nor was it possible to see his lordship, and acquit him of gusto in the task. It was plain he gloried in the exercise of his trained faculties, in the clear sight which pierced at once into the joint of fact, in the rude, unvarnished gibes with which he demolished every figment of defence. He took his ease and jested, unbending in that solemn place with some of the freedom of the tavern; and the rag of man with the flannel round his neck was hunted gallowsward with jeers.

Duncan had a mistress, scarce less forlorn and greatly older than himself, who came up, whimpering and curtseying, to add the weight of her betrayal. My lord gave her the oath in his most roaring voice, and added an intolerant warning.

"Mind what ye say now, Janet," said he. "I have an e'e upon ye, I'm ill to jest with."

Presently, after she was tremblingly embarked on her story, "And what made ye do this, ye auld runt?" the Court interposed. "Do ye mean to tell me ye was the panel's mistress?"

"If you please, ma loard," whined the female.

"Godsake! ye made a bonny couple," observed his lordship; and there was something so formidable and ferocious in his scorn that not even the galleries thought to laugh.

The summing up contained some jewels.

"These two peetiable creatures seem to have made up thegither, it's not for us to explain why."—"The panel, who (whatever else he may be) appears to be equally ill set-out in mind and boady."—"Neither the panel nor yet the old wife appears to have had so much common sense as even to tell a lie when it was necessary." And in the course of sentencing, my lord had this *obiter dictum:* "I have been the means, under God, of haanging a great number, but never just such a disjaskit rascal as yourself." The words were strong in themselves; the light and heat and detonation of their delivery, and the savage pleasure of the speaker in his task, made them tingle in the ears.

When all was over, Archie came forth again into a changed world. Had there been the least redeeming greatness in the crime, any obscurity, any dubiety, perhaps he might have understood. But the culprit stood, with his sore throat, in the sweat of his mortal agony, without defence or excuse: a thing to cover up with blushes: a being so much sunk beneath the zones of sympathy that pity might seem harmless. And the judge had pursued him with a monstrous, relishing gaiety, horrible to be conceived, a trait for nightmares. It is one thing to spear a tiger, another to crush a toad; there are aesthetics even of the slaughter-house; and the loathsomeness of Duncan Jopp enveloped and infected the image of his judge.

Archie passed by his friends in the High Street with incoherent words and gestures. He saw Holyrood in a dream, remembrance of its romance awoke in him and faded; he had a vision of the old radiant stories, of Queen Mary and Prince Charlie, of the hooded stag, of the splendour and crime, the velvet and bright iron of the past; and dismissed them with a cry of pain. He lay and moaned in the Hunter's Bog, and the heavens were dark above him and the grass of the field an offence. "This is my father," he said. "I draw my life from him; the flesh upon my bones is his, the bread I am fed with is the wages of these horrors." He recalled his mother, and ground his forehead in the earth. He thought of flight, and where was he to flee to? of other lives, but was there any life worth living in this den of savage and jeering animals?

The interval before the execution was like a violent dream. He met his father; he would not look at him, he could not speak to him. It seemed there was no living creature but must have been swift to recognise that imminent animosity; but the hide of the Justice-Clerk remained impenetrable. Had my lord been talkative, the truce could never have subsisted; but he was by fortune in one of his humours of sour silence; and under the very guns of his broadside, Archie nursed the enthusiasm of rebellion. It seemed to him, from the top of his nineteen years' experience, as if he were marked at birth to be the perpetrator of some signal action, to set back fallen Mercy, to overthrow the usurping devil that sat, horned and hoofed, on her throne. Seductive Jacobin figments, which he had often refuted at the Speculative, swam up in his mind and startled him as with voices: and he seemed to himself to walk accompanied by an almost tangible presence of new beliefs and duties.

On the named morning he was at the place of execution. He saw the fleering rabble, the flinching wretch produced. He looked on for a while at a certain parody of devotion, which seemed to strip the wretch of his last claim to manhood. Then followed the brutal instant of extinction, and the paltry dangling of the remains like a broken jumping-jack. He had been prepared for something terrible, not for this tragic meanness. He stood a moment silent, and then—"I denounce this God-defying murder," he shouted; and his father, if he must have disclaimed the sentiment, might have owned the stentorian voice with which it was uttered.

Frank Innes dragged him from the spot. The two handsome lads followed the same course of study and recreation, and felt a certain mutual attraction, founded mainly on good looks. It had never gone deep; Frank was by nature a thin, jeering creature, not truly susceptible whether of feeling or inspiring friendship; and the relation between the pair was altogether on the outside, a thing of common knowledge and the pleasantries that spring from a common acquaintance. The more credit to Frank that he was appalled by Archie's outburst, and at least conceived the design of keeping him in sight, and, if possible, in hand for the day. But Archie, who had just defied—was it God or Satan?—would not listen to the word of a college companion.

"I will not go with you," he said. "I do not desire your company, sir; I would be alone."

"Here, Weir, man, don't be absurd," said Innes, keeping a tight hold upon his sleeve. "I will not let you go until I know what you mean to do with yourself; it's no use brandishing that staff." For indeed at that moment Archie had made a sudden—perhaps a warlike—movement. "This has been the most insane affair; you know it has. You know very well that I'm playing the good Samaritan. All I wish is to keep you quiet."

"If quietness is what you wish, Mr. Innes," said Archie, "and you will promise to leave me entirely to myself, I will tell you so much, that I am going to walk in the country and admire the beauties of nature."

"Honour bright?" asked Frank.

"I am not in the habit of lying, Mr. Innes," retorted Archie. "I have the honour of wishing you good-day."

"You won't forget the Spec.?" asked Innes.

"The Spec.?" said Archie. "O no, I won't forget the Spec."

And the one young man carried his tortured spirit forth of the city and all the day long, by one road and another, in an endless pilgrimage of misery; while the other hastened smilingly to spread the news of Weir's access of insanity, and to drum up for that night a full attendance at the Speculative, where further eccentric developments might certainly be looked for. I doubt if Innes had the least belief in his prediction; I think it flowed rather from a wish to make the story as good and the scandal as great as possible; not from any ill-will to Archie—from the mere pleasure of beholding interested faces. But for all that his words were prophetic. Archie did not forget the Spec.; he put in an appearance there at the due time, and, before the evening was over, had dealt a memorable shock to his companions. It chanced he was the president of the night. He sat in the same room where the Society still meets—only the portraits were not there: the men who afterwards sat for them were then but beginning their careers. The same lustre of many tapers shed its light over the meeting; the same chair, perhaps, supported him that so many of us have sat in since. At times he seemed to forget the business of the evening, but even in these periods he sat with a great air of energy and determination. At times he meddled bitterly, and launched with defiance those fines which are the precious and rarely used artillery of the president. He little thought, as he did so, how he resembled his father, but his friends remarked upon it, chuckling. So far, in his high place above his fellow-students, he seemed set beyond the possibility of any scandal; but his mind was made up—he was determined to fulfil the sphere of his offence. He signed to Innes (whom he had just fined and who had just impeached his ruling) to succeed him in the chair, stepped down from the platform, and took his place by the chimney-piece, the shine of many wax tapers from above illuminating his pale face, the glow of the great red fire relieving from behind his slim figure. He had to propose, as an amendment to the next subject in the case-book, "Whether capital punishment be consistent with God's will or man's policy?"

A breath of embarrassment, of something like alarm, passed round the room, so daring did these words appear upon the lips of Hermiston's only son. But the amendment was not seconded; the previous question was promptly moved and unanimously voted, and the momentary scandal smuggled by. Innes triumphed in the fulfilment of his prophecy. He and Archie were now become the heroes of the night; but whereas every one crowded about Innes, when the meeting broke up, but one of all his companions came to speak to Archie.

"Weir, man! That was an extraordinary raid of yours!" observed this courageous member, taking him confidentially by the arm as they went out.

"I don't think it a raid," said Archie grimly. "More like a war. I saw that poor brute hanged this morning, and my gorge rises at it yet."

"Hut-tut," returned his companion, and, dropping his arm like something hot, he sought the less tense society of others.

Archie found himself alone. The last of the faithful—or was it only the boldest of the curious?—had fled. He watched the black huddle of his fellow-students draw off down and up the street, in whispering or boisterous gangs. And the isolation of the moment weighed upon him like an omen and an emblem of his destiny in life. Bred up in unbroken fear himself, among trembling servants and in a house which (at the least ruffle in the master's voice) shuddered into silence, he saw himself on the brink of the red valley of war, and measured the danger and length of it with awe. He made a detour in the glimmer and shadow of the streets, came into the back stable lane, and watched for a long while the light burn steady in the judge's room. The longer he gazed upon that illuminated window-blind, the more blank became the picture of the man who sat behind it, endlessly turning over sheets of process, pausing to sip a glass of port, or rising and passing heavily about his book-lined walls to verify some reference. He could not combine the brutal judge and the industrious, dispassionate student; the connecting link escaped him; from such a dual nature it was impossible he should predict behaviour; and he asked himself if he had done well to plunge into a business of which the end could not be foreseen? and presently after, with a sickening decline of confidence, if he had done loyally to strike his father? For he had struck him—defied him twice over and before a cloud of witnesses—struck him a public buffet before crowds. Who had called him to judge his father in these precarious and high questions? The office was usurped. It might have become a stranger; in a son—there was no blinking it—in a son, it was disloyal. And now, between these two natures so antipathetic, so hateful to each other, there was depending an unpardonable affront: and the providence of God alone might foresee the manner in which it would be resented by Lord Hermiston.

These misgivings tortured him all night and arose with him in the winter's morning; they followed him from class to class, they made him shrinkingly sensitive to every shade of manner in his companions, they sounded in his ears through the current voice of the professor; and he brought them home with him at night unabated and indeed increased. The cause of this increase lay in a chance encounter with the celebrated Dr. Gregory. Archie stood looking vaguely in the lighted window of a book-shop, trying to nerve himself for the approaching ordeal. My lord and he had met and parted in the morning as they had now done for long, with scarcely the ordinary civilities of life; and it was plain to the son that nothing had yet reached the father's ears. Indeed, when he recalled the awful countenance of my lord, a timid hope sprang up in him that perhaps there would be found no one bold enough to carry tales. If this were so, he asked himself, would he begin again? and he found no answer. It was at this moment that a hand was laid upon his arm, and a voice said in his ear, "My dear Mr. Archie, you had better come and see me."

He started, turned round, and found himself face to face with Dr. Gregory. "And why should I come to see you?" he asked, with the defiance of the miserable.

"Because you are looking exceedingly ill," said the doctor, "and you very evidently want looking after, my young friend. Good folk are scarce, you know; and it is not every one that would be quite so much missed as yourself. It is not every one that Hermiston would miss."

And with a nod and a smile, the doctor passed on.

A moment after, Archie was in pursuit, and had in turn, but more roughly, seized him by the arm.

"What do you mean? what did you mean by saying that? What makes you think that Hermis—my father would have missed me?"

The doctor turned about and looked him all over with a clinical eye. A far more stupid man than Dr. Gregory might have guessed the truth; but ninety-nine out of a hundred, even if they had been equally inclined to kindness, would have blundered by some touch of charitable exaggeration. The doctor was better inspired. He knew the father well; in that white face of intelligence and suffering, he divined something of the son; and he told, without apology or adornment, the plain truth.

"When you had the measles, Mr. Archibald, you had them gey and ill; and I thought you were going to slip between my fingers," he said. "Well, your father was anxious. How did I know it? says you. Simply because I am a trained observer. The sign that I saw him make, ten thousand would have missed; and perhaps—*perhaps*, I say, because he's a hard man to judge of—but perhaps he never made another. A strange thing to consider! It was this. One day I came to him: 'Hermiston,' said I, 'there's a change.' He never said a word, just glowered at me (if ye'll pardon the phrase) like a wild beast. 'A change for the better,' said I. And I distinctly heard him take his breath."

The doctor left no opportunity for anti-climax; nodding his cocked hat (a piece of antiquity to which he clung) and repeating "Distinctly" with raised eyebrows, he took his departure, and left Archie speechless in the street.

The anecdote might be called infinitely little, and yet its meaning for Archie was immense. "I did not know the old man had so much blood in him." He had never dreamed this sire of his, this aboriginal antique, this adamantine Adam, had even so much of a heart as to be moved in the least degree for another—and that other himself, who had insulted him! With the generosity of youth, Archie was instantly under arms upon the other side: had instantly created a new image of Lord Hermiston, that of a man who was all iron without and all sensibility within. The mind of the vile jester, the tongue that had pursued Duncan Jopp with unmanly insults, the unbeloved countenance that he had known and feared for so long, were all forgotten; and he hastened home, impatient to confess his misdeeds, impatient to throw himself on the mercy of this imaginary character.

He was not to be long without a rude awakening. It was in the gloaming when he drew near the doorstep of the lighted house, and was aware of the figure of his father approaching from the opposite side. Little daylight lingered; but on the door being opened, the strong yellow shine of the lamp gushed out upon the landing and shone full on Archie, as he stood, in the old-fashioned observance of respect, to yield precedence. The judge came without haste, stepping stately and firm; his chin raised, his face (as he entered the lamplight) strongly illumined, his mouth set hard. There was never a wink of change in his expression; without looking to the right or left, he mounted the stair, passed close to Archie, and entered the house. Instinctively, the boy, upon his first coming, had made a movement to meet him; instinctively he recoiled against the railing, as the old man swept by him in a pomp of indignation. Words were needless; he knew all—perhaps more than all—and the hour of judgment was at hand.

It is possible that, in this sudden revulsion of hope and before these symptoms of impending danger, Archie might have fled. But not even that was left to him. My lord, after hanging up his cloak and hat, turned round in the lighted entry, and made him an imperative and silent gesture with his thumb, and with the strange instinct of obedience, Archie followed him into the house.

All dinner-time there reigned over the judge's table a palpable silence, and as soon as the solids were despatched he rose to his feet.

"M'Killop, tak' the wine into my room," said he; and then to his son: "Archie, you and me has to have a talk."

It was at this sickening moment that Archie's courage, for the first and last time, entirely deserted him. "I have an appointment," said he.

"It'll have to be broken, then," said Hermiston, and led the way into his study.

The lamp was shaded, the fire trimmed to a nicety, the table covered deep with orderly documents, the backs of law-books made a frame upon all sides that was only broken by the window and the doors.

For a moment Hermiston warmed his hands at the fire, presenting his back to Archie; then suddenly disclosed on him the terrors of the Hanging Face.

"What's this I hear of ye?" he asked.

There was no answer possible to Archie.

"I'll have to tell ye, then," pursued Hermiston. "It seems ye've been skirling against the father that begot ye, and one of his Maijesty's judges in this land; and that in the public street, and while an order of the Court was being executit. Forbye which, it would appear that ye've been airing your opeenions in a Coallege Debatin' Society"; he paused a moment: and then, with extraordinary bitterness, added: "Ye damned eediot."

"I had meant to tell you," stammered Archie. "I see you are well informed."

"Muckle obleeged to ye," said his lordship, and took his usual seat. "And so you disapprove of caapital punishment?" he added.

"I am sorry, sir, I do," said Archie.

"I am sorry, too," said his lordship. "And now, if you please, we shall approach this business with a little more parteecularity. I hear that at the hanging of Duncan Jopp—and, man! ye had a fine client there—in the middle of all the riffraff of the ceety, ye thought fit to cry out, 'This is a damned murder, and my gorge rises at the man that haangit him.' "

"No, sir, these were not my words," cried Archie.

"What were yer words, then?" asked the judge.

"I believe I said, 'I denounce it as a murder!' " said the son. "I beg your pardon—a God-defying murder. I have no wish to conceal the truth," he added, and looked his father for a moment in the face.

"God, it would only need that of it next!" cried Hermiston. "There was nothing about your gorge rising, then?"

"That was afterwards, my lord, as I was leaving the Speculative. I said I had been to see the miserable creature hanged, and my gorge rose at it."

"Did ye, though?" said Hermiston. "And I suppose ye knew who haangit him?"

"I was present at the trial; I ought to tell you that, I ought to explain. I ask your pardon beforehand for any expression that may seem undutiful. The position in which I stand is wretched," said the unhappy hero, now fairly face to face with the business he had chosen. "I have been reading some of your cases. I was present while Jopp was tried. It was a hideous business. Father, it was a hideous thing! Grant he was vile, why should you hunt him with a vileness equal to his own? It was done with glee—that is the word—you did it with glee; and I looked on, God help me! with horror."

"You're a young gentleman that doesna approve of caapital punishment," said Hermiston. "Weel, I'm an auld man that does. I was glad to get Jopp haangit, and what for would I pretend I wasna? You're all for honesty, it seems; you couldn't even steik your mouth on the public street. What for should I steik mines upon the Bench, the King's officer, bearing the sword, a dreid to evil-doers, as I was from the beginning, and as I will be to the end! Mair than enough of it! Heedious! I never gave twa thoughts to heediousness, I have no call to be bonny. I'm a man that gets through with my day's business, and let that suffice."

The ring of sarcasm had died out of his voice as he went on; the plain words became invested wlth some of the dignity of the Justice-seat.

"It would be telling you if you could say as much," the speaker resumed. "But ye cannot. Ye've been reading some of my cases, ye say. But it was not for the law in them, it was to spy out your father's nakedness, a fine employment in a son. You're splairging; you're running at lairge in life like a wild nowt. It's impossible you should think any longer of coming to the Bar. You're not fit for it; no splairger is. And another thing: son of mines or no son of mines, you have flung fylement in public on one of the Senators of the Coallege of Justice, and I would make it my business to see that ye were never admitted there yourself. There is a kind of a decency to be observit. Then comes the next of it—what am I to do with ye next? Ye'll have to find some kind of a trade, for I'll never support ye in idleset. What do ye fancy ye'll be fit for? The pulpit? Na, they could never get diveenity into that bloackhead. Him that the law of man whammles is no likely to do muckle better by the law of God. What would ye make of hell? Wouldna your gorge rise at that? Na, there's no room for splairgers under the fower quarters of John Calvin. What else is there? Speak up. Have ye got nothing of your own?"

"Father, let me go to the Peninsula," said Archie. "That's all I'm fit for—to fight."

"All? quo' he!" returned the judge. "And it would be enough too, if I thought it. But I'll never trust ye so near the French, you that's so Frenchifeed."

"You do me injustice there, sir," said Archie. "I am loyal; I will not boast; but any interest I may have ever felt in the French—"

"Have ye been so loyal to me?" interrupted his father.

There came no reply.

"I think not," continued Hermiston. "And I would send no man to be a servant to the King, God bless him! that has proved such a shauchling son to his own faither. You can splairge here on Edinburgh street, and where's the hairm? It doesna play buff on me! And if there were twenty thousand eediots like yourself, sorrow a Duncan Jopp would hang the fewer. But there's no splairging possible in a camp; and if you were to go to it, you would find out for yourself whether Lord Well'n'ton approves of caapital punishment or not. You a sodger!" he cried, with a sudden burst of scorn. "Ye auld wife, the sodgers would bray at ye like cuddies!"

As at the drawing of a curtain, Archie was aware of some illogicality in his position, and stood abashed. He had a strong impression, besides, of the essential valour of the old gentleman before him, how conveyed it would be hard to say.

"Well, have ye no other proposeetion?" said my lord again.

"You have taken this so calmly, sir, that I cannot but stand ashamed," began Archie.

"I'm nearer voamiting, though, than you would fancy," said my lord.

The blood rose to Archie's brow.

"I beg your pardon, I should have said that you had accepted my affront. . . . I admit it was an affront; I did not think to apologise, but I do, I ask your pardon; it will not be so again, I pass you my word of honour. . . . I should have said that I admired your magnanimity with—this—offender," Archie concluded with a gulp.

"I have no other son, ye see," said Hermiston. "A bonny one I have gotten! But I must just do the best I can wi' him, and what am I to do? If ye had been younger, I would have wheepit ye for this rideeculous exhibeetion. The way it is, I have just to grin and bear. But one thing is to be clearly understood. As a faither, I must grin and bear it; but if I had been the Lord Advocate instead of the Lord Justice-Clerk, son or no son, Mr. Erchibald Weir would have been in a jyle the night."

Archie was now dominated. Lord Hermiston was coarse and cruel; and yet the son was aware of a bloomless nobility, an ungracious abnegation of the man's self in the man's office. At every word, this sense of the greatness of Lord Hermiston's spirit struck more home; and along with it that of his own impotence, who had struck—and perhaps basely struck—at his own father, and not reached so far as to have even nettled him.

"I place myself in your hands without reserve," he said.

"That's the first sensible word I've had of ye the night," said Hermiston. "I can tell ye, that would have been the end of it, the one way or the other; but it's better ye should come there yourself, than what I would have had to hirstle ye. Weel, by my way of it—and my way is the best—there's just the one thing it's possible that ye might be with decency, and that's a laird. Ye'll be out of hairm's way at the least of it. If ye have to rowt, ye can rowt amang the kye; and the maist feck of the caapital punishment ye're like to come across'll be guddling trouts. Now, I'm for no idle lairdies; every man has to work, if it's only at peddling ballants; to work, or to be wheeped, or to be haangit. If I set ye down at Hermiston, I'll have to see you work that place the way it has never been workit yet; ye must ken about the sheep like a herd; ye must be my grieve there, and I'll see that I gain by ye. Is that understood?"

"I will do my best," said Archie.

"Well, then, I'll send Kirstie word the morn, and ye can go yourself the day after," said Hermiston. "And just try to be less of an eediot!" he concluded, with a freezing smile, and turned immediately to the papers on his desk.

CHAPTER IV

OPINIONS OF THE BENCH

LATE THE same night, after a disordered walk, Archie was admitted into Lord Glenalmond's dining-room, where he sat, with a book upon his knee, beside three frugal coals of fire. In his robes upon the Bench, Glenalmond had a certain air of burliness: plucked of these, it was a may-pole of a man that rose unsteadily from his chair to give his visitor welcome. Archie had suffered much in the last days, he had suffered again that evening; his face was white and drawn, his eyes wild and dark. But Lord Glenalmond greeted him without the least mark of surprise or curiosity.

"Come in, come in," said he. "Come in and take a seat. Carstairs" (to his servant), "make up the fire, and then you can bring a bit of supper," and again to Archie, with a very trivial accent: "I was half expecting you," he added.

"No supper," said Archie. "It is impossible that I should eat."

"Not impossible," said the tall old man, laying his hand upon his shoulder, "and, if you will believe me, necessary."

"You know what brings me?" said Archie, as soon as the servant had left the room.

"I have a guess, I have a guess," replied Glenalmond. "We will talk of it presently—when Carstairs has come and gone, and you have had a piece of my good Cheddar cheese and a pull at the porter tankard: not before."

"It is impossible I should eat," repeated Archie.

"Tut, tut!" said Lord Glenalmond. "You have eaten nothing to-day, and I venture to add, nothing yesterday. There is no case that may not be made worse; this may be a very disagreeable business, but if you were to fall sick and die, it would be still more so, and for all concerned—for all concerned."

"I see you must know all," said Archie. "Where did you hear it?"

"In the mart of scandal, in the Parliament House," said Glenalmond. "It runs riot below among the Bar and the public, but it sifts up to us upon the Bench, and rumour has some of her voices even in the divisions."

Carstairs returned at this moment, and rapidly laid out a little supper; during which Lord Glenalmond spoke at large and a little vaguely on indifferent subjects, so that it might be rather said of him that he made a cheerful noise, than that he contributed to human conversation; and Archie sat upon the other side, not heeding him, brooding over his wrongs and errors.

But so soon as the servant was gone, he broke forth again at once. "Who told my father? Who dared to tell him? Could it have been you?"

"No, it was not me," said the judge; "although—to be quite frank with you, after I had seen and warned you—it might have been me. I believe it was Glenkindie."

"That shrimp!" cried Archie.

"As you say, that shrimp," returned my lord; "although really it is scarce a fitting mode of expression for one of the senators of the College of Justice. We were hearing the parties in a long, crucial case, before the fifteenth; Creech was moving at some length for an infeftment; when I saw Glenkindie lean forward to Hermiston with his hand over his mouth and make him a secret communication. No one could have guessed its nature from your father; from Glenkindie, yes, his malice sparked out of him a little grossly. But your father, no. A man of granite. The next moment he pounced upon Creech. 'Mr. Creech,' says he, 'I'll take a look of that sasine,' and for thirty minutes after," said Glenalmond, with a smile, "Messrs. Creech and Co. were fighting a pretty uphill battle, which resulted, I need hardly add, in their total rout. The case was dismissed. No, I doubt if ever I heard Hermiston better inspired. He was literally rejoicing *in apicibus juris*."

Archie was able to endure no longer. He thrust his plate away and interrupted the deliberate and insignificant stream of talk. "Here," he said, "I have made a fool of myself, if I have not made something worse. Do you judge between us—judge between a father and a son. I can speak to you; it is not like . . . I will tell you what I feel and what I mean to do; and you shall be the judge," he repeated.

"I decline jurisdiction," said Glenalmond, with extreme seriousness. "But, my dear boy, if it will do you any good to talk, and if it will interest you at all to hear what I may choose to say when I have heard you, I am quite at your command. Let an old man say it, for once, and not need to blush: I love you like a son."

There came a sudden sharp sound in Archie's throat. "Ay," he cried, "and there it is! Love! Like a son! And how do you think I love my father?"

"Quietly, quietly," says my lord.

"I will be very quiet," replied Archie. "And I will be baldly frank. I do not love my father; I wonder sometimes if I do not hate him. There's my shame; perhaps my sin; at least, and in the sight of God, not my fault. How was I to love him? He has never spoken to me, never smiled upon me; I do not think he ever touched me. You know the way he talks? You do not talk so, yet you can sit and hear him without shuddering, and I cannot. My soul is sick when he begins with it; I could smite him in the mouth. And all that's nothing. I was at the trial of this Jopp. You were not there, but you must have heard him often; the man's notorious for it, for being—look at my position! he's my father and this is how I have to speak of him—notorious for being a brute and cruel and a coward. Lord Glenalmond, I give you my word, when I came out of that Court, I longed to die—the shame of it was beyond my strength: but I—I—" he rose from his seat and began to pace the room in a disorder. "Well, who am I? A boy, who have never been tried, have never done anything except this twopenny impotent folly with my father. But I tell you, my lord, and I know myself, I am at least that kind of a man—or that kind of a boy, if you prefer it—that I could die in torments rather than that any one should suffer as that scoundrel suffered. Well, and what have I done? I see it now. I have made a fool of myself, as I said in the beginning; and I have gone back, and asked my father's pardon, and placed myself wholly in his hands—and he has sent me to Hermiston," with a wretched smile, "for life, I suppose—and what can I say? he strikes me as having done quite right, and let me off better than I had deserved."

"My poor, dear boy!" observed Glenalmond. "My poor, dear and, if you will allow me to say so, very foolish boy! You are only discovering where you are; to one of your temperament, or of mine, a painful discovery. The world was not made for us; it was made for ten hundred millions of men, all different from each other and from us; there's no royal road there, we just have to sclamber and tumble. Don't think that I am at all disposed to be surprised; don't suppose that I ever think of blaming you; indeed I rather admire! But there fall to be offered one or two observations on the case which occur to me and which (if you will listen to them dispassionately) may be the means of inducing you to view the matter more calmly. First of all, I cannot acquit you of a good deal of what is called intolerance. You seem to have been very much offended because your father talks a little sculduddery after dinner, which it is perfectly licit for him to do, and which (although I am not very fond of it myself) appears to be entirely an affair of taste. Your father, I scarcely like to remind you, since it is so trite a commonplace, is older than yourself. At least, he is *major* and *sui juris,* and may please himself in the matter of his conversation. And, do you know, I wonder if he might not have as good an answer against you and me? We say we sometimes find him *coarse,* but I suspect he might retort that he finds us always dull. Perhaps a relevant exception."

He beamed on Archie, but no smile could be elicited.

"And now," proceeded the judge, "for 'Archibald on Capital Punishment.' This is a very plausible academic opinion; of course I do not and I cannot hold it; but that's not to say that many able and excellent persons have not done so in the past. Possibly, in the past also, I may have a little dipped myself in the same heresy. My third client, or possibly my fourth, was the means of a return in my opinions. I never saw the man I more believed in; I would have put my hand in the fire; I would have gone to the cross for him; and when it came to trial he was gradually pictured before me, by undeniable probation, in the light of so gross, so cold-blooded, and so black-hearted a villain, that I had a mind to have cast my brief upon the table. I was then boiling against the man with even a more tropical temperature than I had been boiling for him. But I said to myself: 'No, you have taken up his case; and because you have changed your mind it must not be suffered to let drop. All that rich tide of eloquence that you prepared last night with so much enthusiasm is out of place, and yet you must not desert him, you must say something.' So I said something, and I got him off. It made my reputation. But an experience of that kind is formative. A man must not bring his passions to the Bar—or to the Bench," he added.

The story had slightly rekindled Archie's interest. "I could never deny," he began—"I mean I can conceive that some men would be better dead. But who are we to know all the springs of God's unfortunate creatures? Who are we to trust ourselves where it seems that God Himself must think twice before He treads, and to do it with delight? Yes, with delight. *Tigris ut aspera.*"

"Perhaps not a pleasant spectacle," said Glenalmond. "And yet, do you know, I think somehow a great one."

"I've had a long talk with him to-night," said Archie.

"I was supposing so," said Glenalmond.

"And he struck me—I cannot deny that he struck me as something very big," pursued the son. "Yes, he is big. He never spoke about himself; only about me. I suppose I admired him. The dreadful part—"

"Suppose we did not talk about that," interrupted Glenalmond. "You know it very well, it cannot in any way help that you should brood upon it, and I sometimes wonder whether you and I—who are a pair of sentimentalists—are quite good judges of plain men."

"How do you mean?" asked Archie.

"*Fair* judges, I mean," replied Glenalmond. "Can we be just to them? Do we not ask too much? There was a word of yours just now that impressed me a little when you asked me who we were to know all the springs of God's unfortunate creatures. You applied that, as I understood, to capital cases only. But does it—I ask myself—does it not apply all through? Is it any less difficult to judge of a good man or of a half-good man, than of the worst criminal at the bar? And may not each have relevant excuses?"

"Ah, but we do not talk of punishing the good," cried Archie.

"No, we do not talk of it," said Glenalmond. "But I think we do it. Your father, for instance."

"You think I have punished him?" cried Archie.

Lord Glenalmond bowed his head.

"I think I have," said Archie. "And the worst is, I think he feels it! How much, who can tell, with such a being? But I think he does."

"And I am sure of it," said Glenalmond.

"Has he spoken to you, then?" cried Archie.

"O no," replied the judge.

"I tell you honestly," said Archie, "I want to make it up to him. I will go, I have already pledged myself to go, to Hermiston. That was to him. And now I pledge myself to you, in the sight of God, that I will close my mouth on capital punishment and all other subjects where our views may clash, for— how long shall I say? when shall I have sense enough? —ten years. Is that well?"

"It is well," said my lord.

"As far as it goes," said Archie. "It is enough as regards myself, it is to lay down enough of my conceit. But as regards him, whom I have publicly insulted? What am I to do to him? How do you pay attentions to a—an Alp like that?"

"Only in one way," replied Glenalmond. "Only by obedience, punctual, prompt, and scrupulous."

"And I promise that he shall have it," answered Archie. "I offer you my hand in pledge of it."

"And I take your hand as a solemnity," replied the judge. "God bless you, my dear, and enable you to keep your promise. God guide you in the true way, and spare your days, and preserve to you your honest heart." At that, he kissed the young man upon the forehead in a gracious, distant, antiquated way; and instantly launched, with a marked change of voice, into another subject. "And now, let us replenish the tankard; and I believe, if you will try my Cheddar again, you would find you had a better appetite. The Court has spoken, and the case is dismissed."

"No, there is one thing I must say," cried Archie. "I must say it in justice to himself. I know—I believe faithfully, slavishly, after our talk—he will never ask me anything unjust. I am proud to feel it, that we have that much in common, I am proud to say it to you."

The judge, with shining eyes, raised his tankard. "And I think perhaps that we might permit ourselves a toast," said he. "I should like to propose the health of a man very different from me and very much my superior—a man from whom I have often differed, who has often (in the trivial expression) rubbed me the wrong way, but whom I have never ceased to respect and, I may add, to be not a little afraid of. Shall I give you his name?"

"The Lord Justice-Clerk, Lord Hermiston," said Archie, almost with gaiety; and the pair drank the toast deeply.

It was not precisely easy to re-establish, after these emotional passages, the natural flow of conversation. But the judge eked out what was wanting with kind looks, produced his snuff-box (which was very rarely seen) to fill in a pause, and at last, despairing of any further social success, was upon the point of getting down a book to read a favourite passage, when there came a rather startling summons at the front door, and Carstairs ushered in my Lord Glenkindie, hot from a midnight supper. I am not aware that Glenkindie was ever a beautiful object, being short, and gross-bodied, and with an expression of sensuality comparable to a bear's. At that moment, coming in hissing from many potations, with a flushed countenance and blurred eyes, he was strikingly contrasted with the tall, pale, kingly figure of Glenalmond. A rush of confused thought came over Archie—of shame that this was one of his father's elect friends; of pride, that at the least of it Hermiston could carry his liquor; and last of all, of rage, that he should have here under his eyes the man that had betrayed him. And then that too passed away; and he sat quiet, biding his opportunity.

The tipsy senator plunged at once into an explanation with Glenalmond. There was a point reserved yesterday, he had been able to make neither head nor tail of it, and seeing lights in the house, he had just dropped in for a glass of porter—and at this point he became aware of the third person. Archie saw the cod's mouth and the blunt lips of Glenkindie gape at him for a moment, and the recognition twinkle in his eyes.

"Who's this?" said he. "What? is this possibly you,

Don Quickshot? And how are ye? And how's your father? And what's all this we hear of you? It seems you're a most extraordinary leveller, by all tales. No king, no parliaments, and your gorge rises at the macers, worthy men! Hoot, toot! Dear, dear me! Your father's son too! Most rideeculous!"

Archie was on his feet, flushing a little at the reappearance of his unhappy figure of speech, but perfectly self-possessed. "My lord—and you, Lord Glenalmond, my dear friend," he began, "this is a happy chance for me, that I can make my confession and offer my apologies to two of you at once."

"Ah, but I don't know about that. Confession? It'll be judeecial, my young friend," cried the jocular Glenkindie. "And I'm afraid to listen to ye. Think if ye were to make me a convert!"

"If you would allow me, my lord," returned Archie, "what I have to say is very serious to me; and be pleased to be humorous after I am gone!"

"Remember, I'll hear nothing against the macers!" put in the incorrigible Glenkindie.

But Archie continued as though he had not spoken. "I have played, both yesterday and to-day, a part for which I can only offer the excuse of youth. I was so unwise as to go to an execution; it seems I made a scene at the gallows; not content with which, I spoke the same night in a college society against capital punishment. This is the extent of what I have done, and in case you hear more alleged against me, I protest my innocence. I have expressed my regret already to my father, who is so good as to pass my conduct over—in a degree, and upon the condition that I am to leave my law studies." . . .

CHAPTER V

WINTER ON THE MOORS

1. At Hermiston

THE ROAD to Hermiston runs for a great part of the way up the valley of a stream, a favourite with anglers and with midges, full of falls and pools, and shaded by willows and natural woods of birch. Here and there, but at great distances, a byway branches off, and a gaunt farmhouse may be descried above in a fold of the hill; but the more part of the time, the road would be quite empty of passage and the hills of habitation. Hermiston parish is one of the least populous in Scotland; and, by the time you came that length, you would scarce be surprised at the inimitable smallness of the kirk, a dwarfish, ancient place seated for fifty, and standing in a green by the burn-side among two-score gravestones. The manse close by, although no more than a cottage, is surrounded by the brightness of a flower-garden and the straw roofs of bees; and the whole colony, kirk and manse, garden and graveyard, finds harbourage in a grove of rowans, and is all the year round in a great silence broken only by the drone of the bees, the tinkle of the burn, and the bell on Sundays. A mile beyond the kirk the road leaves the valley by a precipitous ascent, and brings you a little after to the place of Hermiston, where it comes to an end in the back-yard before the coach-house. All beyond and about is the great field of the hills; the plover, the curlew, and the lark cry there; the wind blows as it blows in a ship's rigging, hard and cold and pure; and the hill-tops huddle one behind another, like a herd of cattle, into the sunset.

The house was sixty years old, unsightly, comfortable; a farmyard and a kitchen-garden on the left, with a fruit wall where little hard green pears came to their maturity about the end of October.

The policy (as who should say the park) was of some extent, but very ill reclaimed; heather and moor-fowl had crossed the boundary wall and spread and roosted within; and it would have tasked a landscape gardener to say where policy ended and unpolicied nature began. My lord had been led by the influence of Mr. Sheriff Scott into a considerable design of planting; many acres were accordingly set out with fir, and the little feathery besoms gave a false scale and lent a strange air of a toy-shop to the moors. A great, rooty sweetness of bogs was in the air, and at all seasons an infinite melancholy piping of hill birds. Standing so high and with so little shelter, it was a cold, exposed house, splashed by showers, drenched by continuous rains that made the gutters to spout, beaten upon and buffeted by all the winds of heaven; and the prospect would be often black with tempest, and often white with the snows of winter. But the house was wind and weather proof, the hearths were kept bright, and the rooms pleasant with live fires of peat; and Archie might sit of an evening and hear the squalls bugle on the moorland, and watch the fire prosper in the earthy fuel, and the smoke winding up the chimney, and drink deep of the pleasures of shelter.

Solitary as the place was, Archie did not want neighbours. Every night, if he chose, he might go down to the manse and share a "brewst" of toddy with the minister—a hare-brained ancient gentleman, long and light and still active, though his knees were loosened with age, and his voice broke continually in childish trebles—and his lady wife, a heavy, comely dame, without a word to say for herself beyond good-even and good-day. Harum-scarum, clodpole young lairds of the neighbourhood paid him the compliment of a visit. Young Hay of Romanes rode down to call, on his crop-eared pony; young Pringle of Drumanno came up on his bony grey. Hay remained on the hospitable field, and must be carried to bed; Pringle got somehow to his saddle about 3 A.M., and (as Archie stood with the lamp on the upper doorstep) lurched, uttered a senseless view-holloa, and vanished out of the small circle of illumination like a wraith. Yet a minute or two longer the clatter of his break-neck flight was audible, then it was cut off by the intervening steepness of the hill; and again, a great while after, the renewed beating of phantom horsehoofs, far in the valley of the Hermiston, showed that the horse at least, if not his rider, was still on the homeward way.

There was a Tuesday club at the "Crosskeys" in Crossmichael, where the young bloods of the countryside congregated and drank deep on a percentage of the expense, so that he was left gainer who should have drunk the most. Archie had no great mind to this diversion, but he took it like a duty laid upon him, went with a decent regularity, did his manfullest with the liquor, held up his head in the local jests, and got home again and was able to put up his horse, to the admiration of Kirstie and the lass that helped her. He dined at Driffel, supped at Windielaws. He went to the new year's ball at Huntsfield and was made welcome, and thereafter rode to hounds with my Lord Muirfell, upon whose name, as that of a legitimate Lord of Parliament, in a work so full of Lords of Session, my pen should pause reverently. Yet the same fate attended him here as in Edinburgh. The habit of solitude tends to perpetuate itself, and an austerity of which he was quite unconscious, and a pride which seemed arrogance, and perhaps was chiefly shyness, discouraged and offended his new companions. Hay did not return more than twice, Pringle never at all, and there came a time when Archie even desisted from the Tuesday Club, and became in all things—what he had had the name of almost from the first—the Recluse of Hermiston. High-nosed Miss Pringle of Drumanno and high-stepping Miss Marshall of the Mains were understood to have had a difference of opinion about him the day after the ball—he was none the wiser, he could not suppose himself to be remarked by these entrancing ladies. At the ball itself my Lord Muirfell's daughter, the Lady Flora, spoke to him twice, and the second time with a touch of appeal, so that her colour rose and her voice trembled a little in his ear, like a passing grace in music. He stepped back with a heart on fire, coldly and not ungracefully excused himself, and a little after watched her dancing with young Drumanno of the empty laugh, and was harrowed at the sight, and raged to himself that this was a world in which it was given to Drumanno to please, and to himself only to stand aside and envy. He seemed excluded, as of right, from the favour of such society—seemed to extinguish mirth wherever he came, and was quick to feel the wound, and desist, and retire into solitude. If he had but understood the figure he presented, and the impression he made on these bright eyes and tender hearts; if he had but guessed that the Recluse of Hermiston, young, graceful, well spoken, but always cold, stirred the maidens of the county with the charm of Byronism when Byronism was new, it may be questioned whether his destiny might not even yet have been modified. It may be questioned, and I think it should be doubted. It was in his horoscope to be parsimonious of pain to himself, or of the chance of pain, even to the avoidance of any opportunity of pleasure; to have a Roman sense of duty, an instinctive aristocracy of manners and taste; to be the son of Adam Weir and Jean Rutherford.

* * *

2. Kirstie

Kirstie was now over fifty, and might have sat to a sculptor. Long of limb, and still light of foot, deep-breasted, robust-loined, her golden hair not yet mingled with any trace of silver, the years had but caressed and embellished her. By the lines of a rich and vigorous maternity, she seemed destined to be the bride of heroes and the mother of their children; and behold, by the iniquity of fate, she had passed through her youth alone, and drew near to the confines of age, a childless woman. The tender ambitions that she had received at birth had been, by time and disappointment, diverted into a certain barren zeal of industry and fury of interference. She carried her thwarted ardours into housework, she washed floors with her empty heart. If she could not win the love of one with love, she must dominate all by her temper. Hasty, wordy, and wrathful, she had a drawn quarrel with most of her neighbours, and with the others not much more than armed neutrality. The grieve's wife had been "sneisty"; the sister of the gardener who kept house for him had shown herself "upsitten"; and she wrote to Lord Hermiston about once a year demanding the discharge of the offenders, and justifying the demand by much wealth of detail. For it must not be supposed that the quarrel rested with the wife and did not take in the husband also—or with the gardener's sister, and did not speedily include the gardener himself. As the upshot of all this petty quarrelling and intemperate speech, she was practically excluded (like a lightkeeper on his tower) from the comforts of human association; except with her own in-door drudge, who, being but a lassie and entirely at her mercy, must submit to the shifty weather of "the mistress's" moods without complaint, and be willing to take buffets or caresses according to the temper of the hour. To Kirstie, thus situate and in the Indian summer of her heart, which was slow to submit to age, the gods sent this equivocal good thing of Archie's presence. She had known him in the cradle and paddled him when he misbehaved; and yet, as she had not so much as set eyes on him since he was eleven and had his last serious illness, the tall, slender, refined, and rather melancholy young gentleman of twenty came upon her with the shock of a new acquaintance. He was "Young Hermiston," "the laird himsel' ": he had an air of distinctive superiority, a cold straight glance of his black eyes, that abashed the woman's tantrums in the beginning, and therefore the possibility of any quarrel was excluded. He was new, and therefore immediately aroused her curiosity; he was reticent, and kept it awake. And lastly he was dark and she fair, and he was male and she female, the everlasting fountains of interest.

Her feeling partook of the loyalty of a clanswoman, the hero-worship of a maiden aunt, and the idolatry due to a god. No matter what he had asked of her, ridiculous or tragic, she would have done it and joyed to do it. Her passion, for it was nothing less, entirely filled her. It was a rich physical pleasure to make his bed or light his lamp for him when he was absent, to pull off his wet boots or wait on him at dinner when he returned. A young man who should have so doted on the idea, moral and physical, of any woman, might be properly described as being in love, head and heels, and would have behaved himself accordingly. But Kirstie—though her heart leaped at his coming footsteps—though, when he patted her shoulder, her face brightened for the day—had not a hope or thought beyond the present moment and its perpetuation to the end of time. Till the end of time she would have had nothing altered, but still continue delightedly to serve her idol, and be repaid (say twice in the month) with a clap on the shoulder.

I have said her heart leaped—it is the accepted phrase. But rather, when she was alone in any chamber of the house, and heard his foot passing on the corridors, something in her bosom rose slowly until her breath was suspended, and as slowly fell again with a deep sigh, when the steps had passed and she was disappointed of her eyes' desire. This perpetual hunger and thirst of his presence kept her all day on the alert. When he went forth at morning, she would stand and follow him with admiring looks. As it grew late and drew to the time of his return, she would steal forth to a corner of the policy wall and be seen standing there sometimes by the hour together, gazing with shaded eyes, waiting the exquisite and barren pleasure of his view a mile off on the mountains. When at night she had trimmed and gathered the fire, turned down his bed, and laid out his night-gear—when there was no more to be done for the king's pleasure, but to remember him fervently in her usually very tepid prayers, and go to bed brooding upon his perfections, his future career, and what she should give him the next day for dinner—there still remained before her one more opportunity; she was still to take in the tray and say good-night. Sometimes Archie would glance up from his book with a preoccupied nod and a perfunctory salutation which was in truth a dismissal; sometimes—and by degrees more often—the volume would be laid aside, he would meet her coming with a look of relief; and the conversation would be engaged, last out the supper, and be prolonged till the small hours by the waning fire. It was no wonder that Archie was fond of company after his solitary days; and Kirstie, upon her side, exerted all the arts of her vigorous nature to ensnare his attention. She would keep back some piece of news during dinner to be fired off with the entrance of the supper tray, and form as it were the *lever de rideau* of the evening's entertainment. Once he had heard her tongue wag, she made sure of the result. From one subject to another she moved by insidious transitions, fearing the least silence, fearing almost to give him time for an answer lest it should slip into a hint of separation. Like so many people of her class, she was a brave narrator; her place was on the hearthrug and she made it a rostrum, miming her stories as she told them, fitting them with vital detail, spinning them out with endless "quo' he's" and "quo' she's," her voice sinking into a whisper over the supernatural or the horrific; until she would suddenly spring up in affected surprise, and pointing to the clock, "Mercy, Mr. Archie!" she would say, "whatten a time o' night is this of it! God forgive me for a daft wife!" So it befell, by good management, that she was not only the first to begin these nocturnal conversations, but invariably the first to break them off. So she managed to retire and not to be dismissed.

3. A Border Family

Such an unequal intimacy has never been uncommon in Scotland, where the clan spirit survives; where the servant tends to spend her life in the same service, a helpmeet at first, then a tyrant, and at last a pensioner; where, besides, she is not necessarily destitute of the pride of birth, but is, perhaps, like Kirstie, a connection of her master's, and at least knows the legend of her own family, and may count kinship with some illustrious dead. For that is the mark of the Scot of all classes: that he stands in an attitude towards the past unthinkable to Englishmen, and remembers and cherishes the memory of his forebears, good or bad; and there burns alive in him a sense of identity with the dead even to the twentieth generation. No more characteristic instance could be found than in the family of Kirstie Elliott. They were all, and Kirstie the first of all, ready and eager to pour forth the particulars of their genealogy, embellished with every detail that memory had handed down or fancy fabricated; and, behold! from every ramification of that tree there dangled a halter. The Elliotts themselves have had a chequered history; but these Elliotts deduced, besides, from three of the most unfortunate of the border clans—the Nicksons, the Ellwalds, and the Crozers. One ancestor after another might be seen appearing a moment out of the rain and the hill mist upon his furtive business, speeding home, perhaps, with a paltry booty of lame horses and lean kine, or squealing and dealing death in some moorland feud of the ferrets and the wild cats. One after another closed his obscure adventures in mid-air, triced up to the arm of the royal gibbet or the Baron's dule-tree. For the rusty blunderbuss of Scots criminal justice, which usually hurt nobody but jurymen, became a weapon of precision for the Nicksons, the Ellwalds, and the Crozers. The exhilaration of their exploits seemed to haunt the memories of their descendants alone, and the shame to be forgotten. Pride glowed in their bosoms to publish their relationship to "Andrew Ellwald of the Laverockstanes, called 'Unchancy Dand,' who was justifeed wi' seeven mair of the same name at Jeddart in the days of King James the Sax." In all this issue of crime and misfortune, the Elliotts of Cauldstaneslap had one boast which must appear legitimate: the males were gallow-birds, born outlaws, petty thieves, and deadly brawlers; but, according to the same tradition, the females were all chaste and faithful. The power of ancestry on the character is not limited to the inheritance of cells. If I buy ancestors by the gross from the benevolence of Lyon King of Arms, my grandson (if he is Scottish) will feel a quickening emulation of their deeds. The men of the Elliotts were proud, lawless, violent as of right, cherishing and prolonging a tradition. In like manner with the women. And the woman, essentially passionate and reckless, who crouched on the rug, in the shine of the peat fire, telling these tales, had cherished through life a wild integrity of virtue.

Her father Gilbert had been deeply pious, a savage disciplinarian in the antique style, and withal a notorious smuggler. "I mind when I was a bairn getting mony a skelp and being shoo'd to bed like pou'try," she would say. "That would be when the lads and their bit kegs were on the road. We've had the riffraff of two-three counties in our kitchen, mony's the time, betwix' the twelve and the three; and their lanterns would be standing in the forecourt, ay, a score o' them at once. But there was nae ungodly talk permitted at Cauldstaneslap; my faither was a consistent man in walk and conversation; just let slip an aith, and there was the door to ye! He had that zeal for the Lord, it was a fair wonder to hear him pray, but the faim'ly has aye had a gift that way." This father was twice married, once to a dark woman of the old Ellwald stock, by whom he had Gilbert, presently of Cauldstaneslap; and, secondly, to the mother of Kirstie. "He was an auld man when he married her, a fell auld man wi' a muckle voice—you could hear him rowting from the top o' the Kye-skairs," she said; "but for her, it appears she was a perfit wonder. It was gentle blood she had, Mr. Archie, for it was your ain. The country-side gaed gyte about her and her gowden hair. Mines is no to be mentioned wi' it, and there's few weemen has mair hair than what I have, or yet a bonnier colour. Often would I tell my dear Miss Jeannie—that was your mother, dear, she was cruel ta'en up about her hair, it was unco tender, ye see—'Hoots, Miss Jeannie,' I would say, 'just fling your washes and your French dentifrishes in the back o' the fire, for that's the place for them; and awa' down to a burn side, and wash yersel' in cauld hill water, and dry your bonny hair in the caller wind o' the muirs, the way that my mother aye washed hers, and that I have aye made it a practice to have wishen mines—just you do what I tell ye, my dear, and ye'll give me news of it! Ye'll have hair, and routh of hair, a pigtail as thick's my arm,' I said, 'and the bonniest colour like the clear gowden guineas, so as the lads in kirk'll no can keep their eyes off it!' Weel, it lasted out her time, puir thing! I cuttit a lock of it upon her corp that was lying there sae cauld. I'll show it ye some of thir days if ye're good. But, as I was sayin', my mother—"

On the death of the father there remained golden-haired Kirstie, who took service with her distant kinsfolk, the Rutherfords, and black-a-vised Gilbert, twenty years older, who farmed the Cauldstaneslap, married, and begot four sons between 1773 and 1784, and a daughter, like a postscript, in '97, the year of Camperdown and Cape St. Vincent. It seemed it was a tradition in the family to wind up with a belated girl. In 1804, at the age of sixty, Gilbert met an end that might be called heroic. He was due home from market any time from eight at night till five in the morning, and in any condition from the quarrelsome to the speechless, for he maintained to that age the goodly customs of the Scots farmer. It was known on this occasion that he had a good bit of money to bring home; the word had gone round loosely. The laird had shown his guineas, and if anybody had but noticed it, there was an ill-looking, vagabond crew, the scum of Edinburgh, that drew out of the market long ere it was dusk and took the hill-road by Hermiston, where it was not to be believed that they had lawful business. One of the country-side, one Dickieson, they took with them to be their guide, and dear he paid for it! Of a sudden, in the ford of the Broken Dykes, this vermin clan fell on the laird, six to one, and him three parts asleep, having drunk hard. But it is ill to catch an Elliott. For a while, in the night and the black water that was deep as to his saddle-girths, he wrought with his staff like a smith at his stithy, and great was the sound of oaths and blows. With that the ambuscade was burst, and he rode for home with a pistol-ball in him, three knife wounds, the loss of his front teeth, a broken rib and bridle, and a dying horse. That was a race with death that the laird rode. In the mirk night, with his broken bridle and his head swimming, he dug his spurs to the rowels in the horse's side, and the horse, that was even worse off than himself, the poor creature! screamed out like a person as he went, so that the hills echoed with it, and the folks at Cauldstaneslap got to their feet about the table and looked at each other with white faces. The horse fell dead at the yard gate, the laird won the length of the house and fell there on the threshold. To the son that raised him he gave the bag of money. "Hae," said he. All the way up the thieves had seemed to him to be at his heels, but now the hallucination left him—he saw them again in the place of the ambuscade—and the thirst of vengeance seized on his dying mind. Raising himself and pointing with an imperious finger into the black night from which he had come, he uttered the single command, "Brocken Dykes," and fainted. He had never been loved, but he had been feared in honour. At that sight, at that word, gasped out at them from a toothless and bleeding mouth, the old Elliott spirit awoke with a shout in the four sons. "Wanting the hat," continues my author, Kirstie, whom I but haltingly follow, for she told this tale like one inspired, "wanting guns, for there wasna twa grains o' pouder in the house, wi' nae mair weepons than their sticks into their hands, the fower o' them took the road. Only Hob, and that was the eldest, hunkered at the door-sill where the blood had rin, fyled his hand wi' it, and haddit it up to Heeven in the way o' the auld Border aith. 'Hell shall have her ain again this nicht!' he raired, and rode forth upon his earrand." It was three miles to Brocken Dykes, down hill, and a sore road. Kirstie had seen men from Edinburgh dismounting there in plain day to lead their horses. But the four brothers rode it as if Auld Hornie were behind and Heaven in front. Come to the ford, and there was Dickieson. By all tales, he was not dead, but breathed and reared upon his elbow, and cried out to them for help. It was at a graceless face that he asked mercy. As soon as Hob saw, by the glint of the lantern, the eyes shining and the whiteness of the teeth in the man's face, "Damn you!" says he; "ye hae your teeth, hae ye?" and rode his horse to and fro upon that human remnant. Beyond that, Dandie must dismount with the lantern to be their guide; he was the youngest son, scarce twenty at the time. "A' nicht long they gaed in the wet heath and jennipers, and whaur they gaed they neither knew nor cared, but just followed the bluid-stains and the footprints o' their faither's murderers. And a' nicht Dandie had his nose to the grund like a tyke, and the ithers followed and spak' naething, neither black nor white. There was nae noise to be heard, but just the sough of the swalled burns, and Hob, the dour yin, risping his teeth as he gaed." With the first glint of the morning they saw they were on the drove-road, and at that the four stopped and had a dram to their breakfasts, for they knew that Dand must have guided them right, and the rogues could be but little ahead, hot foot for Edinburgh by the way of the Pentland Hills. By eight o'clock they had word of them—a shepherd had seen four men "uncoly mishandled" go by in the last hour. "That's yin a piece," says Clem, and swung his cudgel. "Five o' them!" says Hob. "God's death, but the faither was a man! And him drunk!" And then there befell them what my author termed "a sair misbegowk," for they were overtaken by a posse of mounted neighbours come to aid in the pursuit. Four sour faces looked on the reinforcement. "The Deil's broughten you!" said Clem, and they rode thenceforward in the rear of the party with hanging heads. Before ten they had found and secured the rogues, and by three of the afternoon, as they rode up the Vennel with their prisoners, they were aware of a concourse of people bearing in their midst something that dripped. "For the boady of the saxt," pursued Kirstie, "wi' his head smashed like a hazel-nit, had been a' that nicht in the chairge o' Hermiston Water, and it dunting in on the stanes, and grunding it on the shallows, and flinging the deid thing heels-ower-hurdie at the Fa's o' Spango; and in the first o' the day, Tweed had got a hold o' him and carried him off like a wind, for it was uncoly swalled, and raced wi' him, bobbing under braesides, and was long playing with the creature in the drumlie lynns under the castle, and at the hinder end of all cuist him up on the sterling of Crossmichael brig. Sae there they were a'thegither at last (for Dickieson had been brought in on a cart long syne), and folk could see what mainner o' man my brither had been that had held his head again sax and saved the siller, and him drunk!" Thus died of honourable injuries and in the savour of fame Gilbert Elliott of the Cauldstaneslap; but his sons had scarce less glory out of the business. Their savage haste, the skill with which Dand had found and followed the trail, the barbarity to the wounded Dickieson (which was like an open secret in the county), and the doom which it was currently supposed they had intended for the others, struck and stirred popular imagination. Some century earlier the last of the minstrels might have fashioned the last of the ballads out of that Homeric fight and chase; but the spirit was dead, or had been reincarnated already in Mr. Sheriff Scott, and the degenerate moorsmen must be content to tell the tale in prose, and to make of the "Four Black Brothers" a unit after the fashion of the "Twelve Apostles" or the "Three Musketeers."

Robert, Gilbert, Clement, and Andrew—in the proper Border diminutives, Hob, Gib, Clem, and Dand Elliott—these ballad heroes, had much in common; in particular, their high sense of the family and the family honour; but they went diverse ways, and prospered and failed in different businesses. According to Kirstie, "they had a' bees in their bonnets but Hob." Hob the laird was, indeed, essentially a decent man. An elder of the Kirk, nobody had heard an oath upon his lips, save, perhaps, thrice or so at the sheep-washing, since the chase of his father's murderers. The figure he had shown on that eventful night disappeared as if swallowed by a trap. He who had ecstatically dipped his hand in the red blood, he who had ridden down Dickieson, became, from that moment on, a stiff and rather graceless model of the rustic proprieties; cannily profiting by the high war prices, and yearly stowing away a little nest-egg in the bank against calamity; approved of and sometimes consulted by the greater lairds for the massive and placid sense of what he said, when he could be induced to say anything; and particularly valued by the minister, Mr. Torrance, as a right-hand man in the parish, and a model to parents. The transfiguration had been for the moment only; some Barbarossa, some old Adam of our ancestors, sleeps in all of us till the fit circumstance shall call it into action; and, for as sober as he now seemed, Hob had given once for all the measure of the devil that haunted him. He was married, and, by reason of the effulgence of that legendary night, was adored by his wife. He had a mob of little lusty, barefoot children who marched in a caravan the long miles to school, the stages of whose pilgrimage were marked by acts of spoliation and mischief, and who were qualified in the country-side as "fair pests." But in the house, if "faither was in," they were quiet as mice. In short, Hob moved through life in a great peace—the reward of any one who shall have killed his man, with any formidable and figurative circumstance, in the midst of a country gagged and swaddled with civilisation.

It was a current remark that the Elliotts were "guid and bad, like sanguishes"; and certainly there was a curious distinction, the men of business coming alternately with the dreamers. The second brother, Gib, was a weaver by trade, had gone out early into the world to Edinburgh, and come home again with his wings singed. There was an exaltation in his nature which had led him to embrace with enthusiasm the principles of the French Revolution, and had ended by bringing him under the hawse of my Lord Hermiston in that furious onslaught of his upon the Liberals, which sent Muir and Palmer into exile and dashed the party into chaff. It was whispered that my lord, in his great scorn for the movement, and prevailed upon a little by a sense of neighbourliness, had given Gib a hint. Meeting him one day in the Potterrow, my lord had stopped in front of him: "Gib, ye eediot," he had said, "what's this I hear of you? Poalitics, poalitics, weaver's poalitics, is the way of it, I hear. If ye arena a'thegither dozened with eediocy, ye'll gang your ways back to Cauldstaneslap and ca' your loom, and ca' your loom, man!" And Gilbert had taken him at the word and returned, with an expedition almost to be called flight, to the house of his father. The clearest of his inheritance was that family gift of prayer of which Kirstie had boasted; and the baffled politician now turned his attention to religious matters—or, as others said, to heresy and schism. Every Sunday morning he was in Crossmichael, where he had gathered together, one by one, a sect of about a dozen persons, who called themselves "God's Remnant of the True Faithful," or, for short, "God's Remnant." To the profane they were known as "Gib's Deils." Bailie Sweedie, a noted humorist in the town, vowed that the proceedings always opened to the tune of "The Deil Fly Away with the Exciseman," and that the sacrament was dispensed in the form of hot whisky-toddy; both wicked hits at the evangelist, who had been suspected of smuggling in his youth, and had been overtaken (as the phrase went) on the streets of Crossmichael one Fair day. It was known that every Sunday they prayed for a blessing on the arms of Buonaparte. For this, "God's Remnant," as they were "skailing" from the cottage that did duty for a temple, had been repeatedly stoned by the bairns, and Gib himself hooted by a squadron of Border volunteers in which his own brother, Dand, rode in a uniform and with a drawn sword. The "Remnant" were believed, besides, to be "antinomian in principle," which might otherwise have been a serious charge, but the way public opinion then blew it was quite swallowed up and forgotten in the scandal about Buonaparte. For the rest, Gilbert had set up his loom in an outhouse at Cauldstaneslap, where he laboured assiduously six days of the week. His brothers, appalled by his political opinions, and willing to avoid dissension in the household, spoke but little to him; he less to them, remaining absorbed in the study of the Bible and almost constant prayer. The gaunt weaver was dry-nurse at Cauldstaneslap, and the bairns loved him dearly. Except when he was carrying an infant in his arms, he was rarely seen to smile—as, indeed, there were few smilers in that family. When his sister-in-law rallied him, and proposed that he should get a wife and bairns of his own, since he was so fond of them, "I have no clearness of mind upon that point," he would reply. If nobody called him in to dinner, he stayed out. Mrs. Hob, a hard, unsympathetic woman, once tried the experiment. He went without food all day, but at dusk, as the light began to fail him, he came into the house of his own accord, looking puzzled. "I've had a great gale of prayer upon my specrit," said he. "I canna mind sae muckle's what I had for denner." The creed of God's Remnant was justified in the life of its founder. "And yet I dinna ken," said Kirstie. "He's maybe no more stock-fish than his neeghbours! He rode wi' the rest o' them, and had a good stammach to the work, by a' that I hear! God's Remnant! The deil's clavers! There wasna muckle Christianity in the way Hob guided Johnny Dickieson, at the least of it; but Guid kens! Is he a Christian even? He might be a Mahommedan or a Deevil or a Fireworshipper, for what I ken."

The third brother had his name on a door-plate, no less, in the city of Glasgow, "Mr. Clement Elliott," as long as your arm. In this case, that spirit of innovation which had shown itself timidly in the case of Hob by the admission of new manures, and which had run to waste with Gilbert in subversive politics and heretical religions, bore useful fruit in many ingenious mechanical improvements. In boyhood, from his addiction to strange devices of sticks and string, he had been counted the most eccentric of the family. But that was all by now; and he was a partner of his firm, and looked to die a bailie. He too had married, and was rearing a plentiful family in the smoke and din of Glasgow; he was wealthy, and could have bought out his brother, the cock-laird, six times over, it was whispered; and when he slipped away to Cauldstaneslap for a well-earned holiday, which he did as often as he was able, he astonished the neighbours with his broadcloth, his beaver hat, and the ample plies of his neckcloth. Though an eminently solid man at bottom, after the pattern of Hob, he had contracted a certain Glasgow briskness and *aplomb* which set him off. All the other Elliotts were as lean as a rake, but Clement was laying on fat, and he panted sorely when he must get into his boots. Dand said, chuckling: "Ay, Clem has the elements of a corporation." "A provost and corporation," returned Clem. And his readiness was much admired.

The fourth brother, Dand, was a shepherd to his trade, and by starts, when he could bring his mind to it, excelled in the business. Nobody could train a dog like Dandie; nobody, through the peril of great storms in the winter time, could do more gallantly. But if his dexterity were exquisite, his diligence was but fitful; and he served his brother for bed and board, and a trifle of pocket-money when he asked for it. He loved money well enough, knew very well how to spend it, and could make a shrewd bargain when he liked. But he preferred a vague knowledge that he was well to windward to any counted coins in the pocket; he felt himself richer so. Hob would expostulate: "I'm an amature herd." Dand would reply, "I'll keep your sheep to you when I'm so minded, but I'll keep my liberty too. Thir's no man can coandescend on what I'm worth." Clem would expound to him the miraculous results of compound interest, and recommend investments. "Ay, man?" Dand would say; "and do you think, if I took Hob's siller, that I wouldna drink it or wear it on the lassies? And, anyway, my kingdom is no of this world. Either I'm a poet or else I'm nothing." Clem would remind him of old age. "I'll die young, like Robbie Burns," he would say stoutly. No question but he had a certain accomplishment in minor verse. His "Hermiston Burn," with its pretty refrain—

> "I love to gang thinking whaur ye gang linking,
> Hermiston burn, in the home";

his "Auld, auld Elliotts, clay-cauld Elliotts, dour, bauld Elliotts of auld," and his really fascinating piece about the Praying Weaver's Stone, had gained him in the neighbourhood the reputation, still possible in Scotland, of a local bard; and, though not printed himself, he was recognised by others who were and who had become famous. Walter Scott owed to Dandie the text of the "Raid of Wearie" in the "Minstrelsy"; and made him welcome at his house, and appreciated his talents, such as they were, with all his usual generosity. The Ettrick Shepherd was his sworn crony; they would meet, drink to excess, roar out their lyrics in each other's faces, and quarrel and make it up again till bedtime. And besides these recognitions, almost to be called official, Dandie was made welcome for the sake of his gift through the farmhouses of several contiguous dales, and was thus exposed to manifold temptations which he rather sought than fled. He had figured on the stool of repentance, for once fulfilling to the letter the tradition of his hero and model. His humorous verses to Mr. Torrance on that occasion—"Kenspeckle here my lane I stand"—unfortunately too indelicate for further citation, ran through the country like a fiery cross; they were recited, quoted, paraphrased, and laughed over as far away as Dumfries on the one hand and Dunbar on the other.

These four brothers were united by a close bond, the bond of that mutual admiration—or rather mutual hero-worship—which is so strong among the members of secluded families who have much ability and little culture. Even the extremes admired each other. Hob, who had as much poetry as the tongs, professed to find pleasure in Dand's verses; Clem, who had no more religion than Claverhouse, nourished a heartfelt, at least an open-mouthed, admiration of Gib's prayers; and Dandie followed with relish the rise of Clem's fortunes. Indulgence followed hard on the heels of admiration. The laird, Clem, and Dand, who were Tories and patriots of the hottest quality, excused to themselves, with a certain bashfulness, the radical and revolutionary heresies of Gib. By another division of the family, the laird, Clem, and Gib, who were men exactly virtuous swallowed the dose of Dand's irregularities as a kind of clog or drawback in the mysterious providence of God affixed to bards, and distinctly probative of poetical genius. To appreciate the simplicity of their mutual admiration it was necessary to hear Clem, arrived upon one of his visits, and dealing in a spirit of continuous irony with the affairs and personalities of that great city of Glasgow where he lived and transacted business. The various personages, ministers of the church, municipal officers, mercantile bigwigs, whom he had occasion to introduce, were all alike denigrated, all served but as reflectors to cast back a flattering sidelight on the house of Cauldstaneslap. The Provost, for whom Clem by exception entertained a measure of respect, he would liken to Hob. "He minds me o' the laird there," he would say. "He has some of Hob's grand, whunstane sense, and the same way with him of steiking his mouth when he's no very pleased." And Hob, all unconscious, would draw down his upper lip and produce, as if for comparison, the formidable grimace referred to. The unsatisfactory incumbent of St. Enoch's Kirk was thus briefly dismissed: "If he had but twa fingers o' Gib's, he would waken them up." And Gib, honest man! would look down and secretly smile. Clem was a spy whom they had sent out into the world of men. He had come back with the good news that there was nobody to compare with the Four Black Brothers, no position that they would not adorn, no official that it would not be well they should replace, no interest of mankind, secular or spiritual, which would not immediately bloom under their supervision. The excuse of their folly is in two words: scarce the breadth of a hair divided them from the peasantry. The measure of their sense is this: that these symposia of rustic vanity were kept entirely within the family, like some secret ancestral practice. To the world their serious faces were never deformed by the suspicion of any simper of self-contentment. Yet it was known. "They hae a guid pride o' themsel's!" was the word in the country-side.

Lastly, in a Border story, there should be added their "two-names." Hob was The Laird. "Roy ne puis, prince ne daigne"; he was the laird of Cauldstaneslap—say fifty acres—*ipsissimus*. Clement was Mr. Elliott, as upon his door-plate, the earlier Dafty having been discarded as no longer applicable, and indeed only a reminder of misjudgment and the imbecility of the public; and the youngest, in honour of his perpetual wanderings, was known by the sobriquet of Randy Dand.

It will be understood that not all this information was communicated by the aunt, who had too much of the family failing herself to appreciate it thoroughly in others. But as time went on, Archie began to observe an omission in the family chronicle.

"Is there not a girl too?" he asked.

"Ay: Kirstie. She was named for me, or my grandmother at least—it's the same thing," returned the aunt, and went on again about Dand, whom she secretly preferred by reason of his gallantries.

"But what is your niece like?" said Archie at the next opportunity.

"Her? As black's your hat! But I dinna suppose she would maybe be what you would ca' *ill-looked* a'thegither. Na, she's a kind of a handsome jaud—a kind o' gipsy," said the aunt, who had two sets of scales for men and women—or perhaps it would be more fair to say that she had three, and the third and the most loaded was for girls.

"How comes it that I never see her in church?" said Archie.

" 'Deed, and I believe she's in Glesgie with Clem and his wife. A heap good she's like to get of it! I dinna say for men folk, but where weemen folk are born, there let them bide. Glory to God, I was never far'er from here than Crossmichael."

In the meanwhile it began to strike Archie as strange, that while she thus sang the praises of her kinsfolk, and manifestly relished their virtues and (I may say) their vices like a thing creditable to herself, there should appear not the least sign of cordiality between the house of Hermiston and that of Cauldstaneslap. Going to church of a Sunday, as the lady housekeeper stepped with her skirts kilted, three tucks of her white petticoat showing below, and her best India shawl upon her back (if the day were fine) in a pattern of radiant dyes, she would sometimes overtake her relatives preceding her more leisurely in the same direction. Gib of course was absent: by skreigh of day he had been gone to Crossmichael and his fellow-heretics; but the rest of the family would be seen marching in open order: Hob and Dand, stiff-necked, straight-backed six-footers, with severe dark faces, and their plaids about their shoulders; the convoy of children scattering (in a state of high polish) on the wayside, and every now and again collected by the shrill summons of the mother; and the mother herself, by a suggestive circumstance which might have afforded matter of thought to a more experienced observer than Archie, wrapped in a shawl nearly identical with Kirstie's, but a thought more gaudy and conspicuously newer. At the sight, Kirstie grew more tall—Kirstie showed her classical profile, nose in air and nostril spread, the pure blood came in her cheek evenly in a delicate living pink.

"A braw day to ye, Mistress Elliott," said she, and hostility and gentility were nicely mingled in her tones. "A fine day, mem," the laird's wife would reply with a miraculous curtsey, spreading the while her plumage—setting off, in other words, and with arts unknown to the mere man, the pattern of her India shawl. Behind her, the whole Cauldstaneslap contingent marched in closer order, and with an indescribable air of being in the presence of the foe; and while Dandie saluted his aunt with a certain familiarity as of one who was well in court, Hob marched on in awful immobility. There appeared upon the face of this attitude in the family the consequences of some dreadful feud. Presumably the two women had been principals in the original encounter, and the laird had probably been drawn into the quarrel by the ears, too late to be included in the present skin-deep reconciliation.

"Kirstie," said Archie one day, "what is this you have against your family?"

"I dinna complean," said Kirstie, with a flush. "I say naething."

"I see you do not—not even good-day to your own nephew," said he.

"I hae naething to be ashamed of," said she. "I can say the Lord's Prayer with a good grace. If Hob was ill, or in preeson or poverty, I would see to him blithely. But for curtchying and complimenting and colloguing, thank ye kindly!"

Archie had a bit of a smile: he leaned back in his chair. "I think you and Mrs. Robert are not very good friends," says he slily, "when you have your India shawls on?"

She looked upon him in silence, with a sparkling eye but an indecipherable expression; and that was all that Archie was ever destined to learn of the battle of the India shawls.

"Do none of them ever come here to see you?" he inquired.

"Mr. Archie," said she, "I hope that I ken my place better. It would be a queer thing, I think, if I was to clamjamfry up your faither's house—that I should say it!—wi' a dirty, black-a-vised clan, no ane o' them it was worth while to mar soap upon but just mysel'! Na, they're all damnifeed wi' the black Ellwalds. I have nae patience wi' black folk." Then, with a sudden consciousness of the case of Archie, "No that it maitters for men sae muckle," she made haste to add, "but there's naebody can deny that it's unwomanly. Long hair is the ornament o' woman ony way; we've good warrandise for that—it's in the Bible—and wha can doubt that the Apostle had some gowden-haired lassie in his mind—Apostle and all, for what was he but just a man like yersel'?"

CHAPTER VI

A LEAF FROM CHRISTINA'S PSALM-BOOK

ARCHIE WAS sedulous at church. Sunday after Sunday he sat down and stood up with that small company, heard the voice of Mr. Torrance leaping like an ill-played clarionet from key to key, and had an opportunity to study his moth-eaten gown and the black thread mittens that he joined together in prayer, and lifted up with a reverent solemnity in the act of benediction. Hermiston pew was a little square box, dwarfish in proportion with the kirk itself, and enclosing a table not much bigger than a footstool. There sat Archie, an apparent prince, the only undeniable gentleman and the only great heritor in the parish, taking his ease in the only pew, for no other in the kirk had doors. Thence he might command an undisturbed view of that congregation of solid plaided men, strapping wives and daughters, oppressed children, and uneasy sheep-dogs. It was strange how Archie missed the look of race; except the dogs, with their refined foxy faces and inimitably curling tails, there was no one present with the least claim to gentility. The Cauldstaneslap party was scarcely an exception; Dandie perhaps, as he amused himself making verses through the interminable burden of the service, stood out a little by the glow in his eye and a certain superior animation of face and alertness of body; but even Dandie slouched like a rustic. The rest of the congregation, like so many sheep, oppressed him with a sense of hob-nailed routine, day following day—of physical labour in the open air, oatmeal porridge, peas bannock, the somnolent fireside in the evening, and the nightlong nasal slumbers in a box-bed. Yet he knew many of them to be shrewd and humorous, men of character, notable women, making a bustle in the world and radiating an influence from their low-browed doors. He knew besides they were like other men; below the crust of custom, rapture found a way; he had heard them beat the timbrel before Bacchus—had heard them shout and carouse over their whisky-toddy; and not the most Dutch-bottomed and severe faces among them all, not even the solemn elders themselves, but were capable of singular gambols at the voice of love. Men drawing near to an end of life's adventurous journey—maids thrilling with fear and curiosity on the threshold of entrance—women who had borne and perhaps buried children, who could remember the clinging of the small dead hands and the patter of the little feet now silent—he marvelled that among all those faces there should be no face of expectation, none that was mobile, none into which the rhythm and poetry of life had entered. "O for a live face," he thought; and at times he had a memory of Lady Flora; and at times he would study the living gallery before him with despair, and would see himself go on to waste his days in that joyless, pastoral place, and death come to him, and his grave be dug under the rowans, and the Spirit of the Earth laugh out in a thunder-peal at the huge fiasco.

On this particular Sunday, there was no doubt but that the spring had come at last. It was warm, with a latent shiver in the air that made the warmth only the more welcome. The shallows of the stream glittered and tinkled among bunches of primrose. Vagrant scents of the earth arrested Archie by the way with moments of ethereal intoxication. The grey, Quakerish dale was still only awakened in places and patches from the sobriety of its winter colouring; and he wondered at its beauty; an essential beauty of the old earth it seemed to him, not resident in particulars but breathing to him from the whole. He surprised himself by a sudden impulse to write poetry—he did so sometimes, loose, galloping octosyllabics in the vein of Scott—and when he had taken his place on a boulder, near some fairy falls and shaded by a whip of a tree that was already radiant with new leaves, it still more surprised him that he should find nothing to write. His heart perhaps beat in time to some vast indwelling rhythm of the universe. By the time he came to a corner of the valley and could see the kirk, he had so lingered by the way that the first psalm was finishing. The nasal psalmody, full of turns and trills and graceless graces, seemed the essential voice of the kirk itself upraised in thanksgiving. "Everything's alive!" he said; and again cries it aloud, "thank God, everything's alive!" He lingered yet a while in the kirkyard. A tuft of primroses was blooming hard by the leg of an old, black table tombstone, and he stopped to contemplate the random apologue. They stood forth on the cold earth with a trenchancy of contrast; and he was struck with a sense of incompleteness in the day, the season, and the beauty that surrounded him—the chill there was in the warmth, the gross black clods about the opening primroses, the damp earthy smell that was everywhere intermingled with the scents. The voice of the aged Torrance within rose in an ecstasy. And he wondered if Torrance also felt in his old bones the joyous influence of the spring morning; Torrance, or the shadow of what once was Torrance, that must come so soon to lie outside here in the sun and rain with all his rheumatisms, while a new minister stood in his room and thundered from his own familiar pulpit? The pity of it, and something of the chill of the grave, shook him for a moment as he made haste to enter.

He went up the aisle reverently, and took his place in the pew with lowered eyes, for he feared he had already offended the kind old gentleman in the pulpit, and was sedulous to offend no further. He could not follow the prayer, not even the heads of it. Brightnesses of azure, clouds of fragrance, a tinkle of falling water and singing birds, rose like exhalations from some deeper, aboriginal memory, that was not his, but belonged to the flesh on his bones. His body remembered; and it seemed to him that his body was in no way gross, but ethereal and perishable like a strain of music; and he felt for it an exquisite tenderness as for a child, an innocent, full of beautiful instincts and destined to an early death. And he felt for old Torrance—of the many supplications, of the few days—a pity that was near to tears. The prayer ended. Right over him was a tablet in the wall, the only ornament in the roughly masoned chapel—for it was no more; the tablet commemorated, I was about to say the virtues, but rather the existence of a former Rutherford of Hermiston; and Archie, under that trophy of his long descent and local greatness, leaned back in the pew and contemplated vacancy with the shadow of a smile between playful and sad, that became him strangely. Dandie's sister, sitting by the side of Clem in her new Glasgow finery, chose that moment to observe the young laird. Aware of the stir of his entrance, the little formalist had kept her eyes fastened and her face prettily composed during the prayer. It was not hypocrisy, there was no one further from a hypocrite. The girl had been taught to behave: to look up, to look down, to look unconscious, to look seriously impressed in church, and in every conjuncture to look her best. That was the game of female life, and she played it frankly. Archie was the one person in church who was of interest, who was somebody new, reputed eccentric, known to be young, and a laird, and still unseen by Christina. Small wonder that, as she stood there in her attitude of pretty decency, her mind should run upon him! If he spared a glance in her direction, he should know she was a well-behaved young lady who had been to Glasgow. In reason he must admire her clothes, and it was possible that he should think her pretty. At that her heart beat the least thing in the world; and she proceeded, by way of a corrective, to call up and dismiss a series of fancied pictures of the young man who should now, by rights, be looking at her. She settled on the plainest of them—a pink short young man with a dish face and no figure, at whose admiration she could afford to smile; but for all that, the consciousness of his gaze (which was really fixed on Torrance and his mittens) kept her in something of a flutter till the word Amen. Even then, she was far too well-bred to gratify her curiosity with any impatience. She resumed her seat languidly—this was a Glasgow touch—she composed her dress, rearranged her nosegay of primroses, looked first in front, then behind upon the other side, and at last allowed her eyes to move, without hurry, in the direction of the Hermiston pew. For a moment they were riveted. Next she had plucked her gaze home again like a tame bird who should have meditated flight. Possibilities crowded on her; she hung over the future and grew dizzy; the image of this young man, slim, graceful, dark, with the inscrutable half-smile, attracted and repelled her like a chasm. "I wonder, will I have met my fate?" she thought, and her heart swelled.

Torrance was got some way into his first exposition, positing a deep layer of texts as he went along, laying the foundations of his discourse, which was to deal with a nice point in divinity, before Archie suffered his eyes to wander. They fell first of all on Clem, looking insupportably prosperous, and patronising Torrance with the favour of a modified attention, as of one who was used to better things in Glasgow. Though he had never before set eyes on him, Archie had no difficulty in identifying him, and no hesitation in pronouncing him vulgar, the worst of the family. Clem was leaning lazily forward when Archie first saw him. Presently he leaned nonchalantly back; and that deadly instrument, the maiden, was suddenly unmasked in profile. Though not quite in the front of the fashion (had anybody cared!), certain artful Glasgow mantua-makers, and her own inherent taste, had arrayed her to great advantage. Her accoutrement was, indeed, a cause of heart-burning, and almost of scandal, in that infinitesimal kirk company. Mrs. Hob had said her say at Cauldstaneslap. "Daftlike!" she had pronounced it. "A jaiket that'll no meet! Whaur's the sense of a jaiket that'll no button upon you, if it should come to be weet? What do ye ca' thir things? Demmy brokens, d'ye say? They'll be brokens wi' a vengeance or ye can win back! Weel, I have naething to do wi' it—it's no good taste." Clem, whose purse had thus metamorphosed his sister, and who was not insensible to the advertisement, had come to the rescue with a "Hoot, woman! What do you ken of good taste that has never been to the ceety?" And Hob, looking on the girl with pleased smiles, as she timidly displayed her finery in the midst of the dark kitchen, had thus ended the dispute: "The cutty looks weel," he had said, "and it's no very like rain. Wear them the day, hizzie; but it's no a thing to make a practice o'." In the breasts of her rivals, coming to the kirk very conscious of white under-linen, and their faces splendid with much soap, the sight of the toilet had raised a storm of varying emotion, from the mere unenvious admiration that was expressed in a long-drawn "Eh!" to the angrier feeling that found vent in an emphatic "Set her up!" Her frock was of straw-coloured jaconet muslin, cut low at the bosom and short at the ankle, so as to display her *demi-broquins* of Regency violet, crossing with many straps upon a yellow cobweb stocking. According to the pretty fashion in which our grandmothers did not hesitate to appear, and our great-aunts went forth armed for the pursuit and capture of our great-uncles, the dress was drawn up so as to mould the contour of both breasts, and in the nook between, a cairngorm brooch maintained it. Here, too, surely in a very enviable position, trembled the nosegay of primroses. She wore on her shoulders—or rather, on her back and not her shoulders, which it scarcely passed—a French coat of sarsenet, tied in front with Margate braces, and of the same colour with her violet shoes. About her face clustered a disorder of dark ringlets, a little garland of yellow French roses surmounted her brow, and the whole was crowned by a village hat of chipped straw. Amongst all the rosy and all the weathered faces that surrounded her in church, she glowed like an open flower—girl and raiment, and the cairngorm that caught the daylight and returned it in a fiery flash, and the threads of bronze and gold that played in her hair.

Archie was attracted by the bright thing like a child. He looked at her again and yet again, and their looks crossed. The lip was lifted from her little teeth. He saw the red blood work vividly under her tawny skin. Her eye, which was great as a stag's, struck and held his gaze. He knew who she must be—Kirstie, she of the harsh diminutive, his housekeeper's niece, the sister of the rustic prophet, Gib—and he found in her the answer to his wishes.

Christina felt the shock of their encountering glances, and seemed to rise, clothed in smiles, into a region of the vague and bright. But the gratification was not more exquisite than it was brief. She looked away abruptly, and immediately began to blame herself for that abruptness. She knew what she should have done, too late—turned slowly with her nose in the air. And meantime his look was not removed, but continued to play upon her like a battery of cannon constantly aimed, and now seemed to isolate her alone with him, and now seemed to uplift her, as on a pillory, before the congregation. For Archie continued to drink her in with his eyes, even as a wayfarer comes to a well-head on a mountain, and stoops his face, and drinks with thirst unassuageable. In the cleft of her little breasts the fiery eye of the topaz and the pale florets of primrose fascinated him. He saw the breasts heave, and the flowers shake with the heaving, and marvelled what should so much discompose the girl. And Christina was conscious of his gaze—saw it, perhaps, with the dainty plaything of an ear that peeped among her ringlets; she was conscious of changing colour, conscious of her unsteady breath. Like a creature tracked, run down, surrounded, she sought in a dozen ways to give herself a countenance. She used her handkerchief—it was a really fine one—then she desisted in a panic; "He would only think I was too warm." She took to reading in the metrical psalms, and then remembered it was sermon-time. Last she put a "sugar-bool" in her mouth, and the next moment repented of the step. It was such a homely-like thing! Mr. Archie would never be eating sweeties in kirk; and, with a palpable effort, she swallowed it whole, and her colour flamed high. At this signal of distress Archie awoke to a sense of his ill-behaviour. What had he been doing? He had been exquisitely rude in church to the niece of his housekeeper; he had stared like a lackey and a libertine at a beautiful and modest girl. It was possible, it was even likely, he would be presented to her after service in the kirkyard, and then how was he to look? And there was no excuse. He had marked the tokens of her shame, of her increasing indignation, and he was such a fool that he had not understood them. Shame bowed him down, and he looked resolutely at Mr. Torrance: who little supposed, good, worthy man, as he continued to expound justification by faith, what was his true business: to play the part of derivative to a pair of children at the old game of falling in love.

Christina was greatly relieved at first. It seemed to her that she was clothed again. She looked back on what had passed. All would have been right if she had not blushed, a silly fool! There was nothing to blush at, if she *had* taken a sugar-bool. Mrs. MacTaggart, the elder's wife in St. Enoch's, took them often. And if he had looked at her, what was more natural than that a young gentleman should look at the best-dressed girl in church? And at the same time, she knew far otherwise, she knew there was nothing casual or ordinary in the look, and valued herself on its memory like a decoration. Well, it was a blessing he had found something else to look at! And presently she began to have other thoughts. It was necessary, she fancied, that she should put herself right by a repetition of the incident, better managed. If the wish was father to the thought, she did not know or she would not recognise it. It was simply as a manœuvre of propriety, as something called for to lessen the significance of what had gone before, that she should a second time meet his eyes, and this time without blushing. And at the memory of the blush, she blushed again, and became one general blush burning from head to foot. Was ever anything so indelicate, so forward, done by a girl before? And here she was, making an exhibition of herself before the congregation about nothing! She stole a glance upon her neighbours, and behold! they were steadily indifferent, and Clem had gone to sleep. And still the one idea was becoming more and more potent with her, that in common prudence she must look again before the service ended. Something of the same sort was going forward in the mind of Archie, as he struggled with the load of penitence. So it chanced that, in the flutter of the moment when the last psalm was given out, and Torrance was reading the verse, and the leaves of every psalm-book in church were rustling under busy fingers, two stealthy glances were sent out like antennæ among the pews and on the indifferent and absorbed occupants, and drew timidly nearer to the straight line between Archie and Christina. They met, they lingered together for the least fraction of time, and that was enough. A charge as of electricity passed through Christina, and behold! the leaf of her psalm-book was torn across.

Archie was outside by the gate of the graveyard, conversing with Hob and the minister and shaking hands all round with the scattering congregation, when Clem and Christina were brought up to be presented. The laird took off his hat and bowed to her with grace and respect. Christina made her Glasgow curtsey to the laird, and went on again up the road for Hermiston and Cauldstaneslap, walking fast, breathing hurriedly with a heightened colour, and in this strange frame of mind, that when she was alone she seemed in high happiness, and when any one addressed her she resented it like a contradiction. A part of the way she had the company of some neighbour girls and a loutish young man; never had they seemed so insipid, never had she made herself so disagreeable. But these struck aside to their various destinations or were out-walked and left behind; and when she had driven off with sharp words the proffered convoy of some of her nephews and nieces, she was free to go on alone up Hermiston brae, walking on air, dwelling intoxicated among clouds of happiness. Near to the summit she heard steps behind her, a man's steps, light and very rapid. She knew the foot at once and walked the faster. "If it's me he's wanting, he can run for it," she thought, smiling.

Archie overtook her like a man whose mind was made up.

"Miss Kirstie," he began.

"Miss Christina, if you please, Mr. Weir," she interrupted. "I canna bear the contraction."

"You forget it has a friendly sound for me. Your aunt is an old friend of mine, and a very good one. I hope we shall see much of you at Hermiston?"

"My aunt and my sister-in-law doesna agree very well. Not that I have much ado with it. But still when I'm stopping in the house, if I was to be visiting my aunt, it would not look considerate-like."

"I am sorry," said Archie.

"I thank you kindly, Mr. Weir," she said. "I whiles think myself it's a great peety."

"Ah, I am sure your voice would always be for peace!" he cried.

"I wouldna be too sure of that," she said. "I have my days like other folk, I suppose."

"Do you know, in our old kirk, among our good old grey dames, you made an effect like sunshine."

"Ah, but that would be my Glasgow clothes!"

"I did not think I was so much under the influence of pretty frocks."

She smiled with a half look at him. "There's more than you!" she said. "But you see I'm only Cinderella. I'll have to put all these things by in my trunk; next Sunday I'll be as grey as the rest. They're Glasgow clothes, you see, and it would never do to make a practice of it. It would seem terrible conspicuous."

By that they were come to the place where their ways severed. The old grey moors were all about them; in the midst a few sheep wandered; and they could see on the one hand the straggling caravan scaling the braes in front of them for Cauldstaneslap, and on the other, the contingent from Hermiston bending off and beginning to disappear by detachments into the policy gate. It was in these circumstances that they turned to say farewell, and deliberately exchanged a glance as they shook hands. All passed as it should, genteelly; and in Christina's mind, as she mounted the first steep ascent for Cauldstaneslap, a gratifying sense of triumph prevailed over the recollection of minor lapses and mistakes. She had kilted her gown, as she did usually at that rugged pass; but when she spied Archie still standing and gazing after her, the skirts came down again as if by enchantment. Here was a piece of nicety for that upland parish, where the matrons marched with their coats kilted in the rain, and the lasses walked barefoot to kirk through the dust of summer, and went bravely down by the burnside, and sat on stones to make a public toilet before entering! It was perhaps an air wafted from Glasgow; or perhaps it marked a stage of that dizziness of gratified vanity, in which the instinctive act passed unperceived. He was looking after! She unloaded her bosom of a prodigious sigh that was all pleasure, and betook herself to run. When she had overtaken the stragglers of her family, she caught up the niece whom she had so recently repulsed, and kissed and slapped her, and drove her away again, and ran after her with pretty cries and laughter. Perhaps she thought the laird might still be looking! But it chanced the little scene came under the view of eyes less favourable; for she overtook Mrs. Hob marching with Clem and Dand.

"You're shürely fey,* lass!" quoth Dandie.

"Think shame to yersel', miss!" said the strident Mrs. Hob. "Is this the gait to guide yersel' on the way hame frae kirk? You're shürely no sponsible the day! And anyway I would mind my guid claes."

"Hoot!" said Christina, and went on before them,

*Strange, like people at the time of approaching disaster or death.

head in air, treading the rough track with the tread of a wild doe.

She was in love with herself, her destiny, the air of the hills, the benediction of the sun. All the way home, she continued under the intoxication of these sky-scraping spirits. At table she could talk freely of young Hermiston; gave her opinion of him off-hand and with a loud voice, that he was a handsome young gentleman, real well-mannered and sensible-like, but it was a pity he looked doleful. Only—the moment after—a memory of his eyes in church embarrassed her. But for this inconsiderable check, all through meal-time she had a good appetite, and she kept them laughing at table, until Gib (who had returned before them from Crossmichael and his separative worship) reproved the whole of them for their levity.

Singing "in to herself" as she went, her mind still in the turmoil of a glad confusion, she rose and tripped upstairs to a little loft, lighted by four panes in the gable, where she slept with one of her nieces. The niece, who followed her, presuming on "Auntie's" high spirits, was flounced out of the apartment with small ceremony, and retired, smarting and half tearful, to bury her woes in the byre among the hay. Still humming, Christina divested herself of her finery, and put her treasures one by one in her great green trunk. The last of these was the psalm-book; it was a fine piece, the gift of Mistress Clem, in distinct old-faced type, on paper that had begun to grow foxy in the warehouse—not by service—and she was used to wrap it in a handkerchief every Sunday after its period of service was over, and bury it end-wise at the head of her trunk. As she now took it in hand the book fell open where the leaf was torn, and she stood and gazed upon that evidence of her bygone discomposure. There returned again the vision of the two brown eyes staring at her, intent and bright, out of that dark corner of the kirk. The whole appearance and attitude, the smile, the suggested gesture of young Hermiston came before her in a flash at the sight of the torn page. "I was surely fey!" she said, echoing the words of Dandie, and at the suggested doom her high spirits deserted her. She flung herself prone upon the bed, and lay there, holding the psalm-book in her hands for hours, for the more part in a mere stupor of unconsenting pleasure and unreasoning fear. The fear was superstitious; there came up again and again in her memory Dandie's ill-omened words, and a hundred grisly and black tales out of the immediate neighbourhood read her a commentary on their force. The pleasure was never realised. You might say the joints of her body thought and remembered, and were gladdened, but her essential self, in the immediate theatre of consciousness, talked feverishly of something else, like a nervous person at a fire. The image that she most complacently dwelt on was that of Miss Christina in her character of the Fair Lass of Cauldstaneslap, carrying all before her in the straw-coloured frock, the violet mantle, and the yellow cobweb stockings. Archie's image, on the other hand, when it presented itself was never welcomed—far less welcomed with any ardour, and it was exposed at times to merciless criticism. In the long vague dialogues she held in her mind, often with imaginary, often with unrealised interlocutors, Archie, if he were referred to at all, came in for savage handling. He was described as "looking like a stirk," "staring like a caulf," "a face like a ghaist's." "Do you call that manners?" she said; or, "I soon put him in his place." " '*Miss Christina, if you please, Mr. Weir!*' says I, and just flyped up my skirt tails." With gabble like this she would entertain herself long whiles together, and then her eye would perhaps fall on the torn leaf, and the eyes of Archie would appear again from the darkness of the wall, and the voluble words deserted her, and she would lie still and stupid, and think upon nothing with devotion, and be sometimes raised by a quiet sigh. Had a doctor of medicine come into that loft, he would have diagnosed a healthy, well-developed, eminently vivacious lass lying on her face in a fit of the sulks; not one who had just contracted, or was just contracting, a mortal sickness of the mind which should yet carry her towards death and despair. Had it been a doctor of psychology, he might have been pardoned for divining in the girl a passion of childish vanity, self-love *in excelsis*, and no more. It is to be understood that I have been painting chaos and describing the inarticulate. Every lineament that appears is too precise, almost every word used too strong. Take a finger-post in the mountains on a day of rolling mists; I have but copied the names that appear upon the pointers, the names of definite and famous cities far distant, and now perhaps basking in sunshine; but Christina remained all these hours, as it were, at the foot of the post itself, not moving, and enveloped in mutable and blinding wreaths of haze.

The day was growing late and the sunbeams long and level, when she sat suddenly up, and wrapped in its handkerchief and put by that psalm-book which had already played a part so decisive in the first chapter of her love-story. In the absence of the mesmerist's eye, we are told nowadays that the head of a bright nail may fill his place, if it be steadfastly regarded. So that torn page had riveted her attention on what might else have been but little, and perhaps soon forgotten; while the ominous words of Dandie—heard, not heeded, and still remembered—had lent to her thoughts, or rather to her mood, a cast of solemnity, and that idea of Fate—a pagan Fate, uncontrolled by any Christian deity, obscure, lawless, and august—moving undissuadably in the affairs of Christian men. Thus even that phenomenon of love at first sight, which is so rare and seems so simple and violent, like a disruption of life's tissue, may be decomposed into a sequence of accidents happily concurring.

She put on a grey frock and a pink kerchief, looked at herself a moment with approval in the small square of glass that served her for a toilet mirror, and went softly downstairs through the sleeping house that resounded with the sound of afternoon snoring. Just outside the door, Dandie was sitting with a book in his hand, not reading, only honouring the Sabbath by a sacred vacancy of mind. She came near him and stood still.

"I'm for off up the muirs, Dandie," she said.

There was something unusually soft in her tones that made him look up. She was pale, her eyes dark and bright; no trace remained of the levity of the morning.

"Ay, lass? Ye'll have yer ups and downs like me, I'm thinkin'," he observed.

"What for do ye say that?" she asked.

"O, for naething," says Dand. "Only I think ye're mair like me than the lave of them. Ye've mair of the poetic temper, tho' Guid kens little enough of the poetic taalent. It's an ill gift at the best. Look at yoursel'. At denner you were all sunshine and flowers and laughter, and now you're like the star of evening on a lake."

She drank in this hackneyed compliment like wine, and it glowed in her veins.

"But I'm saying, Dand"—she came nearer him—"I'm

for the muirs. I must have a braith of air. If Clem was to be speiring for me, try and quaiet him, will ye no?"

"What way?" said Dandie. "I ken but the ae way, and that's leein'. I'll say ye had a sair heed, if ye like."

"But I havena," she objected.

"I daursay no," he returned. "I said I would say ye had; and if ye like to nay-say me when ye come back, it'll no mateerially maitter, for my chara'ter's clean gane a'ready past reca'."

"O, Dand, are ye a leear?" she asked, lingering.

"Folks say sae," replied the bard.

"Wha says sae?" she pursued.

"Them that should ken the best," he responded. "The lassies, for ane."

"But, Dand, you would never lee to me?" she asked.

"I'll leave that for your pairt of it, ye girzie," said he. "Ye'll lee to me fast eneuch, when ye hae gotten a jo. I'm tellin' ye and it's true; when you have a jo, Miss Kirstie, it'll be for guid and ill. I ken: I was made that way mysel', but the deil was in my luck! Here, gang awa' wi' ye to your muirs, and let me be; I'm in an hour of inspiraution, ye upsetting tawpie!"

But she clung to her brother's neighbourhood, she knew not why.

"Will ye no gie's a kiss, Dand?" she said. "I aye likit ye fine."

He kissed her and considered her a moment; he found something strange in her. But he was a libertine through and through, nourished equal contempt and suspicion of all womankind, and paid his way among them habitually with idle compliments.

"Gae wa' wi' ye!" said he. "Ye're a dentie baby, and be content wi' that!"

That was Dandie's way; a kiss and a comfit to Jenny—a bawbee and my blessing to Jill—and good-night to the whole clan of ye, my dears! When anything approached the serious, it became a matter for men, he both thought and said. Woman, when they did not absorb, were only children to be shoo'd away. Merely in his character of connoisseur, however, Dandie glanced carelessly after his sister as she crossed the meadow. "The brat's no that bad!" he thought with surprise, for though he had just been paying her compliments, he had not really looked at her. "Hey! what's yon?" For the grey dress was cut with short sleeves and skirts, and displayed her trim strong legs clad in pink stockings of the same shade as the kerchief she wore round her shoulders, and that shimmered as she went. This was not her way in undress; he knew her ways and the ways of the whole sex in the country-side, no one better; when they did not go barefoot, they wore stout "rig and furrow" woollen hose of an invisible blue mostly, when they were not black outright; and Dandie, at sight of this daintiness, put two and two together. It was a silk handkerchief, then they would be silken hose; they matched—then the whole outfit was a present of Clem's, a costly present, and not something to be worn through bog and briar, or on a late afternoon of Sunday. He whistled. "My denty May, either your heid's fair turned, or there's some ongoings!" he observed, and dismissed the subject.

She went slowly at first, but ever straighter and faster for the Cauldstaneslap, a pass among the hills to which the farm owed its name. The Slap opened like a doorway between two rounded hillocks; and through this ran the short cut to Hermiston. Immediately on the other side it went down through the Deil's Hags, a considerable marshy hollow of the hill tops, full of springs, and crouching junipers, and pools where the black peat-water slumbered. There was no view from here. A man might have sat upon the Praying Weaver's Stone a half-century, and seen none but the Cauldstaneslap children twice in the twenty-four hours on their way to the school and back again, an occasional shepherd, the irruption of a clan of sheep, or the birds who haunted about the springs, drinking and shrilly piping. So, when she had once passed the Slap, Kirstie was received into seclusion. She looked back a last time at the farm. It still lay deserted except for the figure of Dandie, who was now seen to be scribbling in his lap, the hour of expected inspiration having come to him at last. Thence she passed rapidly through the morass, and came to the farther end of it, where a sluggish burn discharges, and the path for Hermiston accompanies it on the beginning of its downward way. From this corner a wide view was opened to her of the whole stretch of braes upon the other side, still sallow and in places rusty with the winter, with the path marked boldly, here and there by the burn-side a tuft of birches, and—two miles off as the crow flies—from its enclosures and young plantations, the windows of Hermiston glittering in the western sun.

Here she sat down and waited, and looked for a long time at these far-away bright panes of glass. It amused her to have so extended a view, she thought. It amused her to see the house of Hermiston—to see "folk"; and there was an indistinguishable human unit, perhaps the gardener, visibly sauntering on the gravel paths.

By the time the sun was down and all the easterly braes lay plunged in clear shadow, she was aware of another figure coming up the path at a most unequal rate of approach, now half running, now pausing and seeming to hesitate. She watched him at first with a total suspension of thought. She held her thought as a person holds his breathing. Then she consented to recognise him. "He'll no be coming here, he canna be; it's no possible." And there began to grow upon her a subdued choking suspense. He *was* coming; his hesitations had quite ceased, his step grew firm and swift; no doubt remained; and the question loomed up before her instant: what was she to do? It was all very well to say that her brother was a laird himself; it was all very well to speak of casual intermarriages and to count cousinship, like Auntie Kirstie. The difference in their social station was trenchant; propriety, prudence, all that she had ever learned, all that she knew, bade her flee. But on the other hand the cup of life now offered to her was too enchanting. For one moment, she saw the question clearly, and definitely made her choice. She stood up and showed herself an instant in the gap relieved upon the sky line; and the next, fled trembling and sat down glowing with excitement on the Weaver's Stone. She shut her eyes, seeking, praying for composure. Her hand shook in her lap, and her mind was full of incongruous and futile speeches. What was there to make a work about? She could take care of herself, she supposed! There was no harm in seeing the laird. It was the best thing that could happen. She would mark a proper distance to him once and for all. Gradually the wheels of her nature ceased to go round so madly, and she sat in passive expectation, a quiet, solitary figure in the midst of the grey moss. I have said she was no hypocrite, but here I am at fault. She never admitted to herself that she had come up the hill to look for Archie. And perhaps after all she did not know, perhaps came as a stone falls. For the steps of love in the young, and especially in girls, are instinctive and unconscious.

In the meantime Archie was drawing rapidly near, and he at least was consciously seeking her neighbourhood. The afternoon had turned to ashes in his mouth; the memory of the girl had kept him from reading and drawn him as with cords; and at last, as the cool of the evening began to come on, he had taken his hat and set forth, with a smothered ejaculation, by the moor path to Cauldstaneslap. He had no hope to find her, he took the off chance without expectation of result and to relieve his uneasiness. The greater was his surprise, as he surmounted the slope and came into the hollow of the Deil's Hags, to see there, like an answer to his wishes, the little womanly figure in the grey dress and the pink kerchief sitting little, and low, and lost, and acutely solitary, in these desolate surroundings and on the weather-beaten stone of the dead weaver. Those things that still smacked of winter were all rusty about her, and those things that already relished of the spring had put forth the tender and lively colours of the season. Even in the unchanging face of the death-stone, changes were to be remarked; and in the channeled lettering, the moss began to renew itself in jewels of green. By an afterthought that was a stroke of art, she had turned up over her head the back of the kerchief; so that it now framed becomingly her vivacious and yet pensive face. Her feet were gathered under her on the one side, and she leaned on her bare arm, which showed out strong and round, tapered to a slim wrist, and shimmered in the fading light.

Young Hermiston was struck with a certain chill. He was reminded that he now dealt in serious matters of life and death. This was a grown woman he was approaching, endowed with her mysterious potencies and attractions, the treasury of the continued race, and he was neither better nor worse than the average of his sex and age. He had a certain delicacy which had preserved him hitherto unspotted, and which (had either of them guessed it) made him a more dangerous companion when his heart should be really stirred. His throat was dry as he came near; but the appealing sweetness of her smile stood between them like a guardian angel.

For she turned to him and smiled, though without

rising. There was a shade in this cavalier greeting that neither of them perceived; neither he, who simply thought it gracious and charming as herself; nor yet she, who did not observe (quick as she was) the difference between rising to meet the laird, and remaining seated to receive the expected admirer.

"Are ye stepping west, Hermiston?" said she, giving him his territorial name after the fashion of the countryside.

"I was," said he, a little hoarsely, "but I think I will be about the end of my stroll now. Are you like me, Miss Christina? The house would not hold me. I came here seeking air."

He took his seat at the other end of the tombstone and studied her, wondering what was she. There was infinite import in the question alike for her and him.

"Ay," said she. "I couldna bear the roof either. It's a habit of mine to come up here about the gloaming when it's quaiet and caller."

"It was a habit of my mother's also," he said gravely. The recollection half startled him as he expressed it. He looked around. "I have scarce been here since. It's peaceful," he said, with a long breath.

"It's no like Glasgow," she replied. "A weary place, yon Glasgow! But what a day have I had for my hame-coming, and what a bonny evening!"

"Indeed, it was a wonderful day," said Archie. "I think I will remember it years and years until I come to die. On days like this—I do not know if you feel as I do—but everything appears so brief, and fragile, and exquisite, that I am afraid to touch life. We are here for so short a time; and all the old people before us—Rutherfords of Hermiston, Elliotts of the Cauldstaneslap—that were here but a while since riding about and keeping up a great noise in this quiet corner—making love too, and marrying—why, where are they now? It's deadly commonplace, but, after all, the commonplaces are the great poetic truths."

He was sounding her, semi-consciously, to see if she could understand him; to learn if she were only an animal the colour of flowers, or had a soul in her to keep her sweet. She, on her part, her means well in hand, watched, womanlike, for any opportunity to shine, to abound in his humour, whatever that might be. The dramatic artist, that lies dormant or only half awake in most human beings, had in her sprung to his feet in a divine fury, and chance had served her well. She looked upon him with a subdued twilight look that became the hour of the day and the train of thought; earnestness shone through her like stars in the purple west; and from the great but controlled upheaval of her whole nature there passed into her voice, and ran in her lightest words, a thrill of emotion.

"Have you mind of Dand's song?" she answered. "I think he'll have been trying to say what you have been thinking."

"No, I never heard it," he said. "Repeat it to me, can you?"

"It's nothing wanting the tune," said Kirstie.

"Then sing it me," said he.

"On the Lord's Day? That would never do, Mr. Weir!"

"I am afraid I am not so strict a keeper of the Sabbath, and there is no one in this place to hear us unless the poor old ancient under the stone."

"No that I'm thinking that really," she said. "By my way of thinking, it's just as serious as a psalm. Will I sooth it to ye, then?"

"If you please," said he, and, drawing near to her on the tombstone, prepared to listen.

She sat up as if to sing. "I'll only can sooth it to ye," she explained. "I wouldna like to sing out loud on the Sabbath. I think the birds would carry news of it to Gilbert," and she smiled. "It's about the Elliotts," she continued, "and I think there's few bonnier bits in the book-poets, though Dand has never got printed yet."

And she began, in the low, clear tones of her half voice, now sinking almost to a whisper, now rising to a particular note which was her best, and which Archie learned to wait for with growing emotion:—

"O they rade in the rain, in the days that are gane,
In the rain and the wind and the lave,
They shoutit in the ha' and they routit on the hill,
But they're a' quaitit noo in the grave.
Auld, auld Elliotts, clay-cauld Elliotts, dour,
bauld Elliotts of auld!"

All the time she sang she looked steadfastly before her, her knees straight, her hands upon her knee, head cast back and up. The expression was admirable throughout, for had she not learned it from the lips and under the criticism of the author? When it was done, she turned upon Archie a face softly bright, and eyes gently suffused and shining in the twilight, and his heart rose and went out to her with boundless pity and sympathy. His question was answered. She was a human being tuned to a sense of the tragedy of life; there were pathos and music and a great heart in the girl.

He arose instinctively, she also; for she saw she had gained a point, and scored the impression deeper, and she had wit enough left to flee upon a victory. They were but commonplaces that remained to be exchanged, but the low, moved voices in which they passed made them sacred in the memory. In the falling greyness of the evening he watched her figure winding through the morass, saw it turn a last time and wave a hand, and then pass through the Slap; and it seemed to him as if something went along with her out of the deepest of his heart. And something surely had come, and come to dwell there. He had retained from childhood a picture, now half obliterated by the passage of time and the multitude of fresh impressions, of his mother telling him, with the fluttered earnestness of her voice, and often with dropping tears, the tale of the "Praying Weaver," on the very scene of his brief tragedy and long repose. And now there was a companion piece; and he beheld, and he should behold for ever, Christina perched on the same tomb, in the grey colours of the evening, gracious, dainty, perfect as a flower, and she also singing—

> "Of old, unhappy far off things,
> And battles long ago,"

of their common ancestors now dead, of their rude wars composed, their weapons buried with them, and of these strange changelings, their descendants, who lingered a little in their places, and would soon be gone also, and perhaps sung of by others at the gloaming hour. By one of the unconscious arts of tenderness the two women were enshrined together in his memory. Tears, in that hour of sensibility, came into his eyes indifferently at the thought of either; and the girl, from being something merely bright and shapely, was caught up into the zone of things serious as life and death and his dead mother. So that in all ways and on either side, Fate played his game artfully with this poor pair of children. The generations were prepared, the pangs were made ready, before the curtain rose on the dark drama.

In the same moment of time that she disappeared from Archie, there opened before Kirstie's eyes the cup-like hollow in which the farm lay. She saw, some five hundred feet below her, the house making itself bright with candles, and this was a broad hint to her to hurry. For they were only kindled on a Sabbath night with a view to that family worship which rounded in the incomparable tedium of the day and brought on the relaxation of supper. Already she knew that Robert must be withinsides at the head of the table, "waling the portions"; for it was Robert in his quality of family priest and judge, not the gifted Gilbert, who officiated. She made good time accordingly down the steep ascent, and came up to the door panting as the three younger brothers, all roused at last from slumber, stood together in the cool and the dark of the evening with a fry of nephews and nieces about them, chatting and awaiting the expected signal. She stood back; she had no mind to direct attention to her late arrival or to her labouring breath.

"Kirstie, ye have shaved it this time, my lass," said Clem. "Whaur were ye?"

"O, just taking a dander by mysel'," said Kirstie.

And the talk continued on the subject of the American War, without further reference to the truant who stood by them in the covert of the dusk, thrilling with happiness and the sense of guilt.

The signal was given, and the brothers began to go in one after another, amid the jostle and throng of Hob's children.

Only Dandie, waiting till the last, caught Kirstie by the arm. "When did ye begin to dander in pink hosen, Mistress Elliott?" he whispered slily.

She looked down; she was one blush. "I maun have forgotten to change them," said she; and went in to prayers in her turn with a troubled mind, between anxiety as to whether Dand should have observed her yellow stockings at church, and should thus detect her in a palpable falsehood, and shame that she had already made good his prophecy. She remembered the words of it, how it was to be when she had gotten a jo, and that that would be for good and evil. "Will I have gotten my jo now?" she thought with a secret rapture.

And all through prayers, where it was her principal business to conceal the pink stockings from the eyes of the indifferent Mrs. Hob—and all through supper, as she made a feint of eating and sat at the table radiant and constrained—and again when she had left them and come into her chamber, and was alone with her sleeping niece, and could at last lay aside the armour of society—the same words sounded within her, the same profound note of happiness, of a world all changed and renewed, of a day that had been passed in Paradise, and of a night that was to be heaven opened. All night she seemed to be conveyed smoothly upon a shallow stream of sleep and waking, and through the bowers of Beulah; all night she cherished to her heart that exquisite hope; and if, towards morning, she forgot it a while in a more profound unconsciousness, it was to catch again the rainbow thought with her first moment of awaking.

CHAPTER VII

ENTER MEPHISTOPHELES

Two days later a gig from Crossmichael deposited Frank Innes at the doors of Hermiston. Once in a way, during the past winter, Archie, in some acute phase of boredom, had written him a letter. It had contained something in the nature of an invitation, or a reference to an invitation—precisely what, neither of them now remembered. When Innes had received it, there had been nothing further from his mind than to bury himself in the moors with Archie; but not even the most acute political heads are guided through the steps of life with unerring directness. That would require a gift of prophecy which has been denied to man. For instance, who could have imagined that, not a month after he had received the letter, and turned it into mockery, and put off answering it, and in the end lost it, misfortunes of a gloomy cast should begin to thicken over Frank's career? His case may be briefly stated. His father, a small Morayshire laird with a large family, became recalcitrant and cut off the supplies; he had fitted himself out with the beginnings of quite a good law library, which, upon some sudden losses on the turf, he had been obliged to sell before they were paid for; and his bookseller, hearing some rumour of the event, took out a warrant for his arrest. Innes had early word of it, and was able to take precautions. In this immediate welter of his affairs, with an unpleasant charge hanging over him, he had judged it the part of prudence to be off instantly, had written a fervid letter to his father at Inverauld, and put himself in the coach for Crossmichael. Any port in a storm! He was manfully turning his back on the Parliament House and its gay babble, on porter and oysters, the racecourse and the ring; and manfully prepared, until these clouds should have blown by, to share a living grave with Archie Weir at Hermiston.

To do him justice, he was no less surprised to be going than Archie was to see him come; and he carried off his wonder with an infinitely better grace.

"Well, here I am!" said he, as he alighted. "Pylades has come to Orestes at last. By the way, did you get my answer? No? How very provoking! Well, here I am to answer for myself, and that's better still."

"I am very glad to see you, of course," said Archie. "I make you heartily welcome, of course. But you surely have not come to stay, with the Courts still sitting; is that not most unwise?"

"Damn the Courts!" says Frank. "What are the Courts to friendship and a little fishing?"

And so it was agreed that he was to stay, with no term to the visit but the term which he had privily set to it himself—the day, namely, when his father should have come down with the dust, and he should be able to pacify the bookseller. On such vague conditions there began for these two young men (who were not even friends) a life of great familiarity and, as the days drew on, less and less intimacy. They were together at meal-times, together o' nights when the hour had come for whisky-toddy; but it might have been noticed (had there been any one to pay heed) that they were rarely so much together by day. Archie had Hermiston to attend to, multifarious activities in the hills, in which he did not require, and had even refused, Frank's escort. He would be off sometimes in the morning and leave only a note on the breakfast-table to announce the fact; and sometimes with no notice at all, he would not return for dinner until the hour was long past. Innes groaned under these desertions; it required all his philosophy to sit down to a solitary breakfast with composure and all his unaffected good-nature to be able to greet Archie with friendliness on the more rare occasions when he came home late for dinner.

"I wonder what on earth he finds to do, Mrs. Elliott?" said he one morning, after he had just read the hasty billet and sat down to table.

"I suppose it will be business, sir," replied the housekeeper drily, measuring his distance off to him by an indicated curtsey.

"But I can't imagine what business!" he reiterated.

"I suppose it will be *his* business," retorted the austere Kirstie.

He turned to her with that happy brightness that made the charm of his disposition, and broke into a peal of healthy and natural laughter.

"Well played, Mrs. Elliott!" he cried; and the housekeeper's face relaxed into the shadow of an iron smile. "Well played indeed!" said he. "But you must not be making a stranger of me like that. Why, Archie and I were at the High School together, and we've been to College together, and we were going to the Bar together, when—you know! Dear, dear me! what a pity that was! A life spoiled, a fine young fellow as good as buried here in the wilderness with rustics; and all for what? A frolic, silly, if you like, but no more. God, how good your scones are, Mrs. Elliott!"

"They're no mines, it was the lassie made them," said Kirstie; "and, saving your presence, there's little sense in taking the Lord's name in vain about idle vivers that you fill your kyte wi'."

"I daresay you're perfectly right, ma'am," quoth the imperturbable Frank. "But as I was saying, this is a pitiable business, this about poor Archie; and you and I might do worse than put our heads together, like a couple of sensible people, and bring it to an end. Let me tell you, ma'am, that Archie is really quite a promising young man, and in my opinion he would do well at the Bar. As for his father, no one can deny his ability, and I don't fancy any one would care to deny that he has the deil's own temper—"

"If you'll excuse me, Mr. Innes, I think the lass is crying on me," said Kirstie, and flounced from the room.

"The damned, cross-grained, old broom-stick!" ejaculated Innes.

In the meantime, Kirstie had escaped into the kitchen, and before her vassal gave vent to her feelings.

"Here, ettercap! Ye'll have to wait on yon Innes! I canna haud myself in. 'Puir Erchie!' I'd 'puir Erchie' him, if I had my way! And Hermiston with the deil's ain temper! God, let him take Hermiston's scones out of his mouth first. There's no a hair on ayther o' the Weirs that hasna mair spunk and dirdum to it than what he has in his hale dwaibly body! Settin' up his snash to me! Let him gang to the black toon where he's mebbe wantit—birling on a curricle—wi' pimatum on his heid—making a mess o' himsel' wi' nesty hizzies—a fair disgrace!" It was impossible to hear without admiration Kirstie's graduated disgust, as she brought forth, one after another, these somewhat baseless charges. Then she remembered her immediate purpose, and turned again on her fascinated auditor. "Do ye no hear me, tawpie? Do ye no hear what I'm tellin' ye? Will I have to shoo ye into him? If I come to attend to ye, mistress!" And the maid fled the kitchen, which had become practically dangerous, to attend on Innes's wants in the front parlour.

Tantaene irae? Has the reader perceived the reason? Since Frank's coming there were no more hours of gossip over the supper-tray! All his blandishments were in vain; he had started handicapped on the race for Mrs. Elliott's favour.

But it was a strange thing how misfortune dogged him in his efforts to be genial. I must guard the reader against accepting Kirstie's epithets as evidence; she was more concerned for their vigour than for their accuracy. Dwaibly, for instance; nothing could be more calumnious. Frank was the very picture of good looks, good humour, and manly youth. He had bright eyes with a sparkle and a dance to them, curly hair, a charming smile, brilliant teeth, an admirable carriage of the head, the look of a gentleman, the address of one accustomed to please at first sight and to improve the impression. And with all these advantages, he failed with every one about Hermiston; with the silent shepherd, with the obsequious grieve, with the groom who was also the ploughman, with the gardener and the gardener's sister—a pious, down-hearted woman with the shawl over her ears—he failed equally and flatly. They did not like him, and they showed it. The little maid, indeed, was an exception; she admired him devoutly, probably dreamed of him in her private hours; but she was accustomed to play the part of silent auditor to Kirstie's tirades and silent recipient of Kirstie's buffets, and she had learned not only to be a very capable girl of her years, but a very secret and prudent one besides. Frank was thus conscious that he had one ally and sympathiser in the midst of that general union of disfavour that surrounded, watched, and waited on him in the house of Hermiston; but he had little comfort or society from that alliance, and the demure little maid (twelve on her last birthday) preserved her own counsel, and tripped on his service, brisk, dumbly responsive, but inexorably unconversational. For the others, they were beyond hope and beyond endurance. Never had a young Apollo been cast among such rustic barbarians. But perhaps the cause of his ill-success lay in one trait which was habitual and unconscious with him, yet diagnostic of the man. It was his practice to approach any one person at the expense of some one else. He offered you an alliance against the some one else; he flattered you by slighting him; you were drawn into a small intrigue against him before you knew how. Wonderful are the virtues of this process generally; but Frank's mistake was in the choice of the some one else. He was not politic in that; he listened to the voice of irritation. Archie had offended him at first by what he had felt to be rather a dry reception, had offended him since by his frequent absences. He was besides the one figure continually present in Frank's eye; and it was to his immediate dependants that Frank could offer the snare of his sympathy. Now the truth is that the Weirs, father and son, were surrounded by a posse of strenuous loyalists. Of my lord they were vastly proud. It was a distinction in itself to be one of the vassals of the "Hanging Judge," and his gross, formidable joviality was far from unpopular in the neighbourhood of his home. For Archie they had, one and all, a sensitive affection and respect which recoiled from a word of belittlement.

Nor was Frank more successful when he went farther afield. To the Four Black Brothers, for instance, he was antipathetic in the highest degree. Hob thought him too light, Gib too profane. Clem, who saw him but for a day or two before he went to Glasgow, wanted to know what the fule's business was, and whether he meant to stay here all session time! "Yon's a drone," he pronounced. As for Dand, it will be enough to describe their first meeting, when Frank had been whipping a river and the rustic celebrity chanced to come along the path.

"I'm told you're quite a poet," Frank had said.

"Wha tell 't ye that, mannie?" had been the unconciliating answer.

"O, everybody!" says Frank.

"God! Here's fame!" said the sardonic poet, and he had passed on his way.

Come to think of it, we have here perhaps a truer explanation of Frank's failures. Had he met Mr. Sheriff Scott, he could have turned a neater compliment, because Mr. Scott would have been a friend worth making. Dand, on the other hand, he did not value sixpence, and he showed it even while he tried to flatter. Condescension is an excellent thing, but it is strange how one-sided the pleasure of it is! He who goes fishing among the Scots peasantry with condescension for a bait will have an empty basket by evening.

In proof of this theory Frank made a great success of it at the Crossmichael Club, to which Archie took him immediately on his arrival; his own last appearance on that scene of gaiety. Frank was made welcome there at once, continued to go regularly, and had attended a meeting (as the members ever after loved to tell) on the evening before his death. Young Hay and young Pringle appeared again. There was another supper at Windielaws, another dinner at Driffel; and it resulted in Frank being taken to the bosom of the county people as unreservedly as he had been repudiated by the country folk. He occupied Hermiston after the manner of an invader in a conquered capital. He was perpetually issuing from it, as from a base, to toddy parties, fishing parties, and dinner parties, to which Archie was not invited, or to which Archie would not go. It was now that the name of The Recluse became general for the young man. Some say that Innes invented it; Innes, at least, spread it abroad.

"How's all with your Recluse to-day?" people would ask.

"O, reclusing away!" Innes would declare, with his bright air of saying something witty; and immediately interrupt the general laughter which he had provoked much more by his air than his words, "Mind you, it's all very well laughing, but I'm not very well pleased. Poor Archie is a good fellow, an excellent fellow, a fellow I always liked. I think it small of him to take his little disgrace so hard and shut himself up. 'Grant that it is a ridiculous story, painfully ridiculous,' I keep telling him. 'Be a man! Live it down, man!' But not he. Of course it's just solitude, and shame, and all that. But I confess I'm beginning to fear the result. It would be all the pities in the world if a really promising fellow like Weir was to end ill. I'm seriously tempted to write to Lord Hermiston, and put it plainly to him."

"I would if I were you," some of his auditors would say, shaking the head, sitting bewildered and confused at this new view of the matter, so deftly indicated by a single word. "A capital idea!" they would add, and wonder at the *aplomb* and position of this young man, who talked as a matter of course of writing to Hermiston and correcting him upon his private affairs.

And Frank would proceed, sweetly confidential: "I'll give you an idea, now. He's actually sore about the way that I'm received and he's left out in the county—actually jealous and sore. I've rallied him and I've reasoned with him, told him that every one was most kindly inclined towards him, told him even that *I* was received merely because I was his guest. But it's no use. He will neither accept the invitations he gets, nor stop brooding about the ones where he's left out. What I'm afraid of is that the wound's ulcerating. He had always one of those dark, secret, angry natures—a little underhand and plenty of bile—you know the sort. He must have inherited it from the Weirs, whom I suspect to have been a worthy family of weavers somewhere; what's the cant phrase?—sedentary occupation. It's precisely the kind of character to go wrong in a false position like what his father's made for him, or he's making for himself, whichever you like to call it. And for my part, I think it a disgrace," Frank would say generously.

Presently the sorrow and anxiety of this disinterested friend took shape. He began in private, in conversations of two, to talk vaguely of bad habits and low habits. "I must say I'm afraid he's going wrong altogether," he would say. "I'll tell you plainly, and between ourselves, I scarcely like to stay there any longer; only, man, I'm positively afraid to leave him alone. You'll see, I shall be blamed for it later on. I'm staying at a great sacrifice. I'm hindering my chances at the Bar, and I can't blind my eyes to it. And what I'm afraid of is, that I'm going to get kicked for it all round before all's done. You see, nobody believes in friendship nowadays."

"Well, Innes," his interlocutor would reply, "it's very good of you, I must say that. If there's any blame going, you'll always be sure of *my* good word, for one thing."

"Well," Frank would continue, "candidly, I don't say it's pleasant. He has a very rough way with him; his father's son, you know. I don't say he's rude—of course, I couldn't be expected to stand that—but he steers very near the wind. No, it's not pleasant; but I tell ye, man, in conscience I don't think it would be fair to leave him. Mind you, I don't say there's anything actually wrong. What I say is that I don't like the looks of it, man!" and he would press the arm of his momentary confidant.

In the early stages I am persuaded there was no malice. He talked but for the pleasure of airing himself. He was essentially glib, as becomes the young advocate, and essentially careless of the truth, which is the mark of the young ass; and so he talked at random. There was no particular bias, but that one which is indigenous and universal, to flatter himself and to please and interest the present friend. And by thus milling air out of his mouth, he had presently built up a presentation of Archie which was known and talked of in all corners of the county. Wherever there was a residential house and a walled garden, wherever there was a dwarfish castle and a park, wherever a quadruple cottage by the ruins of a peel-tower showed an old family going down, and wherever a handsome villa with a carriage approach and a shrubbery marked the coming up of a new one—probably on the wheels of machinery—Archie began to be regarded in the light of a dark, perhaps a vicious mystery, and the future developments of his career to be looked for with uneasiness and confidential whispering. He had done something disgraceful, my dear. What, was not precisely known, and that good kind young man, Mr. Innes, did his best to make light of it. But there it was. And Mr.

Innes was very anxious about him now; he was really uneasy, my dear; he was positively wrecking his own prospects because he dared not leave him alone. How wholly we all lie at the mercy of a single prater, not needfully with any malign purpose! And if a man but talks of himself in the right spirit, refers to his virtuous actions by the way, and never applies to them the name of virtue, how easily his evidence is accepted in the court of public opinion!

All this while, however, there was a more poisonous ferment at work between the two lads, which came late indeed to the surface, but had modified and magnified their dissensions from the first. To an idle, shallow, easy-going customer like Frank, the smell of a mystery was attractive. It gave his mind something to play with, like a new toy to a child; and it took him on the weak side, for like many young men coming to the Bar, and before they have been tried and found wanting, he flattered himself he was a fellow of unusual quickness and penetration. They knew nothing of Sherlock Holmes in those days, but there was a good deal said of Talleyrand. And if you could have caught Frank off his guard, he would have confessed with a smirk that, if he resembled any one, it was the Marquis de Talleyrand-Périgord. It was on the occasion of Archie's first absence that this interest took root. It was vastly deepened when Kirstie resented his curiosity at breakfast, and that same afternoon there occurred another scene which clinched the business. He was fishing Swingleburn, Archie accompanying him, when the latter looked at his watch.

"Well, good-bye," said he. "I have something to do. See you at dinner."

"Don't be in such a hurry," cries Frank. "Hold on till I get my rod up. I'll go with you; I'm sick of flogging this ditch."

And he began to reel up his line.

Archie stood speechless. He took a long while to recover his wits under this direct attack; but by the time he was ready with his answer, and the angle was almost packed up, he had become completely Weir, and the hanging face gloomed on his young shoulders. He spoke with a laboured composure, a laboured kindness even; but a child could see that his mind was made up.

"I beg your pardon, Innes; I don't want to be disagreeable, but let us understand one another from the beginning. When I want your company, I'll let you know."

"O!" cries Frank, "you don't want my company, don't you?"

"Apparently not just now," replied Archie. "I even indicated to you when I did, if you'll remember—and that was at dinner. If we two fellows are to live together pleasantly—and I see no reason why we should not—it can only be by respecting each other's privacy. If we begin intruding—"

"O, come! I'll take this at no man's hands. Is this the way you treat a guest and an old friend?" cried Innes.

"Just go home and think over what I said by yourself," continued Archie, "whether it's reasonable, or whether it's really offensive or not; and let's meet at dinner as though nothing had happened. I'll put it this way, if you like—that I know my own character, that I'm looking forward (with great pleasure, I assure you) to a long visit from you, and that I'm taking precautions at the first. I see the thing that we—that I, if you like—might fall out upon, and I step in and *obsto principiis*. I wager you five pounds you'll end by seeing that I mean friendliness, and I assure you, Francie, I do," he added, relenting.

Bursting with anger, but incapable of speech, Innes shouldered his rod, made a gesture of farewell, and strode off down the burn-side. Archie watched him go without moving. He was sorry, but quite unashamed. He hated to be inhospitable, but in one thing he was his father's son. He had a strong sense that his house was his own and no man else's; and to lie at a guest's mercy was what he refused. He hated to seem harsh. But that was Frank's look-out. If Frank had been commonly discreet, he would have been decently courteous. And there was another consideration. The secret he was protecting was not his own merely; it was hers: it belonged to that inexpressible she who was fast taking possession of his soul, and whom he would soon have defended at the cost of burning cities. By the time he had watched Frank as far as the Swingleburnfoot, appearing and disappearing in the tarnished heather, still stalking at a fierce gait, but already dwindled in the distance into less than the smallness of Lilliput, he could afford to smile at thc occurrence. Either Frank would go, and that would be a relief—or he would continue to stay, and his host must continue to endure him. And Archie was now free—by devious paths, behind hillocks and in the hollow of burns—to make for the trysting-place where Kirstie, cried about by the curlew and the plover, waited and burned for his coming by the Covenanter's Stone.

Innes went off down-hill in a passion of resentment, easy to be understood, but which yielded progressively to the needs of his situation. He cursed Archie for a cold-hearted, unfriendly, rude, rude dog; and himself still more passionately for a fool in having come to Hermiston when he might have sought refuge in almost any other house in Scotland. But the step, once taken, was practically irretrievable. He had no more ready money to go anywhere else; he would have to borrow from Archie the next club-night; and ill as he thought of his host's manners, he was sure of his practical generosity. Frank's resemblance to Talleyrand strikes me as imaginary; but at least not Talleyrand himself could have more obediently taken his lesson from the facts. He met Archie at dinner without resentment, almost with cordiality. You must take your friends as you find them, he would have said. Archie couldn't help being his father's son, or his grandfather's, the hypothetical weaver's, grandson. The son of a hunks, he was still a hunks at heart, incapable of true generosity and consideration: but he had other qualities with which Frank could divert himself in the meanwhile, and to enjoy which it was necessary that Frank should keep his temper.

So excellently was it controlled that he awoke next morning with his head full of a different, though a cognate subject. What was Archie's little game? Why did he shun Frank's company? What was he keeping secret? Was he keeping tryst with somebody, and was it a woman? It would be a good joke and a fair revenge to discover. To that task he set himself with a great deal of patience, which might have surprised his friends, for he had been always credited not with patience so much as brilliancy; and little by little, from one point to another, he at last succeeded in piecing out the situation. First he remarked that, although Archie set out in all the directions of the compass, he always came home again from some point between the south and west. From the study of a map, and in consideration of the great expanse of untenanted moorland running in that direction towards the sources of the Clyde, he laid his finger on Cauldstaneslap and two other neighbouring farms, Kingsmuirs and Polintarf. But it was difficult to advance farther. With his rod for a pretext, he vainly visited each of them in turn; nothing was to be seen suspicious about this trinity of moorland settlements. He would have tried to follow Archie, had it been the least possible, but the nature of the land precluded the idea. He did the next best, ensconced himself in a quiet corner, and pursued his movements with a telescope. It was equally in vain, and he soon wearied of his futile vigilance, left the telescope at home, and had almost given the matter up in despair, when, on the twenty-seventh day of his visit, he was suddenly confronted with the person whom he sought. The first Sunday Kirstie had managed to stay away from kirk on some pretext of indisposition, which was more truly modesty; the pleasure of beholding Archie seeming too sacred, too vivid for that public place. On the two following, Frank had himself been absent on some of his excursions among the neighbouring families. It was not until the fourth, accordingly, that Frank had occasion to set eyes on the enchantress. With the first look, all hesitation was over. She came with the Cauldstaneslap party; then she lived at Cauldstaneslap. Here was Archie's secret, here was the woman, and more than that—though I have need here of every manageable attenuation of language—with the first look, he had already entered himself as rival. It was a good deal in pique, it was a little in revenge, it was much in genuine admiration: the devil may decide the proportions! I cannot, and it is very likely that Frank could not.

"Mighty attractive milkmaid," he observed, on the way home.

"Who?" said Archie.

"O, the girl you're looking at—aren't you? Forward there on the road. She came attended by the rustic bard; presumably, therefore, belongs to his exalted family. The single objection! for the Four Black Brothers are awkward customers. If anything were to go wrong, Gib would gibber, and Clem would prove inclement; and Dand fly in danders, and Hob blow up in gobbets. It would be a Helliott of a business!"

"Very humorous, I am sure," said Archie.

"Well, I am trying to be so," said Frank. "It's none too easy in this place, and with your solemn society, my dear fellow. But confess that the milkmaid has found favour in your eyes, or resign all claim to be a man of taste."

"It is no matter," returned Archie.

But the other continued to look at him, steadily and quizzically, and his colour slowly rose and deepened under the glance, until not impudence itself could have denied that he was blushing. And at this Archie lost some of his control. He changed his stick from one hand to the other, and—"O, for God's sake, don't be an ass!" he cried.

"Ass? That's the retort delicate without doubt," says Frank. "Beware of the home-spun brothers, dear. If they come into the dance, you'll see who's an ass. Think now, if they only applied (say) a quarter as much talent as I have applied to the question of what Mr. Archie does with his evening hours, and why he is so unaffectedly nasty when the subject's touched on—"

"You are touching on it now," interrupted Archie, with a wince.

"Thank you. That was all I wanted, an articulate confession," said Frank.

"I beg to remind you—" began Archie.

But he was interrupted in turn. "My dear fellow, don't. It's quite needless. The subject's dead and buried."

And Frank began to talk hastily on other matters, an art in which he was an adept, for it was his gift to be fluent on anything or nothing. But although Archie had the grace or the timidity to suffer him to rattle on, he was by no means done with the subject. When he came home to dinner he was greeted with a sly demand, how things were looking "Cauldstaneslap ways." Frank took his first glass of port out after dinner to the toast of Kirstie, and later in the evening he returned to the charge again.

"I say, Weir, you'll excuse me for returning again to this affair. I've been thinking it over, and I wish to beg you very seriously to be more careful. It's not a safe business. Not safe, my boy," said he.

"What?" said Archie.

"Well, it's your own fault if I must put a name on the thing; but really, as a friend, I cannot stand by and see you rushing head down into these dangers. My dear boy," said he, holding up a warning cigar, "consider! What is to be the end of it?"

"The end of what?"—Archie, helpless with irritation, persisted in this dangerous and ungracious guard.

"Well, the end of the milkmaid; or, to speak more by the card, the end of Miss Christina Elliott of the Cauldstaneslap."

"I assure you," Archie broke out, "this is all a figment of your imagination. There is nothing to be said against that young lady; you have no right to introduce her name into the conversation."

"I'll make a note of it," said Frank. "She shall henceforth be nameless, nameless, nameless, Gregarach! I make a note besides of your valuable testimony to her character. I only want to look at this thing as a man of the world. Admitted she's an angel—but, my good fellow, is she a lady?"

This was torture to Archie. "I beg your pardon," he said, struggling to be composed, "but because you have wormed yourself into my confidence—"

"O, come!" cried Frank. "Your confidence? It was rosy but unconsenting. Your confidence, indeed? Now, look! This is what I must say, Weir, for it concerns your safety and good character, and therefore my honour as your friend. You say I wormed myself into your confidence. Wormed is good. But what have I done? I have put two and two together, just as the parish will be doing to-morrow, and the whole of Tweeddale in two weeks, and the Black Brothers—well, I won't put a date on that; it will be a dark and stormy morning! Your secret, in other words, is poor Poll's. And I want to ask of you as a friend whether you like the prospect? There are two horns to your dilemma, and I must say for myself I should look mighty ruefully on either. Do you see yourself explaining to the Four Black Brothers? or do you see yourself presenting the milkmaid to papa as the future lady of Hermiston? Do you? I tell you plainly, I don't!"

Archie rose. "I will hear no more of this," he said, in a trembling voice.

But Frank again held up his cigar. "Tell me one thing first. Tell me if this is not a friend's part that I am playing?"

"I believe you think it so," replied Archie. "I can go as far as that. I can do so much justice to your motives. But I will hear no more of it. I am going to bed."

"That's right, Weir," said Frank heartily. "Go to bed

and think over it; and I say, man, don't forget your prayers! I don't often do the moral—don't go in for that sort of thing—but when I do, there's one thing sure, that I mean it."

So Archie marched off to bed, and Frank sat alone by the table for another hour or so, smiling to himself richly. There was nothing vindictive in his nature; but, if revenge came in his way, it might as well be good, and the thought of Archie's pillow reflections that night was indescribably sweet to him. He felt a pleasant sense of power. He looked down on Archie as on a very little boy whose strings he pulled—as on a horse whom he had backed and bridled by sheer power of intelligence, and whom he might ride to glory or the grave at pleasure. Which was it to be? He lingered long, relishing the details of schemes that he was too idle to pursue. Poor cork upon a torrent, he tasted that night the sweets of omnipotence, and brooded like a deity over the strands of that intrigue which was to shatter him before the summer waned.

CHAPTER VIII

A NOCTURNAL VISIT

KIRSTIE HAD many causes of distress. More and more as we grow old—and yet more and more as we grow old and are women, frozen by the fear of age—we come to rely on the voice as the single outlet of the soul. Only thus, in the curtailment of our means, can we relieve the straitened cry of the passion within us; only thus, in the bitter and sensitive shyness of advancing years, can we maintain relations with those vivacious figures of the young that still show before us and tend daily to become no more than the moving wall-paper of life. Talk is the last link, the last relation. But with the end of the conversation, when the voice stops and the bright face of the listener is turned away, solitude falls again on the bruised heart. Kirstie had lost her "cannie hour at e'en"; she could no more wander with Archie, a ghost if you will, but a happy ghost, in fields Elysian. And to her it was as if the whole world had fallen silent; to him, but an unremarkable change of amusements. And she raged to know it.

The effervescency of her passionate and irritable nature rose within her at times to bursting point.

This is the price paid by age for unseasonable ardours of feeling. It must have been so for Kirstie at any time when the occasion chanced; but it so fell out that she was deprived of this delight in the hour when she had most need of it, when she had most to say, most to ask, and when she trembled to recognise her sovereignty not merely in abeyance but annulled. For, with the clairvoyance of a genuine love, she had pierced the mystery that had so long embarrassed Frank. She was conscious, even before it was carried out, even on that Sunday night when it began, of an invasion of her rights; and a voice told her the invader's name. Since then, by arts, by accident, by small things observed, and by the general drift of Archie's humour, she had passed beyond all possibility of doubt. With a sense of justice that Lord Hermiston might have envied, she had that day in church considered and admitted the attractions of the younger Kirstie; and with the profound humanity and sentimentality of her nature, she had recognised the coming of fate. Not thus would she have chosen. She had seen, in imagination, Archie wedded to some tall, powerful, and rosy heroine of the golden locks, made in her own image, for whom she would have strewed the bride-bed with delight; and now she could have wept to see the ambition falsified. But the gods had pronounced, and her doom was otherwise.

She lay tossing in bed that night, besieged with feverish thoughts. There were dangerous matters pending, a battle was toward, over the fate of which she hung in jealousy, sympathy, fear, and alternate loyalty and disloyalty to either side. Now she was reincarnated in her niece, and now in Archie. Now she saw, through the girl's eyes, the youth on his knees to her, heard his persuasive instances with a deadly weakness, and received his overmastering caresses. Anon, with a revulsion, her temper raged to see such utmost favours of fortune and love squandered on a brat of a girl, one of her own house, using her own name—a deadly ingredient—and that "didna ken her ain mind an' was as black's your hat." Now she trembled lest her deity should plead in vain, loving the idea of success for him like a triumph of nature; anon, with returning loyalty to her own family and sex, she trembled for Kirstie and the credit of the Elliotts. And again she had a vision of herself, the day over for her old-world tales and local gossip, bidding farewell to her last link with life and brightness and love; and behind and beyond, she saw but the blank butt-end where she must crawl to die. Had she then come to the lees? she, so great, so beautiful, with a heart as fresh as a girl's and strong as womanhood? It could not be, and yet it was so; and for a moment her bed was horrible to her as the sides of the grave. And she looked forward over a waste of hours, and saw herself go on to rage, and tremble, and be softened, and rage again, until the day came and the labours of the day must be renewed.

Suddenly she heard feet on the stairs—his feet, and soon after the sound of a window-sash flung open. She sat up with her heart beating. He had gone to his room alone, and he had not gone to bed. She might again have one of her night cracks; and at the entrancing prospect, a change came over her mind; with the approach of this hope of pleasure, all the baser metal became immediately obliterated from her thoughts. She rose, all woman, and all the best of woman, tender, pitiful, hating the wrong, loyal to her own sex—and all the weakest of that dear miscellany, nourishing, cherishing next her soft heart, voicelessly flattering, hopes that she would have died sooner than have acknowledged. She tore off her night-cap, and her hair fell about her shoulders in profusion. Undying coquetry awoke. By the faint light of her nocturnal rush, she stood before the looking-glass, carried her shapely arms above her head, and gathered up the treasures of her tresses. She was never backward to admire herself; that kind of modesty was a stranger to her nature; and she paused, struck with a pleased wonder at the sight. "Ye daft auld wife!" she said, answering a thought that was not; and she blushed with the innocent consciousness of a child. Hastily she did up the massive and shining coils, hastily donned a wrapper, and with the rushlight in her hand, stole into the hall. Below stairs she heard the clock ticking the deliberate seconds, and Frank jingling with the decanters in the dining-room. Aversion rose in her, bitter and momentary. "Nesty tippling puggy!" she thought; and the next moment she had knocked guardedly at Archie's door and was bidden enter.

Archie had been looking out into the ancient blackness, pierced here and there with a rayless star; taking the sweet air of the moors and the night into his bosom deeply; seeking, perhaps finding, peace after the manner of the unhappy. He turned round as she came in, and showed her a pale face against the window-frame.

"Is that you, Kirstie?" he asked. "Come in!"

"It's unco late, my dear," said Kirstie, affecting unwillingness.

"No, no," he answered, "not at all. Come in, if you want a crack. I am not sleepy, God knows!"

She advanced, took a chair by the toilet-table and the candle, and set the rushlight at her foot. Something—it might be in the comparative disorder of her dress, it might be the emotion that now welled in her bosom—had touched her with a wand of transformation, and she seemed young with the youth of goddesses.

"Mr. Erchie," she began, "what's this that's come to ye?"

"I am not aware of anything that has come," said Archie, and blushed, and repented bitterly that he had let her in.

"O, my dear, that'll no dae!" said Kirstie. "It's ill to blend the eyes of love. O, Mr. Erchie, tak' a thocht ere it's ower late. Ye shouldna be impatient o' the braws o' life, they'll a' come in their saison, like the sun and the rain. Ye're young yet; ye've mony cantie years afore ye. See and dinna wreck yersel' at the outset like sae mony ithers! Hae patience—they telled me aye that was the owercome o' life—hae patience, there's a braw day coming yet. Gude kens it never cam' to me; and here I am, wi' nayther man nor bairn to ca' my ain, wearying a' folks wi' my ill tongue, and you just the first, Mr. Erchie!"

"I have a difficulty in knowing what you mean," said Archie.

"Weel, and I'll tell ye," she said. "It's just this, that I'm feared. I'm feared for ye, my dear. Remember, your faither is a hard man, reaping where he hasna sowed and gaithering where he hasna strawed. It's easy speakin', but mind! Ye'll have to look in the gurley face o'm, where it's ill to look, and vain to look for mercy. Ye mind me o' a bonny ship pitten oot into the black and gowsty seas—ye're a' safe still, sittin' quait and crackin' wi' Kirstie in your lown chalmer; but whaur will ye be the morn, and in whatten horror o' the fearsome tempest, cryin' on the hills to cover ye?"

"Why, Kirstie, you're very enigmatical to-night—and very eloquent," Archie put in.

"And, my dear Mr. Erchie," she continued, with a change of voice, "ye maunna think that I canna sympathise wi' ye. Ye maunna think that I havena been young mysel'. Lang syne, when I was a bit lassie, no twenty yet—" She paused and sighed. "Clean and caller, wi' a fit like the hinney bee," she continued. "I was aye big and buirdly, ye maun understand; a bonny figure o' a woman, though I say it that suldna—built to rear bairns—braw bairns they suld hae been, and grand I would hae likit it! But I was young, dear, wi' the bonny glint o' youth in my e'en, and little I dreamed I'd ever be tellin' ye this, an auld, lanely, rudas wife! Weel, Mr. Erchie, there was a lad cam' courtin' me, as was but naetural. Mony had come before, and I would nane o' them. But this yin had a tongue to wile the birds frae the lift and the bees frae the foxglove bells. Deary me, but it's lang syne. Folk have dee'd sinsyne and been buried, and are forgotten, and bairns been born and got merrit and got bairns o' their ain. Sinsyne woods have been plantit, and have grawn up and are bonny trees, and the joes sit in their shadow; and sinsyne auld estates have changed hands, and there have been wars and rumours of wars on the face of the earth. And here I'm still—like an auld droopit craw—lookin' on and craikin'! But, Mr. Erchie, do ye no think that I have mind o' it a' still? I was dwalling then in my faither's house; and it's a curious thing that we were whiles trysted in the Deil's Hags. And do ye no think that I have mind of the bonny simmer days, the lang miles o' the bluid-red heather, the cryin' o' the whaups, and the lad and the lassie that was trysted? Do ye no think that I mind how the hilly sweetness ran about my hairt? Ay, Mr. Erchie, I ken the way o' it—fine do I ken the way—how the grace o' God takes them, like Paul of Tarsus, when they think it least, and drives the pair o' them into a land which is like a dream, and the world and the folks in 't are nae mair than clouds to the puir lassie, and heeven nae mair than windle-straes, if she can but pleesure him! Until Tam dee'd—that was my story," she broke off to say, "he dee'd, and I wasna at the buryin'. But while he was here, I could take care o' mysel'. And can yon puir lassie?"

Kirstie, her eyes shining with unshed tears, stretched

out her hand towards him appealingly; the bright and the dull gold of her hair flashed and smouldered in the coils behind her comely head, like the rays of an eternal youth; the pure colour had risen in her face; and Archie was abashed alike by her beauty and her story. He came towards her slowly from the window, took up her hand in his and kissed it.

"Kirstie," he said hoarsely, "you have misjudged me sorely. I have always thought of her, I wouldna harm her for the universe, my woman!"

"Eh, lad, and that's easy sayin'," cried Kirstie, "but it's nane sae easy doin'! Man, do ye no comprehend that it's God's wull we should be blendit and glamoured, and have nae command over our ain members at a time like that? My bairn," she cried, still holding his hand, "think o' the puir lass! have pity upon her, Erchie! and O, be wise for twa! Think o' the risk she rins! I have seen ye, and what's to prevent ithers? I saw ye once in the Hags, in my ain howf, and I was wae to see ye there—in pairt for the omen, for I think there's a weird on the place—and in pairt for pure nakit envy and bitterness o' hairt. It's strange ye should forgather there tae! God! but yon puir, thrawn, auld Covenanter's seen a heap o' human natur' since he lookit his last on the musket-barrels, if he never saw nane afore," she added, with a kind of wonder in her eyes.

"I swear by my honour I have done her no wrong," said Archie. "I swear by my honour and the redemption of my soul that there shall none be done her. I have heard of this before. I have been foolish, Kirstie, but not unkind, and, above all, not base."

"There's my bairn!" said Kirstie, rising. "I'll can trust ye noo, I'll can gang to my bed wi' an easy hairt." And then she saw in a flash how barren had been her triumph. Archie had promised to spare the girl, and he would keep it; but who had promised to spare Archie? What was to be the end of it? Over a maze of difficulties she glanced, and saw, at the end of every passage, the flinty countenance of Hermiston. And a kind of horror fell upon her at what she had done. She wore a tragic mask. "Erchie, the Lord peety you, dear, and peety me! I have buildit on this foundation"—laying her hand heavily on his shoulder—"and buildit hie, and pit my hairt in the buildin' of it. If the hale hypothec were to fa', I think, laddie, I would dee! Excuse a daft wife that loves ye, and that kenned your mither. And for His name's sake keep yersel' frae inordinate desires; haud your heart in baith your hands, carry it canny and laigh; dinna send it up like a bairn's kite into the collieshangie o' the wunds! Mind, Maister Erchie dear, that this life's a' disappointment, and a mouthfu' o' mools is the appointed end."

"Ay, but Kirstie, my woman, you're asking me ower much at last," said Archie, profoundly moved, and lapsing into the broad Scots. "Ye're asking what nae man can grant ye, what only the Lord of heaven can grant ye if He see fit. Ay! And can even He? I can promise ye what I shall do, and you can depend on that. But how I shall feel—my woman, that is long past thinking of!"

They were both standing by now opposite each other. The face of Archie wore the wretched semblance of a smile; hers was convulsed for a moment.

"Promise me ae thing," she cried, in a sharp voice. "Promise me ye'll never do naething without telling me."

"No, Kirstie, I canna promise ye that," he replied. "I have promised enough, God kens!"

"May the blessing of God lift and rest upon ye, dear!" she said.

"God bless ye, my old friend," said he.

CHAPTER IX

AT THE WEAVER'S STONE

IT WAS LATE in the afternoon when Archie drew near by the hill path to the Praying Weaver's Stone. The Hags were in shadow. But still, through the gate of the Slap, the sun shot a last arrow, which sped far and straight across the surface of the moss, here and there touching and shining on a tussock, and lighted at length on the gravestone and the small figure awaiting him there. The emptiness and solitude of the great moors seemed to be concentrated there, and Kirstie pointed out by that finger of sunshine for the only inhabitant. His first sight of her was thus excruciatingly sad, like a glimpse of a world from which all light, comfort, and society were on the point of vanishing. And the next moment, when she had turned her face to him and the quick smile had enlightened it, the whole face of nature smiled upon him in her smile of welcome. Archie's slow pace was quickened; his legs hasted to her though his heart was hanging back. The girl, upon her side, drew herself together slowly and stood up, expectant; she was all languor, her face was gone white; her arms ached for him, her soul was on tip-toes. But he deceived her, pausing a few steps away, not less white than herself, and holding up his hand with a gesture of denial.

"No, Christina, not to-day," he said. "To-day I have to talk to you seriously. Sit ye down, please, there where you were. Please!" he repeated.

The revulsion of feeling in Christina's heart was violent. To have longed and waited these weary hours for him, rehearsing her endearments—to have seen him at last come—to have been ready there, breathless, wholly passive, his to do what he would with—and suddenly to have found herself confronted with a grey-faced, harsh schoolmaster—it was too rude a shock. She could have wept, but pride withheld her. She sat down on the stone, from which she had arisen, part with the instinct of obedience, part as though she had been thrust there. What was this? Why was she rejected? Had she ceased to please? She stood here offering her wares, and he would none of them! And yet they were all his! His to take and keep, not his to refuse though! In her quick petulant nature, a moment ago on fire with hope, thwarted love and wounded vanity wrought. The schoolmaster that there is in all men, to the despair of all girls and most women, was now completely in possession of Archie. He had passed a night of sermons, a day of reflection; he had come wound up to do his duty; and the set mouth, which in him only betrayed the effort of his will, to her seemed the expression of an averted heart. It was the same with his constrained voice and embarrassed utterance; and if so—if it was all over—the pang of the thought took away from her the power of thinking.

He stood before her some way off. "Kirstie, there's been too much of this. We've seen too much of each other." She looked up quickly and her eyes contracted. "There's no good ever comes of these secret meetings. They're not frank, not honest truly, and I ought to have seen it. People have begun to talk; and it's not right of me. Do you see?"

"I see somebody will have been talking to ye," she said sullenly.

"They have—more than one of them," replied Archie.

"And whae were they?" she cried. "And what kind o' love do ye ca' that, that's ready to gang round like a whirligig at folk talking? Do ye think they havena talked to me?"

"Have they indeed?" said Archie, with a quick breath. "That is what I feared. Who were they? Who has dare—?"

Archie was on the point of losing his temper.

As a matter of fact, not any one had talked to Christina on the matter; and she strenuously repeated her own first question in a panic of self-defence.

"Ah, well! what does it matter?" he said. "They were good folk that wished well to us, and the great affair is that there are people talking. My dear girl, we have to be wise. We must not wreck our lives at the outset. They may be long and happy yet, and we must see to it, Kirstie, like God's rational creatures and not like fool children. There is one thing we must see to before all. You're worth waiting for, Kirstie! worth waiting for a generation; it would be enough reward."—And here he remembered the schoolmaster again, and very unwisely took to following wisdom. "The first thing that we must see to is that there shall be no scandal about for my father's sake. That would ruin all; do ye no see that?"

Kirstie was a little pleased, there had been some show of warmth of sentiment in what Archie had said last. But the dull irritation still persisted in her bosom; with the aboriginal instinct, having suffered herself, she wished to make Archie suffer.

And besides, there had come out the word she had always feared to hear from his lips, the name of his father. It is not to be supposed that, during so many days with a love avowed between them, some reference had not been made to their conjoint future. It had in fact been often touched upon, and from the first had been the sore point. Kirstie had wilfully closed the eye of thought; she would not argue even with herself; gallant, desperate little heart, she had accepted the command of that supreme attraction like the call of fate, and marched blindfold on her doom. But Archie, with his masculine sense of responsibility, must reason; he must dwell on some future good, when the present good was all in all to Kirstie; he must talk—and talk lamely, as necessity drove him—of what was to be. Again and again he had touched on marriage; again and again been driven back into indistinctness by a memory of Lord Hermiston. And Kirstie had been swift to understand and quick to choke down and smother the understanding; swift to leap up in flame at a mention of that hope, which spoke volumes to her vanity and her love, that she might one day be Mrs. Weir of Hermiston; swift, also, to recognise in his stumbling or throttled utterance the death-knell of these expectations, and constant, poor girl! in her large-minded madness, to go on and to reck nothing of the future. But these unfinished references, these blinks in which his heart spoke, and his memory and reason rose up to silence it before the words were well uttered, gave her unqualifiable agony. She was raised up and dashed down again bleeding. The recurrence of the subject forced her, for however short a time, to open her eyes on what she did not wish to see; and it had invariably ended in another disappointment. So now again, at the mere wind of its coming, at the mere mention of his father's name—who might seem indeed to have accompanied them in their whole moorland courtship, an awful figure in a wig with an ironical and bitter smile, present to guilty consciousness—she fled from it head down.

"Ye havena told me yet," she said, "who was it spoke?"

"Your aunt for one," said Archie.

"Auntie Kirstie?" she cried. "And what do I care for my Auntie Kirstie?"

"She cares a great deal for her niece," replied Archie, in kind reproof.

"Troth, and it's the first I've heard of it," retorted the girl.

"The question here is not who it is, but what they say, what they have noticed," pursued the lucid schoolmaster. "That is what we have to think of in self-defence."

"Auntie Kirstie, indeed! A bitter, thrawn auld maid that's fomented trouble in the country before I was born, and will be doing it still, I daur say, when I'm deid! It's in her nature; it's as natural for her as it's for a sheep to eat."

"Pardon me, Kirstie, she was not the only one," interposed Archie. "I had two warnings, two sermons, last night, both most kind and considerate. Had you been there, I promise you you would have grat, my dear! And they opened my eyes. I saw we were going a wrong way."

"Who was the other one?" Kirstie demanded.

By this time Archie was in the condition of a hunted beast. He had come, braced and resolute; he was to trace out a line of conduct for the pair of them in a few cold, convincing sentences; he had now been there some time, and he was still staggering round the outworks and undergoing what he felt to be a savage cross-examination.

"Mr. Frank!" she cried. "What nex', I would like to ken?"

"He spoke most kindly and truly."

"What like did he say?"

"I am not going to tell you; you have nothing to do with that," cried Archie, startled to find he had admitted so much.

"O, I have naething to do with it!" she repeated, springing to her feet. "A'body at Hermiston's free to pass their opinions upon me, but I have naething to do wi' it! Was this at prayers like? Did ye ca' the grieve into the consultation? Little wonder if a'body's talking, when ye make a'body yer confidants! But as you say, Mr. Weir, most kindly, most considerately, most truly, I'm sure—I have naething to do with it. And I think I'll better be going. I'll be wishing you good evening, Mr. Weir." And she made him a stately curtsey, shaking as she did so from head to foot, with the barren ecstasy of temper.

Poor Archie stood dumbfounded. She had moved some steps away from him before he recovered the gift of articulate speech.

"Kirstie!" he cried. "O, Kirstie woman!"

There was in his voice a ring of appeal, a clang of mere astonishment that showed the schoolmaster was vanquished.

She turned round on him. "What do ye Kirstie me for?" she retorted. "What have ye to do wi' me? Gang to your ain freends and deave them!"

He could only repeat the appealing "Kirstie!"

"Kirstie, indeed!" cried the girl, her eyes blazing in her white face. "My name is Miss Christina Elliott, I would have ye to ken, and I daur ye to ca' me out of it. If I canna get love, I'll have respect, Mr. Weir. I'm come of decent people, and I'll have respect. What have I done that ye should lightly me? What have I done? What have I done? O, what have I done?" and her voice rose upon the third repetition. "I thocht—I thocht—I thocht I was sae happy!" and the first sob broke from her like the paroxysm of some mortal sickness.

Archie ran to her. He took the poor child in his arms, and she nestled to his breast as to a mother's, and clasped him in hands that were strong like vices. He felt her whole body shaken by the throes of distress, and had pity upon her beyond speech. Pity, and at the same time a bewildered fear of this explosive engine in his arms, whose works he did not understand, and yet had been tampering with. There arose from before him the curtains of boyhood, and he saw for the first time the ambiguous face of woman as she is. In vain he looked back over the interview; he saw not where he had offended. It seemed unprovoked, a wilful convulsion of brute nature. . . .

APPENDIX

THE PROJECTED CONCLUSION OF "WEIR OF HERMISTON"

Stevenson's stepdaughter, Belle Strong, to whom he dictated the novel on his deathbed, told his literary friend, Sir Sidney Colvin, his plans for the remainder of the book. In an editorial note to the first edition (1896) of the story, Colvin wrote:

Archie persists in his good resolution of avoiding further conduct compromising to young Kirstie's good name. Taking advantage of the situation thus created, and of the girl's unhappiness and wounded vanity, Frank Innes pursues his purpose of seduction; and Kirstie, though still caring for Archie in her heart, allows herself to become Frank's victim. Old Kirstie is the first to perceive something amiss with her, and believing Archie to be the culprit, accuses him, thus making him aware for the first time that mischief has happened. He does not at once deny the charge, but seeks out and questions young Kirstie, who confesses the truth to him; and he, still loving her, promises to protect and defend her in her trouble. He then has an interview with Frank Innes on the moor, which ends in a quarrel, and in Archie killing Frank beside the Weaver's Stone. Meanwhile the Four Black Brothers, having become aware of their sister's betrayal, are bent on vengeance against Archie as her supposed seducer. But their vengeance is forestalled by his arrest for the murder of Frank. He is tried before his own father, the Lord Justice-Clerk, found guilty, and condemned to death. Meanwhile the elder Kirstie, having discovered from the girl how matters really stand, informs her nephews of the truth; and they, in a great revulsion of feeling in Archie's favour, determine on an action after the ancient manner of their house. They gather a following, and after a great flight break the prison where Archie lies confined, and rescue him. He and young Kirstie thereafter escape to America. But the ordeal of taking part in the trial of his own son has been too much for the Lord Justice-Clerk, who dies of the shock. "I do not know," adds the amanuensis, "what becomes of old Kirstie, but that character grew and strengthened so in the writing that I am sure he had some dramatic destiny for her."

BIBLIOGRAPHY

WORKS BY STEVENSON

An Inland Voyage, 1878 travel
Picturesque Notes on Edinburgh, 1878 travel
Travels with a Donkey in the Cevennes, 1879 travel
Virginibus Puerisque, 1881 essays
Familiar Studies of Men and Books, 1882 essays
New Arabian Nights, 1882 stories
The Silverado Squatters, 1883 travel
Treasure Island, 1883 Novel (Signet Classic 0451–519175)
A Child's Garden of Verses, 1885 poetry
More New Arabian Nights, 1885 stories
Prince Otto, 1885 novel
The Strange Case of Dr. Jekyll and Mr. Hyde, 1886 story (Signet Classic 0451–521382)
Kidnapped, 1886 novel (Signet Classic 0451–519728)
Memories and Portraits, 1887 essays
Underwoods, 1887 poetry
The Merry Men, 1887 stories
The Black Arrow, 1888 novel
The Master of Ballantrae, 1889 novel
The South Seas: A Record of Three Cruises, 1890 travel
Ballads, 1891 poetry
Across the Plains, 1892 travel
A Footnote to History, 1892 essays on Samoa
The Wrecker, 1892 novel
Island Nights' Entertainments, 1893 stories
Catriona, 1893 novel
The Ebb-Tide, 1894 novel
Songs of Travel, 1895 poetry
St. Ives, 1897 novel

CRITICISM

Aldington, Richard. *Portrait of a Rebel: The Life and Work of Robert Louis Stevenson.* London, 1957.

Calder, Jenni. *RLS: A Life Study.* London, 1980.

Chesterton, G.K. *Robert Louis Stevenson.* New York, 1928.

Daiches, David. *Robert Louis Stevenson.* Norfolk, Conn., 1947.

Eigner, Edwin. *Robert Louis Stevenson and Romantic Tradition.* Princeton, 1966.

Furnas, J.C. *Voyage to Windward: The Life of Robert Louis Stevenson.* New York, 1951.

James, Henry. "Robert Louis Stevenson," in *Partial Portraits.* London, 1888, pp. 137–174.

Kiely, Robert. *Robert Louis Stevenson and the Fiction of Adventure.* Cambridge, Mass., 1964.

Pope-Hennessy, James. *Robert Louis Stevenson.* London, 1974.

Saposnik, Irving. *Robert Louis Stevenson.* New York, 1974.